CAT   Cat crimes for the holidays

04

Cat Crimes for the Holidays

EDITED BY
Martin H. Greenberg,
Ed Gorman, and Larry Segriff

DONALD I. FINE BOOKS

DONALD I. FINE BOOKS

Published by the Penguin Group

Penguin Putnam Inc., 375 Hudson Street, New York, New York 10014, U.S.A.

Penguin Books Ltd, 27 Wrights Lane, London W8 5TZ, England

Penguin Books Australia Ltd, Ringwood, Victoria, Australia

Penguin Books Canada Ltd, 10 Alcorn Avenue, Toronto, Ontario, Canada
M4V 3B2

Penguin Books (N.Z.) Ltd, 182–190 Wairau Road, Auckland 10, New Zealand

Penguin Books Ltd, Registered Offices: Harmondsworth, Middlesex, England

First published by Donald I. Fine Books,
an imprint of Penguin Putnam Inc.

First Printing, November, 1997

10 9 8 7 6 5 4 3 2 1

LIBRARY OF CONGRESS CATALOGING-IN-PUBLICATION DATA:

Cat crimes for the holidays / edited by Martin H. Greenberg, Ed Gorman and
Larry Segriff.

p.   cm.

ISBN 1-556-11503-2

1. Detective and mystery stories, American.   2. Holidays—Fiction.
3. Crime—Fiction.   4. Cats—Fiction.   I. Greenberg, Martin Harry.
II. Gorman, Edward.   III. Segriff, Larry.

PS648.C7C4   1997

813'.08720833—dc21   97-12736
                                                                        CIP

Printed in the United States of America

Set in New Caledonia

Contents

Cat Crimes
for the Holidays

Introduction

It's not easy being a cat. You have a lot of responsibilities. You have to keep grouchy human beings entertained all the time, and you have to pretend you really missed them a lot when they come back home.

The thing is, just as human beings need holidays, so do cats.

The little stinkers simply get tuckered out. That's why we've put the two subjects together in this book . . . to show people that cats enjoy holidays just as much as humans do.

What we like about these stories is that they give the cats a lot of credit for helping to solve the mysteries. Cats make much better sleuths than one might think—at least when they're awake they do (and cats have been known to stay awake for up to an hour and a half a day).

So get out those deerstalker caps and settle in for some holiday excitement.

With your favorite cat in your lap, of course.

—THE EDITORS

Dr. Couch Saves a Cat

Nancy Pickard

"It may seem terrible," the old veterinarian admitted to his grand-daughter, "that I was so worried about a cat when there was a person who had just passed on. But it was an awfully nice cat, and the human being wasn't much to brag about, I'm sorry to say."

"Tell me about the cat, Grandpa."

"A child after my own heart."

The old man smiled at the ten-year-old whose hair was the same shade of shiny walnut that his had been seventy years ago and who was a stringbean, as he had been in his youth, and who also had inherited his unusual shade of light brown eyes. Her name was Frances—which she hated, except for the fact that she was named after him—and so she went by Frankie. His name was Franklin Couch. Everybody except the child—even his own daughters, sometimes—called him Dr. Frank. He was a formal sort of man with most people, a trait he deeply regretted when he gauged the emotional distance between him and his daughters. With animals and small children, however, he was magic. Butterflies landed on him, shy little house spiders climbed down walls until they were face-to-face in conversation with him, wild doves allowed him to pick them up and cradle them in his hands before gently putting them back down again. Dogs who barked, lunged, and bit at every other vet bared their teeth in goofy smiles at Dr. Frank. Cats he'd never met before rubbed their foreheads hard against his own and tapped their paws against his cheeks, their claws politely tucked away.

Children such as his own granddaughter tended to run up to his side and slip their hands into his. His daughters had done that, too, when they were little, but now he couldn't recall the last time he'd

1

held their hands. Adults of the human species were a puzzle to him, mysteries to which he knew he hadn't a clue. His wife, Lorraine, was long dead, so he couldn't ask her how to reach his own girls again. It was when she died that he'd felt them slipping away; it was Lorraine, he then understood, who had long bridged the gap between them.

Dr. Frank observed the pert, upturned face of his granddaughter, whom he loved so much it made his heart swell and hurt, and felt sad at the thought of one day watching her, too, disappear into the mists of adulthood.

"Meow," she teased him.

He heard her and smiled.

It was how she called him out of the reveries into which he often sank these days, like an old dog in a patch of sunlight. His grandchild knew him well, he thought ruefully: If his phone barked instead of rang, he'd probably answer it more often.

"It's a murder story," he warned her. "Are you sure you want to hear it?"

"Oh, yes! As long as only people die. No animals, right?"

"I promise no animals die in this story."

"Okay, then."

He knew exactly how she felt and couldn't agree with her more.

"The victim was a man named Joseph Becker," he said, settling back into the easy chair while she also settled herself more comfortably in the crook of his right arm, squeezed into the tiny space between him and the side of his chair. He heard her give a contented little sigh, and he felt like giving one just like it himself. "Joe Becker was a good-looking man in his thirties who was a partner in a small business that, um—" Dr. Couch thought, searching for a simple method of getting across to a ten-year-old the idea of a middleman, "—that bought crops that farmers grew and sold them to big businesses. Most of the young men of our generation had gone off to fight in World War Two, but Joe Becker couldn't go, because he had flat feet."

Young Dr. Franklin Couch hadn't gone to war, either, not because he was a veterinarian, but because he was an only son who was already the sole support of a wife, two little daughters, and, to a lesser degree, his elderly parents. Often he wondered how his life would have been different if he'd served in the military—whether his life would have continued at all. There were times when he felt embarrassed among men of his own generation who had gone to Europe or the South Pacific or Asia. He suspected that feeling of embarrassment—which was partly guilt, but mostly just the sense of being an outsider—may have had something to do with why he had never made any close friends of his own age. It was almost as if he and other men his age didn't have much in common. They had the war. He had dogs and cats, birds and kids; and those were his social peers, it seemed.

On the whole, that was all right with him.

He'd never told anyone how he felt about himself and the war, not even Lorraine. She'd have told him he was silly, that it was a great accomplishment for a man to support a family and to serve his community, as he had done. But her words wouldn't have changed his feelings, he knew. And so there had never been any point in telling her.

"Meow?" said his granddaughter.

"Oh, yes. Joe Becker. Well, the unfortunate young man was found one Sunday in the autumn of nineteen forty-four, bashed in the head with a frying pan in his kitchen in his apartment. I knew Becker, you see, and I also knew all of the people who were considered suspects in his murder. Or at least I knew their pets. Becker, for instance, had a lovely little Siamese named Annie."

"Is that the cat you worried about, Grandpa?"

"That's the cat. But there were also all of the suspects and *their* animals. Some of the suspects had access but no opportunity, and some of them had opportunity but no motive, and—"

"What's a motive, Grandpa?"

He realized he was going to have to slow down and tell the story in a simple, logical fashion so the child could follow him. "A motive, Frankie, is a stupid reason for doing a bad thing."

"Like what?"

"Like the ex-wife, who wished Becker was dead so she could sell the apartment building they both still owned together, the one where they were both residing in separate units at the time that he was killed. The ex-wife, Mary Becker, was in apartment One-A, and Becker himself was in Two-B."

"Was she pretty?"

"Who? Mrs. Becker? I don't recall, but she had the ugliest old marmalade tom you ever saw. Name of JamPot. I certainly remember that. I'm sure he hated it; I would. JamPot! Some people have no sense of propriety or dignity when it comes to naming their animals! Poor JamPot. I don't think that cat ever won a single fight he was in, to judge by the number of times she'd had to bring him round to me to get him fixed up and stitched. He probably should have been neutered, although that might not have solved his problem. I've seen plenty of neutered toms'd take Mike Tyson out in two rounds. No, I suspect JamPot just had bad timing—always throwing his punches late, so to speak. He used to take a swipe at me when I treated him, but I always got my hand away in time. Poor timing, that was JamPot's problem.

"Anyway, the trouble with his owner as a suspect was that she had motive and access, but she apparently didn't have opportunity. The ex-Mrs. Becker claimed she was in Chicago visiting her mother at the time that her former husband was killed. From the police point of view, Mary Becker had bad timing, just like her cat."

"You always say people are like their animals."

"Do I always say that?"

"About once a day that I know of." She grinned up at him, her neck cocked as if she were looking up at the sun. "You probably say it other times when I'm not around."

He laughed, utterly delighted to be teased.

Adults, he knew, were rather intimidated by him, by his size, his age, his reputation. They tended to treat him with a reserve and respect he supposed they thought he deserved. On the whole, he much preferred to be teased.

"So, Grandpa, what's access? What's opportunity?"

Her grandfather was amused and pleased that he didn't have to explain *neutered* to her, but he did have to explain the legal parlance of a homicide investigation. You could tell she hung around vets and not lawyers! Good child! He quirked a bushy silver eyebrow at her and pretended to look stern.

"Access is being able to pull up a chair to the bookcase so you can reach my private collection of Hershey's Kisses with Almonds!"

He observed her eyes get large and her face grow pink.

"Opportunity is when you're in my office alone and I'm in the bathroom with the door closed!"

He watched her scrunch up her face so tight that her eyes shut.

"And motive is . . ." He waited for her eyes to open, and then he smiled at her. "Well, in the case of Hershey's Kisses, it's *not* a stupid and bad reason; it's a perfectly understandable and intelligent one, which is a wish for a taste of chocolate."

"I didn't take any pieces of candy!"

"When?"

"When what?"

"When didn't you take any?"

She thought about that, examined the twinkle in his eyes, and said judiciously, "Almost never."

Her grandfather guffawed, enormously impressed at how sharp she was. "That's a good one, Frankie!" He chuckled. "You almost never didn't take any!"

"Grandpa?"

"Yes?"

"I don't really like almonds."

"Then they will never darken my candy bowl again. But listen, child, you could break your neck climbing up on that chair." She was just like her miniature dachshund, he thought with pride, always aiming for things that were way above her head. "I'll put the bowl on a lower shelf. Now, do you want to hear about any of the other suspects in my little murder mystery?"

"I do! Especially the parts about their pets that you knew. And especially the part where you were worried about Mr. Becker's cat. Annie. The Siamese."

"Well, here's what happened," he began again happily. "You know about the victim now?"

"Joe Becker," the child recited. "Bashed. Frying pan."

"Where?"

"Kitchen of where he lived. Um." She thought hard. "Apartment Two-A."

"No, Two-B. Remember, his ex-wife lived in One-A."

"Wait, wait!" commanded the child, excitedly. "Let me say it! Her name was Sherry, and she had a big marmalade tom named JamPot who never won any fights, and she couldn't have done it, because she was . . . someplace else."

"Her name was Mary," he corrected, gently, fully sympathetic to the fact that it was easier to recall the names of animals than people. "And it was Chicago. But you got everything else right. And what might have been her reason for wanting him dead?"

"She wanted his apartment?"

"She wanted to own the whole building so she could sell it."

Frankie lifted a delicate brown eyebrow. "Greedy pig."

"People often are, unfortunately. Now let me tell you about the other suspects in the murder."

"And their motives, opportunities, and excess."

"Access, although you do have a point there." He laughed. "Excess! Yes indeed, you would certainly find that was true in almost any murder case, I suspect. There would be an excess of something, wouldn't there, whether it was greed, or fear, or whatever."

"Other suspects," she reminded him.

"Yes. Well, there was Nancy Okawa, for instance, who had a nervous, skinny little white tomcat. She had access because she was Becker's girlfriend and so she had a key to his apartment, and she had opportunity, because she was in and out of the apartment all the time, but she didn't have any apparent motive."

"Like wanting chocolate," Frankie commented.

"Exactly. Apparently there wasn't anything the equivalent of chocolate that Nancy Okawa wanted that would require the death of her boyfriend, Joe Becker. She said she loved him madly. She appeared to be grief-stricken."

"What was her cat's name, Grandpa?"

"Lightning."

Frankie reacted disdainfully. "Sounds like a horse's name to me."

"I know, but it was perfect, because he was full of electricity."

The child laughed, and Dr. Couch knew she was picturing in her agile, imaginative mind a skinny white cat that was constantly jumping and racing about.

"You're too young to know this," her grandfather continued, "but there is a clue to the victim's character in the name of his girlfriend. Can you possibly guess what it is?"

Frankie frowned in heavy thought, and repeated to herself several

times in a low voice, "Nancy Okawa, Nancy Okawa, Nancy Okawa."
Suddenly she brightened. "Was she, like, Japanese? Is that the clue?"

"Very good! Nancy wasn't 'like' Japanese; she was a child of Japanese parents who had immigrated to this country soon after she was born. These days people feel free to fall in love with anybody they want to, but in those days there was a lot of prejudice when a white person went around with a person of a different race, not to mention the fact that this country was at war with Japan, so a lot of people looked on Nancy Okawa as the enemy. She had even lived in a concentration camp with her parents for a time in California. Now what does this suggest to you about the character of our victim, Joseph Becker?"

"He didn't care what anybody thought?" Frankie guessed.

"Brilliant child. That is exactly right, although it wasn't precisely the same thing as courage or even tolerance. Becker was just an aggressive, imperious sort of fellow who didn't let anybody or anything stand in the way of what he wanted, not other people's prejudices, not even a war."

"He sounds like a Siamese."

"Some Siamese, you're right. But his lovely Annie was elegantly imperious, like a benevolent queen, while he had always struck me as being a bit of a thug. I should tell you that Annie was a housecat, Frankie. Becker never, never, never allowed her to go outside or anywhere else, for that matter, because he wanted to breed her and make money from her litters."

Again the delicate eyebrow lifted. "Greedy pig."

"There's a lot of that to go around in this story," her grandfather admitted. "Perhaps I should tell you how I became involved."

"Yes!"

"It was simple, really. I received a summons from the man who was our police chief at the time. He sent one of his fellows over to fetch me, because Annie had crawled up on top of Joe Becker's shower-curtain pole, and she was hissing at all of the police officers and she wouldn't come down. He just wanted me to come get her and take her away from the scene of the murder."

"So you saw it!" The child's light brown eyes were huge with awe.

"Blood and all," her grandfather agreed.

They both nodded in mutual satisfaction.

"I saw Becker's body in the kitchen," the old man told her. "And I got a good look around the whole apartment, because Annie gave me quite a little chase!"

They smiled, then laughed together, he at the memory of his undignified pursuit of the furious feline and she at the idea of her big old grandfather racing around after a cat.

"I brought her home with me," he continued. "And I examined her, because she had a little blood on her, and that's when I discovered she was—"

But the eager, curious child interrupted him. "What'd you see in Mr. Becker's apartment? Was it full of cops? Did you find any clues? Was his girlfriend there?"

"No, but his upstairs neighbor was, because he always looked after Annie whenever Joe Becker was traveling on business. It was the neighbor who called the police to tell them he'd found the body. His name was Alastair Reynolds, and he owned a local bakery."

She wasn't interested in that. "Did he have a pet?"

"Everybody in this story had a pet." Her grandfather smiled. "Alastair Reynolds, the baker, had a big, sweet-natured tom named, appropriately enough, Sugar. Sugar was one of my favorite patients. He was a handsome fellow, all soft and shiny black except for three white paws. He looked as if he had stepped in the flour when his owner was baking bread."

Frankie pressed her hands against her grandfather's upper right arm and worked her fingers up and down as if she were a baker kneading bread or a cat kneading his arm. If he could have purred, he would have at that perfect moment in his long life.

"I haven't told you about the partner yet, have I?"

"Whose partner? Mr. Becker's? Tell me, tell me."

"Yes, Joe Becker's partner in the food distribution business was a big blond fellow who never smiled, by the name of Quentin Dees. He didn't have any cats or even a wife, but he did have three Doberman pinschers that he kept locked up behind a high fence at his house. I do believe they were the most sinister dogs I ever met, because they prowled constantly but never made a sound. Instead of barking at strangers, those three dogs would come together in a trio at the fence line and bare their teeth at you. It was worth your life to step onto that property unannounced."

Frankie shivered pleasurably in the crook of his arm and whispered, "What did he call them?"

"He didn't give them names. He would just call *Dog* in a sharp, high voice, and they all three would obey him instantly."

"I don't like that man, Grandpa!"

"No reason you should, Frankie."

The child suddenly looked excited. "I'll bet he killed Mr. Becker, didn't he?"

"Well, now wait," he cautioned. "Let's not rush to any conclusions. You may be right, or you may not. Hop up and get us a handful of Hershey's Kisses, and we'll examine the evidence. They're not on the upper shelf anymore, Frankie; they're on top of my desk. In case you hadn't noticed."

She grinned and scooted down from his lap.

When she hopped back up, she had a double handful of candy to pour into his own cupped hands. Fastidiously, Frankie picked the plain Hersheys without nuts out of the pile he patiently held for her. Only when she was finished did he shift the remaining sweets to his left palm so that he could open the silver wrappings with his right hand. For a few contented moments, grandfather and grandchild rustled paper and chewed chocolate together. "When you're older," he observed, "you'll like the almond ones better."

"Yuk."

They allowed the foil and the little white streamers to drift to the carpet below them.

"I am thinking," Dr. Frank said, as with a bare finger he dabbed a speck of chocolate off a corner of her mouth, "that there may be no way you can guess the truth about this story, because you don't have the memories of wartime that adults have. There is certain crucial information that you're missing—at least one clue that a grownup might be able to surmise just from what I have told you so far—but if I tell you what it is, you'll guess the truth immediately." He surreptitiously wiped his brown fingertip on the underside of the upholstered arm of the chair. "What should I do, Frankie, tell you or not tell you?"

"Don't tell me! Let me guess!"

"All right." He wrinkled his forehead in thought, and when he did, his granddaughter kissed the side of his face. As if her kiss had given him inspiration, he suddenly smiled brightly and said, "I know. There's another way to allow you to figure out the truth, and you don't even have to be eighty years old to do it. What I started to tell you earlier was that when I brought Annie home with me, I examined her because she had a little blood on her."

"Was she hurt?"

Her grandfather realized that although he had promised her no animals would die in the story, he had neglected to guarantee that none of them would be harmed at all.

"No, no," he assured her, quickly. "It was her owner's blood, not hers. No, when I examined her I discovered that what Annie was, was pregnant."

"But he never let her out of the apartment!"

Her grandfather gave her a meaningful stare. "Exactly!"

"Is that the clue?" she asked, excitedly.

He merely smiled and said nothing to assist her.

The child thought and thought, but she was only ten years old, and finally she cried out in frustration, "I don't get it! How can I tell who killed Mr. Becker from just knowing that Annie was going to have kittens?"

Dr. Frank hugged and patted her. "You'll get it. I'll tell you a bit more of the story, and then you'll figure out why that clue is so important."

"Okay," she said a little sulkily.

Her grandfather thought for a moment about how to tell the remainder of it so that it would be impossible for her to guess wrong. "At first," he continued, "the police were sure the girlfriend did it, probably just because she was of Japanese ancestry. But even they had to admit she didn't seem to have any motive for killing him, and she was too short to have been able to reach up and clobber him so effectively with the frying pan."

"He could have been bending over," Frankie pointed out.

"Perhaps they didn't think of that," her grandfather said, keeping his expression quite serious.

The child looked once again satisfied with her own intelligence.

"Then, when they couldn't pin it on her, they decided the wife did it, because she did have a motive . . ."

"But no opportunity!" Frankie crowed.

"That's right."

"I told you the mean partner did it—I told you he did it!"

"Well, Frankie, that is very astute character analysis on your part, because the police discovered that Joe Becker and Quentin Dees had also been partners in an illegal business called the black market. During wartime, you see, certain goods were what was called rationed, which meant that the most important substances, like flour and sugar and butter and rubber and nylon, were put aside for the war effort, leaving only a little for the rest of us to share for domestic purposes on the home front." He gazed into her eyes, which was a little like looking backwards through time into a photograph of his own eyes when he was a boy. "Do you understand what I just said?"

"Do I *have* to understand it?" she asked candidly.

Her grandfather laughed. "No, not really. I'll just say one more thing about it, which is that these men were diverting some of the goods they bought from farmers and selling those goods illegally to private individuals instead of to the government."

"Is that why his partner killed him?"

"The police arrested his partner, Quentin Dees, after they discovered the illegal business the two men had been conducting. Dees admitted that Joe Becker had decided to get out of the business, because it was getting too dangerous and he was afraid of getting caught. They accused Quentin Dees of killing him to prevent him from ever telling anybody what they had been doing."

"That was his . . . motive?"

Dr. Frank nodded.

"Did he have"—carefully she pronounced it—"access?"

"And opportunity? Yes, indeed. He had a key to the apartment, and he was even seen leaving there the morning that Becker was killed. The neighbor reported hearing the two men yelling at each other and then seeing Dees leave by the front door."

"That was dumb!"

"For a murderer, yes."

"Is that the end of the story?" She didn't look entirely satisfied, her grandfather noticed. He certainly didn't want to disappoint her.

"Not exactly," he said. "There is one more loose end we have to tie up. Can you think what it is?"

He could almost see all the many details of the story he had told her going rapidly through her bright mind as she reviewed them, searching for the loose end. He could even tell when, a second before she announced it, she found it.

"Annie!" she shouted triumphantly. "Her kittens!"

"One kitten," the old vet said. "Annie only had one kitten in that first litter. Can you imagine what it looked like, Frankie?"

"A Siamese, of course."

"No, it didn't look very much like a Siamese."

Suddenly, the child's eyes grew wide and her mouth dropped open. "Oh, my gosh! What did it look like, Grandpa, what did it look like?"

"What *could* it look like, Frankie?"

"Oh, gosh, oh, gosh, let me remember all the cats!" She was bouncing up and down on his lap, so excited she couldn't stay still. "There was the skinny little white tom that Mr. Becker's girlfriend owned, and there was the pretty black tom with white paws that the upstairs neighbor owned, and there was the ugly old marmalade tom that the ex-wife owned. Grandpa! The partner owned dogs! He didn't kill Mr. Becker! He didn't kill Mr. Becker, did he?!"

"No, Frankie, he didn't."

"Whichever tomcat that Annie's kitten looked like, it was that cat's owner that killed him, wasn't it?"

"Yes, it was, Frankie."

"Don't tell me, don't tell me!"

For a few long moments, the child sat deep in thought.

When she finally looked up at him, she looked much calmer, even sure of herself. "JamPot's owner was in Chicago, so she didn't do it. Lightning's owner really loved Mr. Becker, and she didn't have any reason to kill him, so she didn't do it. Grandpa, was the baby kitty black with three white paws?"

Solemnly, he nodded. "Just as if he had stepped in flour."

"It was the neighbor," Frankie announced, with equal solemnity. Then she looked frustrated again. "But why did he do it? He had opportunity—because he was there that Sunday. And he had access, I guess—because he must have had a key if he was taking care of Annie when Mr. Becker traveled. But what was his motive, Grandpa?"

He smiled at her. "That's the part you'd have to be a grownup to have guessed. Remember I said he was a local baker, Frankie? What do bakers need to do their job? Things like flour, butter, and sugar, all of which were rationed and difficult for small bakers to get in the quantities they needed in order to keep their businesses going. The upstairs neighbor was a very ambitious man who wanted his little bakery to *grow*, not merely keep going. He'd been purchasing black-market goods from Mr. Becker, and when Becker announced he couldn't do that anymore, he flew into a rage and grabbed the frying pan and beat him with it."

"Oh," said Frankie, nodding wisely.

"As for the cats," her grandfather concluded, "as you may imagine, the baker wasn't a very ethical person. He knew how persnickety Mr. Becker was about Annie, but he didn't care. So when Mr. Becker was out of town, sometimes he left the doors open, and his own sweet black tomcat followed him inside. And that's how it happened."

"But Grandpa, you always say that people are like their cats. If Sugar was really so sweet, how could her owner be such a bad man?"

He smiled at her. "The baker had a very nice wife."

"So Sugar the boy cat fell in love with Annie the girl cat, and they had a baby kitty named—?"

"Cupcake."

"Did they get married?"

"No, dear, they had Cupcake out of wedlock."

A noise at the doorway made both of them look around.

There stood Frankie's mother, who was Dr. Frank's youngest daughter, looking in at them.

"Dad," she said, "do you think a story like that is appropriate for a child her age?"

"Oh, dear, I don't know. I'm sorry! Do you think . . ."

"Let's wait until she's a little older, shall we?"

"Oh, well, yes, if you think so . . ."

"Yes," his daughter continued, "we can wait awhile longer for the birds and the bees."

Her father thought: *Birds and bees? That was what she objected to?* As he lifted Frankie off his lap so she could run to her mother, he happily thought: *Great! If that's all the problem is, next time I'll tell Frankie about the dog who caught a serial murderer!*

At the doorway, the child turned around to ask one last question. "What happened to Sugar and Annie and Cupcake, Grandpa?"

"Sugar stayed with the baker's nice wife," he told her. "And I gave Annie and Cupcake to a kind family who lived in the country. I drove them both out together on Arbor Day of that year, and it was wonderful to get to see Annie run and play outside for once in her life. I even got to see her climb a tree, as if she were celebrating her own personal, very first Arbor Day."

"Oh, Dad," said his daughter, laughing.

But his granddaughter nodded, as if she understood everything perfectly. They smiled at each other as her mother gently pulled her from the room. After a moment of sitting still and listening to their departure, Dr. Frank bent over to begin to pick up the silver foil and white paper streamers that littered the carpet at his feet.

Iä Iä Iä-Iä! Cthulouie!
A Midnight Louie Adventure

Carole Nelson Douglas

I. THE CALL OF À LA CAT

When all Las Vegas is your oyster, it is next to impossible to take a vacation. Where is there to go? It is all here. New York, New York; Monte Carlo; the Luxor hotel pyramid and sphinx; even the wacky world of Oz at the MGM Grand. Just name someplace else, and someone in Las Vegas will have re-created it on a scale that would make epic film director Cecil B. DeMille gnash his dentures with envy.

Nowadays the old town hypes its image with a television commercial. After a visual smorgasbord of the town's newest reconstructions, a voice-over boasts: "Las Vegas, it is like no place else."

Problem is, Las Vegas has become exactly like *every* place else. A dude can hardly scratch up any native sand on which to transact a bit of private personal business.

Still, Las Vegas is my beat, even if it looks more like a movie-studio backlot these days, and I am fond of the old town in spite of all its grand and gaudy excesses. No place offers hot-and-cold running excitement on quite the scale of this multi-personality metropolis on the Mojave, so I am not enthused at the notion of leaving my native turf, even for a business trip, especially not at my signature holiday, Halloween.

"Think of it as a vacation, Louie," Miss Temple Barr coos through my carrier grille.

She is looking guilty, as well she should.

A white stretch limo that extends into next week purrs at the curb outside my home, sweet home, the Circle Ritz condominium and apartment building. Even though I am the original dude in black, twenty pounds of tooth and nail in an ebony fur coat, I am being crated and freighted into the hands of cinemactress Miss Savannah Ashleigh and a cat trainer for a flight to the country's opposite coast. My only consolation for this ignominy is that another carrier inside the limo's dark cocoon shelters my devoutly-to-be-wished-for sweetheart, the Divine Yvette.

"Be good," Miss Temple croons, waving her little hand as I watch her slide away through a tinted glass window, darkly. I hope this is not an omen for the success of this holiday jaunt.

Although I could play the national poster boy for the holiday in question, Halloween is not usually prime time for one of my species and color. Luckily, I am not your average pussycat but a self-appointed feline detective now moonlighting as a jet-setting spokescat. I am no lightweight in any respect, a fact that they carp about at the airport when they hand-carry the Divine Yvette and myself to the gate.

Miss Divine, a Hollywood honey who keeps her weight at a petite seven pounds, travels in a pink canvas carrier emblazoned with her name that hangs from Miss Savannah's shoulder. I am toted by the female trainer, Casey, in a hand-held plastic carrier that scrapes the floor now and then.

"Man, this is a big old boy," the trainer complains, loping along behind the click of Miss Savannah's high heels.

"My little Yvette," Miss Savannah Ashleigh answers with smug possessiveness, "is as light as a feather."

Even I can hear my human travel companion grit her teeth (which are lamentably dull to begin with). Soon, however, I am slung to the cushy leather of a first-class seat. Too bad this plastic shell is between me and it. In the next moment I am thumped onto the airplane carpeting and shoved under the seat ahead, where it is dark and the floorboards thrum like a generator. Forget first class when you are feline and no purebred, so I tune out until I can cut to the chase. In this case, the commercial shoot is slated for a state of the union called Massachusetts.

II. GLAMOR PUSS

Filming cat food commercials may sound glamorous, but I find it to be work. Especially location shoots. Once I am delivered to the set, in short order I find myself afloat on choppy seas, attired in a yellow oilcloth slicker and rainhat to the point of anonymity, being swept toward the Divine Yvette (who is more the Supine Yvette at the moment) by giant fans.

The Divine Yvette is clinging to a red buoy tooth and nail, her indigo eyes wide with a fright more manic than cinematic.

I am an old hand on the bounding main, however, having mastered a dunking in the Treasure Island hotel's pirate-ship cove during one of my cases. And my old man did time on a tuna trawler in the Pacific Northwest, so the sea is in my veins.

This body of waves, however, is not even a first cousin to the sea. We two are adrift on the fan-blown surface of an above-ground swimming pool, circled by a whole crew of potential rescuers, if guys toting expensive videocameras and high-voltage cables can be trusted to leap into the water on missions of mercy for four-footed friends they do not know from Rin-Tin-Tin.

In fact, the camera crew, hired locally—i.e., Ben and Jerry out of New York City—is pretty hip, downright serious, and carries far more equipment than one would need to capture two emoting kittycats for an À La Cat commercial. Perhaps they are from the Method school of feline filming.

The scent of saltwater censers the brisk autumn air, though, for our portable pond is set up on the rocky shingle along the Atlantic Ocean. Beyond us the big waves roll in like anchovy Jell-O, unbroken for thousands of miles save by a low black scowl of rock that looks like a beached sting ray, name of Devil Reef, they say.

My vessel is only a miniature plywood trawler, not the beautiful pea-green boat famed in poesy for romantically inclined pussycats. (And what is so beautiful about pea green, I ask? Especially since it is the color of a pasty-faced human with mal du mer.) If you want a beautiful nautical color, you will find it in the sea-green eyes of the

Divine Yvette, even when she is more than somewhat seasick, as she is at the moment.

"Louie," she wails piteously. "Get me out of here. *Now!*"

What can I do? I am only an actor adrift in my part. But I gallantly throw my weight forward to hasten my arrival at her side. This nearly capsizes my unseaworthy cork, so I bound onto the nearing buoy, which lurches wildly in the waves.

"Cut! Cut!" the director screams from the dry, stable distance.

Water, cold and distinctly wet, laps my darling's curled and clawed little toes. My own tail is as soggy as a salt-drenched cable. Finally the big fans buzz to a dead stop, the waves wane, and Casey wades into the knee-deep water to retrieve us.

"It is a wrap," the director yells.

And wrap it is. The Divine One is soon encompassed by a pink velour bath towel and subsequently cradled in her crooning mistress's arms. I am wrapped in a skimpy brown terrycloth hand towel and crammed dripping into my carrier.

Then we are both whisked back to the Gilman House bed-and-breakfast. If I wanted a change of pace from Las Vegas, I have got it in spades. This burg is so backward it does not even have a McDonald's. I mean, who has ever heard of a half-abandoned coastal Massachusetts fishing town called Innsmouth?

But I understand that we are here because for some reason the fish flock to this backwater, and the area has plenty of local color in the form of fishing boats, buoys, and such.

Now that I am out of the southeaster outfit and ensconced in the dingy bedroom assigned to Casey, I think about what to do for entertainment on an Innsmouth Friday night. This is always a prime fish-eating day of the week in some circles, and in my circles any day is scale day for me. I have not spotted any carp ponds, but the entire bay is teeming with finned creatures, I am given to understand, so I hanker to do a little cruising.

I love bed-and-breakfast places. It is so easy to get in and out of rooms there, what with no chain locks, et cetera. The only television is in the parlor, and there I find Miss Savannah Ashleigh in a turquoise Spandex gym outfit so tight and shiny you would think she was a cellophane-wrapped sausage with a bad case of mold.

She is watching some funky old horror film on the black-and-white television set (I kid you not!) and giggling with the director, Mr. Mitch Marshall, who wears only one earring with his designer jeans and Izod shirts and is the only eligible male (of her species) around.

Sure enough, beside her chair slumps the Divine Yvette's carrier— empty.

I look around and spot my lovely reclining against the wall as far away from the television set as she can manage. Apparently her mistress is viewing one of her old movies.

"Oh, God!" Miss Savannah Ashleigh says. "I cannot believe I was ever desperate enough to make this Reggie Borman film. It was supposed to be set right around here, but of course we filmed it in California. Look at me! I am wearing *bell-bottoms*!"

"I cannot believe you are old enough to have ever worn bell-bottoms," Mr. Mitch Marshall says with the insincere tone of guys in bars trying to manage a pickup.

I ankle over to the wall to pitch some woo of my own.

"Hello there, Beautiful, I see that you are out of your customary container."

"My mistress took me out for a lap session, but then that lying Lothario came along and she forgot all about me. I am not accustomed to being forgotten," she says with a head toss that sets her silver ruff in sensual motion, like a wave of warm, soft velour.

"Then let us escape this dull joint for a night on the town."

"I am not allowed out alone at night or any time else."

"That is as it should be for a delicate little doll like you, but you did not have a suitable escort before who was big and brawny enough to protect you from every eventuality."

The Divine Yvette still looks adorably doubtful, so I jerk my head at her delinquent mistress, who is even now accepting a refill in her glass from a large jug of liquorous nature.

"I am so glad you brought your own," Miss Savannah Ashleigh is cooing to Mr. Mitch Marshall. "This town does not have a liquor store or even a Starbuck's, can you imagine?"

"I can imagine that we will be a lot cozier here tonight," he whispers back. "The loco yokels advised the crew that they have some special Halloween ceremony tonight and we should stay off the streets. A religious observance, I guess."

"Hey, they do not have to encourage me to stay off these nasty, narrow, nauseatingly smelly streets! Why on earth did we end up filming here?"

Mr. Mitch Marshall shrugs. "Lots of fish. For some reason everything has dried up in Innsmouth but the fish and the boats. And with the town so decrepit, there was no city council to demand film permits and paperwork. We can come in and do what we want."

"Oooh, but the place is so creepy." Miss Savannah Ashleigh shivers most unconvincingly, but Mr. Mitch Marshall falls for the act enough to put his arm around her twitching shoulders. "It is much scarier than that old Reggie Borman film, which I guess was based on some stuff by a writer who used to live around here."

"Worry not," he says, "we will hide out here and have our own trick-or-treat party."

They are silent for a while, pursuing courtship rituals that I always try to avoid seeing. Humans are so disgusting. I can tell that the Divine Yvette agrees, for she has turned her face to the wall.

"Ready for a holiday getaway?" I ask.

"How can I? My mistress will notice that my carrier is empty eventually."

"Not if I can help it."

She lifts the airy whiskers above her eyes and watches with rounded pupils when I slink over to the carrier. I spot some sort of lumpish neck pillow on the floor and drag it to the carrier. In two minutes I have stuffed the pillow into the carrier and drawn the zipper shut, using my saber tooth as an implement. I am back at the Divine Yvette's shaded silver side before she can whistle "Cockles and mussels, alive, alive-o."

"Oh, Louie, you are so clever. But what will we do in this Bast-forsaken town if it is as dismal as my mistress and her . . . companion say?"

"Say, I bet I can find some hot spots a pair of hep cats like us would groove on, and besides, your mistress is laboring under a big handicap. Humans do not *like* the smell of fish, especially lots and lots of fish. I can get you some fresh catch wholesale."

All the while I am talking I am nudging the Divine Yvette to her pretty pale little paws and along the wall to the door. It is a rather dingy, dusty wall, so I try to keep her elegant coat from brushing against it. I am nothing if not a gentleman.

We are through the door without anyone's notice and I had seen before that the other crew members had retired to their rooms with whatever private stock they had. For some reason the entire party has been acting a bit depressed ever since we hit town.

But I am exuberant. Here we are, my baby and me, about to step out on our own to paint the town red. It is our first dinner date, and I intend to make it one that the Divine Yvette will never forget.

III. Legend-Shadowed Innsmouth

We inhale the marvelous aroma of the brisk sea air, part cod and halibut, part lobster, part something indescribable.

The Divine Yvette's little rose nose wrinkles. "I must agree with my mistress. Since I have been eating Free-to-be-Feline I have become something of a vegetarian. The odor in the streets certainly is rather . . . fishy."

"*Fishy* is perfume to the feline nation. I am sure that with all these scaled beauties about, our kind patronizes many tasty hideaways down by the waterline. What do you say to a lobster dinner tonight?"

"I do not eat anything I have to remove from a natural casing. I could break a nail."

"I will de-shell the lobster for you, so you have only to nibble on the delicious white meat."

"Oh, very well."

We amble shoulder-to-shoulder down a dark narrow street. High, shuttered houses on both sides hide the stars, and even the moon, but I know that a full one beckons tonight. I can feel its pull in the saltwater within my veins. This will be a momentous evening for Yvette and myself, romantic beyond my imaginings of this moment, which are many and not fit for family consumption.

As I think of consumption, my stomach growls.

"What was that?" The Divine Yvette is cowering in a shadow.

"Nothing, my dear." I improvise quickly. "Probably trick-or-treaters prowling in their mock-monster costumes, making noises to match. We know what real growls are."

She nods, and resumes walking. We are not making tracks for any world speed records. The Divine Yvette walks like Marilyn Monroe, tiny baby steps, each foot crossing in front of the other. It gives her lush tail a delightful rumba motion that must be seen to be appreciated.

I am lagging behind to enjoy the view when she jumps back from an intersection, her fur coat fluffed up like a silvered tumbleweed.

"What is it, my pet?" I inquire in a tone of studly confidence.

"Something . . . someone is down that street."

I peer carefully around the corner, keeping my eyes slit almost shut so they do not reflect the light and draw any undue attention.

This time the Divine Yvette's exquisite nerves are not imagining anything. Shambling figures are indeed doing the hokey pokey down the avenue, such as it is. A fresh wave of fish perfume almost makes *me* swoon, but I cling to consciousness and view their oddly chinless profiles. Some hidden beam of moonlight reflects off their silvered eyes . . . fixed and inexpressive. Their feet barely leave the ground when they walk and they make a scaly, scraping noise as they move that quite intrigues me. My stomach tries to growl again, but I exert all my self-control to quash it. I cannot embarrass the Divine Yvette on our first dinner date by showing too rampant an appetite.

As I am so occupied battling my worse self, a new figure comes into view, one that hops! Yet it is human size. Perhaps all these trick-or-treaters are masquerading as Frankenstein's monster, or at least their impression of him. These Innsmouth types are a backward, isolated, inbred lot, from what I have heard.

None of this disturbs me, however; certain feral clans of my kind have been forced into a dab of inbreeding, with no untoward results other than the usual deplorable population explosion.

There is no population explosion in Innsmouth. From all I have heard, the town has been decimated for decades, and yet so many of these sober Halloween celebrators pass, an entire procession, all of them slobbering and glubbing and squeaking every now and then. And they all seem to be adults, no wee ones out at all.

Despite the heavenly piscine odor, I am touched by a bit of the Divine Yvette's diffidence.

"Let us head for the seaside," I tell her. "I doubt that these trick-or-treaters will be out long, though; few houses look occupied."

"But there are faint lights in the upper stories of some of these ruins," she points out with a well-manicured mitt. "And I have seen strange, humped shadows shuffling past the drawn shades."

"Having a Halloween party, no doubt. Probably dunking for apples. Now, down this alleyway and a few blocks further, and we will be near enough to dip our toes in the tide."

"I do not like water," the Divine Yvette observes in a tone that some might call prissy. Or even pouty. "And my footpads are beginning to hurt from the hard, damp, cold cobblestones."

"Only a street or two more, and I swear the mighty sea itself shall be lapping at our feet as if we were the King and Queen of Tides."

I am relieved to see no more shambling figures as we break onto the shoreline, only a few tented fishing nets, the moonlight visible at last, painting the waves with silver streaks so the ocean looks like a great, purring shaded silver Persian cat asleep in the deep.

I inhale happily. "Ah, nothing like the sea air to enhance an appetite. Is not the moonlight romantic?" I then compare the gently heaving sea to the great, purring shaded silver Persian cat, et cetera.

The Divine Yvette rewards my poetic soul with a coquettish rub against my polished black satin dinner jacket. "What a lovely sentiment, Louie. I should know that you are called Midnight because the nighttime brings out the best in you."

Hey, who needs dinner? By now the exciting fish smell has become as old hat as Sinatra's second-favorite fedora. I can inhale only the heady aroma of pheromones of the feline persuasion, and dare to nuzzle the Divine muzzle.

I am not rebuffed.

This could be my lucky Halloween.

We are dancing cheek to cheek in the moonlight and I think I am in cat heaven, when suddenly the Divine Yvette freezes stiff as a mummy.

I follow the glassy gaze of her aquamarine eyes. She is staring out toward Devil Reef with the concentration of a born predator.

This reaction is unexpected in one who has led such an unnaturally sheltered life. There is not much prey to stare at on Rodeo Drive, unless it is a pink poodle the size of a guinea pig.

"Louie," she breathes in a tone of barely controlled excitement.

My pulses race.

"If the sea is this beautiful, panting, shaded silver Persian whose exquisite coat ripples in the night air, I have news for you."

"Yes, my love?"

"This Persian has *fleas!*"

She sounds most insulted, even peeved, so I gaze more carefully at the gentle moonlit swells between us and the distant Devil Reef.

The waves are aswarm with small dark specks, all moving to land.

"Could it be . . . grunion?" I wonder.

"Grunion?"

"Schools of spawn-happy fish who beach themselves at night. But these fishy full-moon freaks are native to the California coast, naturally . . ."

We hunker down behind a fishnet curtain to watch. As the spots near land, they enlarge and then come lumbering out of the water upright (if you can quite call it that). I am reminded of zombies, of generations of sunken sailors called up from the deep.

Some are robed, others bare and shiny, almost . . . slimy.

The fishy odor gathers into a tidal wave and washes over us with these creatures' passage. It is almost unbearable, even to the feline nose. Yvette buries her little face in my side, trembling with distaste.

I watch the parade pass, scraping and hopping, in an almost human gait, yet quite . . . animal. No, not animal and not quite reptilian, though there is something coldblooded about the moonlit horde humping and jumping ashore. Perhaps ichythoid is the word, a way of saying *fishy* in a more scientific vein.

Now slobbers and croaks come from the passing throng.

We watch until the last ambiguous figure has slithered inland.

"Not lobster," I mutter.

"What did you say, Louie?" comes Yvette's smothered voice.

"Nothing important, my love. I merely said I think we could dine in the French fashion tonight. On frog legs. Lots of very large frog legs . . ."

IV. SHUDDERED WINDOWS

By now even a love-blind Weimaraner would know that something sinister is afoot (or ahop). I tell the Divine Yvette that I will escort her back to the bed-and-breakfast before leaving on a solo investigation. Dinner will have to wait.

She clings to me like a lissome, furred leech. "Do not leave me, Louie! If you do, we will never meet again, I know."

"Do not be silly. I investigate fishy doings all the time, and there is a lot more larceny, felony, and homicide abroad in Vegas than could occur in a puddle in the road like Innsmouth."

So we make our silent, stealthy way back to the byway that hosts the Gilman House. It is not easy. The streets teem with ranks of rank-smelling Halloween revelers, and by now the fishy smell has become a stench redolent of decay.

Occasionally a more human figure moves among the loping, snuffling minions, and that sight chills me more than anything. If anything human lives in this cursed town, it is in service to the misbegotten, mutated multitudes that rule the streets tonight.

We pass an intersection that leads to a square only two blocks away, when I spot an apparent church building, its high thin windows lit by eerie, underwater motes. I glimpse a figure in a trailing robe wearing some sort of Miss America crown, only this tiara gleams with unearthly, unwholesome colors.

Then, amidst the surrounding inarticulate mutters so like a washing seashore, a human voice speaks.

"What about the visitors?"

I stop so suddenly that the Divine Yvette is pressed between me and the wall like a feather duster.

"They are all . . . at the G-G-Gilman House." This second voice has thickened beyond the human, and breaks into high-pitched croaks like a teenage boy's on every other syllable.

The lights from the square cast distorted shadows on the wall opposite us. I will say this for the Divine Yvette: sheltered she may be and scared out of her stripes, but she does not make a peep during this eavesdropping interlude.

"We will come for them later. No outsiders can escape during our semiannual celebration. They might see something to speak of after they leave."

"They will not . . . glug . . . leave."

The speakers are swallowed by the shuffle and hop of many feet, all pouring into the church building as if it were a bottomless pit.

"Come on," I tell my darling. "You must get back to the bed-and-breakfast."

"But you heard! Even that is not safe. My poor mistress! And she is wearing only her second-best workout ensemble. She would die if she were to perish in such a state!"

"No one will perish. I am on the case. I am going to get to the bottom of what is happening here, and then I will stop it."

"One against hundreds?"

"You heard them. They can barely speak, much less think."

"But what will you do?"

"I will infiltrate their ranks to discover who they really are and what this is all about. And then I will think of something."

By now we are back at the shabby door to the bed-and-breakfast. I see that high in the attic a faint light now gleams, but I do not mention this to the Divine Yvette.

"Louie, you are so brave. I cannot let you risk yourself. We will raise an alarm within and—"

"And what?"

"Well, I will yowl like a banshee, then shiver and stand all my hairs on end as if I have had the world's worst permanent wave. My mistress will know that something terrible is happening and insist that I get instant veterinary care and that we all leave immediately."

"You may and she may, but will anyone else rouse themselves in the middle of the night because you might be having a bad hair day? This is not the Hollywood hills, my girl, this is Nowheresville. People have never listened to our kind before. In fact, in this very neck of the woods, a few hundred years ago, during the witchhunts on this very night, they put plenty of our forebears to the torch, too."

"No!"

"Yes! And did you notice something odd about this town?"

"Everything?"

"Besides that. Did you spot anything on four legs beyond the usual wharf rats? Any cats? Any dogs?"

"You think they were all—"

"I think they know better than to hang around Innsmouth, especially on Halloween."

"And especially one of your color, Louie! You must go back. I will investigate. I am not the suspect color, I will—"

"—stand out like a silver Mercedes-Benz in a parking lot full of green Volkswagens."

The Divine Yvette lowers her lashes. "Thank you, Louie. I know you meant that comparison well, but I really consider myself more of the Lamborghini type, possibly a Testarossa."

"Whatever wheels you think you are, baby, they are chrome-plated wire ones. Now go back in like a good girl, and try to calm everyone down."

"It will be hard," she sniffles, "but I will use my most soporific purr. I will even rub against that miserable so-called animal trainer who kept my Free-to-be-Feline away for six hours so I would perform for a bit of nasty, slimy, smelly raw sardine!"

"There is a brave girl."

I paw open a broken-down front window and give the Divine Yvette a lift up via a slightly sharp farewell pat on the rump. What a world-class tail!

Then I am off on errands of a peculiarly repellent nature. Who would think that it would ever be Midnight Louie versus the Fish Folk? All my street days spearing carp from decorative ponds have not been for naught. Although my night-black coat was trouble for my kind in the old days, it does allow me to merge with the dark. I dart from shadow to shadow as I near the square that houses the church.

A religious ceremony, the director had been told, was being held tonight. But what religion? With so many frog-folk present, I might suspect a Roman Catholic bent, but there is nothing remotely French in this town except for the Divine Yvette, and she only has periodic pretensions to being French, having been born and bred in Burbank, California.

I spy the graven letters on another building in the square: Esoteric Order of Dagon. (At first I take it for Order of Dragon, but apparently these debased types in Innsmouth do not know how to spell, because there is no *r* in the word. Actually, sometimes my spelling is a trifle shaky so I am not one to point a paw at others' deficiencies.) But the joint that is jumping is one of the two churches facing the square, a queer edifice with a high, above-ground basement and shuttered windows.

Getting in on the ground floor will be easier, I figure, and besides,

someone left the door open. I boogie in as quietly as a church
mouse . . . which they also do not seem to have in this town. Above
me I hear the thump and jump and slobber and glub and inhuman
croaking of the worshippers.

I have heard and seen a lot of untoward revelry in Las Vegas in my
time, but nothing that compares to what I can only imagine is going
on above.

The fish odor is particularly fetid down here, where the stone and
dirt floor is not only damp but slimy, as if six thousand snails had
done the bunny hop all over the place.

Nobody or nothing appears to be in residence now, dancing or not.
I mince carefully forward to keep from slipping on the slime and
bump right into an altar. Above it hangs an oil lamp that sways as if
we were at sea, but it is just reacting to the uproar above.

Around the stone block are carved strange, coiling creatures and
letters formed into words of no language known on earth, and I have
seen Sanskrit, Cyrillic, Arabic, and plain old Yak on my travels among
the deacquisitioned library books.

Iä-R'eallyeah! Cthulhu phhhht again! Iä! Iä! I can assure one and
all that this is *not* Greek to me. Since the language is so unreadable I
concentrate on the pictographs. My kind was worshipped in ancient
Egypt, so we have a hereditary gift for glyphs.

To study the frieze of strange figures, which runs just below the
top of the altar, I will have to leap on top of it. Ugh! I gather myself
and spring into the oily darkness until the faint lamplight warms my
back.

I crouch atop a stone surface sticky with green ichor, as if those
conga-line snails had given up the ghost here. Above me the cacoph-
ony reaches an unholy pitch. The entire building shakes with the
sound and fury until the shutters rattle on their hinges.

At any moment I expect my sanctuary to be violated by the
humped celebrants, but I crane my neck over the edge and endeavor
to interpret the figures upside down. Actually, they look more attractive that way. I follow the frieze around, spying an island in an immense ocean, with a tribe of humans on bended knee to something
that rises from the sea. Another scene shows a sailing ship amid
ruffled waves . . . with something as huge and humped as Devil
Reef following behind as if towed. The next glyph depicts flying fish

leaping from the waves before a shoreline remarkably like that edging Innsmouth, and a long, low ridge of reef at the rim of the deeper depths.

It is while I am making my sticky circuit of the frieze that my sensitive rear member makes a bit of unexpected contact with something. I freeze myself, wondering what shares the altar top with me. Then I turn, back and tail humped, hair electrified. In the swaying lantern light, I spot a small stone statue, a carving of alien design, showing something so huge and degraded, a mix of sub-aquatic mystery . . . of giant squid and mismated octopus, of shark and serpent and still something that speaks of a human face on the shapeless sac of a head . . . It is as if I am seeing the rotted remains of all hidden bloated beasts of the deeps, reanimated into a revolting new being, into a kind of god so debased that it would give the Devil a good name. Dagon? Or this Cthulhu character?

Whoever, its presence here, and that of its myriad worshippers above, does not bode well for the bodily and mental safety of the À La Cat commercial film crew.

I leap from the altar top down to the slimy floor and bolt into the dark until I find a rickety wooden stairway to the upper regions. Now I can hear faintly human voices chanting, and I run for that last vestige of sanity.

I burst into the upper church unseen, lost in a forest of swaying garments, moisture-darkened along their hems. Croaking, guttural syllables surround me. I weave, overcome by a lethal concentration of fish odor, like cod-liver oil force-fed to a newborn litter. I brush against the revolting vestments and the even more revolting wearers underneath.

And then I smell something else. Expensive leather.

These Innsmouth throwbacks fancy . . . Fendi? Gucci? *Iä! Iä! Versace?* Give me a break! Innsmouth is the antithesis of Rodeo Drive. So I dive under an ichor-soaked robe hem (ick, indeed!), following the scent of designer lambskin, and run right into a black leather backpack. Interesting. Next to it stand the limbs of the creature within. The light leaks through the robe's loose weave, so I unsquinch my eyes and prepare to view the feet I had heard sucking and slurping and slopping and hopping along the Innsmouth byways all night. I expect size-twelve tentacles by now.

I see size-ten Reeboks.

I am not alone.

It only takes a couple of minutes of listening and looking to figure out the situation. I am not the only escapee from the Gilman House Bed-and-Breakfast this Halloween night. Ben and Jerry are out on the town too, in native disguise. So are their cameras, concealed inside the leather bags underneath their disgusting robes. Beneath the raucous uproar, I hear the subtle whirr of hidden tapes recording the goings-on.

Well, well, well. Hello, *Sixty Minutes.*

However, knowing that you are not alone on the *Titanic* may be only momentarily comforting, unlike singing "Nearer, My God, to Thee."

I do not fancy meeting the cat-god Bast with snail-ichor on my tootsies. And I most particularly do not fancy encountering the local deity with the suction-cup manicure and the Bette Davis eyes.

But it cannot be helped. Even if someone human is here recording the distinctly inhuman doings, only the Head Guy can stop the forthcoming carnage. I must go to the top.

V. THE THING FROM THE DEEPS

So I retrace my sticky steps back to the basement, then out the door to the empty streets. I must return to the site of my romantic interlude with the Divine Yvette, but romance is not on my mind.

Unnoticed by any but those who claw like rats at the shuttered windows of the attics as I pass by, I streak through the streets of Innsmouth as if pursued by demons or Dagons.

My route takes me past the bed-and-breakfast, where I am nearly tripped by an extraordinarily luxurious tail that is thrust into my path.

I right myself, sputtering.

The Divine Yvette is posed on the worn stoop, looking adorably determined.

"There are strange creaking and croaking sounds on the floor above our rooms, Louie. I will not be able to get a wink of sleep tonight, anyway. And our valiant cameramen, Ben and Jerry, are missing. I am going with you. Do not try to stop me."

"You have no idea of what I must waken. You have not seen the graven stones, the writhing, rotting heart of Evil grown bloated with the death-swollen carnage of endless eons and bottomless depths. You have not heard the sobbing, gibbering cries of its victims, its worshippers who crawl and hop, croak and creep to lick the pustules of its undulating feet. The horror, the horror!"

My sincerity gives her pause. She shakes her ruff into apple-pie order. "But I have seen and heard my mistress when she first glimpses her unmade-up face in the mirror in the morning. I believe I can face anything. I call upon Bast to protect us."

I want to argue that Bast is a pretty puny god to invoke against the likes of this Cthulhu dude; besides, I did not know that the Divine Yvette had a religious streak.

"Should we not hurry?" she demands.

I cannot argue with that, so I take off again, surprised to find the flying fur of the Divine Yvette at my shoulder. When this babe said she had Lamborghini ambitions, she was not kidding.

We twist and turn through the deserted, damp byways, nearing the seashore and the fetid tide that washed a wave of aquatic flotsam from Hell upon this forgotten Innsmouth shore for Halloween night.

Behind me I hear a soft pattering, like rain. But nothing falls from the sky or wets my tongue when I stick it out. The sound amplifies until it is like a clap of hands at a magician's show. I twist my head, envisioning a Pied Piper's-worth of rats, the only creatures I can imagine sharing this shuddersome town with its loathsome inhabitants.

A mob of racing feet and wind-whipped tails does indeed pursue us: dark hunched forms with pale incisors gleaming.

I lengthen my stride. The Divine Yvette matches me, her pink tongue unrolling with effort. We rush onto the beach and into the moonlight, where I turn back to gauge our pursuers' closeness. Soon we will be rat meat.

But these are exceptionally large rats. As I look I see that all of them are black like me, and some seem . . . charred, and some heads loll at impossible angles. There are dozens and dozens of them, eerily silent, pouring out of the streets of Innsmouth—a legion of black cats, Halloween cats, witches' cats, hunted and hanged and burned by the thousands and millions hundreds of years ago and coming behind us like a many-headed, footed, tailed monster, coming to confront something like the ancient evil that killed them.

"Do not look back," I caution the Divine Yvette so strictly that she actually obeys me. "Our enemy is before us, on that forsaken stretch of rock they call Devil Reef."

Then, facing the sea empty of all apparent living things, including fish, I intone out the words I saw spelled out on the basement altar.

There is silence under the moon, and behind us only the soft, rapid sound of ghost cats panting. The dead do not breathe, and the beast does not come when called. Even if a cat may look at a queen, a cat may not summon a monster.

Yet an ancient antagonism exists between catkind and the denizens of deep water, and in the pallid moonlight I finally see Devil Reef rise, as if the rocks were being driven upward by a tremendous force, an underwater volcano of vengeance and venom.

What hath Bast and Midnight Louie wrought?

The entire dark reef seems to swell, floating, bloating to meet us. Like an oil slick, the shadow darkens the moon-streaked waves, assembling into the bat-black form or a manta ray as large as the dark side of the moon.

Greasy black waves crash over the breakwater stones. They lick their way up the sand, liquid velvet spawned in Hell.

I would retreat but am mindful of the black mass of feline ghouls behind us. Talk about being caught between the Devil and the deep black sea! My only regret is that the Divine Yvette's fate is signed, sealed, and delivered. Nothing will be left of us but an errant whisker by the time this deep-sea leviathan is done.

The body of the beast stretches now from the shore to the reef, as if evil were elastic. It begins to rear up, an amorphous mountain. I see tangled tentacles like the exposed roots of swamp cypress trees and a corpulent, boneless body spreading like pus and a great scaly head with a half-human expression in its twenty-foot-high eyes—flat, silver eyes with bottomless holes of black pinpricks at the soulless center. . . .

Yet there comes another rising. Behind us. The hissing is at first surflike, then it becomes a more sinister sound, resembling hellish fire roaring out of control. I look back, as I urged the Divine Yvette not to do.

The cats . . . the dead cats have risen into a mountain of hissing, spitting forms, black outlined by spectral flames that shoot from gleaming eyes and snarl-shaped mouths.

I blink and look back to the beast from below. It is reaching a height to obscure the moon. Tentacles lash in the ebony ooze of the beach. A whip of suction cups rises above me, then curls around my midsection.

It is like being crushed by an electric eel. I lift off the ground, flailing my feet, my fabled shivs slashing only air.

"Stop that!" the Divine Yvette snarls, "you nasty, scaly, slimy, raw, fishy thing. *Iäääää!*"

Her martial-arts howl would wake the dead, had Bast not done so already. Pale, exquisitely sharpened claws curve into scimitars in the moonlight. Churning limbs attack the tentacle like a buzz-saw.

I feel a sudden sag at my middle and plummet to the sand.

Behind us the cat chorus has reached a pitch that could drown out the clamor of Cthulhu's worshippers, and apparently has.

The black shape on the water shrinks, withdraws, becomes one with Devil Reef. At last the sea is still, and so is the night.

I look behind again. All that masses there is a pile of charred deadwood.

I eye the Divine Yvette, whose unkempt ruff is a spiky silver halo. She looks more than a little like a punk rocker.

Her expression is one of unutterable disgust, but it is not directed at me, I am relieved to say. Instead she is staring towards the sand at our feet.

"Hey!" Things are definitely looking up. "You snared a prime hunk of calimari there. An unusual color. Maybe we should call it blackened calimari. Looks like we can have that seafood dinner for two after all."

Her disgusted look turns in my direction.

"I do not eat sushi," she says. "And who knows where this stuff has been?"

V. ESCAPE FROM INNSMOUTH

Well, it is all over, including the shouting.

By the time the Divine Yvette and I return to the bed-and-break-fast, Ben and Jerry are back, the van that brought us here out front. They are loading the others and their equipment, and urging all possible speed.

Our arrival is greeted with shrieks of relief. We are, after all, the stars of this little epicurean epic. Despite our status, we are tossed unceremoniously into the back of the van, sans carriers.

This allows me to cozy up to the Divine Yvette, who sits washing and washing her feet as if the scent of seafood will never come off.

"I would have liked to have kept it as a souvenir at least," I say, regretting the hunk of Cthulhu left languishing on the beach for the tide to take.

"I suppose you would have had it mounted. Dirty, smelly old dead thing. Males!"

"How did you manage to do so much damage with those dainty little nails of yours?"

"For one thing, they have never been worn down by common activities like street-walking. And my secret for their luxurious length and strength is in the special variety of scratching post I use."

"Oh? I have always found an old fence sufficient."

"Please. I work out indoors, and only on Mommy's best, stretchiest Spandex leotards. This is what also buffs the surface for a special sheen."

She fans the shivs on her right mitt in demonstration while I nod.

The ride back to Boston is exceedingly fast and bumpy. En route, we drowse while Ben and Jerry explain to the others what they think has happened. I listen, trying not to smirk.

"We had an extra, undercover assignment all along," Ben says. "See, we are independent reporters, and word has it that Innsmouth has suffered for decades from unreported, unaddressed toxic waste. That whole bay out there is a pool of putrefaction from the Marsh family refinery."

"Oh," Miss Savannah Ashleigh croons in concern. "Yvette and I drank the water!"

"What we had was well water," Ben assures her. "The remaining residents are not completely unaware of their degraded environment. But did you notice their wan, unhealthy look?"

"They all looked pale, and scaly, and chinless. What they need around here is a good plastic surgeon."

"No," says Jerry firmly. "They need to have the whole bay cleaned up by the EPA. You are right that the 'Innsmouth look' is unhealthy. The skin disease, poor posture, and bone damage are caused by eating tainted fish products. The town was so isolated, and after the pollution got a grip on the place, the neighbors became superstitiously afraid of the poor souls, so that no one in authority was aware of how bad things had become. And then the victims suffered brain damage and made their own decline into a religious cult. It's amazing what isolation and ignorance will do, even in this enlightened age. This is a bigger story than Love Canal, and we've got lots of footage for the evening news. Believe me, once this piece runs, the government will be in here cleaning up their act like gangbusters. Our undercover jaunt will put an end to it all."

"My poor baby!" Miss Savannah Ashleigh pouts, turning in her seat to look at us. "She was lured outdoors by that awful alleycat. I hope she was not exposed to anything toxic."

"No chance. All the action tonight was in that bizarre church."

I beg to differ, but am too polite to say so.

They would be Cthulhu meat, every last one of them, had not I determined the root cause of the commotion and decided to broach the demon on his very own turf and surf.

And, I admit to myself, I would be Cthulhu meat myself, had not the Divine Yvette called on Bast for literal backup and used her awesome shivs on the great big bully from Beyond.

So it was Beauty versus the Beast, and the beast-limb would have been Louie meat if not for the Divine Yvette's delicate sensibilities.

At least I can tell my old man about the Great Old One that got away.

Auld Lang *What?*

Barbara Paul

"I'm gonna kill him, so help me, I'm gonna kill him dead."

"No, you're *not* gonna kill him. Don't talk dumb."

"Well, hell, we can't let him get away with it! We gotta stop him!"

"And how do you propose to do that? Short of killing him."

Gus fell into a vexed silence. He had no idea what to do other than a little homicide, but Conrad didn't seem to cotton to that notion. Gus thought and thought. Finally a new idea came. "Steal it back?"

Conrad nodded approval. "That's better. The only question is *how.*"

That was too much for Gus. He gave up.

Gus was a short, compact man with enormous ears, a combination that left far too many people thinking of a gnome. Gus had long since grown used to the sight of his ears, but his brevity of stature left him with an outlook that occasionally led to regrettable consequences. Not very imaginative or original, Gus used to find self-expression in picking fights with the biggest guy in the bar. Six weeks in traction finally cured him of that, but the attitude persisted.

Conrad's primary advantage in his chosen profession was the averageness of his appearance. Average height, average weight, indeterminate age . . . even his hair was average-colored. He had a face no one remembered, a source of much teenage angst but, he'd learned as he grew older, much better protection than a ski mask. Conrad was the brains of the partnership.

The two men stared sadly at the empty place in the garage where only two hours earlier a new Mercedes had stood. It was *their* Mercedes, Gus and Conrad's—they'd stolen it first. They'd showed it to Harvey and watched him salivate (which is the only reason for displaying one's accomplishments to friends), and then Conrad had gone into the house to get them all beers.

"Why'd you have to leave him alone with it?" Conrad complained.

"I had to take a leak! How'd I know he'd drive the damn thing away?" Gus squinted at the other man. "Who left the keys in the ignition?"

Conrad swore. "All right, so I forgot about the keys. This is the first time we haven't had to pop the ignition in two years. I'm not used to using keys."

They stared at the empty place in the garage some more.

It was Conrad's garage. Conrad's garage was attached to Conrad's house, and Conrad's house was way out in the middle of nowhere— which was the only reason Conrad could afford it. It was so far out that the bus came only once every three hours and a cab ride into the city was sixty bucks, not counting tip. And Harvey had just stolen their only set of wheels.

"How'm I gonna get home?" Gus moaned.

Conrad had been thinking. "He'll have sold the Mercedes by the time we get to him," he speculated. "He must have had a buyer already lined up, someone says, hey Harvey, get me a Mercedes, a spanking brand-new one. And Harvey looks at our Mercedes and knows he can unload it before we can get to him. But how did he get *here?*"

They'd spent the last two hours scouring the neighborhood for the car Harvey had driven. The neighborhood was a bargain-basement housing tract called Pleasant Heights, which was flat as a pancake and not particularly pleasant so as you would notice. Nobody left cars parked on the street in Pleasant Heights, and every garage they'd tried—and they tried them all—had been locked up tight. Hell of a place where you couldn't even borrow a neighbor's car in a pinch.

Conrad looked at his watch. "The last bus leaves at eleven. We got about an hour to work out a plan."

"Last bus? So how do we get back?"

"If the plan works, we drive back . . . in *our* Mercedes."

Gus grinned. "Yeah." They didn't score a Mercedes too often, and they weren't about to let this one get away. "But how do we steal it back, if Harvey's gone and unloaded it?"

"Been thinking about that," Conrad said. "We don't steal it back. We get *Harvey* to steal it back . . . from the guy he unloaded it on."

A slow smile crept over Gus's face. "Yeah. Oh yeah. That's sweet, Conrad." The smile gave way to puzzlement. "How do we do that, exactly?"

"Easy. We take something of Harvey's that he wants back. He wants it back *so bad* he goes and steals the Mercedes for us to get it."

Gus scoffed. "Harvey don't got nothin' like that."

"You sure?"

"Naw, you know how he lives. He's worse off than us. He's got nothin' he cares about except that damn cat he hauls around with him everywhere."

Conrad just looked at him.

Came the dawn. "The cat? We take the cat?"

"Harvey'd do anything for that cat," Conrad pointed out. "He worships that cat. If he had to decide whose life to save, ours or the cat's, he'd go for the cat without even thinking twice. If he was offered a free ticket to Heaven on condition that he gave up the cat, he'd pay for his own ride to Hell. We take that cat, Harvey's gonna do whatever we tell him to do."

Gus was grinning broadly. "I like it."

"It'll be midnight by the time we get to his place. If he's not back yet from delivering the Mercedes, we just take the kitty and leave a note. If he *is* back, we take the kitty and *don't* leave a note. Simple."

Gus liked things simple. "Yeah," he agreed. "Simple."

Harvey was tossing clothes into a suitcase as fast as he could; packing Al's things had taken longer than he'd thought. The tabby sat on the closed suitcase holding all his goodies, eyeing Harvey with a look that said *We're leaving this place?* "We won't be gone long, Al," Harvey assured him. "Just until they get tired of looking for me."

Harvey had a head full of unruly black hair that looked dyed but wasn't. He wore wire-rim glasses and an abstracted air, a combination that allowed him to pass as an academic when the situation called for an alternate persona. Boosting cars wasn't really his thing— that was really Conrad and Gus's line; they had the connections for unloading the product. Besides, Harvey preferred items he could carry . . . and carry without getting a hernia, preferably. But man was not always master of his fate; he'd needed a new Mercedes and there'd been no time for niceties.

Conrad and Gus would be after him, just as soon as they could get in from that residential wasteland where Conrad hung his hat. Harvey had borrowed a Honda Civic to drive out there, and then looked around until he'd found one garage with the door standing open . . . which he'd prudently locked when he left. One resident of Pleasant Heights was in for a surprise the next morning.

Harvey hated doing the dirty to Conrad and Gus; you didn't steal from friends. But he hadn't had a choice; he had to find a new Mercedes before tomorrow night. Harvey had been looking for three days when Conrad called to crow about the spotless model they'd just boosted.

Al stepped into the suitcase Harvey had just finished packing and started to make himself a bed. The man picked him up and crooned, "I'm sorry, big boy, but I have to close that suitcase." He petted the tabby until he heard the familiar purr.

He kept holding the cat although it meant making two trips to move the suitcases from the bedroom to the front door. Harvey was ready to leave when he heard the faint click that meant a lockpick had just nudged a tumbler into place. He grabbed one of the suitcases—Al's—and scuttled back to the bedroom. But there, squatting on the fire escape outside the window, was a big-eared gnome grinning evilly at him.

"You thinking of going someplace, Harvey?" said Conrad's voice from behind him. "Unlock the window—let him in."

With a groan, Harvey put down the suitcase. Still holding Al, he flipped the window latch and Gus crawled inside.

They all went back into the living room of the small apartment. "Harvey, Harvey," Conrad said, shaking his head. "Here we thought you were a friend."

"I was going to send you your share of the money," Harvey said quickly. "Honest, Conrad. I didn't mean to keep it all. I just thought I oughta put some distance between us 'til you had a chance to cool down."

"So you've already unloaded the Mercedes. Okay, Conrad, you can give us the money now. *All* of the money. We don't need you to sell our Mercedes for us."

"I don't have it!" Harvey babbled, beginning to sweat. "I mailed it to myself!" Al squirmed free and jumped to the floor.

Gus was agog. "You trusted real money to the post office?"

"What else could I do? I knew you'd be comin' after me! And I had to get a Mercedes before New Year's Eve or I'd be dead meat!"

Conrad and Gus exchanged a look. "That could do with some explaining," Conrad said.

Harvey sank down on the sofa and wiped his forehead with his arm. "You remember a guy named Whitey? Hustles cameras that fall off trucks."

"He the guy with a tear tattooed on his cheek?" Gus asked.

"That's the guy. Six, seven weeks ago Whitey gimme a call and says he needs help finding a piece. Has to be untraceable and come with a silencer. I find him one, but then Whitey sells one camera too many and the cops pick him up and he can't make delivery on the piece. So he sends me to meet the doctor in his place."

"Who?" Conrad asked. He scooped up the cat and sat down in an armchair.

Harvey cast an anxious look at Al in the lap of the enemy. "Plastic surgeon, lives in Adamsborough." A section of town that was the other end of the economic spectrum from Pleasant Heights. "I meet this guy, he pays full price, no haggling. Then since Whitey is now a guest of the state, the next time the doctor wants something, he calls me."

"So that's a reason to screw your friends?"

Harvey was sweating profusely. "Listen, Conrad, this guy is a cash cow. So when the doctor says 'Get me a late-model Mercedes and get it before New Year's Eve'—I get him a late-model Mercedes. He don't want title papers, nothing . . . just the car. I'd been looking for three days when you called and just happened to mention the new Mercedes in your garage. New Year's Eve is tomorrow—I was running out of time!"

Conrad looked at his watch. "Today, actually. New Year's Eve. Almost one in the ay em. So, Harvey. You mailed yourself the money what, one, two hours ago? That means it won't get delivered today. And no delivery at all on New Year's Day. So we gotta sit around and wait like two and a half days to find out if you're telling the truth or not? We don't want to do that." He looked at Gus. "Do we want to do that?"

"Naw," said Gus. "We don't wanna do that."

"So what you're gonna have to do, Harvey," Conrad said reasonably, "is get us our Mercedes back."

"*What?*" screeched Harvey, which made Al screech and dig his claws into Conrad's thighs, which made Conrad screech.

When they'd all finished screeching and Conrad had unhooked the cat's claws, he explained the plan. "So you see how it goes? If you ever want to see the cat again, you get the Mercedes back."

Gus spent the next three or four minutes reviving Harvey. He'd never seen a man faint before and didn't quite know what to do. Finally a coffee pot full of cold water dumped over Harvey's head did the trick.

Then they had to spend ten minutes listening to Harvey moaning and groaning and threatening and pleading. At one point he made a grab for the cat on Conrad's lap, but Gus courteously escorted him back to the sofa. Harvey rubbed his shoulder. "I think you pulled my arm out of the socket."

"Nah," said Gus. "There weren't no *pop.*"

Harvey took off his glasses and rubbed his eyes. "You guys just don't understand. The doctor lives on an *estate*—you know, big walls, a gate that opens electronically, like that. Adamsborough is full of those. I couldn't get inside, much less drive the Mercedes out through the gate without being stopped."

Hm, that *was* a problem. "That gate's kept locked?" Conrad asked. "All the time?"

"All the time," Harvey agreed. "Except tomorrow night, maybe. Er, tonight, I mean."

"What happens tonight?"

"The doctor's giving a New Year's Eve bash. Lotsa guests coming in. The gate might just be left open."

Gus said, "Go in as a guest."

"I can't, he knows me." Harvey looked at Conrad slyly. "But he don't know you."

The same thought had occurred to Conrad. He stroked Al absently, thinking. "Clothes."

"Monkey suits," Harvey said. Gus groaned.

"It might go," Conrad mused; it was exactly the situation in which his forgettable face worked to best advantage. "I could introduce myself to the doctor twice tonight and he still wouldn't know me the next time he saw me. What's this guy's name?"

Harvey thought twice was a conservative estimate but was too tactful to say so. "Dr. Richard Maximilian. He lives on Shady Oak Drive."

"Maxi-what?" Gus said.

"Maximilian. Like that Hapsburg emperor of Mexico."

"Is there only the one entrance?" Conrad asked.

Gus was frowning. "*Hapsburg* don't sound like a Mexican name."

"Must be a back way in," Harvey said, "but I don't know where it is. I never been inside."

"Might be easier to go out a back way. We have to rent tuxes?"

"Hell, Conrad," Gus said, "there ain't a ready-made tux in the world that'll fit me."

Al had rolled over on his back and was allowing Conrad to tickle his stomach. "You still got that chauffeur's hat?" Conrad asked. "And a black suit?"

Gus's face lit up. "Yeah! I'll be the driver."

"You gonna do it?" Harvey asked, trying not to sound too hopeful.

"We'll need a class-A car. Can't go driving into a party like that in a Chevy."

"You can find one before tonight."

"*We* can find one, Harvey. You and me. Gus, you go out to the doctor's place in Adamsborough and look for a back entrance. Take Myron with you." Myron was a strange young man who worked off and on for a firm that installed burglar alarms; Myron had made *de*installing them his private area of expertise, a specialty that made him much in demand during his off-hours.

Harvey coughed politely. "Myron will want to be paid."

"We'll pay him out of that money you mailed yourself." Conrad ignored the look of anguish on Harvey's face. "Let's see, now. Gus in the driver's seat of an expensive luxury vehicle, me in a tuxedo in the backseat. What's missing from this picture?"

Gus thought a moment. "A broad," he said.

Conrad nodded. "We're going to have to bring Sherry in. If there's a rent-a-cop on the gate tonight, he won't turn a well-dressed couple away unless he's checking a guest list. We won't know that 'til we get there."

They talked some more, trying to think of things that could go wrong. When Conrad and Gus got up to leave, Harvey's face fell when he saw Conrad was still holding on to Al. "You have to take him now?"

"More than ever," Conrad said. "What if we can't get in? All we got to show for our trouble is that cash you mailed yourself. *Then* you get the cat back."

"Al's very sensitive," Harvey said worriedly. "He gets upset easily—so don't yell at him or anything, okay? Wait a sec." He hurried into the bedroom and came back with the suitcase. "This is his food and a couple of toys. Oh—you'll need a litter box." He went into the bathroom.

Gus picked up the suitcase. "Sheesh. Weighs a ton."

Harvey was back with a gray plastic tray and dragging an unopened twenty-pound bag of cat litter. "And here's a box of plastic liners." He handed everything to Gus, who was having a hard time handling it all.

"What about one of those whaddayacallits, pet carriers?" Conrad asked.

Harvey looked shocked. "I'd never put Al in a carrier! A little portable prison? Never!"

"But in a car . . ."

"Al *loves* to ride in cars. He's not like other cats." Harvey's face began to scrunch up. "You're going to take good care of him, aren't you? I mean, you wouldn't really *do* anything to him, would you? Even when you're mad at me?"

"I'll take care of him, Harvey, don't worry about it."

"I mean, he's not like other cats. He's *real* sensitive, you know."

"Yeah, yeah, I'll take *care* of him, dammit!"

There were tears in Harvey's eyes. "Goodbye, Al."

Al didn't say anything.

Down on the street, Conrad left Gus standing on the sidewalk holding Al and surrounded by all the cat's necessities. Before long Conrad was back driving a Dodge Intrepid; he took Al while Gus loaded the car.

Harvey hadn't been exaggerating when he said Al loved to ride in cars, and Al's preferred spot for riding was across the shoulders of the driver. Now, if Al had been a kitten, that would have been cute. But Al was a thick-necked, big-shouldered tabby who weighed twenty-two pounds, all of which was lying across the back of Conrad's neck.

Conrad was stooped forward so far he could barely see over the wheel. "How the hell does Harvey drive like this? Get him off, will you?"

But Al wouldn't be got off. He hissed at Gus and swiped at his hand. "I don't think he wants to move," Gus said, sucking a scratch.

So Conrad drove hunchbacked all the way to Gus's apartment building. Just before he got out, Gus said, "Ya know, we're goin' to a helluva lot of trouble to get that Mercedes back. I know we don't see all that many, but maybe it'd be easier just to look for another one?"

Conrad grinned. "Remember where we're going tonight. Rich man's party, with a lot of rich guests driving rich people cars. *Lots* of rich people cars."

Gus's eyes widened. "We're goin' after more than the Mercedes?"

Conrad nodded. "You, me, Harvey, Myron, and Sherry—that's five cars we can drive away from there tonight . . . including our Mercedes."

Gus laughed out loud. "Five in one go! I like it, I like it!"

Conrad was now bent forward so far his nose was touching the steering wheel. "Say, Gus, I got a long drive back to Pleasant Heights. Do you suppose you could—"

"No animals allowed in this building," Gus said quickly and hurried inside.

Conrad sighed and put the Dodge in gear.

"Whassamadda widdim?" Sherry asked.

"I don't know," Conrad said. "He was all right last night." Al was pacing about, meowing, obviously wanting something. "His litter box is clean. Maybe he just misses Harvey."

"Didja feedim this mornin'?"

Conrad blinked. "Oh." He went out to the Dodge in the garage and brought in Al's suitcase. "I forgot about this." He put the suitcase on the small Formica table in the kitchen and opened it.

"Jesus Christ onna halfshell!" Sherry exclaimed. "Didjever see so many kindsa cat food?" Al jumped up on the table and started nosing among the cans. "Yeah, thass what he wants, awright. Hokay, Al, which one'll it be?" She made a sound of annoyance. "Whoever hearda namin' a cat *Al*?"

Al seemed most interested in Savory Duck with Meaty Juices. Conrad found an empty aluminum pie pan; Sherry dumped in the cat food and put out a bowl of water. "Buy milk, Conrad."

"Milk." As if he didn't have enough to do today. They watched Al chomping away on his Savory Duck for a moment and drifted back into the living room.

"Ya promised to take me to a club on New Year's Eve," Sherry said, stretching out on the sofa. "One a them *expensive* ones."

"This'll be even better," Conrad said. "A private party at a rich doctor's house." He was having trouble standing up straight; crick in his neck.

Sherry allowed as how a private party might be an improvement over a club. Sherry looked like an aristocrat: thin nose, delicate lips, exquisite profile, graceful swanlike neck, naturally gold hair that curled into fine ringlets, a body that was slender without looking anorexic. It was only when she opened her mouth that the illusion was shattered. Sherry got modeling jobs now and then, but she was fired from her only chance at a TV commercial; the director, who'd planned on dubbing in another voice, hadn't allowed for the way Sherry twisted her mouth when she talked. Or tawked. Sherry was aware of the problem and was taking diction lessons. But after six weeks, Conrad could hear no change.

"Gotta clothes prob," she said.

"That blue sequiny thing. Or the white clingy dress."

"No, thass okay, that part," she said. "But it's New Year's Eve."

"So?"

"December thirdy-first, middle a winter?"

"So?"

"*Fur coat*, Conrad. Whaddaya think, I'm gonna go to this rich party in my Lunnon Fog?"

"Oh." He hadn't thought of that.

"An' whadd*ayew* gonna wear for a topcoat? Ya gotta think a things like that."

"Hell." He sat down and made a list. *Fur coat, topcoat, milk for Al. Rent tux. Steal car.* "Gus and Myron'll be here late this afternoon, and Harvey as well. Our last chance to make sure we've thought of everything."

"All I need's a fur coat and I'm set."

"I gotta get going."

Al came strolling in from the kitchen, long pink tongue cleaning off his mouth. He jumped up on the sofa beside Sherry and licked her hand. "Aw," she said.

"Where the hell am I gonna get a fur coat?" Conrad muttered and left.

He drove the Dodge back into the city and left it on a street where it'd be found before long; the car had served its purpose. Harvey was waiting at the Have a Cuppa café and immediately bombarded Conrad with questions about how Al was doing. Conrad assured him the cat was eating and when last seen was curled up happily with Sherry on the sofa.

They headed for the nearest hotel's underground parking. Nothing there more costly than a Cadillac, which Harvey said was what the doctor's servants drove.

At the second hotel they spotted a Lamborghini, but it had The Club locking the steering wheel into place. At the third hotel, they were considering a Chrysler Concorde until they saw the garage ticket hadn't been left on the dashboard.

But at the fourth garage, they were both struck dumb by what they saw. "Is it?" Harvey asked after a moment. "Is it really?"

"It is," Conrad said, as impressed by their good luck as Harvey was. A Rolls-Royce. A no-kidding, honest-to-god, gen-you-wine Rolls-Royce. The garage ticket was tucked into the otherwise unused ashtray.

Harvey stood watch while Conrad got to work. Conrad had never done a Rolls before and it took him a little longer than usual, but soon that noiseless engine was doing its thing. Harvey climbed in.

The garage ticket said the Rolls had been left there late the night before; a different ticket-taker would be on duty now. "Room number, sir?" the man inquired politely.

"Twenty-one-ten," Conrad said.

"Have a nice day."

Conrad had a feeling he would. He drove the Rolls back to the first hotel's parking area and left it there.

Harvey was grinning as they walked away. "Man, are you lucky or what? A Rolls."

"Yeah." Conrad could hardly believe it either. He glanced up at the sky. A lot of what looked like snow clouds up there. He'd just as soon not have bad weather to worry about tonight.

"So," Harvey said, "what's next?"

"You ever boost fur coats, Harvey?"

Harvey shook his head. "The only way to get hold of furs is when they're in transit. They keep 'em in cold-storage vaults, you know. Real hard to get at."

Conrad swore. "I gotta get a coat for Sherry for tonight."

"Oh yeah. So she'll look like the rest of 'em there. The wives and girlfriends."

"And I need one too."

"You want a fur coat?"

"Not a *fur* coat, a topcoat. An expensive one."

Harvey adjusted his glasses. "You think about renting 'em?"

Conrad stopped walking. "You can rent coats?"

"It can be arranged. This guy I know in the rags biz. He'll want a deposit, though. A kinda big one, Conrad."

Conrad looked around; nothing of interest in the immediate vicinity. "Let's go shopping."

They found a Cherokee Laredo that Harvey said would more than satisfy this guy he knew. "But you gotta take the coats back, Conrad. The Cherokee is just a deposit. He won't do business with me again if you don't take 'em back."

"I got it, I got it—I'll take the coats back."

As it turned out, Conrad ended up renting a fur coat for himself after all—mink for him, sable for Sherry. They left the Cherokee with this guy Harvey knew and looked around for transport. They settled on a Pontiac Grand Am, which Harvey would be driving that night.

The snow was still holding off. They had to go four places before they found a still-unrented tuxedo; Conrad was beginning to think they'd left it too late. Then Harvey drove them back to the first hotel parking garage, where Conrad picked up the Rolls and started back to Pleasant Heights.

He remembered to stop for milk on the way.

"A shockin'-pink tuxedo?" Sherry said unbelievingly.

"It was all they had left," Conrad muttered.

"Nobody'll remember yer face fer sure," she remarked. "They'll be too busy lookin' at that tux."

Conrad practiced holding his head high and bouncing along in a self-confident manner. Maybe he could pull it off.

Their meeting late that afternoon had been spent mostly on working out what details they could. Harvey had sat holding Al the whole time.

Gus and Myron, the expert alarm deinstaller, had found the back gate. "The gate opens manually," Myron said nervously; Myron was always nervous. "There's an alarm system, but I'll take care of that tonight. Don't want them noticing the alarm's out too soon."

"Then there's no problem."

"Well, a little one. The gate opens manually from the *inside*. We can't get in that way to pick up the cars unless you come back and open the gate."

"Okay, I'll take care of it. Myron, did you get your driver's license back yet?"

"No, but I borrowed my brother-in-law's. If I'm stopped, I'll have I.D."

Myron was the only one Conrad was worried about. The rest of them were all good, steady drivers—Sherry, the steadiest of the lot. But Myron was one of those people who kept moving the steering wheel constantly; the one time in his life that Conrad had been car sick was the time he'd ridden with Myron.

Gus read his mind. "Myron'll do just fine, Conrad. We had time for a little drivin' lesson this afternoon."

"It's just that they scare me," Myron said nervously. "Those great big machines. Mobile lethal weapons, that's what they are. And these cars tonight are going to be *real* big, I bet."

"You'll do fine," Gus said soothingly. "And if ya don't, I'll kill ya."

Myron squeaked and Conrad hastened to assure him that Gus was joking. They agreed on a shares system, the profit to be divided only when all six cars had been unloaded. Six cars, not five. The Rolls was just too good to give up.

Gus would drive Conrad and Sherry to the doctor's house, drop them off, and then drive straight back to Pleasant Heights. He'd leave the Rolls in Conrad's garage, get in the Pontiac with Harvey and Myron, and Harvey would drive them to the doctor's back gate. The five luxury cars Conrad picked out would leave that way, and the Pontiac would be left behind.

"And the whole thing falls apart if you can't get through the front gate," Harvey said gloomily, stroking Al.

"We'll get through," Gus said ominously. "One way or another."

"Gus has amazing persuasive powers," Conrad added.

They wanted to time it so Conrad and Sherry would arrive shortly before midnight, when the partygoers would be too busy celebrating to pay much attention to a couple of strangers in their midst. Conrad hoped to avoid going into the house at all; the less exposure, the better. Besides, this doctor had had Harvey find a gun for him, and he might not be afraid to use it.

Conrad and Sherry put on their fur coats and got into the backseat of the Rolls. Gus settled in behind the wheel, his chauffeur's cap making his big ears seem even more prominent. "It's gonna snow," he said, and started the engine.

Sherry looked like a queen in her sable; Conrad felt honored just to be sitting beside her. "Now remember," he said, "if we do have to go inside to the party, you don't get into any conversations. All you say is *yes, no, I don't know,* and *thank you.*"

"What a swell party this is gonna be," Sherry grumbled.

"So what do you say?"

"Yes, no, I dunno, thank you."

The *thank you* came out sounding awfully nasal. "Make that *sorry* instead of *thank you.*"

"Somebuddy hands me a drink, I say *Sorry?*"

"Just smile."

They hadn't driven far before the snow that had been holding off all day finally began to fall. Gus spoke from the front seat. "Hey, Conrad, you better go in the house. Freeze your tush hangin' around outside waitin' for us to get there."

"Yeah, I don' wanna stand outside in this," Sherry agreed, peering out at the big snowflakes.

Neither did Conrad. They could sit in one of the cars, but that might be a little noticeable . . . especially if he turned on the engine to start the heater.

Shady Oak Drive in Adamsborough was probably beautiful in the daytime, but at night it looked as if it was lined with those trees that tried to grab Dorothy and Toto. "Jesus!" Gus yelped, making the two in back jump. "Look what's ahead of us!"

Conrad peered past the moving windshield wipers at the car they were following. "Is that a Bentley?"

"Sure as hell looks like it. That'un's gonna be a collector's item in another couple years. Oh, come on, you beautiful Bentley—go to the doctor's party!"

The Bentley heard him. The man stationed at Dr. Richard Maximilian's gate, who'd been toasting the New Year a little early, saw a Bentley followed by a Rolls and just waved them both in. Conrad breathed a sigh of relief; their biggest hurdle was over. The driveway sloped upward slightly and then took a curve to the left before splitting into a circular drive before the house. Better and better; they were out of sight of the gateman.

The driveway was almost filled with parked cars, all of them dollar signs on wheels. The Bentley pulled into one of the last places; Gus drove on by and stopped directly before the front entrance.

"Don't waste any time," Conrad said as he and Sherry got out.

"I know the schedule," Gus growled and pulled away.

"Look at that, Sherry," Conrad said suddenly. "Our Mercedes— Gus's and mine. Parked right there."

"Oh, yeah? You sure that's it?"

"I'm sure. But why did he put a hot Mercedes out here with the guest cars? Why doesn't he keep it in the garage out of sight?"

But he didn't have time to puzzle over it then; a couple in their fifties were getting out of the Bentley. "Remember," he said to Sherry, low, "don't get into any conversations."

"Thanks fer rubbin' it in," she hissed.

The older couple joined them by the door. The Bentley man said, "There's a space behind us where your driver could park."

"Oh, he's running an errand," Conrad said easily. "He'll be back in an hour."

If the Bentley couple thought it odd that a chauffeur should be running errands just as New Year's Eve was about to turn into New Year's Day, they gave no sign. The man pressed the doorbell. Conrad wondered what Dr. Richard Maximilian's friends called him. Richard? Rich? Dick?

The door opened. "Hello, Max," the Bentley man said.

"Happy New Year!" added Mrs. Bentley.

"And the same to you," the man in the doorway said, smiling a welcome. "Come in, come in!"

You knew just by looking at him that this guy could only be a doctor. You'd never mistake him for a lawyer or a politician or a banker; everything about him spelled *doctor*. Mid-forties, good-looking, wearing an air of authority as easily as he wore his tailored tux. A man who controlled life and death. He glanced quizzically at Conrad, visibly trying to put a name to the unremarkable face.

"Max, you've never met my wife," Conrad said smoothly. "Natalie, say hello to our host."

Hello was not in Sherry's authorized vocabulary. "Yes," she said with a smile.

"Yes, indeed," Dr. Max said appreciatively, taking a good look at Sherry. "You're just in time. In five minutes we ring out the old and ring in the new. Here, let me take your coats."

"I'll take care of that," Conrad volunteered. He hung everyone's coats in the entryway closet, delaying taking off his own until the others had disappeared into a room to the right. In the bright entryway lights, his tuxedo looked pinker than ever.

In a room to the left, a small combo was playing for those who wanted to dance. But in the room the others had gone into, to the right, Conrad was happy to find the lighting was subdued; he took his pink tux into a shadow and surveyed the place. Most of the guests were in profitable middle age, the women bright and glittering and the men suave and well pleased with themselves. They all spent hours working out every week, you could tell. The only two younger people in the room both looked like movie stars. Dr. Max was a plastic surgeon, Harvey had said; Conrad wondered how many of the beautiful people here were his patients. The room was noisy, everyone talking and laughing over the music playing from the other room.

But he couldn't see Sherry. Conrad worked his way through the shadowy places to a doorway on the other side. It led to the dining room, where a sumptuous buffet was laid out. The room was packed and the noise level in there was even higher than in the first room. Over in the corner Sherry was listening attentively to something Dr. Max was saying. Conrad snagged a glass of champagne from a passing waiter and stepped back into the first room, staying close to the doorway where he could keep an eye on their host. His tux drew one or two startled glances, but no one said anything.

"Hi, uh, there," a woman in a gold lamé gown said. "Have you seen Edgar?"

"Not recently," Conrad replied. "Have you lost him?"

"Looks like it," she said with a sigh. "Now we'll miss our New Year's kiss."

"Consider a substitute, then. Will I do?"

She laughed lightly. "You'll do very well, but I must confess I've forgotten your first name."

"Roger."

"Roger, right. And I'm Mamie . . . oh, you know that, don't you? Too much of the bubbly, I'm afraid."

Then it was time. The house was filled with the sounds of noisemakers and horns and cries of *Happy New Year!* At least all the television sets weren't tuned to the ball dropping in Times Square. Conrad and Mamie exchanged a chaste kiss.

"Hey, there!" a voice said good-humoredly. "That's my wife you're kissing!"

A short, stout man in a gold lamé dinner jacket that matched his wife's dress came up to them. Conrad dropped a friendly hand on his shoulder and said, "Edgar, the first time I ever get a chance to kiss Mamie, and you have to come along and spoil it."

Edgar laughed, but he had the same uncertain look that everyone got when trying to place Conrad. "Uh, nice tux."

Mamie said, "Roger was just being a gentleman." She held her arms out to Edgar.

While they were welcoming in the New Year, Conrad took another look into the dining room. Dr. Max was smooching Sherry with perhaps more enthusiasm than the occasion called for. When Edgar and Mamie came out of their clinch, Conrad said, "Come with me a minute, will you? I want you both to meet my bride."

"Oh yes," said Mamie brightly, "we'd love to meet her."

With his two new allies in tow, Conrad was able to pry Dr. Max away from Sherry and introduce "Natalie." It worked out well. Dr. Max assumed Edgar and Mamie knew him, and Edgar and Mamie *knew* Dr. Max knew him, since he was so busy bussing Natalie when they approached. Conrad relaxed a little.

A little later he passed some time listening to the Bentley man complaining about his problems with the unions. Then later still Conrad and Edgar loaded up plates at the buffet table and sat down to eat and talk automobiles, a subject Conrad knew well.

When Edgar went back for seconds, Sherry came up and whispered in Conrad's ear, "Can I talk now?" *Kin ah tawk naow?*

"No!" he answered, alarmed. She looked so crestfallen that he added, "Sherry, you're doing so *good*. Don't run any risks now!"

Slightly mollified, she turned away to circulate. Immediately Dr. Max was at her side. Conrad scowled.

Eventually his watch told him it was time; Gus and the other two should be in place. Conrad slipped out to the entryway and got his coat; Sherry would follow in fifteen minutes. Outside, he made a quick circuit of the driveway to select the cars they'd take. His heart was pounding; never before had he seen so much money parked in the same place. One of the cars stopped him cold; when he came out of his daze, he hurried around to the back of the house.

The snow had stopped falling, but the ground was covered and he slipped and slid all the way along to the back gate. The gate was secured by a slide bolt, a big one; Conrad shoved and strained until it finally moved. He pushed open the gate cautiously; no alarm sounded.

Immediately three men got out of the Pontiac parked on the service road. "Yer late," Gus said reprovingly. "Havin' too much fun with the rich and famous?"

"Hey, have I got something to show you! Wait 'til you—Jesus, Harvey! You didn't bring the cat!"

"He wouldn't come without him," Gus said apologetically.

Harvey was cradling Al in his arms. "Why not? You don't need him as a hostage anymore."

Myron was pacing in nervous circles. "Can we get on with it?"

Conrad swore but led them back to the front of the house without saying any more about the cat. Sherry was just coming out of the house as they reached the circular driveway. "You brought Al?" she said to Harvey.

Conrad led them to his find. An almost religious silence filled the air as they stood gaping at the automotive shrine. Only Myron didn't understand. "What is it?"

"It's a Bugatti," Gus said reverentially.

"I've never even seen one in the flesh before," Harvey murmured in awe-hushed tones.

"For what that Bugatti cost," Conrad pointed out, "you could buy five Mercedes." Mercedeses?

"Six, maybe," Gus added. "Speaking of Mercedes . . ."

"It's right up here." He led them to the twice-stolen car.

"What's it doin' out here?"

"Beats me. Harvey, it seems only right that you should drive it back." Conrad used a bottle opener and a loop of wire to raise the hood so he could disable the interior alarm. Then he hooked the door open and popped the ignition, a job he'd performed before on this very car. "There you are, Harve. Take off."

But when Harvey started to get in, Al began to growl and then scream and hiss and fight Harvey. He wriggled free and dashed away.

"Al!" Harvey cried in alarm. "Come back!"

"Keep your voice down," Conrad growled. "Come on, get the Mercedes out of here."

"I'm not leaving without Al!" Harvey lumbered off in the direction the cat had taken.

Conrad ground his teeth; were they going to blow the biggest score of his life because of that damn cat? He seriously considered leaving Harvey behind, but Harvey would talk his head off if he was caught. "Everybody—find Al. Find him fast."

They wasted ten minutes looking in the dark for the reluctant tabby. Conrad was tearing his hair by the time Sherry said, "Here he is."

The cat was crouched under a Maserati Conrad had tagged for

removal. Al wouldn't respond to coaxing, so Harvey got down on his stomach in the snow and pulled the cat out, more gently than Conrad would have done. But when they went back toward the Mercedes, Al began to growl again.

"He doesn't like this car," Harvey said, puzzled. "Maybe I'd better drive the Bugatti."

"*I'm* driving the Bugatti," Conrad snarled and took Al away from Harvey. "He can come with me. Now get going before somebody comes out and sees us." Harvey cast a rueful glance at his cat but did as he was told.

Gus got to drive the Bentley back. All those magic cars had had an effect on Myron, who was eyeing the Maserati Al had been hiding under. But Conrad didn't want their poorest driver handling *that* car; the Maserati was for Sherry. Myron was quite happy when Conrad gave him a red Porsche to drive away.

At last Conrad took possession of the Bugatti. The powerful engine, the luxurious interior, all the little touches that put the Bugatti into a class by itself—driving it was a delight like no other Conrad had ever experienced. *Even better than sex,* he thought euphorically. No vibration, no sound of the engine at all, a feather-touch steering wheel. Conrad floated through the back gate and down the service road. The Bugatti didn't even deign to notice the slipperiness of the road surface.

Conrad luxuriated in every second of the drive back, in spite of the twenty-two pounds of feline weighing down on his neck and shoulders.

After the cars had been stowed in carefully selected hiding places and everyone had grabbed a few hours' sleep, they all assembled at Conrad's house in Pleasant Heights again, at Conrad's request. Also at Conrad's request, Harvey had brought the Mercedes and parked it in Conrad's driveway, since the Rolls was taking up all of the garage space. They tossed a tarp over the car; a Mercedes was not one of your everyday sights in Pleasant Heights.

Gus had stopped at a Roy Rogers on the way and brought them all breakfast. "I like croissants," he announced as he worked his way through four ham, egg, and cheese sandwiches. "They don't get in the way of the food."

They were all feeling cheerful and self-congratulatory after pulling off last night's job; the mood was one of celebration. But Conrad had slept little and the crick in his neck was worse. He'd also been drinking coffee since six a.m. and was feeling the effects. "Something we need to talk about," he said, "but I gotta pee first."

He found Harvey in the bathroom, standing morosely over Al's litter box. "You haven't been scooping," he said accusingly. Conrad finished his business and left Harvey to deal with the litter.

Al had spent the night on the foot of Conrad's bed and had greeted Harvey's arrival in the morning with a big yawn. Once Sherry had gotten there, the cat had picked her lap as the one he wanted to nestle on. Al was the most placid animal Conrad had ever seen, which made last night's hissy fit all the stranger.

"It's that Mercedes," Conrad said when they'd all gathered in the living room. "I'm wondering if we bought ourselves a problem."

Myron the non-car person asked, "Which one's the Mercedes?"

"The one I drove," Harvey said. "The one sitting out in the driveway right now."

"Oh. That one."

Gus said, "What about it, Conrad?"

"It's been bothering me all night," Conrad replied. "Why did Dr. Max put it with the guest cars? Even if his garage was full, there was plenty of space in the back to leave it. And he had it parked right at the top of the circular drive near the front door, like he wanted people to notice it."

Gus was frowning. "Why would he do that?"

"I don't know, Gus, but I think we'd better try to find out." He shifted his weight. "Harvey, the way Al acted when you started to get into the Mercedes—does he do that a lot?"

"He *never* does that," Harvey said flatly. "I've never seen that kind of behavior before. I don't know what got into him."

"Conrad?" Sherry asked. "What ya thinkin'?"

"I'm thinking we got the Mercedes and we got Al. Let's see if it happens again. And for crying out loud, Harvey, hold on to him this time. I don't want to go chasing that friggin' cat all over Pleasant Heights."

Gus was still frowning. "So what the hell does it matter *what* the damn cat does?"

"Don't talk about him like that," Harvey said crossly. "He can hear you."

Gus rolled his eyes.

"Maybe they've got drugs hidden in that car," Myron suggested. "They use dogs to sniff out drugs, don't they? What if cats can be drug-sniffers too?"

"Let's just go see. Sherry, give the cat to Harvey." They all trooped out to the driveway.

But the minute Harvey approached the Mercedes, Al started yowling and hissing and struggling to get free. Harvey backed away, and Al's protest eased down to a low growl.

Myron nodded emphatically. "Drugs."

Conrad moved toward the trunk of the car. "Try back here, Harve."

Al's reaction was stronger than ever.

"Put him back in the house," Conrad said. Harvey did, and Conrad went into the garage for the tools he needed. Gus held up the back of the tarp, and eventually Conrad got the lock open after a couple of false starts.

He raised the lid. Curled inside the trunk was a man none of them had ever seen before, and he was quite dead. A red blossom marked his forehead where the bullet had gone in.

"Well," said Conrad, "now we know what Dr. Max wanted the gun for."

The dead man's name was Lawrence Kiernan, according to the I.D. in his billfold, and he was also a doctor. He'd carried one of those door-opening cards for the Kiernan Clinic for Corrective Surgery. One of Dr. Max's peers, then, and a threat to Dr. Max in some way. Or he was standing in the way of something Dr. Max wanted bad enough to kill for.

"Does Dr. Max work at the Kiernan Clinic?" Conrad asked Harvey.

"I don't know, Conrad." Harvey was hugging Al, miserable and frightened, close to him.

Conrad looked at his friend. "Better stay inside for a while, Harve."

Harvey nodded; he'd already figured it out. He could connect Dr. Max both to the Mercedes and to the gun that fired the bullet that had killed Dr. Kiernan. Harvey was not in an enviable position.

The body was still stiff; rigor mortis hadn't passed yet. Dr. Kiernan couldn't have died more than a few hours earlier—and that meant *during the party.*

"That's the part I don't get," Sherry said. They'd left the body in the Mercedes for the time being and gone back into the house. "How could he off this guy while his whole bloomin' house was full a people? How could he move the body, like, outside—widdout bein' seen? That entryway was bright, Conrad. All those lights?"

"That must be where he killed him. He got this Dr. Kiernan to go with him to the entryway somehow and shot him there, right by the front door. The gun had a silencer, remember, and the party was pretty noisy. Then all he had to do was open the door and lug the guy a few steps to the Mercedes—which he had waiting right there."

Gus nodded, squatting gnomelike on an ottoman. "Then Dr. Max waits until ever'body goes home and runs the Mercedes off a cliff or into the river. And even if the car's recovered, it's hot and can't be traced to him." He grunted. "Woulda been cheaper to use a old Buick."

"He needed something that wouldn't look out of place among his guests' cars," Conrad pointed out. "But that last part didn't happen. His guests start going home, four of them discover their cars have been stolen, Dr. Max sees the Mercedes is gone too. So . . . what is the good doctor doing right now?"

"Laughin' his head off," Gus said glumly.

He probably was, at that. They'd taken his disposal problem off his hands. "So do we just dump the body?" Conrad asked. "I'd like to give him back to Dr. Max."

"That ain't none of our business," Gus said, "that murder. Just dump him."

"Yeah, just dump the body," Harvey said sarcastically. "Forget about me."

"He's right, Gus," Sherry said. "Harve's in deep doo-doo long as Dr. Max's on the loose. *He's* the one oughta get stuck with the body."

Myron cleared his throat. "Police? Leave the car somewhere and phone in an anonymous tip?"

Four heads turned toward him in utter astonishment.

"Bad idea," Myron said hastily. "Forget I said anything."

"Myron," Conrad remonstrated, "that's a perfectly good Mercedes out there! Okay, so it's got a dead body in the trunk. We'll just . . . figure something out."

Myron scratched the back of his neck. "Yeah, well, we better figure it out soon. The cold weather's helping, but he's gonna start smelling, you know. Whatever we're gonna do, we better do it fast."

They all looked at Conrad.

Conrad sat with his arms folded, thinking, for a long time. Eventually he raised an eyebrow and said, "You guys willing to trade the Mercedes in on another car?"

"I didn't think you'd be open on New Year's Day," Myron said.

"Our clinic is open twenty-four hours a day, seven days a week," the receptionist replied primly. "Patients need round-the-clock care, you know."

"Yeah, I guess so. Well, I wanted to ask about getting a nose job."

"Then we'll set up an appointment for a preliminary examination, and the doctor will explain the possibilities to you and set a fee."

"Which doctor?"

"Did you wish to see a particular surgeon?"

"I kinda thought the head guy. Dr. Kiernan."

"Dr. Kiernan is booked four months ahead. Are you willing to wait that long?"

"Naw." Myron appeared to think. "The only other plastic surgeon I heard of is Dr. Maximilian. I don't suppose he's here, is he?"

The receptionist smiled condescendingly. "Dr. Maximilian is one of the owners of this clinic. He and Dr. Kiernan are partners."

"Yeah? Then why isn't it called the Kiernan and Maximilian Clinic?"

"It probably will be, before long. Dr. Maximilian only recently became Dr. Kiernan's partner. But I'm afraid Dr. Maximilian is booked months ahead as well." She flipped a page in her appointment book. "Dr. Smathers can see you next Tuesday. He's an excellent surgeon, and he specializes in nose reconstructions."

"Okay, Dr. Smathers, then," Myron agreed.

He filled out a long questionnaire the receptionist gave him, inventing a name and a medical history for himself. He made an appointment he'd never keep, and left the clinic thinking that it might be a good place for Gus to go get his ears fixed.

Gus wasn't exactly surprised to learn that Dr. Max drove a Ferrari Testarossa; great status symbol, that model. Gus started the Lincoln he'd just liberated and followed the Ferrari to a police station. "Prolly makin' a statement," Gus said to himself. The cops were starting the new year with two new cases, the theft of five luxury cars from the grounds of Dr. Max's house while a party was going on, and the disappearance of Dr. Kiernan from that very same party. Would the cops think the two cases were connected? Of course they would.

When Dr. Max was finished at the police station, he drove to 4 Westminster Place in Adamsborough, the address on Dr. Kiernan's I.D. Another walled-off palace, only this one was on an elevation and Gus could see the front door. Two unmarked cars were parked there. One was a local cop car; Gus could spot those a mile away. The other he thought was a fed car, which meant the FBI, which meant they were thinking kidnapping. A woman opened the door and let Dr. Max in.

Gus felt an uncharacteristic flare of anger. That scumbag Max had done Mrs. Kiernan's husband and now here he was offering sympathy and concern, blah blah blah. Hypocrite. He was a doctor, hadn't he'd taken an oath not to be hypocritical? But he was a killer and a scumbag. Even if he wasn't a threat to Harvey, they oughtn't to let him get away with it.

Dr. Max stayed half an hour and then left. Falling back as far behind as he could without losing him, Gus tailed the Ferrari to still another posh residence in Adamsborough. Gus stopped a kid on a bicycle and asked who lived there. The Langer family, the kid said. Mr. Langer was a lawyer. *Not wasting any time,* Gus thought.

From the lawyer's house, Dr. Max went looking for a gas station that was open; he ended up at a self-service place just outside

Adamsborough. When he'd filled the tank, the doctor sought out the men's room.

Gus left his car grasping the note Conrad had written:

We've got something that belongs to you. We'll get rid of it for a fee. Or we'll return it to you, no charge. We'll call you at the clinic at 6 o'clock.

Gus added a P.S. of his own: *We could have took the Ferrari.*

He stuck the note under a windshield wiper and got out of there.

"Hell, Conrad, I could lose my license!"

"Only if you tell somebody, Jimmy. I'm sure as hell not going to."

Jimmy shook his head. "Too risky. Some other cabby sees my taxi, knows it, sees you or Gus driving, calls the cops—"

"On New Year's Day? How many cabs are out cruising? Everyone's at home sleeping it off. Besides," Conrad added the clincher, "we won't be using it 'til after dark. It won't be on the road more than half an hour, forty-five minutes max. And just think what you're getting in return. Come on, Jimmy—when did you ever get an offer like this before?"

The cab driver sighed. "You're right. I'd be a fool to turn it down. Okay, Conrad, you got a deal."

"Great! Now, what would you like me to get?"

"I'd like a Jaguar," said Jimmy.

Harvey took off his glasses, cleaned them, put them back on. Two minutes later he took them off again, cleaned them again, put them back on. He had the fidgets, sitting in Conrad's house all day while the others set things up. But Conrad had warned him not to stick his nose out of doors until this thing was wrapped up. As if he needed warning.

They were waiting for six o'clock, to call Dr. Max at the clinic. It had to be the clinic, because the doctor's home phone number was unlisted. Sherry had gone out for newspapers, and now everyone was reliving last night's spectacular triumph.

"Lissen at this," Gus said, grinning. "The Bugatti alone is valued at three and a half hundred thou."

"Yowsah!" Myron yelled, waking Al up.

Sherry laughed out loud. "This one cop said—waitaminit, I lost it—here it is. He said, 'Last night's thefts are obviously the work of a sophisticated international ring of car thieves.' Ha! Sophisticated, thass us!"

Conrad hung up the phone. "We've had two offers on the Bugatti already. I'm spreading the word that we have a Rolls and a Mercedes in addition to the four listed in the newspapers." Conrad could tell from the way his contacts had spoken to him that his prestige in the car-removal business had just taken a giant leap upward.

"Dr. Max is quoted here," Myron said, reading. "He says we've come to a sad state if a man can't entertain in his own home without his guests being robbed. He says the moral fiber of this nation degenerates a little more every day."

That high-minded statement was greeted with hoots of laughter. "Damn hypocrite," Gus muttered.

"Nothing in any of the papers about Dr. Kiernan bein' missing," Harvey pointed out.

"There wouldn't be, if they're waiting to hear from kidnappers," Conrad said. "Myron, did that receptionist say how long they'd been partners?"

"Naw, she just said 'recently.' You think that's why he did it? Dr. Max wanted the clinic all to himself?"

"It's a helluva good motive," Conrad said. "Or else the new partnership wasn't working and Dr. Kiernan wanted Dr. Max out."

"Thass not it," Sherry objected. "Dr. Kiernan went to his party, dint he? They hadda be on good terms still."

"That could just be keeping up appearances," Conrad mused. "Well, the cops'll figure that part out. All we have to do is set them on to Dr. Max."

"Yeah, that's all," Harvey said gloomily. "What if it don't work?"

"It has to work. It's the only way I'm gonna get you and Al out of my house." He looked at his watch. "We'd better get going."

"I'll go start the Lincoln," Gus said, putting on his coat. "It's gonna take a while to warm up in this weather." He went outside.

Conrad hesitated, and then said to Sherry: "Do you *swear* you never had a real conversation with Dr. Max?"

"I swear to god, Conrad, I never did. I just said *yes, no,* and *I don't know,* like ya tol' me. I dint need *sorry.* Stop worryin', will ya? He's not gonna connect me to Natalie."

"Okay, then. Remember to ask for some impossibly high sum— make it five million dollars." He grunted. "A million for each of us, if we were really gonna do this. But he won't go for it."

"Okeydoke. Five mil."

Conrad and Myron got their coats and left.

When six o'clock finally rolled around, Harvey put Al down and went to sit next to Sherry by the phone. "Don't be nervous," he said nervously.

"Relax, Harve." She held the receiver so he could listen. She dialed the clinic and asked for Dr. Maximilian; he was there to take the call. "Hiya, Doc. Ya got our note? We got somethin' a yours, we dunno whatcha want done widdit."

"I found a note, yes," Dr. Max said cautiously.

"So ya want us to dispose of the item or not? It'll cost ya."

"How much?"

"Oh, say five—no, make that six mil."

"Six million dollars?" he said incredulously.

Six? Harvey mouthed at her.

Sherry covered the mouthpiece and grinned at him. "One for Al. He found the body, dint he?"

Dr. Max was laughing. "This is a joke, right? Six million—that's absurd."

"Oh, I dunno. I'd pay six mil to stay outta jail, keep my clinic, my house, like that."

"Look, whoever you are, I'm willing to pay a reasonable amount for, er, garbage disposal—"

"Save yer breath, Doc. Not negotiable. Six mil, take it or leave it."

"Then I'll leave it. I can't lay my hands on that kind of money, and even if I could, I wouldn't give it to you. There's nothing to connect me to the item in question. It's your problem now."

Sherry and Harvey exchanged a grin. "Sure thass the way ya wanna play it?" Sherry said. "Not smart, Doc, not smart at all."

He got huffy. "We have no business to conduct. Please do not contact me again."

"That yer final word?"

"That's my final word."

"In that case, ya better take a look in yer garage when ya get home. And do it soon, Doc. Before it starts to smell." She hung up.

Harvey said, "So far so good."

"Yeah." Sherry looked glum. "Now comes the hard part."

They'd argued about the next step—they'd argued long and hard. But there was no getting around it: they were going to have to call in the cops. And it was up to Sherry to give them just enough detail to convince them she knew what she was talking about.

She picked up the phone and tapped out the number.

Dr. Richard Maximilian sat staring at the phone in horror. They couldn't . . . they wouldn't . . . *in his garage?* He grabbed his overcoat and ran from his office toward the clinic parking lot, not even hearing the receptionist's goodbye.

The snow had started again. It was only a little after six but already it was as dark as midnight. Dr. Max bent his head against the wind and made his way to the Ferrari. But when he got in, his expensive status symbol wouldn't start. Cursing, he picked up the car phone; that wasn't working either. Was everything frozen?

He slipped the remote that opened his front gate into a pocket and climbed out of the car. He was heading back to the clinic when he saw a taxi turning the corner. Dr. Max ran out to the street and flagged it down. "Are you free?" he asked the driver.

"Sure am, buddy," said Gus. "Hop in."

When the taxi was out of sight, a Lincoln that had been sitting in the clinic parking lot started its engine and pulled up alongside the Ferrari. Myron waited while Conrad replaced the distributor cap and got Dr. Max's fancy automobile started. Then both cars drove away.

The road Gus was taking cut through a nonresidential wooded area that was black as pitch. No house lights, no street lights, no light at all except the cab's headlights—which showed only road surface and gusting snow.

They were about halfway through the wooded area when the cab's engine began to sputter. "What's the matter?" Dr. Max asked.

"I don't know," Gus said.

The cab lurched a few more feet and rolled to a stop. Flashlight in hand, Gus got out and opened the hood. He poked around in there for what seemed like an eternity before he got back into the cab. He told his passenger, "I dunno what it is, but I could smell rubber burnin'. I'm callin' the dispatcher." Then he grunted. "Radio's not workin'. The whole electrical system is out."

"Oh, wonderful," said Dr. Max in exasperation.

"Look, buddy, I hate to leave you here, but I'm gonna have to go find a phone—"

"Wait! There's a car coming!"

Immediately Gus was out in the road, semaphoring with both arms until the car stopped. "Trouble?" a male voice inquired.

Dr. Max got out of the cab while the other two men were talking. Gus turned to him and said, "It's okay, he's gonna give you a lift." He opened the back door.

Dr. Max climbed in. He got a brief glimpse of the driver's face; no one he knew. "Thank you for stopping."

"Glad to help," Conrad said. "This is no night to be stranded." Gus climbed into the front seat but left the door open.

Conrad handed him a phone. "You wanted to make a call?"

"Yeah, thanks." Gus made a big show of calling the dispatcher and describing his predicament. He handed the phone back to Conrad and turned to Dr. Max in the backseat. "I'm real sorry about this, buddy." He got out of the car.

"Aren't you coming?"

"Naw, I gotta stay with the cab." Gus closed the door, and the car began to move.

"Where do you live?" Conrad asked.

Dr. Max gave him directions and settled back to think about what to do with the problem that awaited him in his garage.

But they'd traveled only half a mile when the car pulled over to the side of the road behind a Lincoln that was parked there. "What's going on?" Dr. Max asked. He watched in disbelief as his rescuer silently got out of the car and climbed into the passenger seat of the Lincoln, which Myron promptly drove away.

What the hell?

A strange feeling came over the doctor, one he hadn't had for years: he was not in control of what was happening. The engine was still running; that man, whoever he was, had left the keys.

It wasn't until Dr. Max got into the driver's seat that he realized he was in a Mercedes. *Not another Mercedes!* Then, slowly, a horrible suspicion entered his head. He turned on the dome light and looked at the interior carefully. No. *Not* another Mercedes. The same one.

God, no. At least it looked like the same one. He rested his forehead against the steering wheel; he *knew* it was the same one. It was all a trick, that business about the body in his garage, a trick to get him into this car. And in the trunk . . . Kiernan must still be there.

Dr. Max peered out into the darkness. Yes, these woods would do as a place to leave the body. He turned off the engine and fumbled the keys out of the ignition. He mustn't be caught in *this* car with *that* in the trunk. But when he tried to open the trunk, he found the lock was jammed; something had been broken off inside it.

He took a number of deep breaths to calm himself, but a sudden gust of wind almost blew him off his feet. He struggled back into the car. Now he was caught in a blizzard as well.

The safest thing to do would be to follow his original plan and just drive the Mercedes into the river right now. But how would he get home? He'd die of hypothermia if he tried to walk back in this weather.

All right; do it tomorrow. Wait until the storm passes. Leave the Mercedes parked outside all night and Kiernan would be a block of ice. Yes.

He started the car and inched slowly forward. The driving was treacherous, but the heavy Mercedes held the road well. At long last he reached Shady Oak Lane and soon turned in to his own driveway. A wave of relief washed over him. His body was sweating and his feet were freezing, but he felt good.

Then . . . he jammed on the brakes, hard, blinded by the sudden glare of light. Light in front and in back of him, light from both sides. Headlights, spotlights. A voice on a bullhorn, saying: "Get out of the car and put both hands on your head." The police.

"I should have paid the six million," Dr. Max said.

Then he was spread-eagled against the Mercedes, patted down for weapons. Like a zombie he watched someone with a crow bar springing open the lid of the trunk. A flash went off as one of the cops took pictures of Kiernan's body. Then his hands were cuffed behind his back as a disembodied voice droned out the words of the Miranda warning.

They drove him to the same police station where he'd gone that morning to make his statement. As he was being taken out of the police car, a taxi drove by, slowing to see what was going on. The passenger's face was pressed against the window; Dr. Max was startled to see it was the man who'd brought him the stolen Mercedes. The cab driver rolled down his window; oddly, he had a cat draped over his shoulders.

"Happy New Year," Conrad said.

Autumn Tethers

Tracy Knight

"Ready to make a delivery, Willie?" Orvin Samuels paused meaningfully. "To . . . Caleb McAllister's?" The grocery store owner arched a shrublike eyebrow as if he expected me to plunge to my knees screaming and begging for mercy.

"Sure," I said with a smile. I'd made deliveries to Mr. McAllister's at least ten times since starting the after-school job at the A&P. The man didn't scare me like he did all the other kids. In fact, the more I saw of him, the more fascinated I became.

The first time I made a delivery he retreated upstairs as soon as he opened the door, but as I continued showing up at his house he began making small talk, chatting about the weather or proudly showing me his pet cat, Philip. I felt special—chosen, even—because everyone else in Elderville, Iowa, shunned Caleb McAllister. My presence seemed to matter.

Being new in town—and a foster child to boot—I hadn't made any real friends, but I enjoyed the challenge of figuring out the mysterious recluse. As far as hobbies went, it was better than breaking windows or classmates' noses, things I was known for.

Mr. Samuels handed me two full sacks of groceries, then wiped a hand over his gleaming bald spot. "Now you be careful, Willie. I heard McAllister was seen last night—"

"Seen . . . *outside?*" That surprised me. The one thing I'd learned about Caleb McAllister was that he never left his home. *Never.*

He nodded. "He was out at the cemetery, wandering around after dark. I'm not sure what it means, but it's unusual for him. Kind of

like President Johnson doing the Peppermint Twist. Just doesn't fit."
Chuckling, he punched me on the arm.

"How'd you find out about this?"

Mr. Samuels winked, grinning the goofy grin that made him fun to
be around. "Willie, this is a small town. Fact is if I passed gas this
afternoon, by suppertime the coffee shop crowd would all be specu-
lating on what I had for lunch."

"Why would he go to the cemetery?"

Shrugging, he said, "Veterans' Day is next week. Maybe he's thinking of our fallen brothers. We've been trying to get him involved in
the Veterans' Day ceremony for years, but . . ." He spun his index
finger near his temple. "You know: one brownie short of a bake sale."

"What happened to him over there in Korea? How did he end up
this way?" I asked as I had before, hoping I'd understand this time.

"No one knows for sure. Sometimes, Willie, war just does this to
people. He was a good soldier. Some of us hometown boys were
stationed together—me, Caleb, Dr. Crist, Mayor Taylor. But Caleb . . . well, something just didn't set right with him, I guess.
When we got back here, he holed up in his house, and he's been
there ever since. Eleven years now. It's a shame. Shell shock, they
call it."

Shell shock. When I tried to imagine it, the only thing I could
picture was that Mr. McAllister had been near a bomb when it
dropped and was still vibrating from the force of the blast, like Wile
E. Coyote on the cartoons after a bundle of Acme TNT blew up in
his paws.

Mr. Samuels flicked at his drooping walrus mustache thoughtfully.
As I watched him, it occurred to me that he had hair almost every
place except on top of his head. He could have combed his ear hair if
he'd wanted to, made a pair of ear beards.

"You hurry back after you make the delivery, Willie. I'm concerned
about Caleb being out last night. Seriously. It doesn't feel right. You
be careful now."

"I will." I nodded and left the store.

As I started walking toward Caleb McAllister's, I took three or four
deep, sighing breaths, marveling at the grand oaks and elms lining
the streets of Elderville. The sky was a palette of dusty cotton balls.

Red and orange leaves glowed against the gray as they fluttered in the crisp autumn air.

Peaceful. It was such a change for me.

I'd lived in Elderville for only two months. After taking me from my home in Des Moines two years before, the State had put me in a succession of foster homes, finally placing me in Elderville with Sam and Martha Gillette. The Gillettes were the closest thing to Ozzie and Harriet Nelson in the real world; they even looked like the TV couple. I hoped they would treat me as gently and fairly as the Nelsons treated their sons. But I didn't count on it.

Troubled twelve-year-old kid, my caseworker had told them as soon as we arrived, the worst boy she'd seen so far in 1964. So it wasn't like anyone had high expectations for me. They all knew I'd fail; it was just a matter of when and how.

Still, I was trying to make the best of it. I smiled and agreed and cooperated with just about everything Mr. and Mrs. Gillette told me, even getting the job at the A&P without any prompting.

Sometimes when life doesn't give you many prizes, you have to look for tiny victories anywhere you can and be happy with the ones you find. When you're adrift, you seek out an anchor. For some reason, here in Elderville my anchor had become Caleb McAllister. He intrigued me just as he intrigued the town and gave me something interesting to concentrate on. And I was actually in a position to find out his secret, to solve the mystery of his life.

"Willie?"

I turned around and saw Luanne Taylor skipping toward me on the sidewalk. I hadn't made any friends at school, but Luanne was the closest thing I had. I'd told her a stupid pun during recess one day, and she'd squirted milk out her nostrils. Since then she'd been smiling at me in the hall and starting conversations whenever she could. I wasn't sure how I felt about that. In my position, you weren't quick to stake your claim on anything.

I gave her a half-smile. "How ya doin', Luanne?"

"Fine." She cocked her head and the dim autumn sunlight made her cheeks take on a warm luster. She had red hair and freckles so thick it looked like someone had sprinkled cinnamon all over her face.

"Where you going?" she asked in her singsong voice. "To Crazy McAllister's?"

"His name's not Crazy," I said sternly. "It's Caleb." It was almost automatic, defending him like that, maybe because I knew what it was like to be an outsider.

She ignored me, still gazing at me with stars in her eyes, smiling at me like I was a Beatle. "Did you hear what happened last night? He was outside."

"I know. Mr. Samuels told me. So what?" I sounded kind of mad and I wasn't sure why.

"Jimmy Flitz and some of his friends have been going down to Crazy's . . . I mean, *Caleb's* house at night. They make bomb noises and pop paper sacks and throw pebbles at the window so he thinks he's in the war again."

"That's stupid."

"Well . . . Jimmy was bragging about it today. They think maybe they've driven him crazy . . . crazy the rest of the way."

"That's *really* stupid. Caleb doesn't hurt anyone."

She fell silent for a moment, apparently sensing that the conversation was going nowhere. Finally she said, "Willie, know something?"

"What?"

Shy smile. Clasping her hands together and twisting her arms like a pretzel, she said, "I think you're really brave going to McAllister's house like this."

Trying the flattery routine. I admit I kind of liked it. "Aw, it's nothin'. He seems nice enough."

"You've seen him?" She opened her eyes wide. "Up close and everything?"

"Sure," I said, walking a little taller.

I wanted to like her so much, but her smile made a critter crawl in my gut. Too many times I'd gotten close to people only to be hurt or torn away from them. No use tying the drifting boat to a dock; temporary anchors were the best I could hope for.

Luanne straightened her neck, proud. "My dad was with Mr. McAllister in Korea."

Suddenly it occurred to me that if my goal was to figure out Caleb McAllister, I needed sources. "What does he say about him?" I asked, trying to seem casual. "Does he know why he won't leave his house?"

She shook her head. "He won't talk about him hardly at all. He did say something about his cat, though. Something about how the cat's kept him alive since they got back. It's all he's got."

We approached Caleb McAllister's ramshackle house at the end of Main Street. The two-story rot-gray building needed a new roof and a good coat of paint. Crooked shutters clattered in the wind. The front storm door hung from one hinge. Besides me, not many people used it, I guessed.

"Well, I gotta get to work, Luanne. See you around."

She smiled and waved. "See you at school, Willie. I *like* you!"

Before I had a chance to protest, she'd laughed and skipped away.

I stepped up onto the porch, then knocked on the door and waited for Mr. McAllister. Usually he answered within a couple of seconds, like he'd been watching out the window, waiting for me.

Not today.

I knocked again, then pressed my ear against the door, only to have it gently creak open.

Odd. It had always been locked before.

"Mr. McAllister?" I said into the darkened house. My voice echoed as if I'd spoken into a barrel.

Nothing. Maybe he was asleep.

I tiptoed through the living room and into the kitchen, then quietly went about putting away the groceries.

I was almost done when I heard a moan.

More curious than scared, I returned to the living room.

Another moan. Coming from upstairs. It was the strangest sound I'd ever heard: low, throaty, mournful. Like a ghost saying goodbye.

I ran up the steps and noticed an open door to my left. Walking in, I saw Mr. McAllister sitting in a chair, facing a window with his head in his hands. At his feet lay his cat Philip, an obese old yellow tabby. The cat was moaning.

"Mr. McAllister?"

He raised his head and turned slowly in my direction.

Startled, I took a step backward. His face was swollen, lips like little balloons, eyes bruised and puffy.

But that wasn't the most surprising thing about his appearance. I was amazed at how nicely he was dressed: sharply ironed slacks and a colorful flannel shirt he had buttoned up all the way. His full head of black hair was neatly parted and shiny with Brylcreem, almost like he was dressed up for something.

The cat yowled weakly.

"Mr. McAllister . . . are you all right? Do you want me to get a doctor for you?"

"No!" Then he pointed to the fat old cat.

Philip the cat was barely moving. His chest heaved with great, ragged sighs.

Tears trickling from his swollen eyes, Caleb gestured again toward the cat, then raised his face to mine. "Philip. He's hurt."

I nodded excitedly. "I can take him to the vet for you. I'd be happy to do it."

I didn't wait for an answer. With great care I placed Philip into one of the sacks I'd brought the groceries in, then realized that because of his weight, double-bagging would be needed.

The cat struggled at first but soon went limp, lying still in the sack, maybe knowing I was there to help.

"I'll come back and tell you what the doctor says. Okay?"

Caleb stood, walked over to me and peeked into the bag. In a voice as faint as yesterday he said, "I'll go . . . I'll go with you. I should be with him. Philip's always been here for me. Always."

Somehow it still surprised me that he talked so clearly, just like any other grownup. I guess I'd expected him to growl or slobber or something. But no. He just sounded like a sad, haunted man.

We left—me holding the heavy sack and Caleb walking so briskly I had trouble keeping up—and headed toward the vet's office.

Within a half-block of the house, Caleb's breath became rough, as if he couldn't get enough air. He was panicking. I wondered how long it had been since he'd been out in the daylight.

I decided to distract him by making conversation. "How long have you had Philip?"

"Twelve years."

"He's getting old then, isn't he?"

He didn't answer.

I cleared my throat and asked, "Where did you get him? Was he a stray?"

"Korea. Snuck him home from Korea."

I saw my opening. "What happened to you in Korea, anyway? Mr. Samuels said something didn't set right with you, and that's why you won't leave your house anymore."

He kept his eyes straight ahead, not even glancing at me. "Sometimes you find out you got nothing to hold on to, so you hold on to whatever you can." He leaned over and looked into the bag. "I hold on to Philip."

"Why don't you have anything to hold on to?"

"It's the way of the world sometimes, the world Shiny made for me."

Shiny? Who was that? An imaginary friend? I didn't understand but I hadn't expected to. "Who hurt you and Philip? It was those kids, wasn't it? The ones who've been bothering you at night."

He didn't answer.

I heard the bikes rolling up behind us, but the last thing I expected was what happened.

It was three junior high kids, Jimmy Flitz and two other boys I recognized but didn't know. Jimmy rode up next to me, snatched the sack carrying Philip from my hands, and started pedaling away, laughing.

"Come back here, Jimmy!" I shouted. "There's a cat in there! It's hurt!"

Now all three boys were laughing. "Look!" one of them called. "We got one of Crazy McAllister's treasures!"

Caleb cried out—not so much saying anything as letting all his fear gush out—and took off in a clumsy sprint. Dead leaves on the sidewalk leapt out of his way as he ran toward the boys.

Two of the boys jumped off their bikes and bolted in different directions, through neighbors' yards and out of sight.

Jimmy Flitz stopped and looked back, eyes round and white like twin moons. He couldn't believe he had Crazy McAllister on his heels.

Caleb ran straight to the boy and grabbed the sack away, again crying out like he was dying. He peeked inside to make sure Philip was okay then looked Jimmy in the eyes, face turning crimson, trembling fist clenched at his side.

"Stop right there, McAllister!"

In all the commotion, none of us had noticed the police car pulling up.

A young deputy dressed in a rumpled blue shirt got out of his car and stomped toward Caleb, hand on his holster. The nameplate on his pocket said he was Deputy Haskins. Truth be told, he looked like a gangly high school kid dressed up for Halloween.

Deputy Haskins grabbed Caleb by the arm and pulled him toward the car.

"My cat!" Caleb said, voice cracking. "Philip's hurt! We can't leave Philip behind!"

I ran to them and pulled at the sack. At first, Caleb resisted. Then he looked into my eyes, nodded, and handed Philip to me.

"I'll take him to the vet for you," I said softly, "and I'll keep him until you're home. I promise."

He nodded again and tried to smile. But I saw something else in his eyes, something like fear or dread, and it went deeper than anything I'd seen in a grownup's eyes before.

"C'mon, McAllister, let's go!" Deputy Haskins barked.

"He wasn't doing anything wrong!" I protested. "That kid tried to kidnap his cat and he was just trying to get it back!"

The deputy frowned and sucked air through his front teeth, making a little whistle. "Listen, son, give me some lip and you'll be taking a ride with us to the county jail. McAllister here's a public nuisance at best, crazy as a loon. We can't have him runnin' around out here."

"But—"

"And if I'm not mistaken, you're the kid who's been in so much trouble. Foster kid, right? Live with the Gillettes? Maybe I should run you in and see if anyone's looking for you."

"You're a big dingleberry!" I yelled, taking off running, hearing Philip's moans as I did.

Deputy Haskins shouted, "Get back here!" But by then I was half a block away.

Dr. Crist, the veterinarian, smiled warmly as he brought Philip out into the waiting room and set him in my lap. Immediately Philip started purring.

Dr. Crist was a middle-aged man, and he wore a blue smock

adorned with clinging samples of animal hair. I knew he must be a nice man, taking care of all the pets.

"He's going to be okay, son," Dr. Crist said. "It was just some bruised ribs. Looks like someone kicked him. I gave him some medicine. He'll probably sleep until tomorrow."

"So I can take him home?"

He sat down in the chair next to me. "Sure can, son. Say, didn't you tell the nurse that this cat belongs to Caleb McAllister?"

"Yes."

He shook his head and smiled. "Goodness, it's hard to believe this old cat's still alive. How do you know Caleb?"

"I deliver his groceries."

Dr. Crist closed his eyes and nodded. "I see. Well, you can tell Caleb that there's no charge."

"That's nice of you."

Dr. Crist stood and started for the examining room. "Caleb and I served together in Korea. I've known him a long time. Good man."

"Then maybe you can answer something. I've been wondering . . . what exactly is the matter with him? And how come people around here don't treat him . . . I don't know . . . like they've known him a long time? Like he's a neighbor?"

Dr. Crist stopped in his tracks. He scrunched up his face like he was figuring out a math problem. "That's a good question, son. I can't say that I completely understand what happened to him in Korea. We all went through the same things over there . . . but everybody's different, I guess. And as to why he's not treated well here in town . . . that's even harder. People want everybody to be the same, I guess, and when someone's different, they begin treating him like he doesn't belong with the rest of us. It's crazy, I know."

It *was* crazy, but I knew exactly what he was talking about. Since leaving my home, I'd been treated like I didn't belong: sometimes quietly, sometimes not so quietly.

I didn't want the discussion to end. Not accepting a person was one thing, attacking him was another. "Someone beat up Mr. McAllister and Philip. Even if they didn't think he belonged, why would they do that?"

Dr. Crist frowned. "Someone beat Caleb up?" He twisted his head to one side, disturbed by the news. "I don't know. Local kids probably did it. A lot of times kids pick up the bad feelings their parents have, but then they go ahead and act on them. It's sad when people don't fit."

"I know."

Philip in tow, I left Dr. Crist's office, surprised to find tears welling in my eyes. I wasn't sure whether I just felt bad for Caleb McAllister or if I also realized that I was in the exact same position as him.

I went by Caleb's house, but he wasn't there. I had pictures in my head of Deputy Haskins shining a bright light in Caleb's face, interrogating him.

Since I wasn't sure when he'd return, I decided to take Philip home with me for the time being. But first I had to stop by the A&P. I was late. It was nearly dark and the chill autumn breeze was beginning to bite.

I knew I was in trouble the minute I entered the store. Josh, a kid who stocked shelves, came up to me with gleaming eyes and a creepy smile.

"Where you been, Willie? Mr. Samuels is hopping mad at you. I think he's down at your house right now."

"It's not my house," I said. "It's a foster home."

"Whatever. You'd better get down there right away. I think he's going to fire you."

Ten minutes later I walked through the front door of the Gillettes' house.

It was worse than I'd expected. Not only were Mr. and Mrs. Gillette sitting on the couch with grim looks on their faces; not only was Orvin Samuels sitting in the recliner, hands crossed over his stomach; but my caseworker, Miss Farley, was there too, and she looked unhappiest of all.

"Where the devil have you been?" Miss Farley asked, almost spitting. She looked like a bleached-blond woman wrestler, all lard and bad attitude.

Everyone else in the room stayed silent. They'd already given up on me.

"I took the groceries to Mr. McAllister's house. Him and his cat were hurt. Well, some kids tried to steal the cat away from us when we were taking it to the vet, and—"

"Willie, stop!" said Miss Farley. "I don't think we're interested in hearing any more."

Mrs. Gillette nodded. In her gentle voice she said, "Willie, we tried so hard to make a good home for you."

"I even gave you a job, against everyone's advice," said Mr. Samuels, no trace of the wry smile I'd learned to enjoy. "I had faith in you, Willie. I didn't think you'd turn out to be so undependable."

Mr. Gillette said nothing, but his pale blue eyes could have burned a hole right through me.

I wanted to protest. "But I was just—"

Miss Farley turned away from me, toward my foster parents. "I'm sorry this didn't work out, Mr. and Mrs. Gillette," she said. "We'll arrange for another placement. We'll have Willie moved tomorrow."

"Stop!" I shouted. "Doesn't anyone want to hear about what I was doing? I was helping someone! I took this cat to the vet for Mr. McAllister! I was helping!"

"Again, I'm sorry," Miss Farley said, as if I hadn't said a word. "Kids like Willie can be so difficult. I've told you what he's been through. His father died in a car accident, and then his mother . . . well, she just couldn't make it alone. Started drinking real bad, quit taking care of Willie. Willie found her dead, and he's never been the same. We've tried ten placements: some with relatives, some with foster families. None of them worked out. He was running away, getting into fights at school. So you folks have nothing to be ashamed of. You did your best. Willie just doesn't seem to have a place in this world."

"You people!" I screamed, pointing my finger at the lot of them. "You give up on people too easy! Just like you gave up on Mr. McAllister!"

Philip yowled in my arms. I was scaring him. I held him close to my chest, like I was cradling a baby. "It's okay, Philip," I cooed.

Mr. Gillette rose from his chair. I'd never seen him tremble with anger before. "Listen, mister, you put that cat outside and march right up to bed!"

That moment I knew the feeling of pure powerlessness. I was paralyzed.

I looked down into Philip's eyes. There was a look of wonder in them, as if he'd never seen another human—outside of Caleb—who loved him.

I turned on my heel and ran out the door.

By the time I reached Caleb's house, both Philip and I were out of breath. I pounded on the front door, but there wasn't an answer.

I peered down the street and saw headlights swinging my direction from the cars pulling out of the Gillettes' driveway. There was no time to lose.

I ran around the side of the house and punched my elbow through a window, then reached in and unlatched it. After lifting up the broken window and crawling in, I carefully placed Philip on an easy chair just inside. Probably happy to be away from my rocking body, he curled himself up and pinched his eyes closed.

"I'll see you, Philip," I said. "You're a good boy."

He opened his eyes for a second, then closed them again. Thanking me.

I stepped back from the house just in time to see the three cars racing down Main Street toward me.

If I stayed a second longer, they'd have me. They would take me back to the Gillettes and keep me prisoner until Miss Farley picked me up tomorrow and hauled me off to another unknown, unfriendly place. I had come to Elderville promising never to run away again. And I'd tried.

I wasn't sure where I was going but I ran as fast as I could. Feet barely skimming the ground, I flew through backyards and across narrow, dimly lit streets: dipping my head below clotheslines, bounding over bushes, snaking around trees.

I reached the north end of town, leaping over a deep ditch and falling to my knees.

It was then I realized where I was.

The cemetery.

Pale silver moonlight glimmered over the rows of headstones, illuminating forgotten names.

But that was the least of it, because there was someone among the cemetery shadows besides me.

Caleb McAllister.

He knelt silently before a simple small stone, hands clasped in front of him in prayer. He hadn't noticed my arrival.

Tempted to jump up and run to him, I hunkered down instead behind a large headstone, then poked my head out just far enough to keep my eyes on him.

He stayed that way for several minutes: silent, reverent.

A hand touched my back.

"Willie?" a small voice said.

I gasped and turned around.

Luanne was crouching behind me. "I followed Mr. McAllister out here," she whispered. "I saw him walking out this way. I knew you wanted to know what his secret is. I thought I might be able to find out something for you."

"Yeah," I said, heart thundering in my chest even as I tried to seem in control. "Thanks a lot."

A loud explosion shattered the night air.

I flattened myself against the earth, feeling Luanne's trembling hands on my arm.

I crawled to the edge of the headstone, looked around it and saw that Caleb had hit the ground, too. He lay on his stomach with his hands clasped over the back of his head.

Another explosion.

Another.

I turned my eyes upward.

Jimmy Flitz was sitting among the branches of a tree, holding a match to the fuse of an M-80.

I shrugged off Luanne's hand and stood.

"Jimmy Flitz! Stop right there!"

My shout must have startled him because Jimmy fell out of the tree like a stone and landed hard on the ground.

His two classmates emerged from behind a nearby mausoleum and ran to Jimmy's side.

I walked toward Caleb, Luanne following closely behind me. Helping him to his feet, I brushed off the front of Caleb's flannel shirt.

"You okay, Mr. McAllister?" I asked.

"Yes. I think so. Thank you."

The other boys pulled Jimmy to his feet. It didn't look like anything was broken, but his face was chalky white.

"Just got the wind knocked out of him," one of the boys said to me, as if I was worried.

I stomped over to them, grabbed Jimmy by the front of his shirt, and yanked him close to me. "If you ever . . . *ever* bother Mr. McAllister again . . . I'm going to track you down and hurt you real, real bad."

His lips curled like worms. He was ready to cry.

"Understand?" I shouted into his face.

He nodded rather politely.

I pushed Jimmy Flitz to the ground. "You three get out of here! Now!"

The three boys scampered out of the graveyard like mice.

I rushed back to where Caleb and Luanne stood.

That moment I felt more useful and important than at any other time in my life. "I don't think you'll be having any more trouble with those boys," I said with confidence.

"Thank you . . . Willie," said Caleb McAllister. "You're a good boy. You're going to be a good man someday. You're loyal, and you would never leave a friend behind. Thank you."

He shook my hand.

Luanne smiled. "You saved Mr. McAllister, Willie. I'm so proud of you." I was afraid she might try to kiss me.

The blush burned my face. I couldn't think of a thing to say.

"I'm going to walk Mr. McAllister part of the way home," Luanne said. "Do you want to come?"

"No, thanks. I've gotta get to the Gillettes. People are waiting for me." I wanted to tell her that I'd be leaving tomorrow, wanted even more to tell her and Caleb goodbye. But I decided not to. I decided to let the moment live just as it was: warm and full.

As I watched Luanne and Caleb walking away hand in hand through the cemetery gloom, my body felt like it might well be glowing. Here I was—Willie the foster boy, the one everyone expected to end up in prison—and I'd rescued a fellow outsider from the wrath of a town that didn't understand him.

I looked down and read the inscription on the headstone where he'd been kneeling.

PHILIP MORRELL
1934–1953
BELOVED SON AND BROTHER
VETERAN OF KOREAN CONFLICT

I understood him even better then. I reasoned that Philip Morrell had been a friend of Caleb and the other Korean veterans in town. He'd been killed in Korea. Losing a friend had been too much for Caleb, so he'd come home and imprisoned himself in his house, maybe feeling guilty that it was Philip who died instead of him. He'd even named his cat after his dead friend, to keep him alive somehow.

A crumpled piece of paper caught my eye. It lay in front of Philip Morrell's headstone, held to the ground by a scattering of gravel.

As I read the short note I realized how wrong I'd been. I'd assumed that the boys were the reason Caleb had been wandering the cemetery, perhaps because their taunting had brought back all the bad memories.

I had been wrong. And it dawned on me who the real culprit was in all of this.

Dear Shiny,

I came to bid Philip goodbye one last time. I apologized to him for all of us. Philip's ghost is now larger than any threats you've made. Like I told you last night, I can't remain silent any longer. I know you're coming for me tonight, and you can have me. At the very worst, Death is nothing . . . and nothing doesn't hurt.

Caleb

Straining every muscle in my body, I raced to Caleb's house.

As I rounded the corner, I turned my head left and saw Luanne skipping down the sidewalk toward her home. Good. I'd hoped she wouldn't be there. I didn't want anything to happen to her. She was my friend.

I stepped through the darkness and up to the window I'd broken.

Peering in, the first thing I noticed was Caleb, tied to a chair in the center of the living room.

Philip was being held tightly in the grasp of the man who had been known to his fellow soldiers as Shiny.

"Go ahead and kill me," Caleb said. "Just let Philip alone. That boy—Willie—he'll take care of him."

"If you're still thinking you've got to tell what you know, I *will* kill you, Caleb," Orvin Samuels said. "But I'll let you watch your cat die first."

"It shouldn't have been my secret in the first place."

"Too late now. You should've stayed home. It was working that way."

Orvin Samuels placed one hand around Philip's neck and began to squeeze.

"Mr. Samuels!" I screamed. "Let go of that cat!"

Startled, Mr. Samuels jerked his head in my direction and released Philip, who hit the floor on all four feet, then scrambled to the stairway and waddled up the steps to safety.

"You!" Mr. Samuels shouted, pointing toward the broken window where I stood. He was sweating so much that his bald spot shone. *Shiny.*

For a moment I toyed with the idea of running to get Deputy Haskins, then dismissed it. By the time I convinced him to come back with me, Caleb might be dead.

Still full of my success at scaring the three boys, I ran around to the front of the house and marched right inside, intent on confronting Mr. Samuels and making him back down.

As soon as I entered the living room, he grabbed me and held me tightly against his body.

"I know what you did!" I lied. "You made Caleb hide what he knew about Philip Morrell's death." It was a guess, sure, but the best guess I could muster.

Immediately his grasp on me weakened.

"This is crazy, Orvin," Caleb said. "Let the boy go."

Mr. Samuels tried to laugh, but it caught in his throat. "This is just a young punk troublemaker. He could tell what he knew to the newspapers, and nobody would believe him."

"But I'll try anyway!" I yelled. "I'll try until someone listens! You can't get away with this!"

"He's right, you know."

The voice came from behind us. As he turned, Mr. Samuels swung me around so I was facing Dr. Crist, who stood in the doorway, hands on his hips.

"Let him go," Dr. Crist said. "It's over, Orvin."

Then Deputy Haskins strode in, his pistol in his hand.

"Give it up, Samuels," Deputy Haskins said in a wavering voice.

Mr. Samuels released me. I promptly went and untied Caleb.

Deputy Haskins handcuffed Mr. Samuels and led him out of the house.

While Caleb went upstairs to retrieve Philip from his hiding place, Dr. Crist came up to me and put a steady hand on my shoulder.

"As soon as you told me Caleb had been beaten, I knew what had happened," he said. "It's sad what people do to one another. Maybe that's why I work with animals instead of people. They're nicer. You can depend on them."

"So what happened in Korea? It was Philip Morrell, wasn't it?"

He nodded. "We were out on patrol one night—Caleb, Philip, Orvin, and me—and Orvin brought along some whiskey. We drank it. We stopped so Philip could relieve himself and . . . that's when it happened."

"What?"

"Orvin knocked the gearshift into reverse and backed over Philip. Ran over him. Killed him." He took a deep breath and continued, "Orvin demanded we tell headquarters that we'd come under fire and that Philip had died as an indirect result of the attack. We went along with it. I don't know why. I guess Orvin had convinced us that it was the thing to do for the sake of Philip's reputation. Philip did receive a posthumous Purple Heart."

"It *wasn't* the war that kept Caleb at home, not really."

"No. Not the Korean War." Frowning, he crossed his arms over his chest. "But it *was* a war of sorts, a war between his loyalty to his friends, his guilt over Philip, and his honesty. Staying home was the best way he could think of to reach a cease-fire, I guess you'd say."

"But what was the real reason you all lied?"

Dr. Crist shrugged. "To hide what happened. To keep our good names so we could come back to our little hometown as heroes. And you know something?"

"What?"

"Tonight, in this town, you're the only hero, son."

The next day, as Miss Farley drove me to Keokuk, where she would place me in yet another foster home, I dreamt of the good I'd done and how things might turn out.

I dreamt that Dr. Crist presented Caleb with a special award at the Veterans Day ceremony, for putting loyalty and honor and friendship—however misguided and unnecessary—ahead of everything else, even his own life.

I dreamt that Caleb was the grand marshal of the Veterans Day parade, riding on the float with Philip on his lap, waving at the crowd and throwing candy to the little children lining the streets of Elderville.

I dreamt that I received an honorary police badge from the sheriff's department in recognition of my role in solving the mystery of Caleb McAllister's isolation and making it possible for him to become part of the world again.

I even dreamt that the school held an assembly in my honor, with a marching band and a special speech from the principal.

None of that happened, of course.

After I moved into the new foster home, I received a few letters from Luanne. She always drew smiles and hearts at the bottom of the page.

She told me that Mr. Samuels had been arrested for assault and battery and put in the county jail for three months. Dr. Crist had paid for the complete remodeling of Caleb's house and promised free lifetime care for Philip. Deputy Haskins was running for sheriff. The Gillettes had a new foster son who behaved himself.

Caleb still didn't leave his house. Apparently the tethers that held him there were so strong, had become so much a part of his life, that he couldn't let them go.

Luanne wrote that she visited him at times and that he smiled when she came, especially when he talked about Philip. Or me.

I started writing to Caleb, and he answered every letter, always telling me how Philip was doing and what the trees outside his windows looked like.

I wrote back and told him that when we were faced with awful problems I was the one who always ran away; he was the one who always stayed home. Perhaps the answer lay between us somewhere. I told him I hoped we'd find that place.

In one letter he wrote that Philip was sick. Old age, he said.

I'd promised Miss Farley and my new foster parents that I was done with being a bad kid. I was going to walk the straight and narrow.

But I ran away one last time, hitching rides all the way to Elderville.

I went to Caleb's house, and we said prayers over Philip's backyard grave.

And I thought about how my short stay in Elderville was a time I shined just a little bit in this world, though few would ever remember but me.

That would have to be enough, I told myself. Sometimes when life doesn't give you many prizes, you have to look for tiny victories anywhere you can and be happy with the ones you find.

But Once a Year

John Lutz

Elana made herself quite clear.

"Jock Leary, if you drink yourself to oblivion this St. Patrick's Day like last and every year, oblivion is what you'll find when you sober up! I'll be far and away!"

But Jock knew she was bluffing. Too kindhearted, she was, to follow through on that sort of threat, actually leaving him to fight life's battle alone. She cared deeply for him, and that was her only flaw. A lovely woman!

"It's not like I get angry and violent when I drink a toot too much," Jock protested. He was a large man with unruly red hair, a florid complexion, and the hopeful blue eyes of a child.

"What you get is stupid and gullible!" Elana said, as she went about getting dressed for her job in the Sheepish Nook souvenir shoppe.

"But it's the annual recognition and celebration of St. Pat, who ridded Ireland of its snakes," Leary said. "An event that comes but once a year."

"Surely more often than that," Elana said.

"No," Jock said thoughtfully, "it comes but once every twelve months."

"As do all dates that are annual holidays," Elana said with disdain. "I was being sarcastic. See what I mean about you being gullible?" She slipped her feet into sensible sales clerk's shoes that nonetheless made her graceful, nyloned calves look even better. "But no, you *wouldn't* see! Not you!"

"I was admiring the fine turn of your ankles," Leary said.

She laughed hopelessly, but he could tell she was pleased by his comment.

"I do love you," he said.

"I know, dammit!"

And out of the house she went to her job selling leprechaun statuettes and woolly socks and sweaters to those who marked Wellin Grove on their travel itineraries. Leary wondered who could resist buying a knickknack or such from Elana. Superb woman!

For Leary, when the noon hour approached, it was off to the Snorting Rooster for a sandwich and a tankard of good stout. Not that he didn't seek honest work when such labor was a possibility. But like many an Irish town, Wellin Grove was in an economic depression, what with the distillery closing last summer, along with the pencil factory, where Leary had put in long and tedious hours listening to supervisors' exhortations to get the lead in.

The Snorting Rooster sat a block off Main Street and was mostly frequented by locals, though a few strays from the flocks of tourists did find their way to the place. It being St. Pat's Day, all of the stools along the bar were occupied, so Leary slid into one of the small wooden booths. The pub smelled pleasantly of stale brew and tobacco smoke. A beautiful melancholy tune was playing on the expensive sound system Danny Blake, the owner and manager, had installed six months ago, hoping to lure more of the tourist trade.

And perhaps the noisesome thing was working to that effect. As Leary exchanged nods with some of those he knew, he noted that there were more strangers than usual in the Snorting Rooster. Perhaps it was the holiday.

Leary had finished his corned beef sandwich and was into his second stout when a small man wearing a tweed coat with a green carnation in its lapel slid into the booth and smiled at him across the table. Leary, ever amiable, smiled back, though he was sure he'd never before laid eyes on the man.

"Name's Star Severson," said the man. "They tell me you're one Jock Leary. I see a fella, I say to myself, is or isn't he gonna be the one?" He spoke rapidly and sibilantly, hissing softly though not exactly lisping. Leary had some difficulty understanding him.

Remembering Elana's stern admonition about being gullible, Leary took a pull of stout and studied this Star Severson across the table. He was one of those men of indeterminate age, maybe forty, maybe sixty. His graying black hair was untrimmed and curled over his ears and about his collar, which was a bit worn and stained. He had a bright and ready creased smile that made you like him right off, and a broken nose that kept him from being too pretty.

"What one?" Leary asked, more curious than he knew was wise.

"The one open-minded man with the wisdom to believe what I have to say about *this*." And with a grand flourish Severson placed a cardboard box about a foot square on the table. Leary was startled to hear movement inside the box, and he saw some air holes punched in its top. Something was alive in there.

"What is it?" he asked.

"It comes with a story," Severson said.

"Ah, doesn't everything?"

Severson tapped the top of the box with his forefinger. "It will bring its recipient luck on this special day," he said earnestly, yet there was a twinkle in his eye.

"Now, now," Leary said, "don't try to play me for a fool and sell me a leprechaun, as was done to an unsuspecting American last year in Belfast."

Severson laughed with a sound oddly like music. "I remember reading about that in the newspaper. A leprechaun, no less! But this is nothing so much as that, my friend." He lowered his voice and his brow. "What I do happen to have here before you is the famous green cat."

"Not so famous that I've heard of it," Leary said. "Besides, such an animal doesn't come in such a color."

"Which makes it a special cat for a special day."

Leary, ever seeking amusement, thought he'd play along with this madman. "And how other than its hue is this cat so special?"

"When you own and care for it this day and this day only, no harm whatsoever can befall you."

"And I suppose such a cat is prohibitively expensive."

Severson leaned back, looked serious, and rubbed his chin. "Expensive? More expensive *not* to obtain it, I'd say." He leaned forward to speak confidentially across the table. "You misunderstand, Jock Leary. What's important is that the cat must change hands. It's up to me to see that such a transaction occurs, and then luck will come to both of us."

"I'll bet."

"And a safe bet it is. For you see, the green cat is yours for no more than the price of a drink."

Leary thought about that and looked dubious. "How do I know you've even a cat in the box? Maybe there's just something in there you're somehow moving around so it sounds alive."

Severson smiled widely. "Maybe *not*. And there's something else about the green cat. On this day only, you may drink your fill and not be in leave of your good senses, and in the morning you'll suffer no ill effects from what you've imbibed in the good cause of St. Pat's Day."

It sounded again as if something moved inside the box, and Severson hadn't a hand near it.

Leary waved to Danny, who wiped his hands on the towel tucked in his belt beneath his substantial paunch and swaggered over to the booth.

"Another pint for me," he said, "and whatever Mr. Severson here might crave."

"An ale will do nicely for me," Severson said, "and with it a twist of lime and a sprinkle of salt."

Danny had begun his career as saloonkeeper behind the bar of a pub on Main Street proper, so he was used to international drinkers and merely nodded at the sort of order he didn't usually get in the Snorting Rooster.

"There is one other thing," Severson said, while they were waiting for their drinks. "You mustn't open the box until I've finished my ale and taken my leave."

Leary, with second thoughts about ordering the man's drink, said, "Why am I not shocked by the request?"

Severson grinned philosophically and shook his head. "I do believe you suspect me of being a miscreant. You need to learn to trust, Jock Leary."

"My wife says I'm too trusting."

"And so you might be, but trusting of the wrong people. That's an important distinction. Trusting is a gift and an instinct. Even though you're a stranger to me, I trust you to believe me just enough and, most importantly, not to mistreat the green cat."

"Never have I mistreated an animal!" Leary proclaimed.

"I know. I could tell. Instinct!"

Danny returned with their drinks, which went on Leary's considerable tab.

Severson drank solemnly and quickly, tilting his head far back. Leary watched the man's Adam's apple ride up and down his scrawny, unwashed neck, then turned his attention to his own drink. He consumed it faster than he might have, perhaps to the pace set by Severson.

For sure now, Leary was working up an honest thirst, and he felt gracious toward this little man who'd been good enough to sell him a lucky cat for the mere price of an ale. He fixed his eye on Danny, waiting until he finished with a couple at the bar, so he could catch his attention and summon him over to the booth.

When finally he caught Danny's eye, he waved for another stout, then generously turned to ask Severson if he cared for another drink.

But Severson was gone.

The box remained.

Danny came over to the booth, carrying a second tankard of stout.

"The little fella who was here a minute ago," Leary said, "ever seen him before?"

"Not to my knowledge," Danny said. "An odd sort is how he struck me."

"Talked in a funny way," Leary said.

Danny shrugged. "Maybe he was Welsh." He placed the stout on the table and withdrew behind the bar, where half a dozen of the regulars were beginning to sing, still fairly in tune and in unison, as the holiday was young.

Leary moved the box over toward him and felt something shift inside it as he set it beside him on the bench. He slowly untied the twine that held the box closed, then raised the cardboard flaps.

Inside was a small green cat.

Not a vivid shamrock green, you understand, but an undeniable green nonetheless.

Leary decided he'd had enough to drink, yet he downed a few more swallows for good measure, then lifted the cat from the box and carried it outside. Such was the condition of the regulars that they didn't notice the animal's strange color. Leary wondered for a moment if he might be in his cups to the extent that only *he* saw the cat as green.

It was a fine cat, gentle and still where it lay cradled in Leary's arm as he walked none too steadily toward Main Street to catch the trolley for home.

Several passersby glanced at him, then at the cat, and smiled in friendly fashion. A man with a green derby and a red nose actually snapped to attention and saluted. Leary would have saluted back but for the cat resting so comfortably on his right arm.

At the corner, he stood swaying north to south while waiting for a string of cars and a foul-smelling tour bus to pass. Finally he lowered his head and, in what he thought was a straight path, started across the street toward the trolley stop.

Suddenly and for no apparent reason the cat yowled and leaped from his grasp. Leary tried to catch it but felt only a fleeting caress of fur along his fingertips. He took several lurching steps after the cat, hearing a bell jangle frantically and repeatedly.

Then there was a rush of air, a roar, and a ferocious crash.

The mere wind of whatever had happened caused Leary to sit down in the middle of the street.

When finally he found his bearings and looked around, he saw the wreckage of the trolley where it had struck the Blackthorn Sweets Shoppe and taken out the front wall. Passengers were emerging from the trolley in a daze, stumbling over the bricks scattered in the street.

The cat! Leary looked all around for it as hands gripped him and helped him to his feet.

The green cat was nowhere to be seen.

"A miracle!" a woman with her gray hair done up in a huge bun was saying over and over.

"Missed you by mere inches, lad," said an elderly man with a cane.

"My cat," mumbled Leary. "The cat I was carrying. Where is my cat off to?"

"I saw no cat," said the woman with the bun. "It was a miracle. You didn't even have time to look up, and it was as if you had second sight and bolted out of harm's way at just the right instant."

"A St. Patrick's Day miracle," the man with the cane confirmed.

"On my dear mother's ashes!" Leary said, beginning to tremble, struck by the firm realization that the green cat had saved his life. Lucky cat indeed!

Made cold sober by his brush with death, Leary politely refused further offer of help and continued on his way.

"A miracle!" repeated the woman behind him.

Sober though he felt, within minutes after arriving home, Leary fell into a stupor in his chair and awoke in his bed the next morning. Someone had kindly removed his shoes and trousers.

"How do you feel?" Elana asked. There was great concern in her voice and on her lovely face. So she had heard about his narrow escape, as she surely would in the ferment of rumor that swirled around sad and quiet Wellin Grove.

Leary told her the tale, directly and without the embellishment of the green cat, as a brave man who'd felt the breeze of the grim reaper's scythe on the back of his neck would speak, with a newfound appreciation and joy of life. When Elana, still spellbound by his words, told him how it dovetailed with what she had heard, she didn't mention a cat he'd been carrying.

Leary decided not to tell Elana about the green cat. This was no time to present her with further evidence that her view of him as gullible was correct. He knew she would scoff at the idea that the cat had saved his life. As far as she knew, as she babied and comforted him, he'd been strolling innocently along his way and by mortal fortune had barely escaped certain death.

But he knew he had not been aware of the trolley's approach, yet *something* had made him lurch out of death's path. A St. Patrick's Day miracle, as the woman with the gray bun had maintained with conviction. And wasn't there such a thing as divine intervention?

The pain in his head and unease in his stomach persisted. The aftermath of yesterday's drink clung to Leary's body and soul as he paced in agony. The luck of the green cat had worked only to a degree.

"How's your head?" the sympathetic Elana asked.

"It feels as if an axe has cleaved it," Leary told her, and with truth.

She moaned sympathetically and hugged him.

"Such a crazy thing, that trolley jumping the track, and on St.

Patrick's Day," she said. "It was a day for insanity. Carrie Muldoon told me her cat Flower went missing yesterday and turned up this morning colored green. Who would do such a cruel thing to a cat?"

Leary's heart jumped in alarm. "Only a madman," he assured her, looking grave. "They tell me a man with a green cat was in one of the pubs yesterday, trying to trade it for a free drink. Probably the Muldoon feline."

"Oh, without doubt," Elana said. "A cat thief and a confidence man, such a criminal will surely roast in a place other than heaven."

"Why would a man go to such trouble for a free glass of ale—or stout or whatever?"

"The heartless fiend was probably in a dozen pubs yesterday, using his green cat to trick the naive and unsuspecting out of free drinks, then following them when they left the pub and retrieving the cat at the first opportunity so he could use it again to deceive the weak-minded."

Leary hadn't thought of that possibility. Leave it to Elana to glimpse an unpleasant truth. So Severson was nothing but a petty crook, a flimflam man. Still, the cat *had* saved a life yesterday.

"A fool who'd fall for such a scam," Elana said, "is born no more than once a year."

"Hmmm." Leary nodded somber agreement, making his headache flare.

At noon, his skull still throbbing painfully, he left the house and walked through the cool day, hoping the bracing air would cause the pain in his head to abate. But it didn't seem to help.

When he took note of his surroundings, he discovered that his steps had naturally led him to the Snorting Rooster. He entered, found that he was one of only half a dozen customers, and had Danny prepare him a hangover remedy of tomato juice with brown sugar and hot sauce mixed in.

But this morning, the usually potent concoction did nothing to calm Leary's heaving stomach or help his pulsating head.

He was staring at the table when he became aware that a body had slid into the booth to sit opposite him. When he looked up, there was Severson. The little man was dressed as he had been yesterday, in his thinly worn shirt and tweedy jacket, but this time without the green carnation in his lapel.

Leary was in no mood to endure scoundrels on this day of painful sobriety. "Go away," he growled.

"I saw what happened yesterday," Severson hissed at him through his cheerful grin. "The green cat saved your life, brought you good fortune just as I promised."

"You're a sham," Leary said. "A cheap confidence man."

"How can you of all people say such a thing?" Severson sounded injured to his quick. "Would you be sitting here alive were it not for me?"

"No," Leary had to admit.

"And now, having used your full portion of luck even before you reached home, and alive though you may be, you're paying dearly for your excesses of yesterday."

"So true," Leary said.

"It happens that way sometimes."

"Small solace." Leary pressed a hand to his aching head.

"I have what you need," Severson said in a low, confidential tone.

"Aw, go away! Please! Do you think I'm the sort of fool born but once a year?"

"A fool? You? By all the saints, no! You weren't a fool yesterday when you obtained the green cat for no more than the price of a pint of ale, were you?"

"As it turned out, no," Leary admitted.

The little man removed a small velvet case of the sort expensive rings come in and set it on the table. He pried back its domed top slowly and with reverence.

Inside on red velvet lay a tuft of what looked like green-tinted fur.

"What is it?" Leary asked, staring at the object.

"It is," Severson said with a smile and a wink, "that which you often hear mention of but seldom see, the real and actual item that never fails its owner."

"So what is it?" Leary repeated impatiently.

Severson seemed to savor his secret even as he divulged it. "What you see before you is a little hair of the dog."

Leary leaned forward.

He was keenly interested.

Cold Turkey

Graham Masterton

"—And as usual, Tarquin wishes all of you a very merry Christmas," said Uncle Philip, stroking the pedigree British Blue cat that sat in his lap. It was obvious, however, that Tarquin was wishing for only one thing. His coppery eyes were fixed on the huge, well-bronzed turkey that had just arrived in the middle of the dining table. His tension was almost palpable. Mandy felt that if the turkey had been capable of twitching just an inch, Tarquin would have launched himself at it, and nothing could have stopped him.

"A very merry Christmas to Tarquin," Kenneth replied, raising his glass. "Long may he live in the lap of luxury." Kenneth was floridly drunk; and two of his shirt buttons were missing; but he was not too drunk to be less-than-subtly sarcastic.

Nicholas raised his glass, too, although Nicholas had remained supremely, remotely sober. A new partner in a firm of Essex Street solicitors couldn't afford to be caught for drunk driving, and besides, he never liked to lose control. His wife Libby, however, was beginning to look distinctly disarranged. She had already pulled one of her crackers and she had awkwardly tugged a purple paper hat over her frizzy ginger hair.

"To Tarquin," said Nicholas, and gave Uncle Philip a waxy, colorless smile. "May all his dreams come true."

"Cats don't have dreams, do they?" frowned Libby.

"Oh, yes," Nicholas assured her, as if he had never met her before. "They have the same kind of dreams as any other creature. Lust, greed, and lost opportunities. Most of all, though, they dream of revenge."

"I don't think Tarquin dreams of revenge, do you, Tarquin?" said

Mandy, reaching over and tickling Tarquin's chin. "I think Tarquin has nice dreams, about mice, and turkey."

Caitlin, arty and vague, threw back her tawny mane and jangled her silver bangles. "I don't think he dreams about mice, either. Cats are too cerebral to dream of mice."

"Cerebral?" laughed Kenneth. "They're not cerebral. They're parasites. They're not much better than tapeworms with fur."

"Kenneth!" Mary scolded him. "We're just about to eat lunch!"

Mary was Mandy's mother. Mandy's father had died in April in a road accident in Newbury, bloody and white in his BMW, with a local doctor holding his hand. His life insurance had scarcely covered the mortgage, and ever since then Mary and Mandy had been living on a smaller and smaller budget. Mandy couldn't remember when she had last bought herself a new skirt.

She thought that Christmases at Box Hill were dull beyond endurance. For three days every year the Chesterton family sat in the gloomy drawing room or the musty-smelling conservatory, picking at soft-centered chocolates and cracking stale Brazil nuts, or bickering aimlessly about politics or who had cheated at Monopoly two Christmases ago and who had ripped the board in half in a rage.

For Mandy, Tarquin was the only consolation. At least he didn't argue and he didn't get drunk. He was so haughty. Apart from Uncle Philip, Mandy was the only member of the family by whom Tarquin would deign to be stroked.

This year there were only eleven of them, including Mandy herself. Ned and Alice had won a safari to Kenya in a competition on the side of a jar of Kenco instant coffee. Poor Uncle David's prostate cancer had spread and he wasn't expected to see the spring. Mind you, he was only a curate, so he didn't really count. Jilly and Michael were having a trial separation after that business with Jilly and the muscular plumber, and so Michael had come on his own, and was tetchy and gloomy and tearful by turns. Kenneth called him "the Surrey Waterworks."

Grace had arrived late, with far too many bags. She had a loud voice and a big face. Mandy had always assumed that she was a lesbian, but her mother said that she was once engaged to be married to a Hungarian violinist. One night, drunk, he had thrown himself off Putney Bridge, and "that was that."

None of the family liked each other much; and none of them felt any affection for Polesden View: this great elaborate red-brick Edwardian pile, with its ugly mansard roof and its gardens full of gelatinous moss and dripping laurels. Mandy thought it was the most depressing house she had ever visited. She was seventeen now—still petite, with glossy dark short-cropped hair and a pixielike face. But she no longer knelt on the windowseats the way she had when she was younger, and peered through the stained-glass windows in the hall, amber and crimson and bottle green. In those days she used to imagine that she could see ladies with capes and umbrellas wandering sadly along the rainswept garden paths. But there were never any ladies; there were only ghosts, and memories, and echoes, and Uncle Philip was the last of them.

They wouldn't have come within fifty miles of Box Hill if it hadn't have been for Uncle Philip. He was the oldest member of the Chesterton family. He was mean, arrogant, and so unremittingly condescending to all of them that Mandy wondered that he didn't grow tired of it. But he had inherited most of the family fortune, which was immense, and none of them were going to displease him until he had gargled his last breath.

Three generations ago, the Chestertons had struck it rich in Rhodesia, and upstairs on the second landing there was still a faded photograph of Uncle Philip's grandfather shaking hands with the diamond magnate Barney Barnato on the terrace of the Natalia Hotel in Durban. In the background, a cheeky black boy was sticking his tongue out.

Apart from Polesden View, Uncle Philip owned a 230-acre farm in Oxfordshire, a seaside house in Southwold on the east coast, and a three-bedroom flat in Cheyne Walk in Chelsea. There were safes stuffed with stocks and bonds, and private deposit boxes crammed with family jewelry. The family may have hated their Christmases here on Box Hill, but none of them were going to risk their inheritance.

Christmas lunch was even more oppressive than ever. It was one of those dark, airless days when the cloud hangs low over the Surrey Downs and the dining-room windows were all steamed up, which made it seem even darker. Uncle Philip sat at the head of the table with Tarquin in his lap, a gaunt silhouette with thin silver hair and gleaming cheekbones where his skin was stretched tightly over his skull. He reminded Mandy of a Halloween mask. He stroked Tarquin with his right hand and twisted his turkey into small pieces with the edge of his fork. Tarquin stared at the half-carved turkey carcass and didn't even blink.

"He looks so hungry, poor thing," said Mandy.

Uncle Philip gave her a wide, emaciated smile. "He has to learn to wait for what he wants, like everybody else. We mustn't spoil him, must we?"

"I suppose not," said Mandy, and stroked Tarquin under his chin until his throat rattled with harsh, catarrhal purring.

Grace said, "Philip . . . I hear you've been ill."

"A bout of the flu, that's all," said Philip. "The Grim Reaper isn't going to get me yet."

"You should think of selling this house. It's so big. It's so damp. It's so impractical."

"It's my home," said Philip. "More than that, it's Tarquin's home. Tarquin would be lost anywhere else."

"Even if you don't move, you should at least think of reassessing your holdings," said Kenneth, after a while. "Some of your older portfolios, well . . ."

Philip didn't even raise his voice. "When I need advice from a bankrupt stockbroker, Kenneth, I'll ask for it. I promise."

"Now come on, Uncle Philip, that's not fair," protested Joy. In the days when Kenneth had been handsome, the blond-haired captain of the village cricket team, Joy had been deliciously pretty, in a scrubbed, country kind of way. Now her face had been disassembled by Kenneth's alcoholism and their children's delinquency. Her young and golden life had vanished and she didn't know where to look for it.

Uncle Philip raised his eyes from his plate, where he had been tirelessly pursuing a Brussels sprout. "Fair, Joy? Fair? You all inherited a hundred thousand each when Father died; and what you did with it afterward was up to you. If you decided to spend it on cars and holidays and ridiculous business ventures, that isn't any concern of mine; and there's nothing about it that isn't *fair*."

He turned to Mandy and laid his hand on top of hers. "What game shall we play after lunch, Mandy? Scrabble? Or shall we play Charades?"

Tarquin had cautiously lifted one paw onto the tablecloth. His eyes were locked onto the turkey as if by laser. Uncle Philip rapped his paw with the flat of his knife, and said, "Tarquin! You can't always have what you want just when you want it!"

Mandy smiled at her mother, and then she said, "Let's play Charades. This family seems to be good at it."

After the turkey came the blue-flaming Christmas pudding, and mince pies with thick Cornish cream. They pulled their crackers and put on paper hats and read out all the jokes. *"Father:* Your hair needs cutting badly. *Son:* No it doesn't . . . it needs cutting well!"

Mandy was too full to eat any more so she helped to clear away the dishes. In the large, pine-paneled kitchen she found Avril, the cook, scraping heaps of sprouts and roast potatoes into the bin. "I don't know why he always orders me to cook so much. Nobody ever eats it. They're all too busy arguing and scoring points off each other. They're all too busy worrying about their inheritance; that's it. That's what Mr. Chesterton says, anyway."

"Doesn't he *ever* believe that we come here because we want to?" said Mandy.

The cook shook her head. "He knows you don't want to. But that's all part of the fun."

"You don't think it's fun, do you?" asked Mandy.

"Yes, miss, I do, in a way. My father used to say that there was nothing that made him laugh more than monkeys dancing for nuts. I didn't really know what he meant until I came here, and saw you lot visiting Mr. Chesterton once every Christmas. No more, because you really can't stand him, can you, the horrible old shriveled-up creature. And no less, because he might decide to cut you out of his will."

Nicholas came in, carrying the remains of the turkey. The cook loosely covered it with a tea towel and put it into the larder to cool. "Turkey," she complained. "I can't stand the stuff. But your Uncle Philip always wants his cold turkey salad on Boxing Day."

Not surprisingly, Tarquin appeared, on a foraging expedition away from the base camp of Uncle Philip's lap. He went up to the cook and rubbed her legs with the flat of his head, and mewed.

"No, Tarquin, you're not having any turkey tonight. He's a terror, you know, when it comes to any kind of birds. Pigeons, chickens, especially duck. He hangs around the larder until I chase him away with the sponge mop."

Mandy hunkered down and stroked Tarquin's soft and fluffy fur. "Surely we could give him just one slice of turkey?"

"Sorry," the cook told her. "Tarquin doesn't get any leftovers until your Uncle Philip's had all of his. Your Uncle Philip will eat a gammon until you can see his teethmarks on the bone, I promise you. Doesn't believe in waste. How do you think he stayed so rich? You've seen his car, haven't you? He bought that in nineteen sixty-two and he won't change it for anything. Waste of money, that's what he calls it. And you should see the meat he expects me to cook with. Neck-end, scrag-end, and skirt. He's mean and he's grumpy and if I were you I wouldn't come for Christmas ever again. You're just making fools of yourselves."

Mandy gave Tarquin one last tickle and then she stood up. "Perhaps you're right. Perhaps we shouldn't come here ever again."

The next morning, Mandy woke up early and went down to the kitchen in her slippers to make herself a cup of coffee. The gloom of the previous day had lifted, and the sun was shining weakly through the trees. In the distance, through a gilded mist, she could see the Surrey Weald and the spire of Dorking church. While she waited for the kettle to boil she switched on the old transistor radio on the windowsill.

"Boxing Day promises to be bright and clear over most of the area, although there is a threat of wintry showers across Essex and Kent . . ."

When she was young, Mandy had always imagined that people held boxing matches on Boxing Day; and she still didn't quite believe her mother's laborious explanation that it was a day when the rich used to give boxes of Christmas leftovers to the poor—any more than she could quite forget her father's joke that the box trees which had given Box Hill its name had real ready-made wooden boxes growing on them, instead of fruit.

The kettle started to dribble, and then to whistle, and she went to the larder to find the coffee jar. The larder door was already slightly open, only three or four inches. But as she approached it she could see the leftover turkey on the marble shelf on the left—and, on the red-and-white tiled floor directly below it, she could see a blue-gray fluffy leg.

She opened the door wide and there was Tarquin, lying on his side, his coppery eyes wide open, and obviously dead.

Uncle Philip sat on a chair in the kitchen with Tarquin in his arms, rocking backward and forward. Tears dripped down his withered cheeks and clung to Tarquin's fur like diamonds.

Kenneth stood in one corner, his eyes half-closed like overripe damsons, his hand pressed against his forehead in the classic gesture of a man who is swearing to himself that he will never touch another alcoholic drink as long as he lives. Nicholas, in his red silk dressing-gown, was calmer and waxier than ever.

"He was eating the leftover turkey," said Paul, Caitlin's husband, who was all dressed up in a bizarre assemblage of socks and track-suit bottoms and a frayed brown sweater.

"But that couldn't have hurt him," said Roger. "We all ate the same turkey, didn't we, and none of us are sick."

"He could have choked," Caitlin suggested.

"He could have had a heart attack. He's almost fourteen, after all."

Paul knelt down beside Uncle Philip's chair and said, "Do you mind if I—you know, touch him?"

Uncle Philip didn't seem to care. He turned away and his face was a mask of terrible distress.

Paul carefully opened Tarquin's jaws. "Look, he didn't vomit, you see. He's still got half-chewed turkey in his mouth." He leaned closer and sniffed, and sniffed again.

"What is it?" asked Nicholas.

"Prussic acid. Or cyanide to you."

"You mean he's been *poisoned*?"

"I used to work for Kodak," said Paul. "You use a lot of potassium cyanide when you're developing photographs, and they taught us to recognize the symptoms. Blue face, blue lips. Well, poor old Tarquin was blue already. But you can't mistake that smell. Sweet, isn't it? One of the pleasantest-tasting poisons there is."

Grace boomed, "Who on earth would want to poison Tarquin?"

"Well, nobody, of course," said Nicholas. "The whole thing was an accident. Somebody must have injected the cold turkey with cyanide after we went to bed last night, with the intention of harming whoever was going to eat it. Fortunately for the intended victim—but very unfortunately for Tarquin—the larder door was accidentally left open."

Caitlin looked aghast. "But we were all planning to leave after breakfast, all of us. We always do on Boxing Day. The only person who would have eaten the turkey was—"

Uncle Philip looked up, although he continued to stroke Tarquin's lifeless head. "Yes," he said. "In fact, I would have thought it was quite obvious. Somebody poisoned the turkey because they wanted to get rid of *me*."

Kenneth looked at Caitlin and Caitlin looked at Paul and Paul looked at Libby. "The house was locked up all night," said Nicholas. "You always switch on the alarm. That means that whoever did it— well, it must have been one of us."

"We should call the police," said Libby.

"But if it's one of us—"

"If it's one of us, the police will find out who it is and presumably charge him or her with attempted murder."

"My God," said Libby. "I simply can't believe that one of us would be capable of such a thing."

"Why not?" Kenneth demanded. "We all have more than enough of a motive, after all. We're all practically broke, and here's Philip sitting on several millions of pounds worth of property and shares . . . and making sure, year by year, that he reminds us how foolish we've been, how wasteful we've been . . ."

"You *have* been foolish, and you *have* been wasteful," said Uncle Philip. He stood up, with Tarquin's heavy dead body cradled in his arms. He circled the kitchen, and his voice was cracking with emotion.

"I always thought that you were rotten, all of you. Rotten through and through. You were each given more money than some people can earn in a lifetime, and each of you wasted it and ended up with nothing. That's why you come here for Christmas, every year, even though you hate me, even though you hate each other, even though you're so bored.

"Well, every Christmas has been my way of showing my contempt for each and every one of you, because I never had any intention of giving you any of my money. I just wanted to see you grovel, year after year. I just wanted to see how low you were prepared to crawl.

"In the whole of my life, I have never come across greed and arrogance like yours. Never. You assumed that I would bequeath you all of my money. You couldn't see that the world is full of far more deserving beneficiaries. But worse than that, you couldn't even wait till I died, could you? One of you tried to poison me. One of you actually tried to murder me. But all you succeeded in doing was killing the one creature who took me for what I was. Tarquin didn't love me because I was wealthy. Tarquin loved me without any conditions at all. I loved him more than life itself, and I can't imagine how I'm going to live without him."

He looked from one to the other with an expression of total wretchedness, and then he walked out of the kitchen with Tarquin still dangling in his arms. The family watched him go, and none of them said a single word.

Only a second later, however, they heard a thumping sound in the hallway and the clatter of a table tipping over. They rushed out of the kitchen to find Uncle Philip lying on his back, his eyes open, his face convulsed, with Tarquin lying on top of him.

"Ambulance!" Nicholas shouted. "Call for an ambulance!"

Detective-Inspector Rogers came into the drawing room where they were all assembled, blowing his nose loudly on a grayish-looking handkerchief.

"Christmas," he complained. "I always get a cold around Christmas."

Nicholas looked at his watch. "I do wish you'd get this over with, Inspector. I was hoping to get back to town before it got dark."

It was New Year's Eve, five days after Boxing Day. During the week, the family had been allowed to return home, but they had all been warned not to leave the southeast of England until the police had completed their preliminary investigations; and Inspector Rogers had been around to each of them, with a long list of penetrating questions. Now they had been called back to Polesden View—as fractious as ever.

"First of all," said Inspector Rogers, "a post-mortem examination has shown that Tarquin the cat died from ingesting hydrocyanic acid, and that the poison entered his system by means of his swallowing a small amount of contaminated turkey.

"If the intention of contaminating the turkey was to cause harm to Mr. Philip Chesterton, almost all of you who were present on Boxing Day had a motive. A mistaken motive, as it turned out, because Mr. Chesterton had no intention of leaving you any money—but you didn't know that at the time."

He walked over to Kenneth and Libby and said, "Your brokerage business is bankrupt, sir, and you desperately need a substantial amount of money to avoid losing your house."

To Grace, he said, "You, madam, after a long period of living alone, have found a partner of whom you are extremely fond. Unfortunately, he is very much younger than you, and you are finding that you keep having to buy him gifts in order to keep him happy. He wants a car, which you can't afford."

He crossed over to Nicholas and said, "Now that you're a partner in your law firm, sir, you want to move into town and live according to your new status . . . amongst other things." Nicholas looked relieved. What nobody else in the family knew was that "other things" referred to his secretary, with whom he had just started an affair.

Inspector Rogers came over to Mary. "Your husband died in spring of last year, leaving you and your daughter almost penniless."

Then he went up to Caitlin. "The lease on your pottery studio has just run out, and unless you can find a new one, you'll be going out of business."

Lastly, he approached Michael. "You're separated from your wife, sir, and she's threatening to divorce you. You're certainly going to need all the funds you can lay your hands on."

Inspector Rogers returned to the center of the room. "To be frank with you, however, there is no evidence that links any of you directly with the contamination of the turkey. It could have been any one of you, or it could have been some of you, or all of you in concert.

"There is also the problem that nobody ate any of the poisoned turkey except for the cat; and poisoning a cat is not exactly a capital offence. It is also unlikely that we can prove beyond a reasonable doubt that whoever poisoned the turkey was specifically intending to kill Mr. Chesterton. It isn't as if the turkey were set out on a plate that was solely intended for him.

"For that reason I am obliged to let you all go about your business, but I must caution you that our investigations will continue and that you should remain available for further questioning."

"Well, thank God for that," said Nicholas. "Sanity at last."

"Not so much sanity, sir," Inspector Rogers corrected him. "More like lack of evidence."

"By the way," said Mary, as they gathered up their coats. "Do you have any idea who *is* going to inherit?"

"Well—this is the funny part," said Inspector Rogers, taking out his handkerchief again and trying to find a dry bit. "The whole estate was supposed to go to Tarquin. All eleven million pounds of it. He would have been the richest cat in the country."

"What!" Kenneth exploded. "Eleven million to a *cat!* It's insane!"

"It's legal, I'm afraid," said Inspector Rogers. "Didn't you read about that woman who gave two million pounds to her spaniel?"

"But Tarquin's dead. Who gets the money now?"

"Let's see . . . something called the British Blue Protection League."

"Bloody cats again," grumbled Kenneth. "I hate bloody cats."

Mandy and her mother drove back to their semi-detached house overlooking Ealing Common in West London, and her mother asked her if she wanted to go out for a curry because she had nothing in the house.

Mandy flopped back on the sagging corduroy sofa and said, "No. I'd rather be hungry."

"Whatever for?"

"Because I'm never going to be hungry again ever; and I want to remember what it's like."

"What on earth are you talking about?"

"I'm talking about Uncle Philip's inheritance."

"I still don't understand you."

"Uncle Philip never believed that any of you loved him, did he? He always thought you were after his money."

"He was right, wasn't he? We didn't, and we were."

"But he knew that Tarquin loved him, and that Tarquin never wanted anything but warmth and food and his bony old lap to sit in."

"So?"

"So none of you used your brains, did you? If you want a cantankerous old man like that to feel good towards you, you don't pretend to like him for what he is, because he won't believe you. In fact he'll be even more suspicious of you than ever. No—you make sure that you win the confidence of somebody he trusts. Or, in Uncle Philip's case, *something* he trusts, which was Tarquin.

"I started to make a fuss over Tarquin because there was nothing else to do at Polesden View. But Tarquin began to trust me, and Uncle Philip began to trust me, too. He gave me bits of money and sweets and he told me that he was going to leave all his inheritance to Tarquin, just to show you how greedy and insincere you all were."

"You *knew* about him giving his inheritance to Tarquin? And you didn't tell us?"

"If I'd told you, you would never have gone down to see him at Christmas, would you, and he wouldn't have trusted me anymore."

"But we suffered all of those horrible, horrible Christmases, and you *knew*?"

Mandy smiled. "We called it our secret, Uncle Philip and me."

"But what was the point, when the money was all going to go to that stupid cat?"

"Oh, Mum! The point was that even the brainiest cats can't look after themselves, can they? Cats can't open bank accounts. They can't even open tins of catfood. When their owners die, cats have to have people to look after them . . . people that their owners trust. And when cats die, they have to leave their money to somebody, don't they?"

Mandy went to the bookcase and tugged out a file. She opened it up so that Mary could see the first page. In official-looking letters, it was headed British Blue Protection League: Annual Accounts. The column under Credits was still blank.

"I put Uncle Philip in touch with them. He never realized it was only me."

"*You* poisoned the turkey," Mary whispered.

Mandy nodded. "And I opened the larder door, so that Tarquin could get in."

"You couldn't have known that Uncle Philip would have a stroke."

"No . . . that was something of a bonus, wasn't it?"

"My God," said Mary. "I can hardly believe it. Eleven million pounds."

"Not until he dies, of course. But we can wait, can't we? It'll give us time to think what we're going to spend it on. You know what I've really always wanted? A dog."

How the July Fourth Cat Saved the Day and Ruined the Night

Jan Grape

"Didn't your mother tell you you'll get freckles if you don't wear your bonnet?" he asked. They had converged on the path leading from the auction barn to the carnival area, and he'd stepped aside to allow Dallas to pass.

It was the first of November in 1872, and opening day of Fort Worth's annual Old Settlers Festival at the Tarrant County fairgrounds. The November nights were cool and crisp, while the days were warm—typical Indian summer weather for north central Texas.

The festival drew a big crowd from around the countryside. It consisted of a carnival with a carousel, a livestock auction, an exhibition of a steam engine, and a county fair.

There had been talk about joining the big state fair over in Dallas, but the citizens of Fort Worth had no real desire to associate with their neighboring city in any endeavor. The folk who made up the City of Dallas thought they were a cut above the folk in Fort Worth anyway. Fort Worth's reputation as a cowtown was widely held. The ironic thing was that the eastern part of the United States thought *all* of Texas was only about twice removed from savages no matter how many airs they put on to the contrary.

Dallas Jamison, who'd been named after the loathsome city that many Fort Worthians loved to hate—because her parents had met and wed there—had never seen the young man before. He was tall, with a reddish-blond mustache and blond hair. He bumped against her arm slightly when he asked about her bonnet as if to punctuate his question.

"My mother is dead," she said and ducked her head. She wasn't used to speaking to strangers.

"I'm, uh, sorry." His tongue somehow tangled in his mouth. He was wearing dark blue bib overalls with a white shirt opened at the neck.

"It's okay. It happened so long ago, I don't remember her too well." Dallas felt the blush start around her neck and move up her face. She reached for the bonnet hanging around her neck in an effort to hide the pinkness she knew even now was reaching her hairline. "So it's my grandmother who always warns me about freckles." She managed to pull the bonnet over her head and tilted it down slightly. Even with the brim shielding her face she could still look upward at him. He's quite handsome, she thought. Maybe his lips were a mite thin, but he did have the most wonderful eyes.

She tried to brush past him then, but he turned right in front of her blocking the way. She stepped back and looked up into his face again.

He didn't say anything for a moment, just held out her pocketbook as she looked at him.

Finally, he said, "You should be more careful when you talk to strangers."

When she didn't take the bag, he dropped it to the grass and quickly walked away. "Wait," she called after him but he kept going and didn't turn back. She stooped, picked up her pocketbook, and brushed off the reddish dust and grassy debris.

She watched him approach a small wagon, painted yellow and red and blue, which stood near a grove of pecan trees some distance away. She followed his path slowly. Signs on the wagon proclaimed the unlimited values and medicinal virtues of Dr. Thaddeus Johnson's Soothing Syrup and Volcanic Ash.

An older man with a full gray beard stood near the wagon and spoke harshly to the young man as he approached. The older man wore a long black coat, even though the day was warm, and a tall-crowned black hat.

Was that Dr. Johnson? Dallas wondered and continued her measured pace towards the wagon. She could hear only their tone, and both men sounded angry. Before she reached them they suddenly climbed into the seat of the wagon and they argued still.

She stopped. The young man took up the reins and slapped them lightly against the roan horse's rump. As the wagon's wheels began moving Dallas saw the old man pitch something. It fell along the side of the road. The black discarded object was small, and it now lay on the rutted path, like a ball of yarn. The colorful wagon, wheels at first turning slowly, picked up speed and disappeared in a cloud of dust.

Dallas turned away and took a tentative step back the way she'd come, but then her curiosity got the better of her. She turned and hurried over to the grove. A skinny black kitten with the tiniest dollop of white fur on top of its head lay hunkered, too afraid to move. Or maybe too injured. When Dallas picked it up, the little cat scratched her arm. She judged the cat's age at three months. "Poor thing. If that horrid man is a doctor he must be a charlatan and a carpetbagger. No reasonable gentleman would throw away a perfectly good mouser."

Dallas talked softly, stroking the trembling cat and rubbing her fingernails under the tiny chin. "I'm going to call you Snowflake," she told the now purring kitten. "And I'm declaring July Fourth as your birthday. That way I can remember it each year." The cat fell asleep in her arms as she walked back to the horse barn to find out how much longer her father, Woodrow Jamison, intended to stay.

Dallas thought about the incident of her purse for several days, but she couldn't understand when or how her pocketbook could have jumped over from her arm to the young man's hand. Some trickery involved, she thought, but what? Well, if he was traveling with a carpetbagger, no telling what a scalawag the young man himself might be.

Snowflake grew and became a constant companion to Dallas, often draping herself across the girl's shoulders. The lonely girl had few close friends.

She had been the delight of her father's life for many years. Woodrow Jamison taught Dallas to ride, shoot, butcher and preserve the game meat, and tan the hides. She learned to piece the hides and make shoes and hats. He taught her how to rope calves, how to test for worms and pregnancy, and how to brand them. When he thought she was old enough, he taught her how to castrate the little bulls.

The one thing he didn't teach was how to understand when he told her one day that it was time for her to learn how to be a lady. She was excited until she realized learning to be feminine meant she could never again hunt or work side by side with Woodrow.

Her father never showed her any affection except for an occasional ruffling of her hair when she was younger. He barely spoke to her nowadays, and Dallas often cried herself to sleep many nights because she was lonely and missed his companionship.

Her grandmother Jamison taught her to cook and clean and tried to teach her to sew and cross-stitch and crochet. Dallas was a passable cook, but she never got the knack for the sewing skills. She was all thumbs.

And Grandmother constantly carped about how much trouble she was and how Dallas was a spawn of the devil and could not be redeemed. Dallas never understood how the old woman's son could be so wonderful and his own daughter—flesh of his flesh and blood of his blood—could be so bad. Grandmother would not explain it either, but Dallas suspected it had something to do with her mother. She kept hoping for courage to ask her father one day.

The feline companion gave the young woman the only reason for laughter each day. Snowflake's antics—like batting a twig of yarn across the floor or chasing after the girl—were her only relief in a dreary day. Often when she played with Snowflake, Dallas thought about the young man she'd met the day she rescued the cat and wondered whatever became of him.

In May of 1876, she saw him again. It had been nearly four years and he looked even more handsome than she remembered. He walked into the Methodist church with an older woman and two school-age girls and a little boy. The woman and children had hair ranging from strawberry blonde to cotton-top white on the little boy. The children's eyes all were the same shade of electric blue as the young man's and their facial features showed the same square jaw. Most likely they were his wife and family, thought Dallas. The strangers seated themselves on the left side facing the pulpit and two rows from the front.

"Who is that young man?" Woodrow Jamison asked Dallas. He sat himself in their pew, located on the fourth row back, right-hand side.

"What young man?"

"The one who keeps turning to stare at you so impudently?"

"I don't know, Papa. Is he really looking at me or at someone behind me?" She felt no qualms about not telling her father she'd seen the young man before because she honestly didn't know who he was. She'd certainly not even been formally introduced to him.

"If he doesn't stop staring, his wife's going to take a rolling pin to him when they get home."

For a married man to look at another woman in such a manner was unforgivable. Maybe he wasn't married to the older woman, Dallas thought. But he must be, those youngsters sure looked like his seed.

After church, Mr. Jamison quickly made his exit out the side door. Dallas figured he'd rush around to the front door and try to gain an introduction to the newcomers.

Dallas took her time, walking slowly towards the side door her father had gone through. She paused to speak with two older women about an upcoming quilting bee for her friend and schoolmate, Linda Toole. Linda would be married in June. She had moved to Fort Worth only two years ago but in that short time had become a close friend to Dallas. As near to a sister as someone could have without being kin, they both declared.

Only a year older than Dallas, Linda had shared all her secrets. Linda's mother had died giving birth to her, which gave the girls a common loss in having to live without a mother.

It was Linda who first suggested that Woodrow Jamison's change towards his daughter started when she began growing bosoms. That struck Dallas as funny and she had laughed, yet realized Linda must be right. Fathers could never be as close to daughters as they could with sons. The idea hurt, but Dallas was able to accept it more easily when there was some reason to explain his attitude. Even if she thought his logic warped.

Dallas exulted in Linda's newfound happiness. Many young women their age married for convenience. But Linda cared deeply for her doctor from Colorado. The only fly in the ointment was that the newlyweds would leave for a honeymoon in San Francisco immediately after the wedding, then move to Boulder when they returned. The girls tried not to let it spoil their last days together.

"Don't forget," said Linda. "We'll be back Independence Day. That's when I'll pack all my things to take to Colorado."

As Dallas discussed colors for Linda's wedding-ring quilt with Mrs. Briggs and Mrs. Lohmann, she watched for the young man and his family out of the corner of her eye.

Finally, she saw them climb into a rickety old buckboard. A sway-backed mule, looking as if she'd never have strength enough to pull five people, strained forward, and the wagon creaked along behind.

Dallas's father joined her and, after greeting the older ladies, offered his arm to his daughter and led her to their buggy.

"Their name is Armstrong," Woodrow said as he helped Dallas into the buggy.

"That new family?"

"Yes." Woodrow Jamison was a large man with a big stomach and it took an extra effort to climb up to the driver's seat. "The woman is a widow and only the little boy is hers. The others are children from previous wives."

"Oh," Dallas said as nonchalantly as she could.

"The young man is the oldest son and his name is Johan, but they call him Hank." Her father picked up the reins and the bay horse started forward. "He asked Brother Taylor who you were."

Dallas didn't know what to say and so she kept quiet, but she felt her face flush and kept her head turned so her father wouldn't see her discomfort.

Mother Nature had decorated the hills, slopes, and canyons along the roadway with wildflower brilliance. The bluebonnets were gone but had been replaced by wild phlox, sleepy daisy, wine cups, and Indian blankets. She kept her attention on the flowers so she wouldn't be tempted suddenly to blurt out something.

"I'll say one thing, missy, I don't like the looks of him," Woodrow said. "I've seen his face before—maybe on a wanted poster at the railway office. In fact, I'm almost sure of it."

"Are you telling me not to speak to the Armstrongs?"

"Of course not. You needn't be impolite to anyone. Just watch yourself if Johan Armstrong happens to be around." Her father cursed sharply as their wagon hit a deep rut. "I would prefer that you not pay any attention whatsoever to that impudent young man."

"Naturally, Papa, whatever you think," Dallas said. At least he didn't forbid me to speak to Hank, she thought. That nickname suited him much better, and in her mind she changed the young man's name to Hank.

Another two weeks passed before she saw Hank again. The church routinely held a covered-dish supper on the last Sunday evening of each month, and the Jamisons attended regularly. When Woodrow drove their buggy into the side churchyard, Dallas noticed the rickety buckboard and the swaybacked mule already hitched to the fence railing in back.

Woodrow helped Dallas unload her baskets of food and watched Hank Armstrong like a hawk as he passed them unloading his buckboard. Armstrong spoke to Woodrow and tipped his hat to the girl.

She greeted the young man briefly and moved to the other end of the food-laden table where her father had placed her things. But for the remainder of the day, every time she glanced his way, Hank looked at her with a smile and sometimes a wink.

Woodrow had not been able to find any proof that Hank was wanted anywhere, but he remained aloof and insisted Dallas do likewise.

When there was only an hour of sunlight left, Woodrow started chomping at the bit to leave for home but the Widow Briggs had other ideas. She asked Woodrow to help her and her daughter load her wagon.

"We can do it, Mother," said Louella Briggs. Louella, an extremely bright young woman, remained a spinster at twenty-five because she was too smart for most men and probably too homely.

Mrs. Briggs searched endlessly for ways to push her daughter into the line-sight of one of Tarrant county's most eligible widowers. Unfortunately, Woodrow Jamison was not the least bit interested in marriage.

"Nonsense," said Woodrow forcing a smile. "It'll only take me a few minutes." He began gathering up their baskets and boxes.

While Woodrow was occupied with the Briggses, Dallas wandered over to watch as a group of young men and boys began playing baseball. Soon Dallas discovered Hank was one of the players and when her father joined her she said she'd like to stay. Woodrow wasn't too keen on the idea, but with Louella Briggs and her mother listening and insisting they should all stay and watch—he couldn't refuse graciously.

That night Dallas dreamed of cornflower blue eyes and Hank's wonderful smile when he knocked a winning home run and raced around the bases in jubilation.

"Papa, I don't want to go to the picnic with Caleb Williamson. Because he's not . . . he's just not my favorite person." The early morning sun beat down on Dallas's head as she helped her father carry the milk cans from the barn to the spring house to cool. Only a few minutes past sunrise and already the heat was building into another scorcher. July had burst on the scene with its usual firecracker heat and endless hours.

"It matters not what you want, missy. You will do as I tell you," said Woodrow. He'd been at the campgrounds all night helping to roast the sides of beef that would be eaten at the picnic and had come home only long enough to help milk their cows.

She knew he was not in the best of moods, having been awake most of the night. And she desperately wanted to say something right then and there in reply but held her tongue between her teeth. Dallas had learned early in life that she could catch more flies with honey than with vinegar—especially when it related to her father.

Now she carefully chose her words. "I didn't mean to sound disrespectful, sir," she said. "Of course, I'll go with Caleb if that's your wish." *But I don't have to like it,* she muttered under her breath.

Caleb Williamson was an older man, thirty-five or forty, and had already buried one wife. He wanted someone to mother his two boys, Walter and Thomas.

The little boys were cute and fun, but Dallas was not ready for such a big responsibility. She wasn't ready to be a farmer's wife and she certainly couldn't imagine herself as a mother.

She wanted to be a happy seventeen-year-old girl—like she actually was, and to find love with someone her own age. Or at least someone nearer to her age. Someone like Hank Armstrong, she thought. Around twenty-one, he most likely was a man of the world but definitely not a rancher. She'd decided long ago she didn't care to marry a rancher.

Woodrow Jamison had farmed and raised cattle, and Dallas appreciated the security her father's labor brought, but she knew from him that the glory days of ranching were drawing to an end. She hoped to find a man who could take her from the land where she'd been raised. She even longed for someone to take her away from Fort Worth—a town known for its cattle drives and meat-packing plants. If the butchering smells didn't churn your stomach then the stink of Trinity River would. All the north side of Fort Worth was not a pleasant place to be, especially in the summer.

Dallas's excitement over the Independence Day picnic had reached a fevered pitch when she climbed out of bed that morning. The day had loomed for weeks—a celebration to end all celebrations—a centennial birthday of the United States.

Most of her waking thoughts were of Hank ever since his youngest sister told her he would be in town for the horse races on July Fourth. "He always races his horse on the Fourth," said Elizabeth.

The day would begin with the barbecue and picnic. Games would be played: footraces, relays, egg-tossing, baseball, and horse racing. Later that night a dance would begin immediately after a fireworks display. Dallas could not imagine anything so grand. Unless it was a chance to see a certain young man named Hank Armstrong race his horse and maybe be asked to dance with him.

Woodrow had expounded loudly regarding Independence Day. "Who would ever have thought that what happened at the Continental Congress way back in seventeen seventy-six was actually the birth of a nation?"

"I don't know, Papa, who?"

"Why, George Washington and Thomas Jefferson and Benjamin Franklin, that's who. Men of vision."

Dallas could remember hearing about the founding fathers at school but she had not really listened. The upcoming picnic and the dance occupied too much of her mind.

"And don't you forget, just last March, Texas itself celebrated a birthday too," Woodrow said. "So we've not yet finished hoorahing for this year."

Dallas had nodded her agreement to whatever her father said and spent her time daydreaming of dancing with a handsome young man.

After the milking, she rushed back in the kitchen to fry the young pullet her father had killed and plucked. The heat would soon get unbearable if she stopped to dawdle. And the potato salad still had to be garnished before she washed and dressed.

"I'll not force you to go with Caleb, Dallas." Woodrow stood in the doorway to the kitchen. "He's only looking for someone to marry to mother his boys."

"You're right, Papa. And I don't know enough about children to be a mother to boys who are half-grown."

Jamison walked outside and paused on the porch to light his pipe. After he got it lit, he said to her through the screen door leading into the kitchen, "I'll ask Caleb if he's offering pay for someone to watch those kids, Dallas. I'm sure that will discourage him."

Dallas stepped to the doorway. "Thank you, Papa."

Jamison grunted as he stepped off the porch and headed back to the fairgrounds near the edge of town.

It was mid-afternoon before Dallas spied Hank leading his horse towards a knot of men. She sauntered in that direction. Hank's conversation with one young man was loud and animated, and they used their hands to punctuate their words. She thought they sounded as if they might break out into fisticuffs at any moment.

Dallas, not wanting to interrupt, backed away to one side. Yet she couldn't help overhearing their conversation.

"So, Armstrong. You think your pony's fast, do ya?" The newcomer, with dark hair and mustache, looked to be near her age or maybe even younger.

"She's done whipped most horses in Tarrant County, John," said Hank.

"Put yore money up on it," said the young man. "I'll be happy to take it all."

"I don't think you've got a prayer. Who's to hold the purse?" Hank wanted to know.

"Sammy Murtaugh."

"Good. He's honest and he's not kin to either of us." Hank watched the young man's face for reaction.

Dallas had no idea who the rawboned young man was, but she didn't think she'd like him much.

John laughed but it was a cruel laugh, one without real mirth. "You im-ply-ing my cousin . . ." He stumbled over the long word.

"I'm not implying anything, John. Don't get riled up. You know you can't ride worth a tinker's damn when you're riled."

The young man laughed again and this time he was sincere about it. Both men took paper money rolls from their pockets, peeled off some bills, and gave them to another man who had just walked up. The man holding the money was older and obviously the earlier-mentioned Sammy Murtaugh.

Dallas felt disgust at Hank's gambling and turned to leave, but he spotted her. He hurried and caught up with her.

"Miss Jamison? Aren't you going to watch me race?" he asked. His dark shirt and pants showed dust from being around the horses, but he projected an air of confidence.

Dallas was glad she'd worn her new green and white plaid dress with a white straw hat to match. She knew they looked good with her dark hair.

"I . . . uh, I'm not so sure. I didn't know you gambled."

"It's not so much gambling as it is an entry fee," Hank said. "Everyone who wants to race puts up their money and the winner takes the pot."

"Oh," she said, relenting a little.

"Would you like some lemonade?"

She nodded and they walked to a booth selling the lemony concoction and he bought two Mason jars full. They walked without talking to the shade of a pin oak tree and stood enjoying the refreshment.

Hank broke the silence first. "Miss Jamison, I'd like the honor of carrying something of yours when I race."

"Something of mine?" she asked. "Whatever do you mean?"

"That lovely locket you are wearing around your neck."

"Oh, I couldn't, Mr. Armstrong. That belonged to my mother."

"Then how about the ribbon from your hat?"

A dark green velvet ribbon encircling the crown of Dallas's hat soon found its way into Hank Armstrong's shirt pocket.

In a few minutes, Hank left to get ready to ride. Dallas took an old quilt from one of her straw baskets and spread it under a huge oak. Her things were at an inconspicuous place near the end of the picnic table groupings. She had asked someone earlier where the races would be held and purposely left her baskets and boxes as close as she dared to that area.

If Woodrow returned unexpectedly, he wouldn't suspect why she lingered nearby.

Linda Toole—Dallas had a hard time recalling her friend's new married name of Hilliard—spotted her and came to sit beside her. "Who are you watching?" asked Linda. "Young Mr. Armstrong?"

"Am I that obvious?"

"Only to those of us who know you well," said Linda with a smile.

"Oh, Linda. Hank's not an outlaw. I'd like for him to come sparking, but how do I convince my father?"

"And how do you know he's a paragon of virtue?"

"I didn't say he's a paragon."

"What about that time he stole your pocketbook from you?"

"He didn't steal it. He . . . well, I'm not sure what he did. Besides, I was just a child. I probably imagined the whole thing."

"Dallas, that's your heart talking now and not your head. Remember what I saw in the Dallas newspaper last month? The description of that bank robber sounded a lot like your young man."

"But . . ."

"You just need to be careful, and don't rush things."

Dallas knew her friend was right, but she still wouldn't change her mind about Hank. Even if all that business about the racing money wasn't exactly on the up and up like he said. Even if he was a gambler.

But if he was a bank robber, then she knew she could not accept that.

While she and Linda talked, numerous horses raced against each other. A pair would race, then the winner of that contest would race another one. The men standing nearby made no pretense of hiding their gambling. Money changed hands in open view of everyone.

Each time it was Hank's turn to race, Dallas stopped talking and watched. He would win and collect money from the men standing in a small knot near the finish line.

Finally, there was only Hank and his horse and the unkempt man he had called John.

As Dallas shifted her head to watch her eye caught an odd movement over to the side. When she turned she saw Snowflake poke her head out of a basket underneath the picnic table. "Kitty, what are you doing here?"

Dallas got up and started towards the cat. She was aware of some raucous laughter over by the racers, but when she looked no one was looking her way. The guffaws continued until Hank and John climbed on their horses, then everything grew quiet.

"Snowflake, come kitty." The cat, obviously trapped inside a small straw basket, had discovered an easy way out. Once Dallas had removed the quilt from the larger container.

The cat ignored Dallas and waddled as fast as she could and jumped up on the oak tree trunk. The cat then stopped and turned to see if Dallas saw her.

"You silly cat. You're going to be a mommy in less than a week. I don't want you falling out of trees."

Snowflake refused to listen and climbed higher up the tree.

Dallas stopped to see what was happening with the horse race. Sammy Murtaugh, the man who held the money, shot off the starter pistol and the racers took off, both animals flying like a house afire.

For a second she watched, oblivious of everything except Hank. Then the horses were nearly lost in a cloud of dust.

She turned back to the cat. "Snowflake, I don't want you using up one of your nine lives. Besides, your babies could be hurt." Dallas climbed up on the picnic table, hoping to pull the cat from the lower branch.

By now Snowflake decided she had had enough adventure and allowed Dallas to take her. The crowd's cheers reminded Dallas of the race. She scratched the cat's backbone and, still standing on the table, turned and quickly realized how much better she could see the horse race from this height.

Dallas saw Hank and John ready to make the turn and head back. The horses were close together and she saw John turn his horse directly into Hank and his mount. The bump looked as if it had been done on purpose.

Neither Hank nor his horse faltered; they kept on running flat out and pounded to the finish line. Hank won but only by a head's-length.

John jumped off his horse and began yelling and cursing at Hank, calling him every name in the book.

Hank stepped down from his horse and spoke to John in a quiet voice. Dallas, still standing on the picnic table, was too far away to hear what he said even though she strained forward.

Hank then said in a normal tone, "John, I won that race fair and square and you know it."

John's curses were still turning the air blue. "Armstrong, you're a lying dog. You bumped me and my horse during that turn. You cheated."

"That is not true, sir." Dallas raised her voice. Everyone turned to look at the woman who dared to interject herself into the males-only proceedings. Dallas put the cat down, scrambled from the table, and hurried over to the group of men. The scent of horses and sweat permeated the air around the group, churning her stomach, but she held her breath until the nausea passed.

She spoke to the young man named John. "You are wrong. In fact, it looked to me like you deliberately bumped into Ha—uh, Mr. Armstrong."

"How could you tell?" Hank asked.

"I had a better view than anyone else because I was standing up on the table over there. I was trying to get my kitty down out from that tree because she's . . . well, never mind why, but you can see ever so much better when you are up higher."

Sammy Murtaugh snorted, then walked over and climbed up on the table. Holding his hand up to shield his eyes from the sun, he turned slowly, looking in every direction. "By gum, she's right. You can see all the way to the river from here."

Woodrow Jamison chose that moment to return from the auction barn. He walked right up to Dallas.

"Missy, what in creation's name are you doing here?"

"I, uh—"

Hank Armstrong said, "Excuse me, sir, but Miss Jamison was settling a disputed race."

"And how and why is she doing that?" asked Jamison.

Sammy Murtaugh and Hank Armstrong hastened to explain. Dallas saw the anger on her father's face as it slowly relaxed. A race involving good horseflesh was one pleasure Jamison enjoyed. But she wouldn't get off easily, she knew.

Snowflake rubbed against Dallas's ankles, mewing softly. The girl picked up the cat and whispered, "Snowflake, you saved the day, getting me to come after you so I could see what happened to Hank. But how did you know that John was going to cause a problem?"

Snowflake just closed her eyes and went to sleep.

While the men sorted events out and explained things to Woodrow's satisfaction, no one noticed what John was doing. Suddenly the young man pulled a gun and grabbed the money bag Murtaugh still held. He also grabbed bills from two or three men who still held their winnings in their hands.

Then John jumped up on the back of Hank Armstrong's horse and started hell-bent for leather for the river.

"Don't shoot him," yelled someone. "You might hit Armstrong's horse."

"But he's getting away," said another.

Hank Armstrong strode to the front of the crowd, placed two fingers into his mouth, and whistled. His horse stopped abruptly, reared up, and the thief fell off, landing with a thud on his backside.

Several men ran and grabbed the dazed crook. One man who'd lost his money began searching John. But they could find only a few bills on his person. Two men twisted his arms and proceeded to march him over to the county sheriff who'd just made his way over from the auction barn.

"But where's the money sack?" someone asked.

The men and Dallas all converged on the spot. She watched Hank walk to his horse, open his saddle bag, and draw out the money sack. "I believe this is what was taken, gentlemen." He passed some bills to three men. "And I believe the remainder is mine, isn't it, Sammy?"

"That's right, Hank. You won that money fair and square. And thanks to Miss Armstrong for setting us straight."

Woodrow Jamison joined them. "And Miss Armstrong is now on her way home," said her father. He physically turned Dallas around and steered her towards their wagon.

The sheriff's voice reached her ears. "Hank Armstrong, you're under arrest."

"For what?" Several male voices asked as one.

"For gambling and disturbing the peace," said the sheriff.

Dallas tried to see what was happening to Hank but her father wouldn't let her look.

"Arrested?" she said. "How could he be arrested?"

Woodrow Jamison kept a stoic face and didn't answer. Neither did Snowflake, who had placed her paws across the girl's shoulders.

As soon as they reached home, Dallas put Snowflake into a straw basket on the front porch and ran upstairs to her bedroom. She began undressing, and planned to stay in bed for the rest of the evening, but flung herself on the bed in the midst of her task, crying. She had shed only a few tears when she heard a horse galloping towards the house.

She jumped up and ran to peek out the window, mindful that she wore only her petticoat and loosened corset. Hank Armstrong got off his horse and strode up to the front porch.

She wanted to talk to him but not looking like some dance-hall floozy. She quickly poured water into the washbasin and wet a soft rag with which to wipe her tear-streaked face and clean herself.

As she brushed her tangled hair she could hear the rumble of voices—Hank's and Woodrow Jamison's—and she couldn't believe her ears when she heard her father laugh. She tied a small white satin bow in her hair after she'd twisted it up in the back.

She quickly relaced her corset and pulled on a dress of red and white dotted swiss that she had planned to wear that evening to the dance.

She cracked open her door just in time to hear her father call up to her. "Dallas? Please come downstairs. Lieutenant Armstrong has something to ask you."

Lieutenant Armstrong? Hank wasn't in the army. What did her father mean? When she reached the front parlor where Hank and Woodrow now sat, there was no sign of a uniform nor any reason to call Hank a lieutenant.

Her father wore a big smile as he stood to meet her. He stared at her briefly before putting his arm around her. Dallas felt shock run through her body. Her father abhorred public displays of affection.

"Enjoy yourself," Woodrow muttered and left the room.

Hank stood with a somewhat addlepated grin on his face.

They looked at each other for a moment and Dallas cleared her throat and said in a voice barely above a whisper, "I guess I'm a bit stunned to find you sitting in my house."

"I'm a bit stunned myself," Hank said.

Snowflake, who'd been napping on a window seat, woke up and waddled over, wanting Dallas to pick her up.

"Do you remember this cat?"

"You've got to be kidding. Is that the one Old Delbert pitched out of the medicine wagon because he was mad at me?"

"I rescued her, and she's a great mouser. I wondered how he could be so cruel as to throw her away."

"Delbert Johnson had a cruel streak a mile wide." Hank held out a finger to Snowflake, who stretched her head up for him to scratch under her chin. "I wouldn't harm a kitty."

Snowflake began purring and rubbing her face against Hank's finger.

Dallas felt much better. Snowflake would never be friendly if Hank had done the pitching. She didn't know what else to say and obviously Hank didn't either, since he kept staring at her while he played with the cat. Soon Snowflake jumped from her arms and strolled away.

That seemed to break the spell. "Would you do me the honor of accompanying me to the dance tonight?" Hank asked.

That wonderful smile she'd dreamed of many times was back on his face. "Only if you tell me how you managed to take my pocketbook from me that day without my knowing it."

Hank laughed. "Magic, pure magic. But a magician never reveals his tricks."

She realized they might explore several possibilities in the coming weeks. "Okay, then tell me what this lieutenant business is? And why aren't you in jail? I heard you arrested. And I know my father *was* against you; why the sudden change?"

"You've got to promise not to tell anyone."

She shook her head solemnly. "Never, ever."

"I hold the ranking as a Texas Ranger."

"And my father knows?"

"It seems. He checked up on me. Went straight to Captain Lee Hall. He originally thought I was an outlaw."

"I know."

"My job is to sometimes pose as a crook in order to arrest bank robbers like that scallywag John Wesley Hardin that we caught today."

"He's a bank robber?"

Hank offered his arm, and began leading her outside. "It's a long story, but I'll tell you all about it on the way to the dance. Your father graciously loaned us your buggy."

"And Dr. Johnson?" she wanted to know.

"I put that crook behind bars for twenty years," he said.

"So you don't go to jail?"

"We have to make it look good. The sheriff here was in on the whole thing."

They reached the buggy, and Snowflake let out a plaintive cry.

Dallas looked and saw the cat curled around a newborn kitten on a blanket spread over the buggy's floor. Another kitten was in the process of making its entrance into the world.

"Oh, Snowflake. You picked the worst possible time." Dallas turned to Hank. "I'm sorry—I'll have to miss the dance this year. Go ahead if you like."

"It's okay. I'll stay with you," said Hank. "There will be other Fourths and other dances."

She could tell he was happy just to be with her.

"Look." Hank pointed. A rocket streaked high in the sky like a shooting star, then popped open, sending red shimmers of light that lit up the darkening clouds.

Dallas watched as another rocket streaked up high. "What a grand Fourth this has turned out to be," she said. "Even if Snowflake did ruin my dance night."

Hank looked at the rocket's glare sparkling in Dallas's eyes. "And a grand beginning for us, wouldn't you say?"

Dallas blushed in the near darkness and then checked to see how Snowflake was doing.

[Author's note: A Lieutenant John B. Armstrong was a Texas Ranger in the 1870s. Lieutenant Lee Hall (also a Texas ranger) did not make the rank of Captain until 1877. John Wesley Hardin, a notorious Texas outlaw during this time period, liked to gamble, race horses and was known as a bank robber. Johan "Hank" Armstrong exists only in my imagination. JG]

Like Father, Like Son

Richard T. Chizmar

Father's Day was always a big deal when I was growing up. The old man loved it. Breakfast in bed. (And let me tell you, back in those days, Mom made a ham and egg omelet so big the plate could barely hold it.) Afternoon barbecue in the back yard. Horseshoes. Ball-tossing. Lots of laughter and silly stuff. And then an evening drive downtown for ice cream cones and milkshakes; all four windows rolled down, cool spring air blushing our cheeks; Dad at the wheel, singing along with the radio in that crazy voice of his, big hands swallowing up the steering wheel; Mom, sitting sideways in the passenger seat, rolling her eyes at us, feigning embarrassment.

There were three of us boys—the three stooges, Dad always called us. I was the oldest and most of the responsibilities fell on my shoulders. Come the big weekend, I was in charge of making sure the lawn was mowed, the hedges clipped, and the sidewalk swept. I was the one every year who bought the card down at Finch's Grocery Mart and made sure that Marty and Lawrence signed it. And most important, I was in charge of organizing the gifts. Of course, back when we were kids, our presents were never very expensive or fancy. Usually just something simple we'd each made in school. Individually wrapped and sealed tight with a few yards of shiny scotch tape so as to prolong the official gift opening ceremony after breakfast.

The first gift I can remember making was an ashtray in the shape of a bullfrog. Painted green, of course. Very bright green. The only frog in class with big yellow teeth, too. Dad loved it. Let out a bellow that rattled the bed frame when he pulled it from the box. Shook my tiny hand and told me how proud he was of me. And he was too; you could just tell.

Then there was the year that Marty gave the old man a wooden pipe-holder for his desktop. Sanded and polished and varnished to a fine finish, it was a thing of beauty; it really was. To this day, I think Marty could've had a successful career as a craftsman; it was that nice a job.

Lawrence, who was the youngest and the brightest, was the writer of the family and for a three-year period in his early teens, he gave the old man an "original Lawrence Finley book" each Father's Day. Each "book" was composed of five short chapters and each chapter ended with a suspenseful cliffhanger. They were typed out in dark, clear script on folded construction paper and carefully stapled down the middle. A remarkably detailed pencil sketch marked the title page of each new volume. The story itself was equally impressive: it featured the old man as an outlaw gunfighter in the Old West. Strong and brave and with a heart of gold. A Wild West Robin Hood with a six-shooter on his hip and a fast white horse named Gypsy. Of all the gifts the three of us gave him back when we were kids, I think these stories were the old man's favorite. Not that he ever would've admitted it, of course.

Years later, when all three of us were over at the university and working good part-time jobs, we each saved up and chipped in for something special: a John Deere riding mower. A brand-spanking-new one with a big red ribbon laced through the steering wheel. We surprised him with it right after breakfast that year, and he flat out couldn't believe his eyes. Neither could we; it was the first time any of us—Mom included—had ever seen the old guy speechless. Makes me smile even now just to think about it. Makes me smile even more when I remember all the times I called home from college and Mom would tell me he couldn't come to the phone right now because he was out cutting the lawn . . . again . . . for the second time that week.

Yes, sir, Father's Day was always a big deal back when I was growing up.

The drive out to Hagerstown Prison takes just under three hours on a good day. I figure the traffic to be a bit heavier than usual this morning, so I leave when it's still dark outside. I ride with the radio off and the heat on; it rained last night and the June air has a nasty little bite to it.

I drive the winding country roads faster than I should, but visiting hours have been extended because of the holiday, and I want to show up a few minutes early to get a head start on the registration forms and to check in the gifts I've brought along with me. In the back seat, I have a big bag of freshly baked chocolate chip cookies, a stack of brand-new paperbacks—westerns, mostly—and a half-dozen pouches of his favorite pipe tobacco.

The road is fairly clear and the trip takes two hours and thirty-five minutes. Plenty of time for a man to think . . . even if he doesn't want to.

When I step out onto the gravel parking lot, the morning sun is shining and the chill has vanished from the air. I can hear birds singing in the trees across the way, and I can't help wondering what they must sound like to the men locked inside these walls.

There are already a scattered handful of visitors waiting inside the lobby. Mostly young women with pale, dirty, restless children. But a few older couples, too. None of them look up at me when I take off my coat and sit down, but the hush of whispering momentarily fades to silence, then picks up again. In all my visits here, I've never once heard anyone speak in a normal tone of voice in this room—only whispers. It's always like this in the waiting room. There's an awkward kind of acceptance here. No one gawks or stares. It's like we're all charter members of the same club—each and every one of us joined together by our love for someone behind these bars and each of us sharing the same white-hot emotions of embarrassment and fear and despair that coming here brings to the surface.

My father has been here for almost three years now. And unless his case is reopened—which is very unlikely—he will remain here until the day he dies. I don't like to think about that, though. I'd rather dream about the day when he might be free again to spend his retirement years back where he belongs—back at the house with me.

But we both know that day will never come. He will never come home again . . . and still the old man claims he has no regrets. Swears he'd do it all over again in a heartbeat. After all, he tells me, I was just protecting my family.

✿   ✿   ✿

Sometimes families just drift apart and it's almost impossible to put a finger on the reason. Age-old secrets remain secret. Hidden feelings remain hidden. Sometimes the family was never really that close in the first place, and it simply took the passage of time to bring this sad fact to light.

But you know, that's the funny thing. We never drifted apart. We remained close right up to a point and then *boom*—it was over. One day we're a family; the next day we're not. It was almost as if Marty and Lawrence had gotten together behind our backs and planned the whole terrible thing.

After college, Marty went into real estate. He married a fairly snobby woman named Jennifer (not Jenny or Jen, but Jennifer) and moved east to Annapolis and earned a six-figure income selling waterfront property to yuppies. By the time he was thirty-five, he'd had two boys of his own, divorced Jennifer after discovering that she'd been unfaithful with a co-worker, and entered into a second marriage, this time with an older woman who also worked in real estate. I've never met her, but her name is Vicki and she has a very pleasant voice and is downright friendly on the telephone (although I've only spoken with her twice).

Lawrence, who turned out to be not only the brightest but the hardest-working Finley boy, put his creative skills to profitable use—he went into advertising. He worked a back-breaking schedule and squirreled away his pennies for damn near a decade, then opened his own small agency in downtown Baltimore when he was still in his early thirties. Just a handful of years later, he was one of the field's fastest risers, appeared regularly in all the trade magazines, and oversaw an operation of some two dozen employees. Last year (and I read this in the newspaper; we haven't spoken in over five years), he opened a second office—in New York City.

But for all of their success, it quickly became apparent that Marty and Lawrence had changed. And for the worse. Sure, there were gifts and cards at Christmas and on birthdays, but that was pretty much it. Mom and Dad and I rarely spoke with the two of them—much less saw them—and whenever friends and neighbors asked, our responses were quick, our smiles forced. For a couple of years we kept trying, we honestly did, but our letters went mostly unanswered, our phone calls ignored. The whole situation made Mom and Dad furious. They'd sit around the dining room table, nibbling at their desserts and say, "If they're so ashamed of their smalltown roots and their smalltown family, then so be it. Couple of big shots is what they think they are. Good riddance to them." But I could see past their bitterness and resentment. At the end of the day, they were just like me—left feeling hurt and confused and abandoned. And it was a miserable feeling, let me tell you. Things like this might happen to other families, but for God's sake, not the Finleys.

And so just like that, we became a family of three.

And, soon after, a family of two.

Mom died in her sleep on Easter weekend 1989, and everyone—including Dad—thought it was a good thing. She'd been suffering something terrible. Lung cancer, if you can believe that. Only fifty-three years old and never smoked a day in her life.

Of course, neither Marty nor Lawrence made it home for the funeral. And if you ask me (and the state police boys *did* ask me in a roundabout way later on), Mom's death coupled with their failure to show up at the service was the final straw. Something inside the old man's mind snapped like a dried twig, and he was never the same again.

Shortly after, he began bringing home the cats. Strays, store-bought—it didn't matter a lick. Sometimes as many as two or three a month. His new family, he called them. The two of us need a family to take care of, he'd say. A family that will stay together and live under the same roof. Just wait and see.

By Christmas later that year, we were living with over twenty cats of various sizes, shapes, and colors. The old man had a name for each and every one of them. And I have to admit, he was right; we were like a family again. He must have felt it, too; he was the happiest I'd seen him in a long time.

Then, just after Easter, right after the first anniversary of Mom's passing, the old man lost it and killed the Benson kid and all hell broke loose.

*   *   *

The drive home takes forever. It's raining again—really coming down now in thick, flapping sheets—and it's all I can do to keep the tires on the road. I change the radio station, try to think of something cheerful, but I can't stop myself from thinking of his eyes. Sparkling with such happiness and love, pleased with my gifts, overjoyed with my presence on his special day. But then, as always, the conversation soon turns and he is asking about his family, and his eyes are transforming into something alien and frightening. Eyes so focused and intense and determined, they belong to someone decades younger; they are the eyes of the stranger who stormed out of the house and chased down the Benson kid that long-ago night.

So that's when I take his trembling hand and gently squeeze and tell him what I always tell him: that they are fine. That I am taking good care of them. That his family is safe and sound, and they are all very happy and healthy.

Before I leave he almost breaks my heart when he thanks me with fat tears streaming down his cheeks, and in a quaking voice tells me that I am the man of the family now, that I am the one responsible for their care.

It is after midnight when I pull into the mud-streaked driveway. In the shine of the headlights, I glimpse a blur of black and white fur flash past me and disappear beneath the front porch. For just one moment, I can't decide if I should laugh or cry.

As for me . . . well, I'm still here. I never did leave this town (except for college and hell, even then, I was back living in my old room ten days after graduation). I never did marry. Never had children. Never made my first million. In fact, you can still find me six days a week working the desk over at the Bradshaw County Library and every other Saturday night taking tickets at the movie theater downtown. Not very exciting, I'm afraid.

But, you know, that's okay with me. I turned forty-six a month ago today. I'm finally starting to lose a little ground—going bald on top and a little pudgy on the bottom. Started wearing glasses a while back too. The kids at the library snicker behind my back once in a while, but they're just being kids; they don't mean anything by it. And sure, I hear the whispering sometimes, I know the stories they tell—about how Old Man Finley went off his rocker and strangled little Billy Benson with his bare hands. And all because he'd set one of the old man's cats on fire.

I know they're starting to talk about me, too: about how I'm just as crazy as my old man was. Spending all that time with a house full of stinky old cats. Just like an old blue-haired spinster.

But you know what? I don't mind. Despite everything, I still like this town. I still like my life. There's just something that feels right about it. That's the best way I can explain it. It just feels *right*.

Sure there are nights—usually after drinking too many beers out on the front porch—when I lay awake in bed and stare off into the darkness and wonder what else my life might amount to. I wonder about Marty and Lawrence and why they did what they did. I wonder about Mom and what she would think about all this if she were still alive. And I can't help but wonder about the old man and those haunted eyes of his and that old green bullfrog ashtray and the evening drives for ice cream we used to take back when I was a little kid. But you know, nothing good ever comes from those thoughts. There are never any easy answers, and those nights are long and lonely and sometimes even a little scary.

But then, when I awake the next morning and feel the sunlight on my face and smell the coffee in the air and hear the purrs of my family as they gather around my ankles, I have all the answers I'll ever need.

And I'll tell you something else . . . like father, like son. I have no regrets. Not a one.

Longevity Has Its Place

Jon L. Breen

Holidays are a big deal at Plantain Point. I guess that's probably true of any retirement community. On a holiday, you impress the families if they visit and cheer up the inmates if they don't. You'd think we senior citizens would welcome another holiday. Theoretically, at least, we don't have that much regular business to interrupt. But when Martin Luther King Day was added to the calendar a few years ago, it was the subject of considerable controversy.

All of us residents of Plantain Point, by definition, were old enough to remember Dr. King's activities first hand. Most of us had supported what he did, at least in spirit, but others hadn't. And even some of his supporters questioned whether he should be the single individual to have his own holiday on the calendar, Washington and Lincoln having been relegated to an all-purpose Presidents' Day that might as well have been honoring James K. Polk and Warren G. Harding.

You've no doubt noticed that the younger generation—even including some who if born a few years earlier would have been standing in the schoolhouse door, teargassing the lunchroom, breaking up the marches with billy clubs, or (in most cases) merely wondering why the black folk were in such an unseemly hurry to claim their rights as United States citizens—all seem to embrace Dr. King. When a revered historical figure is safely dead, you know, you can hang his or her spirit or blessing on whatever position you happen to take at the time. But to those of us who have first-hand memories of the time, it can be more problematical. Not for me, though—not in this case.

When I remarked to my lunch tablemates in the Plantain Point dining room one recent King Day that I had known Martin Luther King, Jr., I got the expected reaction.

"There's old Seb Grady, droppin' names again," said Charlie Fordyce, a retired lawyer who always has the needle out.

"Dropping names?" I protested. "Can I help it if I knew a lot of people? I restrain myself as much as I can."

"Don't mind him, Seb," said Melanie August, a former high school teacher who seems to imagine me a good deal thinner-skinned than I am. "Tell us about it."

"My first meeting with Dr. King had some interesting elements," I began. "A dying millionaire's nutty will. Two abandoned kittens with numbers for names. A copy of T. S. Eliot's cat poems. And a clue that Dr. King was in a unique position to interpret. It was almost like something out of Harry Stephen Keeler."

"Who?" said Melanie.

"You have to remember, Seb, we're all younger than you and don't get all your period allusions," said Charlie, who at eighty-one was easily old enough to have heard of Harry Stephen Keeler.

"Tell us the story, Seb," said my loyal buddy Bill Trethwin, who was the manager of a clothing store in his working years.

"Yeah, go ahead," said Charlie resignedly. "Forget the trailer and roll the feature picture."

"Okay, I will. And you guys are so sharp in the puzzle department, what with your crosswords and jigsaws and minute mysteries, if any one of you can crack the puzzle, I'll host a dinner for the whole lot of you."

"Seb," said Charlie, "all the meals here are free—or, more precisely, included in the price."

"Please," I said with mock offense, "I mean off-base. At the ridiculously expensive restaurant of your choice."

"That's more like it," said Bill, rubbing his hands.

"Must be an impossible puzzle," Charlie muttered.

"Martin Luther King figured it out all right. Listen to this, and I'll tell you when you have all the clues just like Ellery Queen used to do on the radio."

"I told you, Seb, these period references are too obscure—"

"Aw, shut up, Charlie, and listen."

                  ✿   ✿   ✿

Dr. King (I told them) came to speak in Los Angeles early in 1958. It was an unusually wet winter, as I remember. People were still debating the L. Ewing Scott case—he was the guy convicted of murder though they never found his wife's body; it was almost as big a *cause célèbre* then as the O. J. Simpson case has been more recently. The Dodgers were about to play their first season in L.A., and Jack Benny officially turned forty in a TV special—it didn't take. The Soviet Union's *Sputnik II* was in the air; Charlton Heston had signed to make *Ben Hur*; Silky Sullivan was winning horse races; Liz Taylor was married to Mike Todd and had announced her impending retirement from the screen; and I was working one of my less edifying but more short-term-lucrative Hollywood jobs as vice-president of Gustweiler Enterprises.

In this case, VP really meant highly paid fifty-eight-year-old gofer for Grant Gustweiler, who was full of dandy ideas for movie productions, book packages, and sundry other projects that almost never got off the ground. Grant was about forty, an energetic guy with a bad toupee and the disconcerting stare of a contact lens salesman. He'd made just enough of a killing in the aluminum siding business to retire and devote his days to having expensive lunches and working on big deals, but not quite enough to finance any of his projects without help—or maybe, to give him the benefit of the doubt, he was just too smart to use his own money.

You've heard of people being ahead of their time? Grant Gustweiler was such a person, but I don't mean that in an entirely complimentary way. A lot of his failed fifties ideas would have got off the ground in the nineties, not necessarily because they were good ideas but because they suited the temper of our times.

"Now, Seb," Grant said one morning in the plush Wilshire Boulevard office where he invariably gave me my nutty marching orders for the day, "are you familiar with the Reverend Martin Luther King, Jr.?"

"Of course," I said. "The leader of the Montgomery bus boycott. A great man."

"A great *property*," Grant said in a correcting tone.

I started to say something about the dubious taste of referring to a black man as property almost a century after emancipation, but before I could speak, Grant was off on one of his mile-a-minute spiels.

"I saw a book called *Room to Swing,* Seb, by a writer named Ed Lacy. Harper published it last year. I strongly considered it for my next picture." Would have been his first, but who was counting? "Know what's fresh and unusual about this book, Seb? It's about a *Negro* detective. Not a funny Negro detective, but a realistic Negro detective. Here, I think, is an idea whose time has come. But you know what's wrong with it?"

"That somebody already did it?"

"Not at all. What's wrong is this Lacy is a white man. But what a sensation if there were a Negro detective in a story *written by a Negro writer.* And that's where Dr. King comes in."

"What makes you think Dr. King has any interest in writing detective stories?"

"My contacts in New York tell me he's under contract to that very same publisher, Harper and Brothers, for a book about the bus boycott. And who do you think his agent is, Seb?"

"Not you."

"No, but none other than Marie F. Rodell. She used to be one of the great mystery editors—wrote a couple herself."

I didn't see how that proved King himself would have any interest in detective fiction, but I tried to reply reasonably.

"Then maybe we should contact Miss Rodell and sound her out."

"I don't think so, Seb. She and I don't quite see eye to eye." Apparently he'd pitched an idea to her before. For a lot of people, once was enough. "It might be more fruitful to make the suggestion directly to Dr. King himself. He's speaking here in town. I'd like you to go see him."

"Sure, Grant, if that's what you want. But Dr. King is a busy man. He's got a lot going on. Some people are calling him an American Gandhi. Do you think he'll have time to sit down and write—"

"Oh, we'll get somebody else to do the actual writing. Some mystery writer."

"A white writer?"

"I suppose so. There aren't any Negro mystery writers. Are there?"

There were, I knew, but what was the use of saying so?

"Really, the books are just a secondary idea," Grant went on. "What I really want to do is a movie, a big Hollywood movie, about the Montgomery bus boycott."

"You think that's likely to happen?"

"Look at the popularity of movies with Negro themes these days, Seb. Can't you imagine Harry Belafonte on the screen playing Martin Luther King?"

I couldn't, but Grant was paying me good money to be a cat's paw, and anyway I liked the idea of meeting Dr. Martin Luther King, whatever the trumped-up excuse. You see, I knew Bert Williams and other highly paid black acts who had to use the back door, so to speak, in vaudeville days; and I knew Clarence Muse, among other black actors, who tried to make a living in Hollywood of the thirties and forties while still keeping a semblance of dignity. I knew some black ballplayers, too, in the years before Jackie Robinson and Branch Rickey integrated the major leagues. Anyone striving to improve racial justice—and meeting with a degree of success—was somebody I wanted to shake hands with.

First, though, I had to find Dr. King, and it wasn't easy. He was on a tight schedule. Calling all over town and using contacts I didn't even know I had, I finally got a break, learning from a reporter for a local Negro paper that Dr. King intended to squeeze in a visit that afternoon to an old college friend named Esther Corbett—and I might be able to get there ahead of him. I was given an address in a lower-middle-class L.A. neighborhood that I knew was undergoing a demographic adjustment: the blacks were moving in, and the whites were moving out.

It was a small one-story house with flowers in bloom in front of the windows and the lawn immaculately kept, showing the residents had considerable pride in their home. When I stepped on the welcome mat and knocked on the door, however, my reception was something less than welcoming. The door opened a crack and a white man of about thirty peered out at me suspiciously.

"Whatever you're selling—"

I raised a placating hand. "I'm not selling anything. You are expecting the Reverend Martin Luther King?" On the last words, I lowered my voice confidentially.

He didn't seem sure how to answer for a moment. "Yes, we are," he said finally. "Who—?"

I flashed my old private detective license in his face and said, "I'm

Sebastian Grady. I'm working on security for Dr. King's visit. I need to check the place out before he gets here."

"Really? I never thought . . . well, you better come in."

You may be thinking the guy should have been more suspicious of me. After all, I could have been somebody who wanted to kill King as easily as somebody who was working to protect him, and a careful look at my credentials would have led to more questions. But those were simpler times. America hadn't even had its first Kennedy assassination then, and while King may have had reason to watch his back down south, he would have felt fairly safe in L.A.

"My name's Al Corbett," my host said. "This is my wife Esther." As he made the introduction, his eyes gave me a searching look, daring me to react in an offensive way. It couldn't have been easy for an interracial couple in the fifties. Where Corbett was blond and his white skin almost pale, his wife was black as ebony. (Or as one black pal of mine might have put it, "too black for *Ebony*," referring to the Negro media's snobbish preference for lighter skin tones.)

"You're working for M. L., Mr. Grady?" Esther Corbett asked me with a smile.

I, of course, hadn't even known his friends called him M. L., so I made a quick decision not to claim a personal relationship.

"Indirectly," I said. "But I've never actually met him face to face. My job's just to go around ahead of him while he's here in town and make sure things are safe."

"M. L. King is in no danger here, Mr. Grady. But I guess you need to look around, don't you?"

The charade of doing a security check of the compact house— front room, kitchen, bathroom, small master bedroom and smaller guest room—didn't take long. The most interesting thing I saw (and smelled) was a freshly baked peach pie on the kitchen counter. When I was done, I was offered a cup of coffee and a seat in a worn easy chair in the front room. Both Corbetts were openly cordial now, as if I'd passed some sort of test.

"M. L. did a wonderful thing down in Montgomery, Mr. Grady," Esther said.

"Did you expect how he'd turn out when you knew him . . . where was it?"

"In Chester, Pennsylvania, when he was at Crozer Theological

Seminary. My father worked there. And no, I don't think any of us expected him to become the leader he did, but maybe we should have. You see— Sixty-three, you leave Mr. Grady's shoes alone."

A black-and-white kitten was playing with my shoelaces. I always liked cats, so I swooped my hand down and picked him up. I saw a small shape leap over my right shoulder, and now I had two identical kittens in my lap. The second one started licking my hand with his rough feline tongue.

"You called him Sixty-three?" I said. "That's an odd name."

"We didn't name them," said Al Corbett with a touch of asperity in his voice.

"Look at their collars," Esther said.

One kitten's collar had a little bell and a medallion with LXIII engraved on it. Sure enough, the roman numeral sixty-three. I looked at the other kitten's collar. It also had a bell and a medallion, this one with MM engraved on it.

"We just call them Sixty-three and Two-K," Esther said.

I didn't get it right away. "Two-K?" I said.

"Sure, we figured the MM must be the roman numeral two thousand."

"I just have to ask," I said, while scratching Two-K behind the ear with one hand and Sixty-three with the other, "how they got these names."

"They just turned up on our doorstep the day before Christmas," Esther said. "The doorbell rang. I went to the door, saw nobody there, looked down, and there they were. They were snuggled into this basket with a big red ribbon tied around the handle, and they had these labels and those little Christmas bells on their collars. And you know what else was in the basket? A copy of *Old Possum's Book of Practical Cats*."

"Oh, sure, T. S. Eliot! Great stuff. 'Macavity: The Mystery Cat''s my favorite."

"Oh, yes," Esther said, "but I like 'Gus: The Theatre Cat' the best. You remember his great role, Mr. Grady?"

"Sure. 'Firefrorefiddle, the Fiend of the Fell.' "

As you can see, Esther and I were hitting it off great. We'd found kindred spirits—and remember this was years before Andrew Lloyd Webber brought Eliot's cats to the musical stage. As we shared our enthusiasm for *Old Possum,* though, husband Al was looking more and more grim.

"And you don't know who gave you this present?" I asked.

"Oh, we know all right," Al spoke up.

"It was Al's Uncle Artemus," Esther provided, "just before he died. I thought it was sweet."

"It wasn't sweet at all," Al said. "Black and white kittens, Mr. Grady. Mixed race, huh? The old bigot was getting in one last insult."

"He never insulted me the first time, Al Corbett!"

"If you weren't insulted, you were deaf and blind to subtleties, baby. He was making his little snide comment on our marriage, saying we have polka-dot kids in our future."

"Oh, Al," she said, shaking her head.

"My whole family's like that, Mr. Grady, can't accept two people could love each other in spite of an accident of pigmentation."

"Al, I really do think you're misjudging him," Esther said mildly. It was obviously a reprise of a conversation they'd had a dozen times before. "It was a sweet gift, and anyway you shouldn't speak ill of your poor Uncle Artemus." Turning to me, she explained, "He knew he was dying before Christmas, and he passed away just after New Year's. I think sending these kittens was his way of trying to make peace with Al. He may have felt differently when he was younger, but I think as he was dying his attitudes changed. If he meant anything bad toward us with the black and white kittens, why include the book, too? Where's the insult in that? Uncle Artemus was a sweet old man—"

Al Corbett snorted.

"—and I never found," Esther added, raising her voice slightly, "any evidence that he was especially prejudiced."

"What about this damned game he set us to playing in his will then?"

"Liking to play games doesn't mean a person's prejudiced, Al."

I had to ask, "What's the game you mean?" This was getting interesting.

"Old Artemus made tons of money in the car dealership business," Al said. "He also had tons of relatives, but he made it clear to us all long before he popped off that he was leaving what he had to a bunch of nutty charities. Animal homes, things like that. He was determined not to leave a cent to his flesh and blood, even those of us who could use it, and God knows Esther and I could." Al picked up one of the kittens—I think it was Two-K—and started stroking him absentmindedly. Al apparently didn't take out on the kittens his wrath against his late uncle, and this might have helped explain why such an oddly matched couple stayed together.

"He's giving us a fair chance at a piece of that money, Al," Esther said, "and maybe he disinherited the rest of your relatives because he thought as little of them and their narrow attitudes as you do. Did you ever consider that?"

"He didn't exactly disinherit them, Esther. Tell the whole story." Al tossed out a wadded-up tissue wrapped in a rubber band, and we watched the two kittens chase it.

Esther turned to me and explained, "The will says all we have to do is inform the executor of the estate, Uncle Artemus's lawyer, within thirty days of his death which of these two kittens was a gift to Al and which was a gift to me and why and we get one hundred thousand dollars."

"Yeah, that's all we have to do," Al said sarcastically.

"We still might figure it out, you know," Esther said.

"Not worth the effort of taxing our brains in a losing effort. Who knows what went on in that old scoundrel's senile brain? Like I said, he made his pile in the car dealership business, Mr. Grady. You might remember him—he did his own TV commercials, started when he was over sixty and kept doing them till just last year, when he was past seventy. His gimmick was he always appeared with an animal. Artemus Corbett and his faithful friend Fido, except Fido might be a dog one time and a tiger another and an elephant another—"

"Or a chimp or a parrot," I said. "I remember the act well."

"He was already a successful dealer, but the TV ads really made him a bundle. I guess he felt he owed it more to the animals who worked with him in the commercials than he did to his family." The kittens had leapt back into Al's lap, and he was stroking them absentmindedly as he talked. "Uncle Artemus was always crazy about puzzles, and we weren't the only ones to get one. My brother and several cousins got surprise gifts before Christmas, too."

"Not kittens, though," Esther said. "Not living things."

"No, not living things, but each one of them had a follow-up message in the will, too, just like we did, saying if they could solve the puzzle they'd get a hundred thousand dollars from the estate, but all the puzzles were impossible for anybody to solve. They told me. They pondered them and pondered them and finally gave up, realizing he never intended anybody but the old pussies' home to inherit a hundred grand from him. It was just his last joke on all his relatives."

"If all the others were impossible," Esther protested, "that doesn't mean ours is impossible, too. If Uncle Artemus liked us, he might have made ours easier to solve."

Al Corbett sighed heavily. "Could I interest you in a beer, Mr. Grady?"

"Thanks, if you're having one, I'll join you," I said.

Al gently deposited the kittens on the carpet and strode into the kitchen. Esther looked at me with a shake of her head. "He takes everything so hard, Mr. Grady. He's not really as sour and angry as he seems, but he just lets things get on top of him sometimes."

"How'd you folks happen to meet?" I asked.

"My brother was his closest buddy in Korea. When they came back after the war, we struck sparks off each other right away. And it's true Uncle Artemus was just as dubious about a mixed marriage as the rest of his family, at least at first. That's not necessarily prejudice, you know—some people would say it's just practical common sense. Not all my family were thrilled with the idea either. Anyway, Uncle Artemus had a Negro woman as his favorite nurse when he went in the hospital, and I think he took a liking to me when I went to see him. I really did see Uncle Artemus change, Mr. Grady, but Al was never able to believe it. He's one of those people who just can't handle good news." With a whisper, she added, "He wants us to move to Paris."

"France?" I said.

"I don't mean Texas. Al seems to think people like us are more accepted there. He's never been there, doesn't speak a word of French, which I hear could give you more problems in France than my black skin does here, but he wants to just up and go. He thinks the French aren't as prejudiced as Americans, which may be, but I don't know. He's always telling me about Richard Wright, Chester Himes, people like that, American Negroes who made a happier life in France."

"And so should we, darling," Al said, returning from the kitchen. "You'd love it in Paris."

"Who am I, Josephine Baker?"

"You're better, baby," he said, handing me a glass of beer and swooping down to peck Esther on the cheek.

"Be that as it may, this is my country, Al. I'm not about to leave here. Things will get better. They *are* getting better."

"Well, they won't get better enough," Al said. "Not in our lifetime. Maybe in our children's lifetime, but maybe not even then."

"But look how far we've come already." She turned to me for support. "Mr. Grady, I have lived with this skin over twenty-five years. I feel prejudice and disrespect every day of my life, but I also feel things getting better. And aren't I in a position to know? Shouldn't my skin know when things are getting better?"

"There you go again," Al said kiddingly. "The old blacker-than-thou argument."

She grinned back at him. "That's one argument I'm always gonna win, white man."

The Corbetts were obviously undergoing some conflict, but I sensed they were absolutely solid in their love for each other. They had no regrets or recriminations about making their life together, but they had a profound difference of opinion on the country's prospects for racial harmony.

I listened to their discussion a little longer, with his cataloging every slight from an overflowing mental scrapbook and her pointing out every small sign of racial progress. They each seemed to me to be taking an extreme view, but I knew from long experience that's how marital argument works. Then the doorbell rang.

"It must be M. L.!" Esther said brightly.

Her husband, who by his manner seemed to think a visit from the Ku Klux Klan more likely, went to the door and opened it a crack, just as he had for me. But he opened it wide more quickly when he saw who was there.

The Reverend Martin Luther King, Jr., was a smaller man than I'd expected, five foot six or seven. He seemed younger, too, for all he'd accomplished, though I knew he was not yet thirty. He was immaculately dressed in a dark suit and fashionably narrow striped tie. Al Corbett, who obviously hadn't met him before, introduced himself and shook King's hand warmly. King then strode across the room to embrace Esther with a close friend's affection and enthusiasm.

"How's Coretta, M. L.?" Esther asked.

"Wonderful."

"We're all jealous of that lady," Esther said. "She made herself a catch."

"I did all the catching," King protested.

"Maybe so, but you sure cast out a lot of lines before you finally reeled one in." They both laughed at a joke I didn't fully understand until years later.

Finally Esther introduced me, and I shook the great man's hand and said some pretty inarticulate things about my admiration for what he had achieved with the Montgomery bus boycott. I was thankful neither Esther nor Al, who seemed to think of me as a friend now, made any reference to my supposed security role, though I had been ready to finesse it if I had to. I'd decided my best move would be to leave the house when King did, assuming his visit was a short one, and to dutifully present Grant Gustweiler's proposal on the way up the path to the street. That should be long enough to get the inevitable refusal.

King refused a beer but accepted a cup of coffee, and that wonderful-smelling peach pie made its way out from the kitchen. I soon learned Esther was famous in the neighborhood for her pie-baking. In a quiet aside, she confided to me that Uncle Artemus had even complimented her peach pie.

Soon we were all sitting around the living room exchanging small talk, then somewhat larger talk about recent developments in race relations. The latest version of the KKK was reportedly disbanding, and the politicos of Alabama had been forced into eliminating the "segregation oath" that would block any Negro candidates from participating in the Democratic primaries. Esther took these as very hopeful developments, but I thought Dr. King was as reluctant to take much comfort from them as Al was.

At one point, King turned to Al Corbett and said with obvious feeling, "You have a fine lady here, Al. And you both have demonstrated a great deal of courage to enter into a mixed marriage in the present-day United States. I once was very close to marriage to a white girl I met while I was at Crozer."

Esther nodded with a small, sad smile. She knew the story.

"Mind you, I realize now I would not have been wise to marry her.

Coretta is the woman God intended for me, and I never could have carried out my work in the South with a white wife. Whatever course my life would have taken would have been far different. But it was difficult at the time to give up a woman's love because of societal pressures. Tell me now how things are with you two. Has it been difficult?"

They both chimed in that it had been worth it, but from that point their accounts started to diverge. You'll know by now which partner emphasized the difficulties and which the hopefulness. Eventually the conversation got around to the two kittens in the basket and the unconventional will of Uncle Artemus. King listened to the story intently, then pondered it for a few moments in silence.

"A man can't choose his relatives, can he?" Al Corbett said, breaking the silence.

"Your Uncle Artemus sounds like one worth choosing," Martin Luther King said with a smile.

"What do you mean?"

"Well, to propound such a simple riddle for you, he obviously wanted you to have that hundred thousand dollars."

Both Corbetts looked at their guest with blank expressions.

"Must I elucidate?" King asked with a smile.

I chose that point to break off the story and issue the challenge to my tablemates. "Okay," I said, "must he elucidate, or can one of you figure it out?"

With a lawyer's precision, Charlie summed up the problem. "Both kittens were black and white, right?"

"Virtually identical," I said. "Certainly I couldn't tell them apart."

"Then, as I see it, the only variable was the labels on the two medallions. They had to be the clue to which black-and-white kitten was Esther's gift and which was Al's. One said LXIII, pretty clearly the roman numeral sixty-three, and the other said MM, which *they* interpreted to be the roman numeral two thousand."

"M and M's!" Melanie exclaimed. "Uncle Artemus had a sweet tooth. He loved Esther's peach pie. Did they have M and M's back then?"

"Certainly they did," Bill Trethwin said. "But it doesn't make any sense as a clue, and it doesn't fit with the other one, unless there's a confection called LXIII."

"I suppose not," Melanie agreed.

"Let's stick with the numbers," Charlie said. "Sixty-three and two thousand. What could they mean?"

"How about biblical verses?" Bill suggested. "That would certainly be something Martin Luther King was expert in and would be able to interpret."

"The numbers never go that high," Melanie objected.

"Some bibles number all the chapters from beginning to end, don't they?"

"They still don't go that high. But how about numbered lines in *Old Possum's Book of Practical Cats*? There must have been some reason why that gift was included with the kittens."

"Not necessarily," Charlie said. "The old guy just liked cats, that's all. I do think Esther was right, though, that it was a friendly gesture. If he liked cats, he wouldn't entrust a couple of kittens to people he had no use for, and he certainly wouldn't have put in the book, too."

"I don't think there are two thousand lines in *Old Possum*," I said helpfully. "It's a pretty small book." All that got me was three glares from my tablemates, who apparently felt it was cheating to get any help from me once the problem had been set.

"So what else could the numbers mean?" Bill said.

"Statutes," suggested Charlie. "Section numbers in the California codes."

"You mean like the penal code?"

"The probate code would be more appropriate. Or maybe the civil code. If this place just had a decent law library—"

"They want to discourage jailhouse lawyers," I said. It got me three more glares.

"I think they must be years," Bill said.

"What years?" Melanie said.

"Well, the LXIII could represent nineteen sixty-three. You couldn't represent only the last two digits of the year two thousand, since it would just be zeroes, so old Uncle Artemus had to go with the whole MM."

"How about it, Seb, is it years?" Melanie asked.

"Don't ask him!" Charlie protested. "We haven't solved the puzzle yet. We have to deliver a full solution."

"They were both years in the future," Bill said. "JFK was assassinated in nineteen sixty-three. . . ."

"Don't go psychic on me," Charlie said disgustedly. "Nobody in nineteen fifty-eight knew what was going to happen in nineteen sixty-three."

My three tablemates sort of wound down then, running out of fresh ideas, but they wouldn't let me finish the story for them, said they'd come up with their answer over dinner that evening. But when I saw them again at our same table that night, they didn't look any happier. Charlie had been on the phone to a law library.

"There are no probate code sections numbered sixty-three or two thousand," he said. "In the civil code, section sixty-three *now* defines the age of majority, but back in nineteen fifty-eight, the reference would have been to the validity of foreign marriages."

"When two Americans of different races wed, that doesn't equal a foreign marriage, Charlie," Bill pointed out.

"I know that," Charlie said with a withering look. "The code sections are a dead end. What were you guys up to?"

Melanie and Bill had spent their time counting lines and verses in both the Bible and T. S. Eliot, but had come up empty. I was surprised none of them had thought to check a biography of Martin Luther King for clues to the solution. Figuring I'd probably wind up springing for a night on the town anyway, I let them in on the answer.

In answer to Dr. King's teasing question, Esther Corbett said, "M. L., I think you must elucidate."

"In the aftermath of the happenings in Montgomery, my friends in the NAACP made a brave prediction. They projected the eventual end of segregation in the United States of America."

"Praise the Lord," said Esther, as if imagining herself in a church congregation. Listening to King's mellifluous tones, I couldn't blame her.

"And when did they think this momentous event would take place?" Al Corbett inquired sardonically.

King smiled. "They were far, far too optimistic, I fear. They predicted it would happen by the year nineteen sixty-three."

"I'll say they're too optimi—did you say nineteen sixty-three?"

King nodded. "I, on the other hand, advised more caution, and when asked to offer my own estimate for the end of segregation—"

"You said the year two thousand!" Esther exclaimed. "M. L., that was way too pessimistic."

"These two predictions were reported in the press, of course. Now am I right to infer that your Uncle Artemus was aware of your respective opinions about the future of American race relations?"

"Yes, he surely was," Esther said with a smile.

"Then can there be the slightest doubt which kitten was a gift to Al and which to Esther?"

Al Corbett's face lit up then—it had taken him as long to get it as it had me. He reached down and scooped up one of the black-and-white kittens in each hand. "I guess you're my soul brother, Two-K," he said to the one in his left hand. Handing the other over to his wife, he said, "And, baby, old Pollyanna Sixty-three here must belong to you. Thanks a million, M. L.—or anyway, a hundred thousand."

"Thank Uncle Artemus," Martin Luther King said.

Five or six different emotions warring on his face, Al Corbett said, "Too late for that, I guess."

Shortly thereafter, Dr. King said he had to run along, keep up with the exhausting schedule his aides had laid out for him. I made my regrets, too, and we left the two of them discussing whether the hundred thou would take them to Paris or help them fight the good fight here—my own thought was they'd better get on the phone to the old guy's lawyer before they started counting the money.

As we walked to the street, I offered to give Dr. King a lift, but of course he had a car waiting. His armchair detective work had given me a perfect opening to lay out Grant Gustweiler's nutty proposal, but I flubbed it. On purpose. Oh, I made the offer but just weakly enough so he could refuse gracefully. Then I reiterated my best wishes on all his future endeavors and said I hoped we'd meet again some time.

Grant Gustweiler never made a big Hollywood movie about the Montgomery bus boycott, and neither did anybody else, and I hardly need add that Dr. King never fronted a series of detective novels. He went from success to success but sometimes must have felt like a prophet without honor. A local black L.A. paper called him an Uncle Tom for including a message on self-reliance in his L.A. talk. Not long after I met him, that following September after his non-fiction book had come out, Dr. King was stabbed with a letter opener by a woman at a department-store book signing. They saved him, though it was reported in the papers that the point of the weapon was so close to his aorta, if he'd so much as sneezed, it would have killed him. But he didn't sneeze, and so he was around for another ten years of civil rights leadership before his life was finally ended by an assassin's bullet at a Memphis motel.

"Did you ever cross paths with him again, Seb?" Melanie August asked.

"Once, a few years later. But that's a bit more complicated story. Read my memoirs."

"King was still a pretty young man when he died, wasn't he?" Bill Trethwin said.

"He died at thirty-nine," I said. "Never even saw forty. And look at us old farts sitting here. What did we ever do with all our extra decades?"

"Hell, Seb, you've done a lot," Bill protested, as always overreacting to one of my darker mood swings.

"I've had a lot of colorful experiences, a lot of memories, sure, but most of it was just spinning my wheels in terms of any real accomplishment. My biggest achievement will probably be living through the whole twentieth century."

"If you make it," Charlie Fordyce said. Always the needle.

"Oh, I'll make it all right. Dr. King said he had a dream and he'd been to the mountaintop, but he also said, 'Longevity has its place.'"

"Don't remember that one," said Bill.

"He said it in a speech the day before he died. But I guess we'd all agree, there are more important things in life than longevity."

I've lived way over twice as long as Martin Luther King, Jr., and accomplished way under half as much. But I'll see my century through to its end. For what that's worth.

Party Animal

Morris Hershman

Seth's mother phoned just after he got done with an overdue crime scene report. She was cheerful as always, ready to be obliging if necessary, a grade-one mother in nearly every way.

"We're all okay," she said after the exchange of greetings, sparing him a rundown on any late-breaking family news. "I just want to be sure you know we'll be having a Hanukkah dinner on the eighteenth, so you can't say you're not getting enough notice."

Seth hadn't known the date of the holiday start, not having been properly observant since just after his bar mitzvah. "I'll be there if the work doesn't interfere."

"Let somebody else solve one homicide." Mom always said *home*-icide, as if her son earned a living at some kind of social work. "I'll call Andrea and make the invitation twice as official."

It crossed his mind, not for the first time, that he had been luckier than most in drawing civilized parents. They hadn't wanted him going into the force, for instance, but didn't criticize his choice. They had been polite, at least, five months ago, back when Seth took his second wife, a girl of Italian ancestry. Unhappiness was kept to themselves in the time-honored Gordon family tradition: show nothing because your feelings aren't anyone else's business.

He broke the connection after a few added polite interchanges, then looked up at the opening door of his closet of an office. His partner had come striding in.

"We've got some business," Harry Drawhill boomed, offering a memo in one outsized hand. "Let's jump for it."

"Fine. It's sure to take my mind off . . . something else for a while."

*   *   *

He left the twelfth precinct stationhouse in an unmarked car, Harry
next to him and set to ride shotgun if necessary. They found a coven
of spectators in front of the right address, a store on Perry Street in
lower Greenwich Village. A flushed policeman stood before the
scene, saying mechanically, "There's nothing to be seen, move along
now."

Drawhill had passed a card to the uniformed man by the time Seth
was parked and out on the chill December sidewalk, but minutes
rolled by before they could get through the nervous bystanders.

A bright-looking younger uniform who gave his last name as
Napier had been expecting help. Holding his stick adventurously by
three fingers and thumb, a sure sign of not much experience on the
job, Napier told them happily how efficient he and his partner had
been. "We were in the car when the Korean kid whose father owned
this place came running out to call us. My partner stayed in the street
to keep civilians off. I went in, saw what'd happened, and phoned
right away."

Drawhill asked crudely, "Where's the merchandise?"

The middle-aged victim lay on the narrow strip behind the
counter, bloody spots flecking his gray wool shirt and well-worn gray
pants. Near his chest lay a knife with a rough-textured handle, its
blade reddened almost to the haft. A black cat, a male shorthair, had
been standing at the dead man's feet, but moved tentatively and
sociably in the direction of whichever newcomer was talking.

Seth, having eased the animal away before looking more closely at
the knife, heard a gasp behind him.

Drawhill asked the young man crisply, "Did you make all over
yourself, sonny, or what?"

Seth, well aware that Napier's features suddenly looked like raw
dough, said, "First body, I suppose."

"That's right, and I couldn't help—" He brushed the cat away and
became quiet.

"What did you touch, fella?" Seth was gentle. "The knife?"

Napier shuddered while shaking his head. "I wanted to be sure if
there was any breath, so maybe I could give CPU. I bent over him.
On account of the space being so small, I lost my balance."

"Did you touch the knife?"

"There was no blood on my fingers, that's all I know. My left hand touched the floor and I think my right hand came up against—well, the body."

Seth spoke quietly over Drawhill's curses. "We'll try and cover your ass later on, if we have to."

The young patrolman's complexion slowly went back to normal.

By half-past four of that cloudy afternoon, Seth had told the head of the tech squad that a verbal report on fingerprints was to be transmitted to him first, and he'd explain the reasons higher up if he had to. The weapon had been identified by flecks of cardboard clinging to it as a knife used to open cardboard cartons in the store.

He had taken it on himself to tell Homicide Downtown that it didn't look like they could help right now, and to suggest politely that an Assistant D.A. go back into his cage because there had been no movement in the case so far.

Drawhill had been nosing around in the meantime and was able to offer some information. "The victim was fifty-three years old and Korean, named Roe te Dae. His only son is sixteen and calls himself Johnny. A daughter, fourteen, insists on being called Stacey, and one result of the name-changes is that there have been family arguments you could probably hear in Korea."

"Did the parents do much to keep their Americanized kids loyal to old traditions, besides arguing with them?"

"They couldn't supervise the kids twenty-four hours a day. One time the mother told a neighbor that when she and her husband saved enough money they'd be going back to Pyongyang in North Korea and live like royalty. And of course, the kids would come with them."

In other words, the kids were supposed to be foreigners transplanted to America for a short time and hanging on with teeth and fingernails to a rose-tinged past they never knew. If Seth's parents hadn't come out of Russia with its ample history of anti-Semitism, he might have been in the same bag himself until clambering to independence at twenty-one.

"Have you talked to the mother and kids?"

"The mother just came back from Crown Heights, a neighbor says. She'd been in Brooklyn visiting relatives. She and the kids are in their apartment upstairs and mourning. They haven't talked to anybody yet, except to relatives on the phone, I guess."

"We'll have to bust in on them."

"We might not need to talk to them right away if the killer is under lock and key first," Drawhill said surprisingly, and rubbed his heavy hands in pleasure. "A witness who was passing by at just about the time of the killing saw somebody he knows hurrying out of the store and gave us the name and address. If we hustle now, we might crack this one in the next twenty minutes."

Nick Paris was taller and rangier than kids in Seth's day. He took up every inch of stiff chair in the living room of this small apartment at the northeast end of Barrow Street in the Village.

Seth began, evenly as usual, "There's a witness who saw you leaving the Roe te Dae fruit and vegetable store on Perry Street just a little while after three today, when Mr. Dae was killed."

Victor Paris, the kid's father, shot out of the easy chair in which he'd insisted on hearing what might be said.

Nick was speaking now. "I knew the old man, sure. I used to go in there on weekdays around three if I was on the block." And more quickly, "I came to see Johnny. He's—right."

Drawhill snapped, "Right enough to help you sell or buy stolen guns to resell, action like that!"

Nick spoke before his father could protest. "I haven't done nothing like that in a while. Mostly over the last months, me and Johnny used to hang around and—and look for girls. You know what I'm saying?"

Gently but firmly, Seth pulled the boy's thoughts back to his and Drawhill's priorities. "What happened when you came in today?"

"I didn't see Johnny, so I cut out. I never wanted old Dae to keep staring at me like I had just liberated a mango or something—you know what I'm saying?"

"That sounds fine, Nick, but since you admit you were on the scene we've got to ask you to come downtown and give us a statement for our records."

As Drawhill pushed Nick Paris out the door, the father murmured over and over, "I'll do something to help you this time, Nicky, I swear I will."

"The father sent some grease-tongued lawyer to smooth Nick Paris's way, so we had to let him go eventually," Seth told his wife over the nightly scotch at their Brooklyn Heights apartment. "It all took longer than anybody expected, so I'm late."

"I only got home from work twenty minutes ago myself." Andrea was tired though self-possessed. "Time enough to get a call from your mother about a Jewish holiday dinner on the eighteenth—we ought to go. I also got a call from Vinnie inviting us to Christmas dinner on the twenty-fifth. We ought to go there, too."

"It's always fun to see your brother again." He grinned at the prospect.

The phone clattered just as he was emerging from the nightly back-home shower. Harry Drawhill was on the line, his acrid tones practically dissolving the wire.

"We agreed to meet in the Village tomorrow morning and question the Dae family—remember, Seth? Well, now you can forget it. The loot wants to see us first thing."

English translation: the lieutenant wanted to talk about some fresh complication in the case. "Half-past eight at the precinct."

He hung up. Andie, not quite fully dressed, was looking thoughtfully into the freezer compartment of the refrigerator. Seth impulsively approached, smiling, and she turned happily to put her arms around his neck.

"There could be another angle to this," Lieutenant Sean Goodwin said after hearing Seth's preliminary report. "Plenty of Korean store-owners, along with Chinese and Vietnamese, are being bilked by a protection racket. The same old racket of the nineteen twenties and thirties, but with new immigrants and a fresh angle."

"What's the connection to Dae's murder?" Seth asked carefully.

"The collectors are people the storeowners already know, to start with. They could be friends or customers, from what I've been told. They can threaten to notify other countrymen that the particular storeowner isn't giving money to help new immigrants and is a disgrace to their close-knit community. The victim doesn't want to be ostracized, so he pays up."

Seth asked, "But you think Dae wouldn't kick in, so he was killed as a warning to others?"

"It's possible." The brittle-tempered Goodwin refrained from pouring scorn on Seth's caution. "I want you both to look into it. If we make any dent in the closed circle, if we put away a few collectors, enough arrests could follow to give us a chance of stamping out that whole rat's nest."

"We'll work on it," Seth promised.

On the way to the anteroom, from which Seth was going to clock out for both of them while Drawhill requisitioned an unmarked car, Drawhill said, "If you ask me, it's a straight case. Nick Paris fought with his buddy's father and killed him."

"I can't prove you're wrong." Seth smiled pacifically.

There wasn't any trade at the Dae store when they arrived for the delayed questioning. The daughter, Stacey, stood behind the register to take money that wasn't offered, and put in her time reading *Brides* magazine. Most of the fruit crates open to the public were untouched.

The mother, unpacking greenish pears, straightened with no difficulty. A small woman, Mrs. Dae was in firm control of herself. Tears had been halted, sobs pushed back from her scrawny throat. As an exhibition of hiding feelings, it was worthy of Seth's mother or Seth himself.

The black cat moved toward them, friendly as before and meowing a welcome while he rubbed up against Seth's pants legs. Drawhill didn't particularly like cats and dismissed this one irritably when he rubbed his metal-studded vinyl collar against Seth's partner.

The cat, called Lucky by Stacey Dae, portentously, tail up, followed behind Drawhill into the back room. This was a small area with only one window, and it out of reach. The smell of fruit was overpowering. Local roaches most likely got together pretty often to celebrate, and ended by offering good hunting to the black cat called Lucky.

Settled firmly on an upturned crate, the mother spoke in a service-able English. "The American boy killed," she insisted, hard hands folded tautly. "Mr. Dae hated the boy always coming here same time, going out with my son on Friday-Saturday nights, wanting him become Yankee criminal."

Maybe so, but older people were famous for not understanding different groups. When Seth's father had heard that his son's helpful superior was named Goodwin, for instance, he had said thoughtfully, "Maybe it's really Good*man*," taking it for granted that no gentile would help a Jew, which couldn't have been so even when Pop himself was in his twenties.

The questioning proceeded easily. Asked about her alibi, although not so plainly, Mrs. Dae gave the address and phone number of relatives she had visited at the murder time. Stacey Dae, clutching her copy of *Brides* as if for dear life, said vehemently that Nick Paris may have done bad things a long while ago, but now he was every-thing a man should be. Plus which, he was innocent of hurting her father. At the time of the killing, yesterday afternoon at three o'clock or so, she had been walking home from school with a girlfriend.

Lucky, that most affable of beasts, had jumped onto Seth's lap and circled three times before sitting down when Johnny Dae hurried in. Before the sturdy youngster could get out half a dozen words in defense of his friend Nick, he was being asked about his whereabouts at the time of the murder. He had to think before saying he had gone across the street to the Vietnamese restaurant for a pack of cigarettes, a habit of which his father strongly disapproved. Coming back, he had found—"You know what I found."

Did Johnny have any information about countrymen who de-manded protection money from storekeepers like his father? Johnny swore he didn't but promised to get in touch if he heard anything.

By the time Seth was ready to stand up he had petted the cat a little too briskly and scratched a finger on a stud of the cat's collar. He wasn't surprised. He wouldn't have been surprised if blood poisoning set in. It was that kind of case.

"The damned case is still wide open," Seth was saying as he drove himself and Andie from the well-lighted Brooklyn Bridge into lower

Manhattan. "I can pass the store if you're in the mood to see it. Not too far out of the way."

This was late afternoon of the eighteenth and the Gordons were heading happily for the Hanukkah dinner at the home of Seth's parents. For once he was sorry he hadn't been able to go to synagogue with Pop for the reading of the Haftorah on the Sabbath. *Not by might nor by power, said the Lord of Hosts.* The memory of that quote, so appropriate to Gordons young and old, embittered him when he remembered it. Spirit alone was wrong for his job. Power and might solved a lot more cases.

Perry Street was quiet. Residents, intimidated by threats of mugging and stray bullets, tended to stay home after work. The Dae store was already closed, since distant family members who were laboring alongside the widow and children had refused, as Drawhill told Seth, to put in hours without end.

A young man stood pensively in front of the store and looked up towards one particular bedroom light that had suddenly been flicked on in the Dae apartment overhead. Seth could see the outlines of the female behind the shade as she moved, her posture erect and vital with the coltish energy of youth.

Seth pulled up, gesturing Andie to be quiet, and hurried out of the car. He gripped Nick Paris by an arm before the boy could dart away, and held him lightly.

"You have the hots for Stacey Dae? You and Stacey Dae?"

Nick Paris became more agitated. "Look, don't talk about this! Stacey never did anything to deserve having a cop on her tracks."

Seth kept from nodding amusedly at the melodramatic speechifying of this Romeo, just as he couldn't help remembering Juliet poring over a magazine for brides. "You were coming into the store every weekday afternoon at about the same time not to talk with Johnny but to see Stacey coming back from school, maybe even say a few words to her."

Nick's reddening face made the admission for him.

"You'd start out with Johnny Dae on weekend nights, but I suppose Johnny cut away so you could be with Stacey when her folks wouldn't suspect you two were together." He didn't wait for the boy's nod. "Do you intend to marry Stacey Dae?"

"Yes. God, yes!"

Seth looked Nick Paris in the eyes and only then gave the matter some thought. "You have to handle it indirectly."

"What do you mean?"

"First thing tomorrow morning, as a start, you root around for the best job you can get. Then you go to see Mrs. Dae and tell her in Stacey's presence that you're saving to learn a trade so you can support Stacey and a family after the two of you are married."

"Mrs. Dae never liked me. She won't go along with it."

"I think that with Mr. Dae gone, she'll see the good points to having a daughter settled with a husband she's crazy about and a hardworking husband who feels the same about her."

"She won't want Stacey marrying somebody who isn't Korean."

"She'd prefer a Korean husband for Stacey, but she's old enough to know that two people who love each other most of the time can work out their differences and make a good life together."

"What about my father? No, he'll probably want what I want, long as it's honest." He gazed up at his love's window and whispered, "You're worth my best, Stace."

And she'd get his best if Seth and Harry Drawhill could put the real killer under lock and key. The major suspect in the Dae murder had just about been eliminated, not by might or by power but by spirit, like the Lord of Hosts had dictated. The comparison was enough to make a cat laugh, but it wasn't funny at all.

"I heard some of your talk about happiness being possible even for people who marry outside their ethnic group," Andie said when Seth got behind the wheel of the car once again. "Sickeningly sentimental, aren't you?"

"Cruelly accurate is more like it, baby."

They were still grinning at each other when his beeper went off. Seth promptly punched the emergency number on his car phone and was patched through to Reggie Cray, a black man whose job called for examining and evaluating evidence.

"Sorry it took so long to get back to you about the material in the Dae business," Reg began. "All the news is rotten. No prints on the blade. There are prints on the handle, but they belong to Roe te Dae, the dead man."

"Any prints on the clothes he was wearing?"

"Nothing besides his that I could identify. On the shirt and just above the belt line there's a smear that might have been made by the back of a hand. Useless for us."

Good news for young Patrolman Napier—first name Ray, as Seth had typically taken the trouble to find out. Napier had been luckier than he deserved when it came to clothes he had touched without meaning to.

"Okay, Reg, at least I know the story. Thanks."

His parents' co-op apartment on East River Drive was brightly lit when Seth, blinking rapidly, came in with Andie at his side. Marvin, his older brother, stopped playing with little Brandon long enough to smile broadly at Andie and come over to greet them. Naomi, his sister, waved hello but didn't stop talking—about clothing prices, if he knew Nay.

Mom had been chatting with Norma, Marvin's wife. At the sight of Seth with Andie she hurried over, asking interestedly about Andie's brother and his family. Andie's initial apprehensiveness was fading rapidly.

Pop, having come back from synagogue after Marvin, appeared and pecked Andie on the cheek before turning to his younger son. "What's the matter, Shimmy?" Pop asked, using Seth's family name. "Any trouble on the job that you can't handle?"

"I'm not sure yet," Seth answered, grateful that a family night didn't force him in turn into becoming a television critic who had to hand down judgments on cop shows on the tube.

That was when three-year-old Brandon set up a howl. Norma hurried over with motherly solicitude.

"He scratched a finger on the *dreidl*," she said, referring to the four-sided spinning top with a Hebrew letter on each side. "At his age, of course, he could scratch himself on a marshmallow."

Seth's offer of half a dollar for Hanukkah money didn't quiet any son of Marvin's. While Brandon's thumb was being vigorously rubbed, Seth said, "A few days ago, I scratched myself on a cat's collar." Brandon kept crying, not at all impressed. "You don't care? You don't believe me? Why, I've hardly told a lie since the rededication of the Temple, which we're celebrating, and I give you my word—" He snapped his fingers. "That cat collar! That particular special cat collar! I should have known!"

He forced himself to become quiet, well aware that respect and

good manners must cause him to wait before breaking away. He was
tight-lipped during the seating and the benediction, at which Pop lit
the eight candles on the gleaming Menorah with the help of Marvin's
older son.

The Festival of Lights was proceeding when Seth quietly excused
himself and practically ran into Pop's study. The phone was at a right
angle to the new computer table and on the familiar apple-pie-order
desk.

"Harry?" He had reached his partner at home. "I've got the answer to the Dae killing. Nick Paris isn't the perp. I can tell you who is
and how we're going to get proof."

"What've you got and how'd you find it?"

Seth was tempted to answer with a phrase in Hebrew: *Ness godol
hayoh shom,* although it may not have been true in this instance that
a great miracle had happened there. But the notion was worth trea-
suring, if only for a few moments.

"I started remembering the angle that Goodwin brought up, the
protection scam where some friend or relative or customer comes to
a store to collect and the store owner had better pay or be ostracized
by his countrymen. Roe te Dae and his wife wanted to save money
and go back to Korea, where they could live very well among their
own people. Dae wouldn't come across, so a special collector had to
be brought in to rattle or shock or beat him into paying."

"And this special got tough."

"Very tough is more like it." From the dining room, Seth could
hear most family members' voices raised collectively in the *Maoz
Tsur,* which Andie would later tell him ingenuously sounded a lot like
"Rock of Ages." "This perp punched the stubborn man in the stomach. Dae grabbed a knife to defend himself. The perp put his own
stronger hand on Dae's, turning it around, and stabbing him to death.
Which is when his own trouble started."

"His own trouble?"

"The Daes have a black cat who seems to think that if strangers
walk into the store it must be party time, so he comes over. Lucky
was near when the argument turned bad, probably very quickly. He
started to get away, like any cat would, brushing against the perp and
causing him to lose his balance after the stabbing and cut himself on
a metal stud on the cat's collar."

"You yourself scratched a finger on the collar when we were questioning the family," Drawhill mused. "What would it prove, that bit about the perp?"

"We're not talking about a scratch but a cut that drew blood. There's a discoloration on one of the collar studs, and the lab can tell us if it's blood and about how long it's been there and, with an identification from us, whose it is."

"All right, Seth, whose is it? Do you know the name of this special collector you talked about?"

"Who would be more impressive to hire for that job than a uniformed cop?"

"One of ours! Bastard!" Drawhill considered. "He'd want to make the strongest impression by wearing his uniform and wouldn't want to be seen out of his own beat. Two cops were working the neighborhood when this happened. Which one do we tag?"

"I figured that out pretty quick. When we first got to the crime scene, the policeman inside the store was holding his stick with a thumb and three fingers. I thought he was relieving his boredom with carrying the damn thing, but he was actually hiding the finger he had cut."

"His blood type is a matter of record, and details can distinguish it from Dae's on the scene. But we need supplementary evidence."

"Tomorrow morning we start finding out if he's living beyond his means, which is probable if he's done jobs for the protection mob. And we can ask storekeepers, who'll talk if they see an end to what's been happening, Harry. We'll probably hit paydirt on a not very experienced guy like Napier before we bring him in for questioning. Ray Napier, you told me his full name is. Son of a bitch!"

Outside the study door, Seth found Andie waiting to keep any intruder at a distance.

She smiled contentedly. "Your mother just solved a big problem for me. You know that I've been having trouble selling one-bedroom units in a co-op building on West End Avenue here in Manhattan. Well, your mother has a friend who has recently been widowed and belongs to a support group with other recent widows. One or more is sure to be interested in smaller living quarters."

"Great." He'd tell her afterwards that the Dae case was history.

"When I thanked your mother for being so helpful she said, 'After all, you're in the family now. Who does a person try to help if not family?' "

"Right she is." He took her arm. "And now we can go back into the dining room for a high old time with the family. Mine and yours."

I Suppose This Makes Me Sancho

Gary A. Braunbeck

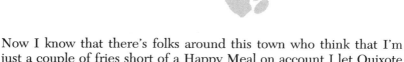

Now I know that there's folks around this town who think that I'm just a couple of fries short of a Happy Meal on account I let Quixote ride around inside my leg sometimes. That's right, I said *inside* my leg, not *on* it—Quixote's my cat, he ain't no dog, and I'm not partial to making off-color jokes about over-friendly hounds, so I'll thank you to get that smutty smirk off your face.

Quixote's nothing special, breed-wise; just a crotchety old tom who kept coming round my back door every night a few summers ago howling for a little food. I'm not the type who usually takes to animals, but that particular summer had been a not-great one for me, what with breaking up with my girlfriend and having to go in for an operation to have the pins replaced in my remaining leg, and I guess I was feeling a bit lonely and blue, and Quixote's coming around every night gave me some company to look forward to—but don't you go feeling sorry for me. I've got plenty of friends here in town and don't never have to be alone if I don't wanna be, but there're times when a soul gets to feeling a little . . . on the outside of things, if you know what I mean. None of which really has anything to do with what happened, but I figured since you asked for all the details, I might as well give you a little personal information, what with this being a—what'd you call it again?—a human interest piece. Stop me if I start to go south while I'm talking. I've never been interviewed by a reporter before.

Now where was I? Oh, yeah; how I came to adopt Quixote.

When it became apparent to me that he was a stray that tended to get in a lot of fights—evidenced by the nightly new scratch or fresh cut—I realized that I just couldn't let him go on by himself much longer. The night following this little epiphany of mine, he shows up at my back door with a serious gash on his side that I knew was gonna shorten his life expectancy something considerable, so I coaxed him into the house with a can of salmon, found an old box to put him in, took him to the twenty-four-hour emergency animal clinic out past Cherry Valley Road, got him all fixed up with stitches and medicine and shots and such (didn't get him declawed, though; didn't like the idea of having him go through the rest of his life unarmed), then brought him back home with me where he immediately set out making himself right at home. He don't take well to strangers most of the time, which comes in handy when I'm sizing up a person: If Quixote don't warm up to them after about, say, a half-hour or thereabouts, they're probably not the type of person likely to win any humanitarian awards.

You're probably wondering why I named him Quixote. Well, part of it's because he saw—and still sees—enemies hidden everywhere. I can't ponder much his opinion of windmills, since there ain't any in these parts, but he's a bit on the paranoid side: the TV he hates on account of all the faces and voices that come out of it (he once actually hissed and jumped at the screen, claws at the ready, when he got a load of that big-ass dumb dog they use on that one Kibbles-and-something-or-other commercial), I'm convinced he thinks the coffee pot is some kind of mad robot out to get him, and I don't even wanna discuss the ongoing battle between him and the vacuum cleaner. The upshot is, Quixote's got himself a suspicious and defensive nature (I can't hold that against him, not when I think about what his life was like on the street before I took him in), and for a while I was afraid things wasn't gonna work out between us, then just this past Veteran's Day something happened that made me not only thankful for his suspicious nature, but also made me realize that maybe it's a good thing that not all cats are the warm and fuzzy, friendly types you see like in them cat food commercials.

Okay, here's what happened: Every Veteran's Day I participate in the annual parade downtown. I usually ride on the Vietnam vets' float with the other guys who was over there, all of us wearing either our dress uniforms or field outfits (depending on which we can still fit our expanding waistlines into) and on account I don't drive, Jimmy Henderson down at the VA office always arranges for somebody to come and pick me up a couple hours ahead of time so's him and me can have ourselves a nice lunch with the other vets that the Ladies' Auxiliary fixes up every year. They lay out quite a buffet for us, the ladies do, and they're more than happy to wait on those vets who can't get around easily on their own. It's damn nice of them, and a fella always comes away feeling appreciated.

Okay, so I get myself all ready and have my dress uniform on. I'd gone on a diet a few months before and lost three inches around the waist just so's I could fit into it; I cut, if I do say so myself, a somewhat dashing figure in that uniform, and there was a young lady named Beth at the Ladies' Auxiliary who I suspected was waiting for me to ask her out on a date, so I wanted to look as handsome as possible, an area in which I need all the help I can get.

Because the arthritis in my good leg was flaring up that day, I was rolling around the house in my wheelchair, looking for my Ken-doll prosthetic. I call it that because it always reminded me of the leg on one of them Ken dolls—you know, Barbie's boyfriend. I'm talking the older Ken doll, the one they was making back in the late sixties, early seventies. It was this big, heavy plastic job, with a wider-than-average circumference where I had to fit it around the stump below my right knee. As you can tell by looking at me, I'm a big guy—six-six, two hundred and sixty-five pounds, most of which is still fairly solid muscle. I made 'em crazy at the Veteran's Hospital when they was trying to fit a prosthetic on me because my legs were so big. I suppose on the day in question I could've gone for that sleek new alloy job they gave me last year—I mean, sure, it *is* a lot stronger and lighter than my old one, but something about the alloy leg makes me feel like I'm slowly being transformed into Ah-nald the way he got to looking in the last reel of *The Terminator* and it sort of gives me the willies. I prefer my Ken-doll leg. Guess I'm just sentimental about it.

Anyway, I finally find the darned thing buried under a pile of laundry in the back room and I slide down out of the chair and get on my side and roll up my right pant leg and start slipping the leg into place when I notice that it seems to have a bit more *heft* to it than usual. I figure it's just on account this is one of my aching arthritis days and I'm in kind of a hurry 'cause I'm all excited about seeing

Beth at the buffet and asking her to meet me after the parade and all that.

I reach into my pockets and slip my hands through the special flaps I made so I can snap the straps into place without having to actually take my pants off—and if you make any pocket-pool jokes, son, this interview's over—and I almost got it all snug and secure when the phone rings. I figured the answering machine would just pick up after three but it didn't. You see, the answering machine is another enemy of Quixote's; he don't like all the buzzing, all the clicking and whirring, he'll have none of it. Some time ago he had figured out that the red indicator light meant that the monster was awake, so if he just jumped up onto the table and pressed his paw against the button *beside* the indicator light, that put the monster to sleep. Well, the monster'd been put out cold today, so the phone keeps ringing and ringing. I get into my chair, my Ken-doll leg still not entirely attached, and do a Mario Andretti over to the phone stand. I snatch up the receiver and put it to my ear and hear Jimmy Henderson on the other end, already chatting away like I'd answered and we was having ourselves a hearty conversation.

". . . know that you always get hit up this time of year by door-to-door donation-seekers, but I just wanted to let you know that the Supporters of American Veterans is a fine organization and has my wholehearted endorsement, so I urge you to give them a little something when they drop by—"

"Jimmy, what the hell're you talking about? You know full well that I donate part of my monthly VA check to vets' charity funds—you helped me arrange it when we set up the Direct Deposit with the bank! How come—"

"—representative will be stopping by in a few minutes to see you and ask for your financial support."

Something in his voice wasn't right. At all. Someone who didn't know Jimmy wouldn't have noticed it, would probably have thought he sounded just fine, real smooth and calm, collected-like, but I'd known Jimmy for quite a few years and could tell when he was nervous because he got this little twang in his voice, mostly at the end of certain words—*financial,* for instance, came out sounding like *finansheeal*—not quite that exaggerated, but you get the idea. I first noticed this when him and me started playing poker with a bunch of other guys every other Thursday; if Jimmy had himself a good hand, he got all nervous and excited inside (but looked as composed as you please outwardly) and would almost always give himself away to me on account of that twang. Jimmy loses a lot at poker.

But this time the twang was a bit different. Jimmy wasn't just nervous.

He was scared. Seriously scared.

"Jimmy, is everything all right?"

"*Of course* it is, Daniel."

He *never* calls me Daniel. Everybody calls me Dan or Danny.

"Then why're you letting these folks hit me up for a donation?"

"She's fine, and the kids're great. Said to tell you hi and they're looking forward to seeing you in the parade today."

Now it was getting not only scary, but weird. Jimmy's a bachelor. I felt my back go rigid in the chair. "What's going on, Jimmy?"

"Sure, I'll be glad to let them know you'll bring your cheesecake recipe. Listen, Daniel, I've got a lot of other guys to call here in the next half-hour or so. An S.A.V. representative'll be over in a few minutes. Give generously—oh, yeah, and make sure you tie that dog of yours up outside, okay? Can't be too safe about tying up the dog."

Then he hung up.

I checked the caller I.D. screen on the phone.

Jimmy had called me from the main office of the VA downtown.

I sat stock-still for several moments, trying to figure out what was wrong and how I was gonna let the police know that there was some kind of an emergency at the VA office.

What tipped me off? Jimmy saying "tying up the dog" right before he hung up. That was a code phrase my unit used over in Vietnam. I'd told Jimmy about it several times. It was a distress call. Translation: We're in deep sewage, send help *now.*

I was picking up the phone to call the police when someone knocked at the door, then turned the knob and just came on in.

Kid must've been in his early twenties but the meanness in his features made him look at least a decade older. He was well-dressed—suit must've put someone back a few hundred—and he was carrying a big donation can with an S.A.V. label on it.

"Mr. Gentry?" he said.

"I don't recall saying you could come in."

He smiled a lizard grin and pushed the door closed, then reached inside his jacket and pulled out the biggest and ugliest semi-automatic pistol I'd ever seen. "I knew the door would be unlocked. Mr. Henderson said you always left it unlocked on Veteran's Day so the person giving you a ride to the parade could just come on in in case you were still getting ready. Please hang up the phone."

I did. I've found it's best not to argue with a semi-aut.

"What the hell do you want, son?"

"I'm not your son, and what I want is the second half of the combination of the safe at the VA office."

I glared at him. "You must've done some serious convincing to get Jimmy to tell you that."

"He'll need a couple of stitches and maybe a bone or two reset, but nothing major."

The local VA office has a policy—not widely known—of cashing checks for certain veterans who don't have Direct Deposit, or don't live in a mailbox-safe neighborhood, or simply prefer to avoid banks. There's usually anywhere between two and ten thousand dollars in that safe during the early part of the month. A lot of vets—and this town's got a bunch—have their checks delivered right to the office so they can go straight to the source and not have to bother with a lot of middlemen.

The checks had been late this month—mine still hadn't arrived— so the money was just sitting there in the safe. Jimmy gets nervous about that, so he always has me change the combination every month—the lock is computerized—and every month instructs me to not tell him what the secondary sequence is. For some reason I don't quite understand, the initial series of codes has to stay the same— some kind of manufacturer's safeguard, I guess—but the secondary sequence can be changed as often as you please. I do volunteer work at the office five days a month right after the checks come, so I'm always the one who gets to open the safe. Makes me feel important, and it's kind of neat to watch this big electronic lockbox go through its circuit-dance when it swings open.

Jimmy insists that we do it this way every month so that in case something like this were to ever happen, he could honestly tell any robbers that he doesn't know the rest of the combination. It's all kind of over-complicated and a bit laughable, because you'd think in a mid-sized town like this, nobody'd be stupid enough to try and rob the VA office.

I shook my head at the kid and said, "Well, you at least picked the right day. I imagine Jimmy's the only one down at the office."

"Bingo. Everyone else is either at the luncheon or the parade site."

"How do I know you ain't gonna kill Jimmy and me once you got what you want?"

He jacked back the slide, chambered a round, and pressed the business end of the pistol against my forehead. "You don't."

I took a deep breath, said a quick prayer, and told him what he wanted to know.

Placing his foot against one of the arms, he pushed my wheelchair back about five feet, the gun still aimed directly at my head, then picked up the phone and punched in the number of the office. "Yeah, I got it." He gave them the secondary sequence.

I cleared my throat to get his attention. "Tell 'em that it's gonna take about two minutes for the safe to finish the whole activation sequence before it opens."

"What?"

I sighed. "Once the sequence is punched in, the safe has all these other built-in security programs it has to shut off before it opens. Takes about two minutes. I don't want your buddies thinking Jimmy and me are trying to pull a fast one."

He passed the information along, then hung up the phone and stood there staring at me.

What I knew that he didn't—what no one but me and Jimmy knew, in fact—was that the sequence I'd given to him *would* open the safe, sure, but this particular sequence would also trigger a silent alarm at the police station.

"How many of you are there?" I asked.

He was feeling cocky, I'm sure, having proved his superior intelligence and manhood by holding a wheelchair-bound man at gunpoint. "Me and the two guys at the office, plus the dozen or so folks we've got down at the parade site, you know, going through the crowd and soliciting donations."

"Nice scam. Kind of like what they did in Cleveland a couple of years ago."

"That's how we got the idea."

"Those folks got caught."

"We won't."

"How do you know?"

He yanked the phone cord from the wall, then stormed over and pressed the gun against my head, looking down at the plastic foot of my prosthesis. " 'Cause a one-legged man can't give chase, and since most of your neighbors are gone, it'll take you at least ten or fifteen minutes to get any help. That is, if you can get out of these." He pulled a set of handcuffs from his back pocket, slapped one end around my wrist, then pulled me over next to the radiator and attached the other end to the main gas pipe. "Out of the chair."

It was a little difficult, but I managed to slide down onto the floor and get myself in a half-comfortable sitting position.

The kid knelt down and tugged on my Ken-doll leg; it budged a little, then stopped.

That's when I felt something uncurl just a tad next to my stump, and realized where Quixote was hiding.

"Can you unbutton or unhook this thing?"

"Sure." I reached in with my free hand—my left one, so you can imagine it was quite a reach—and managed to get the harness unsnapped.

"It's loose," I said, hoisting it up so the foot was almost level with the kid's face.

I could feel Quixote's body tense, could feel him give one of those mean, quiet little growls that he always gave before attacking some evil household appliance, and I *definitely* felt the claws dig in as he readied to spring.

The pain must've shown on my face, because the kid said, "Are you all right?"

He actually sounded concerned, so I decided to play the sympathy card for all I could. "It . . . it h-hurts to put this on and take it off . . . I stepped on a damned mine when I was on patrol one night . . . ouch!"

"Sorry," said the kid, putting on the pistol's safety and shoving it in behind his belt.

"Just . . . just pull it off real quick, will you?"

"Uh, yeah, yeah." He started to tug, then stopped and said, "Look, we, uh . . . we didn't hurt your friend too much, really. We aren't gonna kill anybody. My dad, he was over in Vietnam, too. I wouldn't be part of this if I thought we'd kill any vets. I got too much respect for them."

"Mighty patriotic of you. Will you *please* pull it off quick? The pain's killing me." I suppose I was doing some powerful overacting at this point, but this kid didn't strike me as a closet theater critic, so I figured I was safe.

On his knees, the kid pulled himself straight up, the prosthetic came straight off, and as soon as the leg had cleared away, eleven pounds of paranoid feline fury threw itself straight into his face. His hands flew up to grab Quixote and I expected him to fall backward but he didn't, he fell to the side, and I was able to roll half-over and grab the pistol from his pants, release the safety, and fire three shots into the ceiling.

This would've sent most cats heading for the hills, but it only served to irritate Quixote, who pressed his claws against the kid's throat and sank his teeth into the kid's nose.

"Oh god, get it off me!"

"I really wouldn't move too much if I was you. He don't seem to've taken a shining to you, and I ain't had them claws of his trimmed for a *long* time."

"Uh-huh . . ."

"By the way, son?"

"Uh-huh . . . ?"

"Happy Veteran's Day."

When the kid didn't say anything, Quixote growled and scratched him a bit.

"Uh . . . h-happy Veteran's Day," squeaked the kid.

I felt proud to be a feline-loving American at that moment, I don't mind saying.

Well, you pretty much know the rest. The cops showed up at my house about two minutes later, the guys down at the VA office panicked and gave themselves up—not one of them was older than twenty-two, and they hadn't planned it out as well as they'd thought—and the rest of them were picked up at various spots along the parade route as they tried to solicit donations for their bogus charity.

Quixote rode on the float with me that day, and I even draped one of my medals around his neck to show my appreciation. He sat up at the front of the float, head high, chest out, looking pretty proud of himself.

As for me and Beth—well, I suppose you figured out from your call earlier and from her answering the door that her and me had ourselves that date, and about a hundred others, and we got married a while back and I ain't had a lonely moment since.

The VA decided that maybe keeping all that money in the safe wasn't such a good idea, so now they've arranged it so that the cash is on hand for only three days every month, and there're armed police officers at the office during those three days, and if there's any vet who can't make it to the office during that time, Beth and me are more than happy to go and give them a ride into town.

Those punks split Jimmy's lip and busted his nose, but since he's healed up everyone agrees that it has improved his looks considerably.

As for Quixote and my leg, I took an ice-pick and hammer and made several air holes in the plastic so he can breathe while he's in there, and once a week I strap on the Ken-doll leg (Beth makes me wear my Terminator leg the rest of the time) and take him out for a stroll. He's real comfortable in there. I added a patch of carpeting for him to snuggle up on, and it's quite an odd sensation to feel the inside of your leg purring as you walk around. Sometimes when he gets real happy, that purring gets a bit loud, and the little kids get a real kick out of it.

Quixote's just this week been named the official mascot of our Veteran's Day parade; and, yeah, I suppose this makes me Sancho Panza but I don't care. My cat's as good a soldier as ever I served with.

You'll have to excuse me now; I believe my leg needs to visit the litter box. It was real nice of you to stop by.

Boxing Day

Nick Hassam

(1) Frankie on the telephone:

"So how was the trip?"

"Fine, just fine." The voice on the other end of the line sounds like it could be in the next room, Frankie's outer office. It's a grand title for what is, in reality, only a threadbare-carpeted room containing nothing but boxes. Boxes of Soney Walkmans, Guchi shoes and Ahmani sweaters, all the brand names carefully misspelled. He can see them from where he's sitting, lined up like whorls on the cross-sections of a tree trunk denoting all the deals and scams that are his life.

Frankie is a small-time crook, a con man. But now he's made a move into the big time, and he's nervous about it.

Frankie reaches for the pack of Marlboro Lights and shakes one free. He feels like his old dog, Vegas, been dead now most of twenty years, rummaging around in the dead garden soil of the old house in Queens, looking for treasures. Nodding to the old Vargas calendar he keeps up on the wall simply because he likes the pictures, he grunts and says, "And how's Marcie? She enjoy the flight?"

"Fine," the voice says, "Marcie's fine. She liked the flight."

"Good," says Frankie, "I'm pleased." Actually, Frankie couldn't give a damn about what Marcie thought about the flight, but he's making conversation. People tell him all the time he should make more conversation so he's making it. He considers asking if they had nice seats on the plane and how was the food and did they manage to get the john to flush but he figures, hey, enough making with the conversation already. Time for business.

174

He grunts again and says, "So no problems." He makes it sound like a statement. Positive thinking. Frankie doesn't want problems.

There's a slight pause on the other end of the line, slight but noticeable. Then the voice says, "Well . . .", stretching it out into a long word.

Frankie decides to light the cigarette. He's been thinking about quitting these past few weeks but the closest he's got is sitting chewing on the unlit cigarette until the filter gets to look like secondhand gum. He draws the smoke in deep and feels the tension ease. "So, what? Are you telling me there *were* problems? Huh? What are you telling me here?"

"There's a problem, yeah. One problem."

"You want to tell me what it is, this problem?"

"It's Boston."

Frankie draws in more smoke and watches the fire run down the cigarette. He imagines Boston wandering around London, high as a kite, walking down the street clicking his little claw-fingers to some unheard (by everyone else) melody, maybe wearing a beret and shades like . . .

like a real cool cat, maybe?

. . . like he just soaked up a quarter-million bucks of prime nose-candy.

"The bag's burst and the cat's stoned out of his gourd. Is that it? If that's it then I don't want to know." He waits, listening to the silence. "Okay, tell me. I want to know. *Has* the bag burst?"

"Not as far as I know?"

"How far is that? A long way? A little way?" Frankie shakes his head and smoke envelops him, wafting around like a shroud. "Will you talk to me for crissakes, Mel? What's the problem here?"

"Boston's in kwar . . . kwor . . . what they call it, Frankie?"

"What do they call *what*, Mel? Speak to me. Give me a clue."

"You know . . . you can't visit him."

"You can't vis—look, Mel, think about this, is—" It suddenly makes sense, like those old comic books when there's a lamp clicks on over the character's head. "Quarantine! The cat's in quarantine!"

"That's it. That's where he's at," Mel says, sounding relieved.

"That means he's sick. God! Is he sick?"

"Not as far as I know."

"Mel, we did that one already. If he's in quarantine then he's sick."
Silence.

Frankie stubs out his cigarette and shakes another out of the pack. "You still there, Mel?" he asks.

"Still here."

"Okay." He lights up and pulls it in, deep. "Okay, why's he in quarantine if he's not sick?"

Mel says, "They took him from Marcie at the airport. Said they have to keep him a while, you know, like locked up?"

Being locked up suddenly seems like a luxury vacation to Frankie. There were worse things to consider. "They say anything else?"

The silence indicates that Mel is either nodding or shaking his head. Frankie waits for some kind of verbal sign which.

"They going to keep him away from other animals until they're sure he's okay, they said," says Mel.

"How long?"

"Boxing Day."

Frankie frowns and pulls on the cigarette. "Boxing Day? What the hell's Boxing Day?"

"That's what I said." Mel lets out a throaty chuckle. "I said to this guy, 'What the—' "

"And what did he say, Mel?"

"Day after Christmas. Then we can get him back."

Frankie could feel his eyeballs pushing out of his sockets. "Day after Christmas! God, Mel, that's—"

"Three months is what it is, Frankie."

Three months. If they have to wait until then, Frankie realizes, he'll have been feeding fishes in the East River since Halloween. "We have to get the bag back. We have to get it out of the cat, Mel."

"Guy said we could visit."

"Yeah?"

"Yeah. We can visit him anytime. But he's in a cage, Frankie."

"Okay. You leave it with me and I'll call you back." Frankie makes to put down the telephone and has a second thought. He lifts it back to his ear and shouts, "Mel, you still there?"

"Still here."

"I'm coming over."

"You're coming over? To England?"

"Right."

"When? Now?"

Frankie sighs. "Not this minute, Mel. There's a couple things I need to do first, you know? Like, I have to book a flight, pack a bag . . . little things like that. But I'm coming over. Do nothing until I get there."

"Okay. Can we go out, Frankie, me and Marcie?"

"Sure, go out, have a good time. I'll call you from the hotel lobby when I get in."

"From our hotel, Frankie?"

Frankie smiles like he just had a bad attack of heartburn. "Something like that, Mel. Something like that."

He hangs up and looks at his cigarette. It's burned down to the filter. He reaches for the pack as the door buzzer sounds.

"Yeah," Frankie says into the voicebox.

"Francis, it is I. We need to parlez. Beam me up."

Frankie can hardly get the words out, but eventually he manages it. "Sure, push on the door, Ed," he says.

Then he lights the cigarette.

(2) Frankie in conference:

"So how you doing, Ed? To what do I owe this honor?" Frankie looks at the big man slumping into the chair right in front of his desk, casts a glance at the two neatly dressed thugs who enter the room behind him and stand with their backs against the door.

Edward Kroaeneur shakes his head. "I think I need to see a doctor, Francis," he says, folding his gloves neatly on his crossed legs.

"What is it, you sick?"

"Not so much sick as confused, Francis."

Frankie frowns, looks up at the other guys, but their heads are somewheres else, faces blank. But he knows better. He knows that it may *look* like the lights are on and nobody's home, but one wrong move and there'll be a whole heap of action behind the curtains. He looks back at Ed, tries a half smile, and raises his eyebrows questioningly.

"I am confused because I am hearing voices, Francis." Ed settles back in the chair and straightens the crease on his pants leg. "Voices on the telephone. They call me from London, England. They tell me my delivery has not arrived. They tell me, too, that your man— Milton?"

"Melvin," Frankie says.

"They tell me he said something about a cat. I am wondering if perhaps, though I know you are not a doctor, Francis, I am wondering if perhaps you are able to explain why I hear these voices telling me things I do not want to hear."

Frankie laughs a short, nervous braying noise. "It's a mix-up, Ed, a little prob—well, hey, not even a problem. You know what I'm saying?" He raises his shoulders and, elbows close to his sides, holds his hands out palms up.

Ed Kroaeneur's face breaks into a smile. "Tell me about the mix-up."

Frankie leans back in his chair. "We put the bag into a cat's belly."

Clouds appear on Ed's face, storm clouds gathering out on the ocean of his forehead and sweeping quickly towards the beachhead that are his eyes, little piggy eyes set close together, little piggy eyes that show no compassion.

"Hey, no, the cat felt nothing. Not a thing. It was all done under a full anesthetic. The bag was placed into the outer lining of the stomach, where it could come to no harm, and then he was stitched up good as new. Boston didn't feel a thing."

"Boston? This is the cat in question?"

Frankie nods enthusiastically. "This is the cat." He leans forward. "Shirley—my wife?—she called him Boston on account of he has little reddy-brown markings just above his feet. You know? Like he has red socks?" He looks around at the two guys standing by the door. "And I didn't even know she knew anything about the game!" He laughs.

"And the mix-up?"

"Well, the mix-up came about because we forgot about the quarantine laws. You know? Where you have to put animals into quarantine for a time until they're satisfied they aren't bringing something in."

"Bringing something in?" The clouds, which seemed to have dispersed, returned. There was lightning in them.

"No, no," Frankie says, shaking his head. "Not bringing in something like dope, bringing in something like AIDS or beriberi. Leprosy, maybe. What the hell do I know. Like you said, I'm not a doctor, right?"

"Correct," says Ed, pointing a finger.

Frankie sits back.

"So how long is Boston being detained?"

"Until Boxing Day."

"When is that, Francis?"

Frankie frowns. "Day after Christmas."

Ed laughs. The laugh subsides a little as Ed watches Frankie's face, and then it starts again, loud and raucous. Frankie starts chuckling too.

"Is that Christmas *this* year, Frankie, or next?"

Frankie laughs harder now until he notices that Ed has stopped. "Hey, no, it's Christmas this year, Ed."

Ed Kroaeneur lifts his gloves and gets to his feet. He turns to the man standing immediately behind him and nods, once. Then he says to Frankie, "Well, look on the bright side, Francis. At least this year you will not have to worry about buying any presents."

The man by the door takes something from inside his jacket. It's long and black and metallic-looking, and it has a thick nozzle on the end of it.

Frankie jumps to his feet. "No, Ed, you don't understand. I've got it all sorted. I'm going over. I'm going over to England and I'm going to visit the cat and get the bag out. As God's my judge, Ed, you have to trust me on this!"

Kroaeneur slaps his gloves against his side, considering. The man with the gun lets it hang by his side, waiting for further instructions.

"Very well, Francis. You have until Tuesday, which is the first of October. If I do not hear voices telling me everything is well, we shall need to talk again."

Frankie nods. "Sure, Ed," he says.

The big man turns around. "That will not be necessary on this visit," he tells the man with the gun. "But our friend should be made to appreciate that diversions such as this are costly and tiresome," he says. "However, I do not feel it would be helpful to the current situation for others to be made aware of this lesson in understanding."

Both men nod.

"I'll wait downstairs," Ed says. "I will see you again, Francis."

As the door closes, the two men step into the center of the office. "The boss says for us not to leave marks," one of the men says with a smile.

Frankie steps out from behind his desk. "Oh, is *that* what he said?"

(3) Frankie flying high:

"You okay, honey?"

"I'm fine, Shirley, really fine," Frankie says, coming back from the john and pouring himself into the seat like his ass is full of buckshot. "Will you quit asking me how I am every five seconds." He lets out a sigh as he tries to make himself comfortable.

Shirley turns away from him and looks out of the window, where she sees only more clouds. "You don't *seem* like you're fine," she says softly, her breath misting the glass for a moment and then disappearing.

"Well, no, I'm not fine, now you come to mention it," Frankie says. "I'm still pissing blood and I just dropped a turd that had more kinks in it than a corkscrew." He groans and rubs his stomach. "I think those goons mangled my bowel or my large intestine."

"Well, at least they didn't leave any marks, honey."

Frankie lets out a sharp laugh. "Hey, and don't think I'm not grateful, okay? I'll remember them in my will. Could be I'll need to write one."

Shirley turns around, her face a mask of concern, and says, "Haven't you made one out already?"

"I was kidding you. I was joking, for crissakes."

"Oh."

Frankie shakes his head and flips through the London guidebook he bought at LaGuardia. "What the hell *is* Boxing Day, anyway?" he says to nobody in particular.

"Frankie?"

"Yeah."

"How big is this cat?"

"How big is it? You saw how big it was, you gave the goddamn cat its name."

"So we're talking about Boston, the same Boston I saw already."

"Yes." If she had twice the brains she'd still be only a half-wit, he thinks.

"So, how did you manage to get quarter of a million dollars of coke into Boston's stomach? He must look like an airship."

Frankie closes the guidebook and lays it on his lap. "Shirley, this is a new strain of coke, not a goddamn shipment. It contains some new ingredient . . . I don't know what it is . . . bunch of numbers. But it means you can spread it wider. Like, I mean, you can get more dime bags per deal. You follow me?"

"A prototype."

"A what?"

"A prototype. The specimen that they'll use to mass produce it."

Frankie stares at his wife like he's seeing her for the first time. "You been keeping anything from me here, Shirley?"

"Now why would I do that, honey?"

(4) Frankie comes home:

Frankie says to Shirley, "It's like coming home, you know?"

Shirley is turning around in the cab to get a look at a big store with a whole load of flags hanging outside. "Coming home?"

"Yeah, my old man, his grandfather came over from England. Did I ever tell you that?"

"I don't think you did, honey, no."

The three thousand miles he's just put between himself and Edward Kroaeneur have made him feel easier. Even the pain in his gut feels better and the last time he took a pee it was clear. A little painful but clear.

Frankie settles back in the seat and looks out at the rain-washed streets, looks at the mass of bulbous black London cabs going every which way up and down the little streets, and he feels safe. "You know what?"

"What?"

"I could live here."

"We haven't even been outside yet, honey. How d'you know you could live here?"

Frankie shrugs. "Just feels quieter. More . . . more civilized. Like, it feels like it has more depth. Am I making any sense here?"

Shirley pats him on the knee. "I think I know what you're trying to say, honey," she says. "It has more character, more breeding."

Frankie nods, thinking on that for a second. Then he turns to her and he asks, "You *sure* you're not keeping anything from me?"

"Like what, honey?"

Frankie shrugs. "Seems like you suddenly know a whole lot of things."

Shirley turns to him and she gives a smile, kind of a sad smile. "I guess I read a lot."

"You read a lot? Since when? I don't think I ever saw you reading anything other than the *Enquirer*."

"You're never home to see me doing anything, Frankie. How could you say that? I haven't read an *Enquirer* for years. Only reason we still get it delivered is for you. It's *you* reads the *Enquirer*."

Frankie takes that in. It's true. He *does* read the *Enquirer* and, truth to tell, he's been getting annoyed with it just recently. Like every article has quotes from "pals" or "close sources." He doesn't believe in it anymore. It's then, with the rainy streets of London speeding by the cab window, that he realizes he doesn't believe in a lot of things anymore.

"You think I'm changing, Shirley?"

"Changing in what way, honey?"

He gives another little shrug. Jesus, he thinks, where would my conversation be if I didn't have my shoulders? "Changing like . . . like getting more intense. You know what I mean?"

"You're getting older, Frankie." She looks out of the window. "We're all getting older. Gets to a time when the old things and the old ways—the things and ways that seemed so important once—they no longer seem to matter."

Frankie frowns, gives it some thought.

"Is this Piccadilly Circus?" Shirley shouts through the partly open window which separates them from the driver, breaking the words up to make *Pick a Dilly.*

The man shouts back over his shoulder that it is. He points to some kind of statue right in the middle of the road and says, "And that's—"

"Eros," Shirley says, staring at the statue, making the word sound mystical and wonderful at the same time.

Frankie watches her face from the side and wonders where the years have all gone.

(5) *Frankie and Melvin go shopping:*

"Yes, gentlemen, how may I help you?"

"We'd like to purchase a cat," Frankie tells the man behind the counter.

"*Purchase?*" Mel whispers.

Frankie ignores him.

"A kitten?" the man asks.

Frankie shakes his head. "We were looking for a full-grown cat. One with, like, little orange socks around the feet?"

The man looks surprised. "You want to buy a cat wearing *socks?*"

"Sock *markings,*" Frankie explains. "My, er, my wife's sister, she used to have a cat with orange markings around the feet. We're over here to see her—the sister, not the cat."

The man nods patiently.

"Actually, the cat died."

"I'm sorry to hear that, sir."

"Yeah. So was she. The sister, not—"

"Not the cat, yes. I think I get the picture."

"No, the cat's dead," Mel adds helpfully.

The man nods some more and all three of them stand looking at each other. Next to them, a cockatoo squawks something unintelligible and the man says, "Quite." Frankie isn't sure whether he's referring to the bird or them.

"We only keep kittens here, sir," the man says then. "And not too many at that. And I'm sure we don't have one with those markings."

"Oh."

"Might I suggest you visit the Cat Protection League. They have a shelter over in Clapham. You can get the address from the Yellow Pages. I'm sure you'll be able to find what you want there."

Frankie nods. "Thank you kindly," he says.

Outside the pet store, Mel says, "What's with this *purchase* and *thank you kindly* stuff?"

"Breeding," Frankie says. "Character and breeding."

Mel nods and doesn't ask what Frankie means exactly.

Frankie is pleased for such small mercies.

Later that same day, Frankie and Mel are in a cab heading away from the Cat Protection League's shelter in Clapham, south of the Thames. They have a cat that looks like a dead ringer for Boston. They are heading for the quarantine section of the Immigration and Passport Control buildings at Heathrow Airport. Mel is practicing appearing normal with the cat stuffed down his shirt. It moves around a lot but doesn't hurt.

"How do I look?"

"Fat," Frankie says. "How's it feel?"

Mel considers before answering. "Okay," he says. "It feels okay." He rubs the lump under his shirt. "It feels good."

Frankie frowns.

"Marcie kind of fell for Boston, you know? I think I'm going to have to get her a cat."

"Sounds like—" Frankie was going to say *a pretty crazy idea,* but suddenly it seems to make a whole lot of sense. "A great idea," he says instead. "Sounds like a great idea."

(6) Frankie and Melvin make a fair exchange:

Sometimes the bear eats you, sometimes you eat the bear.

Frankie has heard that saying somewhere, he doesn't remember where or when. But he knows what it means.

Today, he and Melvin have eaten the bear.

Everything has gone incredibly well, timing perfect, with the gods of Irony looking the other way at every stage. Maybe it's a sign, Frankie thinks, heading back into town in yet another black cab, this time with Boston—the real Boston—sitting on his lap.

They got into the quarantine section at Heathrow without any trouble at all. The new cat stayed still under Mel's shirt. The guy who escorted them in to see Boston was called away for a few minutes, giving them time to make the switch. When the guy returned he didn't notice the difference in the cat he now had and the one he'd had a few minutes earlier. Boston stayed still under Mel's shirt. And they got out without any further comments. Except one:

"You certainly do love your cat," the guy had said.

"Yes," Frankie had answered, "I guess I do."

The guy in East Cheam—a strange man who called both Frankie and Mel "matey" and who possessed a bizarre glass eye that continually watched the opposite wall when he was speaking to them—had performed the simple operation, removing the packet, and Frankie had given him the promised thousand dollars. Now, stitched up once again, Boston is groggy. Frankie strokes him and looks across at Mel. He smiles and says, "You know, I been thinking."

"Yeah? About what?"

"Yeah. I been thinking about . . . about *things*."

"Yeah," Mel says, in an ain't-that-the-truth voice, and Frankie realizes that further comment will not lead anywhere.

(7) Frankie delivers the goods:

"You want me to make it now?"

Frankie nods. He and Melvin are in a small office three flights above a sleazy strip joint in Soho. It's dark outside. Frankie has just asked the man to make a call stateside to say the handover has happened.

The man dials the number and speaks. "Yeah, it's me. Sure, everything went fine . . . I suppose," he says, looking questioningly at Frankie. Frankie nods. "Yeah, no problem. I'll put him on."

Frankie takes the receiver. "Ed, it's Frankie."

Ed tells Frankie he did well. Frankie says thanks. Then Frankie tells him he isn't coming back to New York, at least not for a while. Ed asks why.

Frankie turns away from the man watching him and from Mel, who's right now sitting on the sofa stroking the sleeping Boston. "Personal reasons," he says in a soft voice.

(8) Frankie bids farewell to the past:

Frankie and Shirley wave through the huge windows at the disappearing plane. The farewells have been tearful, particularly for Shirley and Marcie, although Frankie, too, has experienced some sense of things changing. Things that can never be the same again.

Frankie has told Mel he can take over the old business.

He has been in touch with his bank and with a realtor, and the apartment on Riverside Drive is already up for sale. The realtor told him he thought he could make a quick deal if that was what Frankie wanted. Frankie told him it was.

The funds from his checking and savings accounts have been transferred from his bank in New York to an account in Lloyds Bank. Frankie picked Lloyds because he felt they needed his support having gone through all the insurance hoo-hah that Shirley told him about. Frankie has not realized that Lloyds Bank and Lloyds of London are two completely different companies and Shirley has seen fit not to tell him. She thinks it's kind of sweet of him to do it.

They have bought a small place in Swiss Cottage, because the area sounded European, and Boston has recovered completely. Frankie, now fifty-six and heading full tilt for fifty-seven, considers himself retired.

"You know," Shirley tells him as she thrusts her hand into Frankie's coat pocket and takes hold of his hand, "I feel a little naughty."

They are outside the main Heathrow terminal and walking to the car park where their Jaguar is waiting to take them home. It's a typically cold October night in London and the atmosphere is damp and foggy and mysterious. All possibilities are there for the taking, it seems.

"Naughty?" Frankie says. "Is that a character-and-breeding word?"

She laughs. "I feel like I just left my husband and ran away with the man I married. Does that make any sense to you?"

Frankie nods. "I'm beginning to see a whole lot of sense in the things you tell me," he says. "There's still one thing I want to know about, though."

She says, "What's that?"

"Eros," Frankie says.

Her laughter echoes in the foggy air.

(8) *Frankie and Shirley on Boxing Day:*

The days and weeks and months have sped by in the lives of Frankie and Shirley the way that days and weeks and months speed by in the lives of us all.

The Tower of London, Madame Tussaud's, Big Ben, the Houses of Parliament . . . so many days filled with discovery and experience and enjoyment. Particularly enjoyment.

They have been up to Stratford, where Shirley took Frankie to see a production of *The Merry Wives of Windsor* ("You've never seen Shakespeare until you've seen him in Stratford," Shirley told her husband in the foyer and Frankie didn't have the heart—or perhaps the nerve—to ask her how she knew that) and they have been across to the southwest coast to see Tintagel Castle, where King Arthur ruled the land from a round table.

And they have been across the Thames to Clapham. Many times.

"You certainly do love your cat," the man tells Shirley and Frankie. "How many times have you been out here to see him?"

Frankie fights off the urge to shrug and instead says, "No more than he deserves." He signs the papers and waits for the man to check through the details. The man looks up and nods, smiling. He hands one copy of the document to Frankie and looks across at Shirley, who is sitting on a chair with Boston on her lap.

"You know," the man says, nodding at Boston, "that cat could be a twin for this fellow." He lifts the cage containing the cat from the shelter onto the desk, his eyes glancing from one to the other. "*Are* they related?"

Frankie slips the paper into his jacket pocket. "Who knows," he says.

"Quite," the man says.

Shirley stands up with Boston, and Frankie picks up the cage with the other cat. Then he stops and glances across at his wife.

"Was there something else?" the man asks.

Shirley frowns at Frankie, wondering what he's thinking about.

"Well, just one thing," he says, "but it isn't anything to do with cats."

The man waves his arms and gives them a big smile. "Well," he says, "if it's anything I can help you with, I'll be happy to do so."

"Boxing Day," says Frankie.

The man looks puzzled. "Yes?"

Frankie says, "Why is it called that?"

"What, Boxing Day?"

Frankie nods.

"Well, it's a traditional day of giving," he says. "The first weekday after Christmas is what it *used* to be; now, of course, it's always December twenty-sixth."

"But why *boxing* day? What's that got to do with giving?"

"Oh," comes the answer. "It comes from Christmas box . . . like a present. That's how people used to pass on their gifts to one another, in a box."

Frankie looks across at Shirley, gives her a smile. She smiles back.

He lifts the small cage containing the cat and walks across to where Shirley is sitting, puts it on her lap next to Boston. "Happy Boxing Day," he says.

"And a happy Boxing Day to you too, honey."

Afoot and light-hearted I take to the open road,
Healthy, free, the world before me,
The long brown path before me leading wherever I choose.
—WALT WHITMAN
from *Song of the Open Road* (1881)

Death of a Glamour Cat

Christine Matthews and Robert J. Randisi

1

"She's been your mother for forty-four years. If anyone should know what she likes, it would be her darling boy."

"Come on, you two spend hours together talking, shopping, gossiping. You know her taste better than I do," he countered over the phone.

"Remember the beautiful nightgown I got her two years ago? She gave it back to me, wrapped up in the same box, as a gift for my last birthday. Said she never cared for it. And the plant we sent her when she moved into her new house? She refused delivery telling the poor florist that he should be ashamed of himself for sending her something half-dead. Besides, if you want to get technical about it, I've only been related to her for three years."

They could go on like this for hours. Thinking about that mile-wide stubborn streak of his wife's, he knew this standoff might last for days. Someone had to be grownup about the whole thing and Gil decided to take the plunge.

"All right, Claire, you win. I'll think of something." He could hear the director shouting in the background and knew their call would be cut short.

"You're such a sweetie," she cooed. "I love it when you take charge. It makes me hot. Are you going to watch the show tonight?" "Sorry, can't. I'm finishing up inventory in the breakfront."

The huge breakfront was filled with first-edition mysteries instead of dishes.

"I'll bring dinner home. How's that?"

"Great. I'll see you later."

As if cued by the hanging up of the phone, a handsome man in his late twenties walked into the bookstore.

"I'm looking for a book on cats," he said when he noticed Gil sitting at his desk. The bookstore had no counter, just a small wooden desk where Gil sat and conducted his business. He had an office in the back with a larger desk, where he did his bookkeeping and other business he could handle after closing—like inventory.

"Animals—aisle three—"

"No," the man corrected, laughing, "not the animal, the play. I'm sorry I didn't make myself clear."

Gil laughed also. "Honest mistake."

"There's this new book I'm kind of excited about. I think it came out last week."

"What's so special about it?"

Now the man's laugh was a nervous one, and he looked embarrassed.

"I'm supposed to be on pages twenty-six and thirty. You see, I'm an actor and I'm in the play. My name's Paul Taylor."

They shook hands and Gil introduced himself.

"We've been touring for two years now," Taylor said, "and we're at the Fox for the next two weeks."

"You know, I just happen to have that book." Gil knew most of his stock by heart and he also knew that *Cats* was coming to the Fox. He had ordered several copies of the book, hoping someone would be moved to look for it after seeing the play. "I'll get it for you."

"That's great!"

The Old Delmar Book Store was housed in a trendy section of St. Louis called University City. Some called it the Loop. It was a stretch of about six long blocks of Delmar that boasted indoor and outdoor restaurants, antique shops, bookstores—two others besides his own—and small specialty shops.

Gil Hunt had owned the shop before the area became trendy, and even before he met and married Claire. The building was one of the oldest on the block.

Gil walked to the back of the store, savoring the sound of the creaking floorboards and the scent of paper and leather bindings. He never got tired of the way the store smelled.

The young man was more impatient than he had first seemed and decided to follow Gil to the shelves in the back, under a staircase. The theatrical section. Gil found the oversized book and held it out to his customer.

"Here you go."

"Thanks. This is great." Excitedly flipping through the pages, he finally stopped at a black and white photo of an actor made up to look like a large cat. "This is me! Old Deuteronomy."

He held the book out for Gil's inspection. The bookstore owner had trouble recognizing the young actor beneath all the makeup, except perhaps for around the eyes. With all that makeup and fur it could have been anyone. And so the older man lied.

"Looks just like you."

"Think so? I'd be in a lot of trouble if I looked like some old, mangy cat. But thanks, you've been great. I'll take it." He snapped the book closed. "It's for my Mom, for Mother's Day."

They walked back to the front of the store, where Gil totaled the purchase. It came to fifty-five dollars and eighty-five cents. When Gil told the man the amount he looked concerned.

"What? Gee, that's a lot."

"These coffee table books can run pretty high."

The young actor pulled out a worn wallet and pulled a velcro tab. Gil could see two twenty-dollar bills in the cash section.

"We take Mastercard and Visa." He hoped that would solve the man's problem.

"Too bad they wouldn't take me. A struggling actor is not a very good credit risk. I've only got forty dollars and that has to last me until next Wednesday."

Suddenly the young man's eyes lit up.

"Say, have you seen the show?"

"Yes, my wife and I saw it in New York."

The man looked crestfallen.

"But my mother hasn't seen it."

The man's face lit up once again.

"Would you like two tickets? I mean, I know we've just met and all, but I really want this book for Sunday. How about if I leave two tickets at the box office for you and your mom?"

"I tell you what, make it three for Sunday and you've got a deal."

"Done!"

"Looks like I owe *you* money now," Gil said. "How about if I gift wrap the book and you can pick out a card from that wall over there to go with it?"

"Thanks, man, you saved my life."

Gil's Mother's Day problem had been solved. He thought about Claire's reaction when she found out that he'd handled it so quickly. If she'd been aroused before . . .

He reminded himself to pick up some wine on the way home.

2

Gil checked his appearance in the bedroom mirror and, satisfied, walked into the living room. The apartment he shared with Claire was in a high-rise building on Brentwood Avenue, in Clayton. He and Claire had moved there after they were first married. With the combined incomes from his store and her job as a hostess on the St. Louis-based Home Mall Channel, they were able to afford the rent. Prior to that he'd lived in a more modest part of town in a small apartment he'd used basically for sleeping. He'd moved there following his separation—and ultimate divorce—from his first wife, because it had been close enough for him to spend time with his two sons. Since that time his wife had taken the boys and moved to New York, so now he got to see them only two or three times a year. It was actually a small price to pay not to have his ex living in the same town.

Okay, not so small . . .

"I'm almost ready," Claire called from her bathroom.

"Take your time. We don't have to pick up my mother for an hour."

Claire came out and he marvelled at how it never went away, that little leap in his stomach when he saw her. He loved the way the apartment smelled of her perfume. Her blonde hair seemed to glow, as did her pale skin. She wore very little makeup because she *needed* so little, she was that pretty.

"You look fabulous," he told her, "and you smell great."

"You," she said, heading right for him, "look like a hunchback."

She reached him and immediately began straightening his sweater, pulling it down so it didn't bunch behind his neck. He thought most husbands would have merely endured her touch in this situation, but he reveled in it. He wondered if it would still be like this in ten years? He hoped so. He knew so.

"How do I look now?" he asked.

"Wonderful," she said, touching his arm, his chest, his beard.

Gil Hunt was forty-four, three years younger than his wife, Claire, but his hair and beard were peppered with gray and this, coupled with her youthful looks, convinced people he was actually older than she.

They had met at a mystery convention in Omaha, Nebraska. He had been a book dealer there, and she was attending with a girlfriend. Circumstances had thrown them together—fittingly for the event, a murder that they had solved—and a whirlwind, long-distance romance had ensued, resulting in her moving to St. Louis to marry him.

As a result of the murder he had become something of a minor celebrity at mystery conventions these days. On the other hand, almost upon her arrival in town she had secured her television job, which made her a celebrity, especially throughout the Midwest.

"We'd better go," she said. "Rose likes us to be early. She's going to complain about having dinner afterward."

"We already explained that to her."

"I know," Claire said, "but she'll complain."

"I'll tell her I had to work—"

"She'll complain."

"Are you saying my mother's a complainer?"

She stared at him. "Hello? Is anyone home? Read my lips. Your . . . mother . . . complains."

He laughed and said, "I know, I know," while he slipped his leather jacket on.

"But I put up with it," Claire said, putting on her coat, "because her son's so doggone cute."

After two kisses they stopped and left the apartment. If they got to a third and fourth they'd be late, and his mother would have even more to complain about.

3

"My doctor says I'm supposed to eat regularly," Rose Hunterelli complained.

"You'll eat, Ma," her son told her. "Believe me, you won't die of hunger."

"I had a small salad for lunch, because I knew my son and daughter-in-law were taking me out to dinner. I *didn't* know dinner would be at midnight."

"Don't exaggerate," Gil said.

Claire, sitting in the back seat of the car, maintained a controlled silence and let her husband handle his own mother.

"Well," Rose said, and sniffed, "it'll be late."

"Not so late."

Hunterelli was Gil's family name. When he first opened his bookstore he realized that with his mail-order business, he'd be on the phone a lot, explaining not only how to pronounce his name but how to spell it. Shortening it to *Hunt* for business purposes seemed the thing to do.

They were driving down Grand Avenue, and finally the Fox Theater came into view. Parking was easy to find since the city had put in the lighted signs that looked as if they had been stolen from cheap motels. They'd even had a lighting ceremony to add some class, but Gil still thought the signs looked tacky.

He headed for one of the lots, trying to ignore his mother's loud sniff.

Glamour Cat checked herself one last time in the mirror. She was known to be fussy about her makeup—in fact, fussy about everything, which caused her to be generally disliked by the rest of the cast.

The door behind her opened.

"I'll be out in a minute."

When no one replied she turned and looked at her uninvited guest. "What do you want? Stop—"

Her protest was cut off by the first blow to the head. The second blow caught her on the way down, and the third and fourth rained on her while she was prone on the floor. The blows had to be hard to have the desired effect through her makeup and costume. They continued after she had lost consciousness, and because she was lying on the floor and there was no give beneath her head they were particularly effective.

The killer dropped the weapon to the floor, where the torn wrapping paper quickly became stained with blood, and left the dressing room, closing the door gently behind.

The curtain went up in half an hour.

4

"Cats?" Rose Hunterelli looked horrified as she read the large letters on the marquee. "You know I'm allergic."

"No, Ma." Gil held back a laugh. "It's a play. A musical."

The old woman's eyes lit up. "Like *The Sound of Music*? What a beautiful story that was."

"It's our gift to you," Claire said. Then she hugged the frail woman. "Happy Mother's Day, Rose."

"Yeah, Ma." Gil hugged and kissed her when Claire stepped aside. "Happy Mother's Day. Now you stay here while I pick up the tickets."

The two women watched as Gil walked into the small ticket office adjoining the theater. When he was out of sight Rose turned to Claire.

"You kids shouldn't have gotten me anything. You know I'm happy just spending time with my favorite people."

"We know," Claire said, even though she knew it was a lie. Rose Hunterelli loved getting presents.

Claire had come to understand and respect her mother-in-law. And she had, after all, given birth to one perfect son. For that reason alone Claire would be eternally grateful. Gil had come into Claire's life when she had given up hope.

That had been five years ago, but to her it felt more like five months. He was still so new to her. His intelligence, warmth, even his finicky mother—she adored everything about him.

"We're all set." Gil held out the tickets for their inspection. "Third row, in the center. Orchestra."

"I hope it's not too loud."

Claire patted her mother-in-law's arm. "It'll be perfect."

As they stood in line to enter the lobby, several women whispered, pointing towards Claire. Finally one of them waved and shouted, "I love your show!"

"Thank you," Claire mouthed, trying not to draw attention to herself. The status of television star fit uncomfortably. Spending time in front of a camera was to her just a job. She was still overwhelmed by the attention it brought her outside the studio. It brought the shyness she had tried to suppress for so many years to the surface.

A young, eager man with thick glasses took their tickets, checked the date, and ripped them in half. "Enjoy the show," he said mechanically, returning the stubs to Gil.

The lobby of the Fox Theater was spectacular. The floor inclined slightly towards the back, where an elaborate staircase led to a private club. Flanking the staircase were two large lions painted gold with ruby eyes. The ceiling was at least fifty feet high and a stained glass window rose above the front doors. On either side of the oblong room, bars manned by tuxedoed bartenders were set up.

"Would you care for a glass of wine, Rose?" Claire asked.

"That would be nice."

"Gil?"

Being catered to was something he had never experienced within the parameters of a marriage before. He enjoyed Claire's attention and made great efforts never to take the gesture for granted. "I'd love a beer."

She leaned closer and said so only he could hear, "You got it, Gilly." She was the only one who dared to call him *Gilly*. She winked and left him with his mother. Knowing he would be watching her walk the long lobby, she stood a little taller.

The theater seemed to be filled with mostly women. A good number of them wore corsages on their jackets and spring dresses. Gil looked down at his mother. The two of them had been through a lot together, and he was proud of the feisty woman.

"I hope you enjoy this, Ma."

"I'm sure I will, son. I always enjoy—"

Before she could finish a speaker buzzed loudly with feedback. Then a man's voice spoke.

"Ladies and gentlemen. Due to circumstances beyond our control the Fox Theater regretfully must cancel this evening's performance . . ."

The crowd started grumbling and complaining, drowning out much of the rest of the announcement.

"What about our tickets?" Rose shouted to her son.

"The announcer is saying something about that now, but I can't make it out."

Claire returned with their drinks. "I wonder what happened?"

Gil steered them to an alcove off the lobby. "Let's stay here until the crowd clears a little. We'll have our drinks and keep out of the way."

"Good idea," Claire said, handing Rose her wine.

It was useless trying to make any sort of conversation. The lobby was jammed with one large disgruntled audience left now with nothing to watch.

As they sipped from their plastic glasses and tried to avoid being trampled or shoved, a door opened behind them. The old theater had many passageways and staircases. This particular door had been concealed by a tapestry curtain. When it opened they were taken by surprise.

"Excuse us. Make way, please." Two police officers stood on either side of a big cat—that is, an actor or actress dressed in full theatrical splendor. Gil guessed it was a man because of the height, and then noticed something familiar.

His hands had been handcuffed behind him and he looked as if his feet were getting tangled. Every so many steps the officers would have to stand him upright to keep him from slumping over.

"The police!" Rose was excited. "Looks like they're gonna haul him into the station."

Suddenly, Gil realized why the handcuffed cast member looked familiar. He grabbed Claire's arm.

"That's the man who got us our tickets."

"The one from the bookstore? How can you be sure?"

"He showed me his picture in the book. He's Deuteronomy."

As if he'd heard his name the big cat turned and looked directly at Gil. He set his legs and pulled the cops to a stop.

"Hey, mister!" he shouted as they yanked him away again. "I didn't do it, mister. I swear, I didn't kill her."

5

Before he could respond Gil saw someone he knew moving through the crowd after the cops.

"That's Sam Harper."

"The writer for the *Dispatch* who shops in your store?" Claire asked.

"He's after the cops," Gil said. "Maybe he knows what happened."

Claire knew her husband was nosy and anxious to find out what was going on.

"Oh, go on," she said, "but I'll get the car. I'll take Rose to her place and then wait for you at home."

"You're wonderful," he said, kissing her and rushing off.

"Where's he going?" he heard his mother ask.

"Never mind him, Rose. You and I will . . ."

Her voice faded away as he pushed through the crowd, trying to catch up to Harper.

"Harper!" he shouted.

The man paused, looked around, then continued on.

"Sam!"

This time he turned and saw Gil.

"Come on," he said, beckoning. "I've got to catch up."

"What's going on?" Gil asked the reporter.

Harper spoke without looking at him, intent on getting through.

"There's been a murder. One of the cast members. The cops just hauled off another one and are probably gonna arrest him."

"Deuteronomy."

"What?"

"That's who they're taking away," Gil said, "an actor named Paul Taylor."

Suddenly Harper grabbed Gil's sleeve.

"You know him?"

"He was in my store the other day. He got us the tickets for today."

Harper's grip tightened and he said, "Stay with me."

When they got outside they saw a police car driving off down the block.

"The meat wagon and M.E.'s car are around the side," Harper said. "Come on."

"Where to?" Gil asked.

"My car," Harper said. "We've got to get to the police station. This is a helluva story."

In the car he said, "Tell me about this actor—what's his name?"

"Paul Taylor. He came into my store and bought a coffee-table book about the show. He showed me his picture inside."

"And that's how you recognized him? Even with all the makeup?"

"Well," Gil said, backing off for a second, "I recognized the character, and Taylor *plays* the character—"

"You mean it might not be him?"

"No, it's him," Gil said. "He spoke to me in the lobby as they were leading him away."

"What did he say to you?"

"That he didn't kill her. It *was* a woman who was killed, wasn't it?"

"Yes," Harper said, "but I don't know who. I managed to talk to one of the detectives for a few minutes, and I got a look at the murder weapon. Real odd."

"What is?"

"The way she was killed."

"How?"

"She was beaten to death," Harper said, "with a book, a big, thick—say, Gil, do you suppose that's the book you sold him?"

6

Claire gave her husband a concerned look as he entered their apartment.

"I would have come to get you."

"Sam gave me a ride."

She embraced him and he closed his eyes for a moment, breathing her in, enjoying the feel of her.

"Are you all right?"

"I'm fine," he said, as they broke apart, "it's the kid I'm worried about."

It was her husband Claire was worried about, ever since he'd called her and told her how the woman was killed.

"Was it the same book?"

He sat on the sofa and nodded.

"You can't feel guilty."

"How would you feel if you'd sold someone a murder weapon?" he asked. A moment later he grabbed her hand.

"You didn't," she said, sitting beside him. "It's not your fault she was killed."

"I know," he said, squeezing her hand, "I know that, I just feel . . ."

"You don't think he did it, do you?"

"If you'd seen how excited he was to get that book," Gil said. "It was for his mother!"

She smiled and touched his cheek tenderly.

"You're such a kind man."

Remarks like that embarrassed him, she knew, and she loved that about him, too.

"What do you want to do?" she asked.

"I want to help him."

"How?"

He shrugged.

"Guess you should start at the theater and ask some questions, poke around."

"That's an idea."

"Has he been charged?" she asked.

"He hadn't been when I left. They were still questioning him."

"Did you get a chance to talk to him?"

"Just briefly. He repeated what he said at the theater, that he didn't do it, and asked me to believe him."

"Why you?"

"He just arrived in town. Maybe he doesn't know anyone else. He's going to need a lawyer." Gil added that last statement as if he'd just realized it.

"I imagine the people with the play will help."

"The people with the play . . ." he said. "I've got to find out who they are."

"Wait." She got up, walked to the dining room table and returned with a program for that day's performance of *Cats*. "Here. I grabbed this on the way out, one for us, one for your mom. I thought she should have a memento of some kind."

7

Getting up at four A.M. and making it to the studio by five-thirty was the pits. But the morning show was Claire's baby.

The makeup woman applied foundation to Claire's face with a small sponge. She chatted almost as quickly as she dabbed.

"Wasn't that just too horrible? What happened last night at the Fox? My cousin's husband's sister, Maureen, works over there. They call her when a new production comes to town and then she gets assigned to one of the stars. She's done 'em all. *Hello Dolly*, *Phantom of the Opera* . . . you name it, she's been there, done that."

Claire hadn't told anyone she'd been at the theater the day before. She knew only too well how one word could start an avalanche of gossip. Being interviewed on *Hard Copy* was not her idea of fun. Too many of her colleagues had found themselves discredited and unemployed after talking to the wrong reporter. But yet . . . anything she could find out to help Gil . . . to ease the guilt he had struggled with last night . . .

"Was Maureen working on any of the *Cats* cast yesterday?"

"No, and she was pissed off. When the crew got to town about a week ago, the people at the theater gave her a call. God, she was so excited. We went out and celebrated."

"Why so special? I thought you said she does this all the time."

The thin woman in the black jumpsuit started applying eyeliner to Claire. "There are shows—and then there are shows. Know what I'm sayin'? *Cats* has been on Broadway for like what? Thirty years? Somethin' like that. One of the big wigs told Maureen that one of the Cats was looking for someone to travel with her. And when the tour was over she needed that someone to stay with her in New York. Someone who could do it all. Hair, makeup, nails, maybe even help out with wardrobe."

"Maureen can do it all?" Claire asked, trying not to move.

"Sure! She's a graduate of the Hollywood Beauty School. It's her dream to make it in the theater or movies. A soap opera, now that's good work. All she needs is to hook up with the right person."

"So what happened?"

"Women can be so catty, you know?" The woman kept speaking, unaware of the pun she had made. "Just because Maureen is gorgeous and talented. I guess Madame Diva felt threatened. Before Maureen even got a chance she was out. Axed. Fired."

"That's a shame."

A bald man with a black headset clamped over his ears stuck his head into the room. "How's it coming?"

"Hold your horses, I'll have her ready in fifteen minutes."

"That's my girl." Pleased with the answer, the man left.

"So?" Claire needed one more bit of information. "Did Maureen get a chance to meet the woman who was killed?"

"Meet her? She was the very same bitch who got her fired. It's like I always say, what goes around comes around."

Claire hurried out of the makeup room, towards the set. There was no time to call Gil with her news. Time was short and there were so many other things to remember.

The director's chair was empty, and as Claire waited for her cue she couldn't help noticing that morning's copy of the *Post-Dispatch* folded across the seat. MURDER AT THE FOX CANCELS SHOW read the bold headlines.

"Claire! You're on in five! Four . . . three . . . two . . . go!"

8

Gil entered the lobby of the Fox. It looked quite different during the day, when it was completely empty. For one thing, it appeared larger. He heard footsteps and turned his head to watch a man come from one of the foyers.

"The tours start in the back, by the—"

"I'm not here for a tour."

"Oh. Is there something else—"

"I'm meeting someone here."

"Who?"

"Me," a voice said, behind them.

"Oh, Mr. DeLay."

"It's all right," DeLay said, "I'll take care of Mr. Hunt."

The man nodded and walked away, leaving Gil with Charles De-Lay, the director of *Cats*.

Gil turned and looked at DeLay. The man was barrel-chested and in his forties, with wavy black hair salted with gray.

"You *are* Mr. Hunt, aren't you?"

"Yes, I am."

They shook hands. It had taken Gil the better part of the morning to track DeLay down on the phone, and then he'd had to convince the man to meet him at the theater.

Gil's day had started with a call from Claire after her morning show. She'd told him what her makeup lady had said about her friend, Maureen.

"All right, Mr. Hunt," DeLay said, "I'm here as you requested. Now what can I do for you?"

"I wanted to talk to you about Paul Taylor."

"What is your interest in Taylor?"

"I met him a few days ago and sold him a book about this play, *Cats*."

DeLay frowned.

"The book he used to kill Brenda Manning?"

Gil recalled reading in the newspaper that the victim, who had played Glamour Cat in the show, was named Brenda Manning.

"I don't think he killed her."

"Really. The police seem to think so. They've charged him."
That was also in the newspaper.

"I realize that, but I'd just like to ask some questions—"

"Are you some sort of a detective?"

"Well, no, but—"

"Then I don't understand—when you said on the phone you were
a writer I thought you wanted an interview—"

"I'm sorry if I gave you that impression."

Actually, Gil wasn't sorry. He'd been vague on the phone and it
had been DeLay who'd asked if he was a writer.

"I'm sure you *said* you were a writer . . ."

"I'm not," Gil said, "although I am involved with books, as a book-
seller."

"Look," DeLay said, "this is a very trying time, and you've brought
me here under false pretenses."

"Don't you want to help Paul?"

"What do *you* think? He's put a halt to my production . . . and
killed a wonderfully talented girl."

Gil had the feeling DeLay had thrown in that last bit as an after-
thought.

"I don't think he killed her."

"You met him a few days ago. What do you know about him?"

"When did you meet him?"

DeLay sputtered a moment, then said, "That's neither here nor
there."

Gil was sure DeLay had met Taylor just before he did. Taylor did
say he had just arrived in town.

"I have very little time for this, Mr. Hunt," DeLay said. "I've got to
find replacements for two cast members."

"I would think the part of Glamour Cat would be difficult to replace at this stage of the play's run."

"Very difficult," DeLay said, "and that's why I haven't got time to
talk to you."

"How well did you know the dead woman?"

"I was her director," he said. "She's been with the show the whole
time. I knew her."

"Wouldn't you like to help Taylor if he didn't kill her?"

"I don't know him."

"That doesn't necessarily preclude you from helping him," Gil argued. "Take me, for instance. I intend to ask questions until I can prove he's innocent."

"That's very admirable, Mr. Hunt." The director's tone was condescending.

"Does the rest of the cast think he's guilty?"

"I can't speak for the rest of the cast."

"Would you mind telling me where the cast is staying?"

"They're spread out," the director said. "Some are at the Hilton, some at the Embassy Suites, some are even at the Drury Inn. You'd have to look around for them."

"Mr. DeLay—"

"That's all, Mr. Hunt," DeLay said. "I have no more time for you. Good day."

The director walked away and left Gil alone in the lobby. Since he was already in the theater, he decided he might as well take a look at the dressing rooms.

It wasn't hard to find the dressing room that had been Brenda Manning's. There was a tape outline on the floor where her body had been. There wasn't much to see beyond that. When he left he found a pay phone and called home.

"It's about time," Claire said. "What did you find out?"

"Only that the director, Charles DeLay, is sure Taylor killed Brenda Manning."

"What's he like?"

"A big, barrel-chested guy in his late forties, black hair turning gray. He seems real convinced that Taylor killed Manning, and I don't know why."

"Did you ask him how well he knew her?"

"Sure I did. He said he was her director."

"That's all?"

Gil knew the tone of Claire's voice. It was her I-know-something-you-don't-know tone.

"All right, tell me."

"He was more than her director."

"How do you know that?"

"I talked to Maureen."

"Your makeup lady's friend, or whatever."

"Right. I got her on the phone and she was only too willing to talk."

"And she says they were having an affair?"

"Yup."

"And you believed her?"

"I think she was telling the truth, Gil."

"No sour grapes?"

"Maybe some. She's no saint, but her story can be checked out with some of the cast. She says they knew, so why would she lie?"

"How did *she* know they were having an affair?"

"She saw them together once," Claire said.

"Why would he lie to me?"

"Oh, Gil, why not? You're not the police. Besides, did he really lie?"

"Well . . . no, he just sort of skirted the issue."

"Why don't you come home and we can figure this out."

"I'll bet you think you already have."

"I think it's him," she said, "Charles DeLay, but come home, Gilly."

"So we can talk?"

"And for other reasons, too."

He smiled at the phone.

"I'm on my way."

Gil hung up and walked to the lot where he'd parked his car.

9

When there was a knock on the door, Claire wondered if Gil had forgotten his key. Even as she opened the door she realized that if he had his car key, he certainly had his door key, too.

"Oh!" There was a man at the door, a tall, barrel-chested man with gray hair who looked surprised. "I'm sorry."

"Can I help you?"

"I . . . was supposed to meet a man here."

"Who?"

"Does Gil Hunt live here?"

"Yes, he does."

"Are you . . . his wife?"

"That's right. Can I help you with something?"

The man seemed confused. He looked up and down the hall, and then back at Claire.

"I'm supposed to meet him here."

"What's your name?"

"It's . . . kind of personal."

"I just talked to him on the phone," she said. "He's on his way home, but he didn't say anything about meeting anyone."

"I—I could wait for him in front of the building."

"If you'd tell me your name—"

"Really," the man said, "I'd rather wait out front."

"Wait a minute," Claire said, suddenly recognizing the man from Gil's description. "You're Mr. DeLay, aren't you? The director of *Cats*?"

"You . . . know me?"

"Mr. DeLay, you talked to my husband already today. Why would he ask you to meet him here?"

Suddenly they both moved. Claire tried to close the door in the man's face but he got his shoulder into it and pushed it open, sending her staggering back. He entered and slammed the door behind him.

"What do you think you're doing?" she yelled.

"Please be quiet, Mrs. Hunt," DeLay said, his tone anguished. "I don't want to hurt you, but your husband—he says he won't stop."

"You did it, didn't you?" she asked. "You killed that poor girl."

"Please . . ."

"My husband will be here any minute."

"I know," DeLay said, "I'm counting on that."

When he took out the gun Claire was surprised at how calm she was. This man had already killed one woman, and he probably wanted to kill Gil—and her—but his heart didn't seem to be in it.

"Tell me what happened?" she asked. "Please, while we wait for Gil."

She was surprised at how readily he responded. How many times had she and Gil watched a movie where this happened, where the killer spilled his guts in the end, and they had a hard time believing it?

"It was her own fault," DeLay said, almost in tears. The gun he was holding was an automatic, and it looked small but deadly. He wasn't pointing it at her, just waving it around as he talked.

"She was going to leave me," he went on, "and leave the show."

"And which was the greater sin?"

"Both," DeLay said. "I made her, Mrs. Hunt, but she was tremendously popular with the audiences. Without her the show would flounder . . . and so would I."

She saw a wedding ring on his hand.

"You're married, and you were having an affair."

"A foolish affair, as it turned out. I loved her, but she never loved me. She told me that to my face. She was leaving me and the show, and I couldn't let her do that."

"But . . . you didn't shoot her. You . . . beat her to death."

"I couldn't bring myself to shoot her," DeLay said. "Isn't that amazing?"

"But you had no problem beating her with that book until she was dead?"

"I didn't mean it," he said. "I . . . I hit her once, and then I couldn't stop."

Claire wondered what would happen when Gil came home. Of course they'd hear his key in the door. Would DeLay shoot her and then Gil, or the other way around?

There was a pewter gargoyle on a table near the sofa, and she started to inch her way over to it.

"I think you're a liar, Mr. DeLay."

He didn't seem to catch what she said right away, then looked at her and said, "What?"

"You had to have taken that book from Paul Taylor's dressing room. You meant to kill her with it and then leave the book behind to frame him. This is not quite the crime of passion you're trying to make it out to be."

Now he adopted an indignant pose. His back straightened and he looked down his nose at her.

"What did you expect? I couldn't just kill her and take the blame. You don't understand. The show needs me, and he had only just arrived."

"That's very noble of you," she said. "You frame a young man so you can go on directing the show, which you say will flounder without Brenda. I'm finding your logic kind of faulty, Mr. DeLay."

"Logic?" The man laughed, humorlessly. "There's perfect logic involved here, woman. Certainly the play will flounder without her, but the publicity her death will bring will make up for that, at least until I can find a suitable replacement."

"So you're going to kill my husband and me and then walk out of here and find her replacement? Is killing just an order of business to you, Mr. DeLay?"

She was still moving sideways, inch by inch.

"I did not do this lightly, Mrs. Hunt," DeLay said, "and I admit, I haven't thought this part out. I didn't know your husband was married. I knocked, but I didn't expect anyone to be here. I thought I'd force the door and wait for him here."

"And shoot him when he got home?"

"He *told* me he wasn't going to stop until he proved that boy innocent. I couldn't just let him—"

"Mr. DeLay, you can't—"

The key in the lock froze both of them. She was still several feet from the gargoyle. She watched his eyes carefully, feeling the sweat running down the side of her face and between her breasts, hoping that his eyes would go to the door, just for a second or two . . . and then they did.

Just as Charles DeLay took his eyes from her to look at the door, she lunged for the gargoyle, grabbed it, and threw it. Never much of an athlete, she could hardly toss Gil his keys or a glove accurately. The gargoyle was no different. It sailed towards DeLay, easily missing him by two feet. But he reflexively raised his arms in front of him to ward off the blow.

"Gil! He has a gun."

Next to the door was a counter, and beneath the counter a couple of stools Gil had bought, which were too high to sit on. They'd been useless up to now, until Gil picked one up, charged at Charles De-Lay, and hit him over the head with it. The stool shattered and DeLay fell to the floor, pulling the trigger of the gun once as he did so.

Gil and Claire stood stock still as the sound of the shot faded. They studied each other for holes first, and then themselves.

"Are you all right?" he asked.

"Yes," she said, "you?"

"I'm fine."

Only then did they fall into each other's arms and hold on tightly.

10

Rose Hunterelli called her son from a pay phone near the entrance of the Admiral. It was Tuesday, Senior's Day at the riverboat casino. The ride down to the riverfront in the tour bus had been filled with gossip, all of it about the arrest of Charles DeLay the day before. Telling her friend, Ava, that she'd catch up, Rose waited impatiently for Gil to answer the phone.

"Old Delmar Book Store."

"It's about time! I just heard about that friend of yours. The *Cats* kid we saw with the police at the theater."

"What did you hear?"

"He's innocent. The director killed that poor girl. They were having an affair, you know."

Gil didn't want to worry his mother and acted surprised. "Really? I haven't read the paper yet."

"You always were a good judge of character, Gil."

"Thanks, Ma."

"I was wondering what you're doing on Sunday," Rose said.

"Sunday? I don't know, why?"

"Well, we never got to see the play and it was my Mother's Day present."

"I'll talk to Claire and get back to you, Ma."

"Good. Well, I gotta get going, Ava's holding a machine for me."

Gil smiled. "Have fun and win big."

"You gotta work the machines, that's the trick."

Before he could say goodbye, she had hung up. Gil sat a moment, studying the phone. He wondered how he would approach Claire with the subject of buying Rose a Mother's Day present . . . again.

To Grandmother's House We Go

Barbara Collins

Lydia May Albright, nine years old, sat in the backseat of her parents' late-model Ford Thunderbird as the car traveled along a snowy two-lane highway in northern Minnesota, with her father at the wheel and her mother beside him. The little girl was wearing a new red corduroy dress with a white lace collar, white tights, and black patent-leather shoes. With her long blond hair, bright blue eyes, tiny button nose, and pink cherub mouth, she looked like a china doll come to life. Next to her, on the back seat, slept the family cat, Fluffy, a white Persian, curled up on the girl's red woollen coat. For never having made the long car trip before, the feline was doing quite well.

Lydia looked out the window of the car at the winter-wonderland scenery whizzing by and couldn't remember *ever* feeling happier.

The snow outside that covered the thick pine tree forests was not the heavy kind good for making snowballs or snowmen—it was the kind of snow that crunched under your shoes when you walked, and it crumbled apart in your hand if you tried to mold it. *This* snow sparkled, just like the glitter on the front of the Thanksgiving greeting card Lydia held in her hand.

She bought the card yesterday with her mother at the Hallmark store in the mall, passing over the more modern and mundane greetings of pumpkins and turkeys for this traditional one. Besides the fake snow, the outside of the card showed a family riding in an old-fashioned sleigh—a father, mother, little boy, and little girl. While she didn't have a brother, the parents looked a lot like hers, and the little girl seemed a mirror image of herself.

211

But she hadn't picked the card because of the glitter or the family in the sleigh, or even because of a poem that was printed throughout and written by a person with the same first name as hers. She had picked the card because of what was *inside.*

Lydia opened the card and smiled at the picture of an old Victorian farm house—just like the house where they were going. And on the front porch stood a plump old woman in an apron and funny cap, her arms outstretched, a look of joy on her grandmotherly face . . .

"Are you still fiddling with that card?" her mother asked, glancing back at her daughter. She sounded cross, but Lydia could see a smile tugging at the corners of her ruby-stained mouth. "It'll be in tatters before we get there," she warned.

Lydia thought her mother looked so pretty in her green coat with plaid velvet collar, and shoulder-length brown hair gathered at the neck with a green velvet bow. Her makeup was heavier than Lydia had ever seen her mother wear; she could have been a movie star.

And for once her mother didn't have a bad headache.

"What's that, dear?" Lydia's father asked her mother. A middle-aged man with dark hair and a handsome, chiseled face, he was wearing a colorful sweater over a pale polo shirt.

"A card she bought for Grandmother," explained Lydia's mother.

"Oh, yes," he replied, looking at his daughter in the rearview mirror. "I saw it on the dining room table. Very nice, Lydia. It reminds me of Thanksgiving with my grandparents when I was a little kid."

And he began to sing the poem which was printed on the card. "Over the river and through the woods to Grandmother's house we go . . ."

Lydia beamed. So the poem was a *song*, too! She listened, enraptured, to her father's deep voice. After a minute her mother joined in. She had a nice voice, too. "Oh, how the wind does blow! It stings the toes and bites the nose, as over the ground we go."

Her parents stopped singing and laughed, her father reaching out with one hand and giving her mother a little hug. And her mother in return leaned toward him, placing a little kiss on his cheek, leaving a faint red mark.

They all were so happy. So very, very happy. Even Fluffy, woken from her nap by their singing, appeared to have a smile on her little furry face.

What a wonderful Thanksgiving this would be!

Not at all like *last* Thanksgiving.

Lydia stared out the car window.

Which seemed like a long, long time ago . . .

"Hurry along, now," Lydia's mother, Brenda, said anxiously. "Make sure you have all of Fluffy's things."

Brenda, in a black parka with its hood pulled up and Fluffy in her arms, stood by the front door of their Tudor home on Lake Minnetonka.

"Why can't we take her with us?" Lydia asked. She hated leaving the cat behind, even for a short while.

"You know Grandmother doesn't like cats."

Lydia, her arms laden with Fluffy's bed and food, moved past her mother, to the front door. "And a lot of other things," the little girl muttered.

Mother and daughter walked across the frozen front lawn toward the big brick Dutch colonial home next door. Behind them, the lake—what Brenda could see of it—seemed forlorn, enveloped by a dense rolling fog. The dreary day fit her dreary mood.

Mrs. Jensen, a widow in her early seventies whose husband had died the year before, answered their knock at her door. She was short and plump, in gray slacks and sweater, a pleasant expression on her fair Scandinavian face. Brenda thought Mrs. Jensen looked like a grandmother, even though the woman didn't have any grandchildren—or even children—of her own.

"Happy Thanksgiving, Mrs. Jensen." Brenda smiled.

"Come in, come in," the elderly woman greeted them.

Brenda and Lydia stepped inside the foyer. The house even smelled like a grandmother's house. Like chocolate chip cookies were baking in the oven. Not like booze and stale cigarettes.

"You're positive taking care of Fluffy won't be any trouble?" Brenda asked.

"Not at all," Mrs. Jensen assured her. "We get along just fine. I'm sure she'll feel at home in no time."

As if in response to that, Fluffy jumped from Brenda's arms to the floor and scampered down the long hall that led to the back of the house.

"She remembers where the kitchen is," Mrs. Jensen laughed.

"Here's Fluffy's things," Lydia said to the elderly woman, setting the items down on the floor. "Don't forget, she gets fed in the morning."

Mrs. Jensen smiled at the little girl. "I won't forget."

"I want to pay you something . . ." Brenda dug in her coat pocket.

"Oh, no," Mrs. Jensen protested. "I won't hear of it."

"But I insist," Brenda replied firmly, and held out a twenty-dollar bill. "We'd have to pay to board her, you know. And this is so much better."

"Well . . ." The older woman hesitated, looking at the money, which she then took and tucked away in a pants pocket.

Brenda and Lydia were about to take leave of the woman when the little girl asked abruptly, "What happened to that lady that was here by the door?"

"You mean the statue?" Mrs. Jensen replied.

"Uh-huh."

"Oh, I got tired of her," Mrs. Jensen said lightly. "So I sold it."

That startled Brenda. "But . . . I thought it was an heirloom," she said, amazed. She remembered Mrs. Jensen telling her about that exquisite bronze statue of a young Egyptian girl with arms outstretched holding a platter for salesmen to leave their calling cards on, and how it had been in the office of the family's wholesale grocery store for generations.

"Well, now, my dear," Mrs. Jensen chided, "you can't afford to be sentimental at my age."

The word *afford* resonated in Brenda's head. Looking past Mrs. Jensen, she noticed that the grand hall tree with its beveled mirror and ornate dragon hooks was also gone. Had the woman gotten tired of that, too? Then something occurred to Brenda. The week before she had seen the van of a real estate firm parked in front of Mrs. Jensen's house. Brenda didn't think much of it at the time, because that company often canvassed their neighborhood in search of leads to potential buyers.

"Mrs. Jensen," Brenda said, alarmed, "you're not selling the house." It came out more a statement than a question.

The old woman's pleasant mask slipped, and her eyes turned moist, but her voice continued to be cheerful. "I'm looking for a smaller place, yes. Now that Harold is gone, this house is really too big for me."

"But you've lived here so long," Brenda moaned. "And we'd miss you terribly." She fought back the tears that sprang to her eyes.

Lydia didn't bother holding back her tears. The little girl fell into the old woman's arms, sobbing uncontrollably.

Then Mrs. Jensen was crying, and Brenda buckled and joined them, and the three stood hugging each other in the foyer.

After a minute, Mrs. Jensen wiped her eyes with a tissue from the pocket of her slacks. "I'm not going very far away," she told them. "Maybe some place further north where it's not so expensive. We'll still see each other."

Brenda smiled bravely for the benefit of Lydia and Mrs. Jensen, but inside she felt sick, like someone close to her had died. "Of *course* we'll still see each other."

"You promise?" Lydia sniffed, looking at Mrs. Jensen.

"Promise," the old woman said, and stroked the little girl's head. Then she returned to her cheerfulness. "Now you must hurry along. There's a bad storm coming, and you have quite a drive up north. Oh . . . wait . . . there's something I want to give you . . ."

The elderly woman left them and walked down the hall, disappearing into the kitchen. Then back she came with a white paper plate of chocolate chip cookies covered with clear wrap.

"Maybe these will pass the time in the car," she said handing the plate to Lydia. "I made them from scratch."

Mother and daughter thanked the woman and left, waving goodbye.

Trudging back across the lawn to their house, Lydia said glumly to her mother, "I wish we were spending Thanksgiving with Mrs. Jensen."

Brenda sighed. "I do, too, honey. I do, too."

The family was quiet on the three-hour trip north from Minnetonka to Brainard to visit Brenda's mother, who still lived in the same farmhouse Brenda grew up in. Brenda's father had died from a stroke seven years ago, when Lydia was only two. Her husband, Robert, had both of his parents living, but they resided in California, and the families rarely got together.

On the other side of St. Cloud, with heavy snow beginning to come down, Brenda said to her husband, "I wish there was something we could do to help Mrs. Jensen."

Robert, behind the wheel, nodded. "I do, too."

Earlier when they were packing the car (and Lydia was out of earshot), Brenda had told him of her fear that the elderly woman had run out of money.

"She should get a nice sum for the house," he had replied. But Brenda reminded him that the Jensens had had to mortgage their home some years ago when the grocery business ran into financial trouble. Now she was sure the woman was selling off her antique furniture, one piece at a time, just to make ends meet.

Brenda felt a familiar tightening in her neck, and one hand went there automatically to massage it, though she knew it would do no good.

"Migraine?" Robert asked, taking his eyes off the road, giving her a funny look, a combination of, "I'm sorry" and "I knew this would happen."

Brenda dug in her purse and pulled out the prescription bottle of sumatriptan tablets. She took one, washing it down with a swig of mineral water she'd brought along. Then she put the pills in the pocket of her cardigan sweater, in case she might need another.

"When will we get there?" Lydia asked from the back seat. The little girl had been quietly reading a book. She was casually dressed (like her parents) in jeans and a sweatshirt. Brenda didn't feel much like making them all dress up. Trips to see her mother were never very festive.

"Too soon," her husband said under his breath.

Brenda closed her eyes, resting her head against the car seat.

She hated her mother, a humorless, whiny, vile witch of a woman. There was no other way to describe her. But what Brenda hated even more than the woman herself was the control she still had over Brenda after all these years. In seconds her mother could beat her down with a few choice words, just as she had when Brenda was a child.

"Robert, pull over!" Brenda cried.

He swerved the car off the two-lane highway onto the snowy shoulder.

Brenda flung open her car door, leaned out, and upchucked the sumatriptan tablet. Her breakfast followed shortly, which she'd had over four hours ago. Her stomach, realizing long before she did that a migraine was coming, had shut itself down.

"Are you all right?" Robert asked softly.

Brenda nodded, involuntary tears sliding down her face. She reached for the bottle of mineral water, rinsed out her mouth, and spat into the snow.

"Would you like a cookie, Mommy?" Lydia asked sympathetically.

Brenda shook her head no.

"Let's turn around and go home," Robert suggested. "We'll stop somewhere and call your mother and tell her you're sick."

"No!" Brenda said firmly. "I feel better. And we're almost there." She wasn't lying, she did feel better, and besides, she'd never hear the end of it if they missed Thanksgiving with her mother. They, after all, were bringing most of the food.

Robert sighed and steered the car back onto the road.

They were silent the rest of the way.

At the farmhouse, Brenda's mother didn't bother to come out on to the dilapidated front porch to greet them. Brenda could see her, scowling from the picture window as they unloaded the car.

As she approached the farmhouse carrying the picnic basket of food, Robert behind her with a suitcase, Lydia bringing up the rear with her books, Brenda felt her stomach lurch again. She closed her eyes and took a deep breath, shutting out childhood memories that floated toward her out of the house like unwelcome ghosts.

She looked up at the old Victorian house and told herself that's all it was: a house, a structure of wood and stone. Nothing more.

She tried to open the wood door with its etched oval window, but the door was locked; it had a special latch that automatically locked whenever the door shut. Robert had installed it for mother last summer after there were some area break-ins.

So where was her mother? Brenda thought. She knocked on the door. She knew her mother had seen them. Just what kind of game was she playing now? Then the door slowly opened and the smell of

turkey greeted her, and suddenly Brenda was filled with hopefulness . . . perhaps this visit would be different.

But then there stood her mother, thin and bony in a drab cotton
dress (where was the new wool one she'd sent her?), a white shawl
around her slumped shoulders, coarse gray hair pulled back in a bun,
cigarette hanging from puckered lips.

"Where the hell have you been?" the old woman said crossly. "The
turkey's been done for an hour. Now it's going to be tough as
leather." Besides the nicotine, her mother's breath smelled of bour-
bon.

"I'm sorry, Mother," Brenda said apologetically. "The traffic was
heavy." Why did she have to lie? Why couldn't she just say that they'd
gotten a late start, or that she was sick along the way? But then that
would be Brenda's fault. And her mother already found enough fault
with Brenda.

Her mother grunted. "You've put on some weight," she said.

"No," Brenda responded neutrally, "I don't think so. Maybe it's
just this sweater."

"Well, you look fat."

Robert set the suitcase down. "It's so nice to see you, too," he said
warmly to his mother-in-law. Which made Brenda smile. Robert's
sarcasm always went right over the old woman's head.

"Hello, Grandmother," Lydia said, keeping her distance.

Her grandmother smiled—a rarity—showing tobacco-stained
stumpy teeth, and reached out to her granddaughter, touching the
little girl's head.

"Such pretty blonde hair," she said, then the smile dropped. "Too
bad it'll most likely turn mousy, like your mother's."

"Thank you," Lydia said politely, having caught on to her father's
way of handling the woman.

"Are you still writing those books?" Brenda's mother asked Robert,
the word *those* coming out disdainfully. She had turned abruptly
away from her guests, heading for the rocking chair by the picture
window.

"That's right," Robert responded, following the woman into the
living room, settling into a rickety wicker chair, "I'm still writing
suspense novels." He sighed and put some exasperation into his

voice. "I wish I could do something more worthwhile, like work in a factory, but the darn things keep selling."

"I don't read trash," the grandmother said acerbically, putting her cigarette out in a blackened ashtray.

Robert nodded thoughtfully, "I remember . . . your taste is more literary . . . tabloids, is it?"

Brenda smiled and took the picnic basket into the back kitchen. Lydia, wisely, had made herself scarce, having disappeared to an upstairs bedroom with her books.

The kitchen was small, with worn linoleum and appliances that had been new when television was young. Several times, Brenda and Robert had offered to give her mother a new kitchen, but the old woman declined, saying she liked things just the way they were. If so, she liked them dirty and dingy, Brenda thought.

She sighed and placed the picnic basket on a formica table. Sometimes she envisioned the house empty, her mother gone. Oh, the things she would do *then*! How she would fix the house up! The front porch repaired, lace curtains in the living room windows, the fireplace roaring . . . all the things she'd never had when she lived here, all the things she had always wanted.

Hugging her arms to herself as if to keep warm, Brenda glanced toward the ceiling and shuddered. She could almost hear the house cry out. And something dawned on her: the house had been as much a victim as she.

"Someday," she whispered. "Someday."

There was a noise at the back door in the kitchen, a scratching sound. Brenda turned away from the table and walked over to the door. She looked out one of the grimy window panes. On the stoop was a yellow tom, shivering in the cold, snow swirling around it, one paw stretched out toward the door.

"Oh, my goodness," she said. "You poor thing."

She tried to open the back door but it was stuck. She gave it another good tug, but the door didn't budge. Probably hadn't been used for years, she thought. But then she noticed that the door had been nailed shut at the top. . . . Her mother's idea of a back-door lock. Brenda went through the kitchen to the living room, where Robert and her mother still sat, but silent now.

"Mother," she said, "there's a cat at the back door." She started to say, *Can it come in?*, but she already knew the answer.

"Leave it be!" the old woman said sharply. "It's been hanging around here for a week and it can either freeze or scat!"

Upset, Brenda turned on her heels and went back to the kitchen. Maybe she could hide the cat in the basement overnight, then put it out in the morning after the storm had passed through. She peered through the back-door window again, but the cat was gone, and she didn't see it anywhere.

"That witch," Brenda muttered as she went back to the table and began emptying the contents of the picnic basket, each with an angry *klunk* onto the table: candied sweet potato casserole, cranberry sauce, dinner rolls, pumpkin pie.

The cranberry sauce was for her mother; no one else in the family liked it. She'd gotten the recipe from Mrs. Jensen, and went to a lot of trouble to make it.

SPICED CRANBERRIES

4 cups cranberries	*5 allspice*
5 cloves	*2 sticks cinnamon*
3 cups sugar	*2 blades mace*

Pick over and wash the berries. Place in a saucepan and cover with cold water. Tie spices in a cheesecloth bag and drop in with the berries. Cook until the berries burst. Remove spices, add sugar, and cook until the mixture is clear. Chill.

Just before serving add one bottle of sumatriptan tablets.

And Brenda plucked the pills from the pocket of her cardigan, crushed them up with two spoons, and stirred the white drug into the red cranberry sauce.

At the table, as if in a dream, Brenda watched calmly as her mother dished the red cranberry sauce onto her plate next to slices of turkey (the meat actually was quite juicy, not tough at all).

Brenda knew what would happen if someone took too many pills; she'd read the insert that came with the tablets warning of an overdose: cardiac arrest.

Her mother took a big bite of the cranberry sauce and chewed. Brenda watched, as detached as the whipped cream sitting on the pumpkin pie.

Suddenly the old woman gagged and spat the food onto her plate, startling both Robert and Lydia.

"That tastes *terrible!*" her mother said, giving Brenda a mean look, wiping her mouth with the back of one hand.

"Must be the sumatriptan," Brenda said sweetly.

"Well, next time use a different spice!" her mother snapped, and stabbed a piece of turkey with her fork.

"Yes, Mother."

Brenda looked over at her daughter, who'd gone back to eating her food, unperturbed. But her husband—a forkful of sweet potato casserole held frozen in the air—was anything *but*; his eyes were wide and frightened.

Robert lay awake in bed next to his wife in an upstairs room of the farmhouse. Outside, the howling snowstorm—which had hit around midnight—rattled the window panes, shaking them with icy hands.

He looked over at his wife, who was sleeping deeply though fitfully, her lovely face a twisted mask of subconscious pain.

It wasn't fair, he thought, that she should go through life tortured by her mother. Wasn't the physical abuse his wife had endured as a child enough? The horror stories she'd told him, waking shivering from nightmares, were enough to fill a season of daytime talk shows. Did the abuse now have to turn psychological?

And what about him? As much as he loved Brenda—which was a lot—he had to admit he was growing weary of the effect that horrible woman was having on Brenda: the moodiness and migraines were casting a pall on their lives that extended even to their bedroom. He tried to be supportive, understanding, but after all, he was only human.

He reached over with one hand, gently smoothing out the furrows on Brenda's brow. She moaned and turned her head away from him. No, it just wasn't fair. He wished that old witch were dead. A meaner person—man or woman—he had never encountered. Even the villains in his books weren't this vile.

Take the treatment of that poor kitty, for instance, the stray Brenda's mother wouldn't let her bring into the house. What the hell harm would that have done? And later, after supper, when Lydia tried to sneak a bowl of milk and a towel onto the ice-covered front porch for the pathetic little creature, the old biddy knocked the bowl from his daughter's hands, making the little girl cry, and chased the cat away with a broom. He could have *killed* that wretched old woman!

Which brought him around to what was really bothering him, what he'd been avoiding thinking about as he lay in bed: that Brenda really *had* tried to kill her mother.

At the table he knew Brenda hadn't been kidding about putting her migraine drug in the cranberry sauce—after all, his wife wasn't much of a kidder. And the look on Brenda's face! He couldn't quite describe it. He'd never seen it before—a kind of madness, like she'd lost her mind, and that really scared the hell out of him.

Later, after Brenda had gone to sleep, he had slipped out of bed and checked the pill bottle she'd left in the pocket of her sweater. It was empty, all right. Earlier, in the car, he had seen it full.

Robert put his hands behind his head and stared up at the cracked ceiling in the dark. No, he could never leave Brenda. He loved her too much. And he could never hurt his daughter, whom he loved even more. Where did that leave him?

Robert sat up in bed. But something had to be done, he thought, before Brenda got another chance to *really* harm her mother . . .

He got out of bed and slipped into his robe, cinching the belt. God, it was cold in there! In woollen socks, he tiptoed out of the bedroom.

He could see light shining under the closed bedroom door across the hall where his mother-in-law slept. There were only two bedrooms upstairs. Their daughter was sleeping on the couch down in the living room.

Good, he thought, the old woman was awake. Maybe they could have a nice heart-to-heart talk. He would be sincere for once.

Lightly he rapped on the door. No answer. Slowly he opened the bedroom door and peeked in.

The woman was asleep on the sagging bed, under the covers, snoring. Even in slumber her face had an unpleasant look. Folded across her rising stomach lay a supermarket tabloid, and in one limp hand dangled a cigarette, smoke spiraling lazily upward, just inches from the paper.

Robert was startled at what he saw. Didn't the crazy woman even know better than to smoke in bed? That smoldering cigarette could catch fire and . . . and . . .

Just a minute, he thought, exhilarated, terrified. This was almost too perfect. All he had to do was back out of the room and wait. Wait until the paper caught fire, and then the blanket, and then the woman herself . . .

But what if the whole house burned down?

What if it did? He'd seen the tormented look on his wife's face every time she approached the farmhouse, steeling herself to go in. Having the house gone would put an end to her tormented memories. And he'd have plenty of time to steer Brenda and Lydia safely to their car. Of course, it would be too late to help her mother. Tragically too late, that is.

He crept toward the bed.

Seized with excitement, heart racing . . . What if his plan took too long to happen? What if he went back to bed waiting for the inevitable and—damn!—fell asleep? No, that was impossible; as excited as he felt, he could never fall asleep, and yet—perhaps he should help things along. . . .

With a finger he ever so gently scooted the corner of the tabloid to the butt of the smoldering cigarette.

With a crackle the tabloid ignited, then the tattered blanket beneath it, the flames dancing quickly . . . and the old woman woke up, eyes popping open like a vampire in its coffin . . .

. . . and with him still standing there!

So he swatted at the flames on the blanket, with the old lady beneath it, and she yelped and started hitting him on the head.

"What the hell are you doing?" she snarled.

"I'm putting out the fire, what do you think?" he snarled back.

The fire was out. Smoke hung heavy in the air.

But instead of appreciation, the old woman pointed to the blackened bedspread and snapped, "Now see what you've done!"

Robert stared speechless at the tattered blanket that, even prior to the fire, had had too many holes in it to count.

His mother-in-law threw back the bedspread, showing bony legs beneath a faded flannel nightgown, and slid out of bed. "Now I'll have to go get another."

Robert's face was burning, but his fire wouldn't be as easily put out—even if his spur-of-the-moment plan had been doused.

"You shouldn't smoke in bed," he said, wagging a finger at her.

"It's my house," she responded defiantly. "I'll do as I damn well please." She paused, then added, "And I *never* had any trouble before!"

He snorted in disgust, and turned, retreating to his room across the hall, where his wife slept unaware of the commotion, because of the squalling storm.

He was disgusted, all right. Disgusted with the stubborn old woman, and disgusted with himself . . . for even considering such a foolish plan . . . and for failing to carry it out.

From the yawning darkness of the upstairs, the grandmother descended to the living room, both her knees and the stairs creaking with every step. She had given her granddaughter two blankets to sleep with on the couch, and she would take one back.

She thought about her son-in-law and frowned. Was she supposed to be *happy* that he had disturbed her sleep, which probably caused the paper to catch fire in the first place? She hadn't even finished reading the story about the clone of Son of Sam framing O.J.! Now she'd have to buy another *Galaxy Star*. Did he think they grew on trees? And what was he doing in her bedroom, anyway? Sick, perverted creep . . . even that disappointment of a daughter of hers deserved better.

Not to mention that his thoughtless action in putting out the flames had ruined her favorite blanket. She had *never* liked that man. He thought he was so superior. Once she'd tried to read one of his books he sent her, but she ended up using it as a door stop. It had too many characters to keep track of, and who did he think he was impressing with all those big words. And the swearing! Christ Almighty. She wouldn't keep filth like that in the house.

Her frown deepened into familiar grooves. She was quite aware that man made fun of her . . . but she never let on. He thought he was so smart. But not as smart as her!

The old woman smiled. Now Brenda, she wasn't smart at all. She could get that girl to jump through a hoop any old time she wanted.

The brief smile settled back into the frown. She had to admit, though, her daughter seemed almost defiant this trip. But the old woman would take care of that. In the morning she'd ask her to go to the cellar for something, then lock her down there for a minute or two (just like when her daughter was little, but only then it was a lot longer). That ought to bring back a nostalgic memory or two.

Lydia could use some discipline, too. That little girl was so spoiled and coddled, she didn't show the proper respect for her elders. But if the grandmother could have just a few days alone with the child, she could turn that around, all right . . . she'd have to manage that, and soon.

She moved slowly toward her granddaughter through the chilly, shadowy living room. She liked the house that way: cold and dark and dreary. She wanted the happy little family to know, when they came for a visit, just what her life was like, just how hard she had it. Sometimes when they arrived, they'd look around for something they had sent—like a new dress or curtains. *Try the trash, why don't you.*

She didn't need *them* to tell *her* what it was that she needed, or how to live, either.

She stood over the small figure of Lydia, curled up on the couch, covered up to her chin with the blankets. The girl was awake, her eyes big and round.

"What is it, Grandma?" she asked.

"Got to have one of those blankets."

"Grandma . . ." The girl started to protest. But her grandmother had already pulled back the top cover, exposing the yellow tom curled up underneath.

"Why, you little . . ." the old woman said through clenched teeth, not sure herself which insolent creature she was cursing at. Then she grabbed the cat by the scruff of its neck.

Lydia began to cry. "Please, Grandmother, it's so cold outside. I'll put it out in the morning."

"I'll put it out now!"

And the grandmother marched to the front door with the terrified cat, opened it, and threw the animal out on the front porch into the blizzard.

"Now *scat!*" she hissed.

But the cat didn't scat or even move, half-lying where it had landed.

"Won't go, will you?" the old woman said. She retreated a few steps to the fireplace and snatched up an old poker.

Her granddaughter, sobbing, ran past her—probably going to summon her parents, the old woman thought. But she didn't care. This was her house, and everyone had damn well better abide by her rules.

The old woman went out onto the porch, into the storm, and threw the poker at the cat, missing her target by a mere inch, the steel rod flying over the animal's head, disappearing into the drifting snow.

The cat screeched and fled—but not out into the yard. The animal ran past the woman back into the house.

And the wind blew, slamming the front door shut, locking the old woman out.

She banged at the front door, but no one saw her. She screamed, but no one heard her. She sank to her knees in the cold, cold snow, fingernails scratching at the front door . . . but no one came to rescue her.

And no one was there to provide her with a blanket, except the snow.

The Ford Thunderbird turned off the two-lane highway and down a winding lane lined with pine trees, their snow-covered boughs shimmering in the late-morning sun.

Lydia leaned forward anxiously in the back seat, peering through the front windshield.

Would they ever get there? she wondered.

Then around the next bend in the lane, there was the farmhouse—just like in the card—but even prettier, with a fresh coat of white paint, the railing on the grand porch repaired, and new lace curtains hanging in the windows.

Lydia's father parked the car in front of the house, next to a trio of birch trees.

"I'll get the suitcases," he said. "Mother, you take in the picnic basket, and Lydia, you're in charge of the cat."

But when he opened the car door, Fluffy leapt from the backseat, over the front, and scampered out before Lydia could even move.

"Fluffy!" Lydia called, afraid that the cat might run away because she'd never been there before. But the feline headed toward the front door of the farmhouse; she knew where she was going.

Then out of the screen door came a plump old woman, in an apron covering a navy dress, her arms outstretched, a look of joy on her grandmotherly face. Staying close by her feet was the yellow tom.

"Hello, Mrs. Jensen," Lydia's father said, coming up the front porch steps, a suitcase in each hand.

"Now," the woman scolded, "I thought we all agreed to call me Grandmother."

He smiled and put the suitcases down and gave the woman a hug. "Hello, Grandmother," he smiled.

"Happy Thanksgiving, Grandmother," said Lydia's mother. "It's so nice to see you."

"Grandmother!" called Lydia, and bounded up the steps and into the woman's arms. She smelled of roasted turkey, her bosom soft and warm.

"Come, let's all go inside," Grandmother said. "We'll have some hot punch in the living room before dinner. I've gotten the fireplace working, you know."

"How wonderful," Lydia's mother exclaimed. "The house looks so beautiful, just like I imagined it could."

Lydia started to follow the group inside but remembered the card she'd left in the backseat of the car.

She turned and hurried back to the Ford, her patent leather shoes crunching on the snow, and retrieved the card. As the little girl stood next to the car, she looked toward the farmhouse. Through the big front picture window she could see the crackling fire in the living room fireplace, and her parents laughing as Grandmother served them punch off the big bronze tray of the Egyptian lady.

Her mother had bought all the things back.

And a smile appeared on Lydia's pretty pink lips.

She wasn't at all sorry about what happened last Thanksgiving. About the front door blowing shut, locking her real grandmother out.

Nor was she sorry that the wind stung the old woman's toes and bit her nose (and worse). Nor was she even sorry she ignored the old woman's cries (staying huddled on the living room steps), which blended with the storm before growing faint, then silent.

Because *that* grandmother wasn't the kind of grandmother a grandmother *should* have been!

The little girl skipped toward the house, card in hand, singing as she went, "Spring over the ground, like a hunting hound, for this is Thanksgiving Day!"

Him. Gone? Good!

Jeremiah Healy

Darragh Galvin walked down the corridor toward her apartment door, juggling the grocery bag and notebook computer as she fumbled with her key case.

DOOR. SHE? FOOD!

From the corridor side of the wooden six-panel, Darragh could hear squeaky mewling mixed with mad scratching just above the saddle of the threshold.

"Pooky, it's me. Leave some of the paint on there, huh?"

Darragh said basically the same thing every day when she arrived home from work, but that had never stopped him yet, and she didn't expect tonight would be any different.

The key finally turned in the lock. As the apartment door swung open, Pooky dashed out, the long-haired brown and yellow calico doing a lightning-speed figure-eight around the corridor. What Darragh called his Dance of Welcome.

As soon as she was inside the apartment, Pooky came dashing back, rubbing his face against her calf nearly hard enough to knock his Mom off-balance.

"God, you'd have made a good football player, Pook'."

Dropping the computer into a living room chair, Darragh moved to the kitchen—just a little galley, really. The grocery bag containing her Valentine's Day fixings went onto the counter by the microwave. Then Darragh bent over the stacked plastic trays under the counter, taking out a small can.

SHE. FOOD? ME!

"Minced turkey, one of your favorites."

Reaching down with her free hand, Darragh felt Pooky rise up on his hind legs, pushing his head into her palm. "Glad to see me, right?" She opened the can. "Even with an extra claw on those front footsies, you'd have some trouble doing this for yourself."

Pooky rubbed his face against Darragh's calf again as she used a dessert fork from the utensils drawer to mush the soft food into the dry cereal left over from the morning meal. When the blend looked right, Darragh set the dish on the linoleum next to the refrigerator.

Watching him tear into his dinner, she thought, *God, I love you, Pookmeister. Almost as much as . . .*

Darragh moved into the living room, stopping at the framed photo of a smiling, dimpled, and clefted male face on the mantel over the fireplace. Thom—with an *H,* he'd said to her the first time they'd met, in a bar near the theater district. From across the room, he was good-looking enough to be an actor. Darragh was wondering about that when she noticed him noticing her, then wending his way toward her stool. But Darragh knew she was attractive, too—the red hair, the green eyes—and Thom's opening line to her ("Are you in a play around here?") showed just the right combination of awareness and compliment. In fact, Thom was the right combination in a lot of ways: stockbroker, six feet tall, medium build but great legs and buns from his tennis days. Other than being a little fixated on money, there was really only one problem with the man.

He was still married.

But separated, as he'd told her, upfront with it that first night. The problem was, the divorce could be messy, since his wife ("Emily; never did like that name, *Em*-ily") had an invalid mother and infantile attitudes about a lot of things, like investing for retirement through buying seven lottery tickets a week. Put simply, Thom had to keep their affair under wraps until his lawyer could drive a rational deal that would free him to plan a rational future.

A future that, rationally, would include Darragh. If she didn't botch the relationship by pushing too hard. (Darragh didn't count her gentle hints about when the divorce was going to become final.) Besides, it was often more convenient entertaining Thom at her apartment rather than insisting on visiting his (*"Em*-ily might have hired a private investigator to stake out my place, luv; I never know what that woman will do next"). And in this age of sexually transmitted plague, there certainly were obvious advantages to seeing a married man.

Which reminded her of what would happen after dinner. Feeling a delicious shiver, Darragh moved back into the kitchen and the grocery bag on the counter, carefully lifting out the veal chops and fresh broccoli and especially the chocolate-Amaretto torte in the shape of two joined hearts.

Thom Wexford sat in his office, spending what he expected would be his last Monday behind the desk. Computer terminal for stock quotes and trades, television screen for CNN, even a VCR for those dead times. "Dead" times? A snorted laugh.

Did I actually just think that?

Then, focusing with his right eye, Thom looked at the tennis trophies in the glass case against one wall. Quite a few of them, too. High school through college and on to the club, nice little display to serve as an icebreaker with new clients, even impress them some with what a Renaissance Man he was. Most never noticed that the last trophy was dated five years earlier. Oh, Thom still played tennis, but he never won trophies anymore. Not since the injury to his left eye.

A fluke, that. Volleying at the net, the ball caromed crazily off the frame of his opponent's racquet and hit him. Result: Eighty percent loss of vision by the time he was tested at the hospital.

That injury soured Thom on the sport for a while. On everything for a while, including hucking the stocks. Drifted from one brokerage house to another, never regaining the touch he'd had with the stocks, like the touch he'd had with the racquet. Depth perception, damned important factor in tennis.

Nothing wrong with his other perceptions, though. Like spotting Darragh across the bar that night six months ago, her falling for him like a ton of bricks. He sensed that lying to the girl right away about his being separated would prove one of those strokes of genius he had from time to time.

"Stroke?" Tennis pun, that.

And Darragh was a red-headed tiger in the sack. Nice change of pace from the ever-duller Emily's rather weak service (there's another; they did creep into one's vocabulary, eh?).

Emily, Emily. Obsessed with her wheelchaired mother and her absurd lottery tickets and her dovetailed belief that good people—daughters who looked after their parents, for example—would be rewarded. With hitting the jackpot, for example.

And damned if she didn't. Last Wednesday, the four-million-dollar bonanza. Pre-tax, a couple hundred thousand a year for the next two decades. Rationally invested, that would throw off . . .

Then Thom frowned. One problem with the rosy financial forecast. Emily's definition of "good people" didn't include husbands who were getting a little something on the side. And Darragh wasn't exactly the first. No, Emily hadn't found out about all of them, but the one last year who'd actually telephoned her—*tele*phoned her, can you imagine the gall?—was enough. Or too much, really. Ultimatum time, Emily called it. One more, Thom, and I'm kicking you out. Which wouldn't have mattered much to him, honestly.

Until last Wednesday, that is.

Yes, the lottery jackpot changed everything. Now Emily was a bit too good to let go, or continue to betray, or risk being betrayed to. As, for example, by a certain redhead scorned.

And Darragh would feel just that way, no matter how he might try to let her down easy. She was more cloying every day he saw her, dropping broader and broader hints (read: prods) about when his divorce would finally go through. Not to mention her escalating demands about their spending more time together.

Like Valentine's Day, for example.

Fortunately, Emily's mother happened to have been born on February 14, and throughout their marriage Thom understood that his wife just *had* to spend that evening sitting next to the wheelchair. Which was just fine, when your affairee believes you're already separated and therefore free to spend that most romantic of calendar days with her.

No, any risk of Darragh contacting Emily out of pique or revenge or whatever was simply too much, given the stakes. And like any good stockbroker, Thom had learned how to deal with risk.

And its management.

Smiling now, Thom Wexford leaned forward, going over the checklist on his desk one more time.

SHE. SMELL? MEAT!

Darragh Galvin went over the recipe one more time. "I have everything in there, Pooky. What do you think?"

The cat rubbed his face against her calf, but Darragh was pretty sure he was reacting more to the veal than the marinade mixed in the casserole dish. Covering the dish with some aluminum foil, she placed it carefully in the refrigerator. "Fire's next, Pookster. Want to help?"

Just a squeaky meow. Darragh was always amazed, a cat as big and strong as her calico with such a little voice. Probably because she had him fixed.

Walking to the mantel in the living room, Darragh looked at Thom's photo again, feeling her heart skip. It was the only thing of his she had in the apartment, given his constant warnings of the dire consequences to the divorce proceedings should *Em*-ily find out about their relationship. But that was tolerable, so long as it was only temporary. And even though Pooky could leap like a gazelle—onto furniture, the kitchen counter, even this mantel—he never wrecked anything, so the photo was safe here and easily remembered for hiding should somebody other than Thom come visiting.

Darragh picked up the brass rack holding the fireplace tools and carried it around the corner into her bedroom. One of the real advantages of an apartment in the city's older buildings: a fireplace in both the living room and the bedroom, the latter just right for romantic evenings. There were disadvantages, too, however. Like cranky heat from rattling radiators, a fire escape looming outside the bedroom window, and rent higher than the Himalayas. When the landlord told her what the apartment would cost, Darragh decided she'd have to economize on furnishings, like having a single set of tools since only one fire would be going at any given time.

WALL. HOLE? FIRE!

Edging Pooky to the side with her foot, Darragh set the tool rack on the hardwood floor next to her bureau. She removed the spark screen and began laying the crumpled newspaper, fatwood sticks, and split logs for the fire that would accompany the one she hoped to kindle in the four-poster behind her.

A pen in his right hand, Thom Wexford made a little tick mark next to each item on the checklist.

Fingerprints? All over the apartment, but since he'd never served in the military or been arrested, etc., his weren't on file anywhere. *Tick.*

Telephone records? Inconclusive, since he'd always used pay phones or someone else's extension at work to call Darragh. *Tick.*

Alibi? Shouldn't need one, but just in case: stop by the Civic Center, buy a standing-room-only ticket for tonight's Agassi-Sampras match. Then set the office VCR to tape the program, allowing him to see all the details tomorrow morning as though he'd been there. *Tick.*

Flowers? Darragh would expect *some*thing. After all, it is Valentine's Day. Easily bought anonymously from a sidewalk vendor. *Tick.*

Witnesses? Shouldn't be a problem. Old building, no doorman. Seven other apartment doors along her corridor, but the tenants kept to themselves, and going up to Darragh's place, he'd never so much as seen one of them. Or been seen by them, which was more to the point. *Tick.*

Photo? Just remember to take the whole frame from the mantel and put it in his briefcase. No other trace of him there. *Tick.*

Murder weapon? Nicely provided by occupant. Smile. *Tick.*

Window? Easy enough, with a facecloth from the bathroom linen cabinet. *Tick.*

Cat?

Thom Wexford thought about the little wretch. Darragh had named it "Pooky," but Thom would have preferred "Pukey." And the disgusting hair balls weren't the worst transgression the thing committed. No, the absolute nadir was the way Pukey hid around the corner of the living room, against the fireplace. Its mutant, six-clawed front paw raised in the air, it somehow sensed in its feline way that Thom's reduced vision limited his ability to spot the ambush coming.

Tearing open his ankle every time he walked from Darragh's bathroom toward the kitchen after taking a shower. Slashed with that paw the way he'd take a tennis ball on the rise, come to think of it. Sweep the ball cross-court for a winner in a three-count movement. Cock the arm. Sweep the ball. Follow through.

Except tonight, perhaps a backhand was called for.

Returning to the checklist, Thom Wexford spoke softly to himself. "*Cat?*" Broader smile. *Tick.*

By the time Darragh finished laying the fire—using the heavy brass poker to angle the unlit logs—she realized Pooky had left her for another go at the food dish. Just as well. She needed to take a bath before Thom arrived, and she hated to close any doors on the cat, because he always wanted to see what he was missing. Thom insisted on the bedroom door being shut when they made love, of course. And to be honest, she didn't think the guy was exactly nuts about cats, especially given Pooky's tendency to attack him after a shower.

Darragh suppressed a giggle. She had to admit, it was kind of funny to see a grown man like Thom hopping around, holding his bleeding ankle, cursing.

But she always found a way to make it up to him.

WATER. HIM? GO!

"Hello, Emily? . . . Yes, I'm still at the off—. . . . I remember that it's her birthday. That's why I'm calling. . . . I certainly do. The tennis match at the Civic Center. . . . Probably not before eleven. . . . Fine, you have a good time, too . . . Right, bye."

Wearing only her robe, Darragh opened the bathroom door, a little surprised that Pooky hadn't been waiting outside it. She drew the sash tight around her waist and walked toward the kitchen, turning the corner by the living room fireplace.

LEG. HIM? NO!

"Carnations, please."

The scabrous man hunching over the large white containers of flowers looked like one of Snow White's dwarfs as Thom Wexford called to him from the driver's window of his BMW.

The man walked across the sidewalk to the curb but carrying a bouquet of roses. "It's Valentine's Day, buddy. How's about getting her these instead?"

Thom thought about it. "How much more than the carnations?"

"These here are ten, the others six."

"Then just the carnations."

Thom was quite certain the dwarf muttered something with the word *bastard* in the middle, but under the circumstances he didn't dare make a fuss over it.

"Oh, there you are."

From his position next to the living room fireplace, Pooky blinked up at Darragh, then began licking his raised right forepaw.

"Caught you in the act, didn't I?"

The calico blinked some more, the soul of innocence.

"Just you behave with Thom tonight. It's special."

And Darragh moved into the kitchen, clanging pots against pans to make the holiday even more so.

"Will this chardonnay be all, sir?"

"Yes."

The clerk rang it up. "A fine selection for Valentine's Day, if I may say."

"Thank you."

And it was, a fifteen-dollar varietal from the Alexander Valley. But no sense in stinting on something he'd be enjoying.

Whether shared or alone.

SMELL. HOT? MEAT!

"You like this, huh, Pook? Well, maybe if you're real good, a couple of scraps will find their way into your food dish."

Darragh took the squeaky meow for agreement on the subject.

✿   ✿   ✿

Parking his car several blocks away, as usual, Thom Wexford walked with the chardonnay in his briefcase and the carnations under his arm. Getting to Darragh's apartment would be the tricky part, but good luck: No one at the main entrance, or on the elevator, or in the corridor of her floor.

Perfect, perfect, perfect.

DOOR. HIM? BAD!

"Happy Valentine's Day, luv."

What Darragh said was, "Oh, thank you, Thom." What she thought was, *Just carnations?* Well, that's probably all the florist had by the time Thom got out of work.

He inclined his head toward the kitchen. "What smells so good?"

She told him.

Then he leaned into her, his lips barely brushing hers, then crushing them a little, his tongue slipping through here and there. "Can dinner wait?" he whispered.

"If you can't."

Smiling, but not completely happy about the schedule reversal, Darragh took the flowers to the kitchen, arranging them in a vase.

Thom looked around the room. No sign of the cat. Probably have to chase the little wretch off a pillow in—no. No, there's Pukey, peering around the side of an armchair like one of the Marx Brothers in a movie.

Over her shoulder, Darragh said, "I think they'll look best up on the mantel, to the doorway side of your photo."

"So long as they remind you of me, luv."

Thom watched her move his photo from the center to the left, so that the frame and the vase balanced each other on the mantel. Have to remember the photo. *Tick.*

Which was when he realized something. No fireplace tools. Almost said as much, too, until he realized something else.

Only one other place in the apartment they could be. *Tick.*

Grinning, he moved up behind Darragh, pressing his pelvis into her rump. "Let's take the wine in with us."

UP. FLOWERS? TASTE!

An hour later, her head resting on her lover's shoulder, Darragh said, "I hate to hear Pooky scratching like that."

Sipping his chardonnay in the afterglow of lovemaking, Thom thought, *Better thy door than me.* Then he looked around the room. The flaring, flickering light from the fireplace made the bedposts seem to dance against the multipaned old windows, especially if he closed his right eye. Rather like a surreal scene from hell through the reduced vision in the left.

When he opened his right eye again, the brass of the poker seemed to glint like gold, reminding him of Emily's jackpot. The gold he couldn't risk losing.

"I have to leave you for a moment, luv."

"Oh, but it's so nice, cuddling like this."

"Sorry, but nature calls."

WATER. GO? NO!

In the bathroom, Thom took a clean facecloth from the linen cabinet and used the flushing of the toilet to mask his re-entry into the bedroom. At the tool rack, he wrapped the facecloth around the handle of the poker to mimic a burglar's glove. Then, hiding the weapon as much as possible behind his bare right leg, Thom tiptoed to Darragh's side of the bed, where one of the floorboards creaked just a bit.

Without opening her eyes, she said, "I didn't hear you coming."

Thom raised the poker over his head. "That was the idea, luv."

HIT. SHE? BAD!

Very carefully, Thom Wexford leaned the poker against the side of the bed near Darragh's body, slipping the facecloth off the handle. She'd made only a low, grunting noise when he struck her, and for all the blood on the sheets and pillow, there was none on the facecloth itself, though some had spattered up and onto his chest. Hmmmmmmmn.

Thom moved to the window, using the cloth first to open the lock and then to lift the window. Cold February air, but he'd be out in it for only moments.

Climbing onto the fire escape, Thom wrapped the facecloth around his fist before punching out the small pane above the window lock, so the glass would fall inward and break on the hardwood floor. Climbing back in and being careful to step past the glass shards, he lowered the window again.

A last glance at his handiwork. Poor Darragh Galvin, another tragic victim of urban burglary gone violent.

Grinning, Thom headed into the bathroom to shower off the drying drops of blood.

WATER? DOOR? HIM!

In his left hand, Thom Wexford carried the wineglass he'd used back toward the kitchen. Flexing his right forearm, he liked the way the facecloth felt, now wrapped again around the handle of the poker. Rather like a racquet's grip when he'd towel it off during a match, and the perfectly ironic way to avenge all those ambushes by the fireplace.

Thom had considered going after the cat before showering, on the off chance that some of its blood also would spatter up on him. But showering first meant he wouldn't have to remain at the crime scene for a dangerously extended length of time to search out the little wretch.

Because Thom knew just where Pukey would be. Standing inside the doorway to the living room, against that fireplace. Mutant fore-paw up to slash at him after his shower.

Yes, well, not this time, eh?

Thom stopped for a moment as something he hadn't anticipated occurred to him. What kind of burglar would kill a cat, too?

Then Thom grinned again. A very *bad* burglar.

HIM? UP! WAIT.

Quite simple, really. The lower creatures are supposedly quite sensitive to emotion, so walk naturally, as if he didn't have a care in the world. Left, right, left. Only instead of leading with his right ankle, he'd bend down a bit and lead with a nice firm backhand. The crosscourt ground stroke, with topspin. Rip the little wretch's head off its neck.

A three-step movement. Cock. Swing. Follow through.

HIM. READY? NO!

"Damn!"

The poker made a slight crunching noise as it glanced off the wall at the base of the fireplace, chipping some of the plaster onto the floor.

"Not there, eh? Well, that's one life you've burned, Pukey."

Knowing he couldn't risk more time in the apartment searching for the little wretch, Thom began to straighten up.

HIM. SOON? NOW!

Thom Wexford's peripheral vision began registering something, but far too slowly for even his honed reflexes to react to it in time.

The pain! "Oh, God!" Searing, indescribable pain from his right eye. Screaming, he dropped the poker and the wineglass. Brought his right hand up to the socket, felt only wet mush there. Then, terrified, brought his hand over to his left eye. It could deliver only a blur, but a red blur. Slippery against his fingers.

"Oh, God! No. No!"

Naked and screaming still, Thom headed toward the fuzzy mass of a front door he could barely make out with his left eye. "Help! Doctor! Help me, oh, God, help!"

Thom managed to undo the lock and burst into the corridor, his screams reverberating as though someone had loosed them inside an echo chamber. Doors were opening, blurs now of lights and bodies, flooding into the hall.

"No. No!" Thom stumbled against the tenants grabbing at his arms. He pulled away, trying to find the elevator, even the stairs.

Other voices yelling, his own mind seizing through the pain into just an internal mantra: *God. Blind? No!*

Everyone seemed unaware of the creature watching it all from the threshold of Darragh Galvin's open door, licking something from its right forepaw and almost . . . smiling?

HIM. GONE? GOOD!

Non-Lethals

Marlys Millhiser

Tuxedo Greene watched the flaps on his entrance vibrate. He'd waged a savage battle to persuade the females to install it. Mostly by regurgitating indoor foliage and Fancy Feast on the sanctuary's furry areas.

Now an intruder was about to invade. The enemy across the alley, perhaps, whose similar entry had given Tuxedo the idea for this one. He hunkered. His tail swept the cool hardness of the food room's floor, prickles exciting his every hair to attention. His ears laid themselves back. The warning moan came up his throat, slow and low. Or it could be a creature who had no sanctuary. They were many and often sick and demented. His rear legs stationed themselves to pounce, his butt wiggling into the optimum position.

But it was a people paw that penetrated the catway. It carried the odor of male. It reached inside to the shoulder, grappling for the mechanism that held the peopleway secure.

Tuxedo leapt to the top of the cold food container to watch the intruder from above. Up close, it smelled of dried skin flakes and bad teeth, its breath like that of a crow.

It stopped partway across the room to shine a light beam up and down and across. People were such kittens when it came to the dark. The blinding beam found Tuxedo.

"Shush, cat." The intruder moved off into the room where the fur began.

Tuxedo remained quiet, adjusting his vision back to the darkness. Drops formed on the end of the water tube to splatter against the hole below when he jumped down to the next level. He paused for a drink and decided the male was interesting.

When he reached the fur, his quarry was quietly ascending the steps on the far wall that led to the sleeping rooms. A rather nice arrangement when you thought about it. Placing bits of regurgitated plant life or dinner or occasional fur balls in a procession up those steps gave him acute gratification. You had to do something with them, and placing them outside alerted enemies to your presence. Especially dangerous when you had a catway into your sanctuary.

Tuxedo glided after the clumsy intruder, who turned at the top of the stairs and fumbled down the hall into the older female's sleeping room, the fur flooring keeping their steps quiet. Tuxedo headed for Libby.

He'd had a real name once—but so long ago he'd forgotten. The females called him Tuxedo. The younger, Libby, sometimes called him Tux. The older female was called Charlie. He preferred the younger. He supposed Charlie was somehow their substitute mother and did his best to please her. But she was cranky and difficult. Still, if his food or water disappeared for long, it was the older female who saw to it that he didn't go without.

Libby was his love. She was fun. He leapt onto her now and slid, along with her slippery covering, up her to jam his nose into the warm spot of her throat. She made gurgling sounds. "Tux, go outside. You got your door now."

She stroked his back, and there was love in her voice even though it was thick with sleep. He kneaded her bare skin, his pleasure at the moment vibrating his being and almost erasing the memory of the cool night he'd planned in the alley and the people intruder with the breath of a crow.

That is until Charlie made a horrendous sound from her sleeping room and the male answered with, "Memorial Day!"

Charlie Greene and her daughter sat taped to straight wooden chairs at the dining room table while the burglar ransacked their Long Beach condo. He threatened to hurt Libby if Charlie screamed again, so she sat silent—waiting for him to discover they didn't have any-thing worth stealing except the computers, Libby's CDs, and the TV, which all sat out in plain sight, so ransacking was hardly necessary.

"No sterling silver?"

"Needs polishing. Too much trouble."

"What kind of woman are you? No family heirlooms? No cash? No drugs?" He looked at Libby. She looked back as if he were a slug in her soup. Both Charlie and her daughter slept in varying forms of the simple T-shirt—but Libby's was simpler than necessary and barely covered her parts. Charlie was no prude, but she was a mother. At the moment a worried one.

"My name's Bill," the burglar said and sat down across from them—the detritus of a busy life and junk mail mounded on the table between them. Charlie couldn't remember them ever eating off it. "And tomorrow's Memorial Day."

Bill the Burglar slammed a fist on the detritus and Charlie's accumulated prospects of winnings from every shyster organization with a celebrity frontman slid to the floor along with the debt prospects of blank checks from credit card companies around the globe. Zillions of dollars in promises and debt. But nothing of value. "And what are you doing about it?"

Being robbed? But Charlie tried, "I thought maybe we'd . . . go out and decorate a grave?"

Libby managed a *duh*-look. "With what? Wallpaper?"

Charlie heard the rubber flaps on the cat door: *Pul-ap.* Now there's something she'd have paid this geek to steal—good old barf-on-everything Tuxedo.

"Decorate a grave? You know about that? Most people think of it as a holiday to leave town or have a picnic." Bill lectured them on Decoration Day. (If Bill was his real name. And if it was, his bulb was pretty dim to tell them so. Unless he planned to leave no witnesses to repeat it and his description.)

Decoration Day, according to the burglar, was not a holiday at all but a day of mourning. A national grieving day set aside to honor those who gave their lives for their country and to decorate their graves, it had been going on since the Civil War. "Or was it the Revolutionary War?"

Charlie had no idea, but if she got the chance to give Bill's description to the police she'd tag him "a longhaired Prince Charles with a perm." But younger and plumper. And with a bald spot reaching from his crown to his forehead.

"Tinsel?" Libby ignored Charlie's warning look and went on with her exterior decorating. "Colored lights? New carpet, drapes, and paint—right?"

Bill Palmer swallowed angst. What could these two know about reality and death? How could this shallow woman who held his soul, his future, his very life in her hands really know about Memorial Day? "It's not fair."

"Don't whine. Nobody ever said life was fair."

"Libby—"

"Well, that's what you always tell me."

Bill pounded the table again and more mail fell to the floor. Did this Charlie Greene have no sense of order and housekeeping? Of course not. Things were probably no better in her office, which he'd narrowly missed getting caught trying to break into. "Hello? Excuse me? *I'm* the burglar here. You two are the victims."

Libby tried to shrug, but he had her taped too tightly. "Silly me."

"Libby, that smart mouth is not appropriate," the disorganized literary agent said to her daughter. "Are you keeping track of reality here?"

"Like, what's he going to do, shoot us? With what?"

"With this." Bill Palmer pulled out the needle and syringe.

"So, um, you're too young to be a 'Nam vet, too old to be the son of one," Libby's mom fished around with old Bill, disgusting Libby by even speaking to the turd. "Am I right in assuming this isn't about the war thing?"

"You didn't even have any screenplays in your house, what kind of an agent are you?"

Libby's mom was a Hollywood literary agent and her daughter would never understand why. There had to be less annoying ways for her to support them. Libby's English teacher had handed over a box of novel manuscript right around grading time for Libby to insist her mom give an opinion on. The latest manager at their favorite diner had begged Charlie to "take a peek" at his screenplay. Libby Greene just knew that if she ever walked into a bank, a robber would hold two city blocks hostage until she promised to make her mom read his stuff. If she ever went to college, the president of it would insist her admittance hinge on whether or not Charlie Greene would sponsor his literary gift to the world. If Libby ever went to Heaven, God would be holding a manuscript in front of the latch on the gates. If she ever got married it would be the preacher. Or worse yet, the groom.

Crud. Libby'd been ruined even before Bill the Burglar entered her life, and it was all her mom's fault.

Movies were cool—but this writing stuff was dragging half of California into the ocean. Didn't anybody have a life?

Old Bill had Charlie driving an ancient station wagon instead of an S.U.V. (sports-utility vehicle). He sat up front, holding the needle to a major blood vessel in the side of her neck. Libby sat in back, wrists taped together behind her and her smart mouth taped shut. She tried to display the taped mouth to every car that passed, but it was too early for most people to be out on a holiday and those who were probably couldn't see her through the morning fog. The wagon was a four-door and she could squirm enough to reach the handle, but it had some kind of dorky kiddie-lock on it controlled from up front. And Bill had her mother's blood vessel at his disposal.

"You had *Soulmates of Blood* for two years, while I rotted living with my parents, working grip for less than nothing . . ."

Gardening supplies filled the back of this heap. Libby, bored with the current conversation and the tiresome slang going around—like, who wants to sound like a twenty-something?—was experimenting with her grandmother's expressions, *crud, turd, heap.* Her friends were beginning to pick it up. Since her mother and grandmother did not get along, Libby had fun rattling the former.

None of which meant she wanted the creep to inject whatever was in that needle into Charlie Greene. Actually, they had no proof it held anything but water. Right?

It was at this point that Libby heard the beginning moans of a catfight in the back of the station wagon and turned to see Tuxedo and Hairy, who lived across the alley, squaring off between the tines of a rake and the blade of a shovel. How did they get in here? Then she registered the gap in the back door—tied together with rope to allow the long black box to hang out.

She and Charlie had been allowed to put on shoes. And sweatpants under their sleep shirts. Bill the Wanna-be had led them to the alley in the opening rays of day—barely seeping through fog—and past the houses of their normally nosy neighbors, who hadn't bothered to notice their abduction. Libby hadn't taken the time to study the box then, but now she recognized it as a possible halfway house for Count Dracula. Not as fancy—but clearly coffin-shaped. She also recognized the smell of car exhaust, too intense for the relatively sparse traffic this early on a holiday.

What, Bill the Turd was going to poison them before they got to the cemetery? Bury them together in the box? Wouldn't there be people around who might notice if, as he insisted, this Memorial Day was for decorating graves? Maybe he was going to kill them before anybody with half a brain got up. But wouldn't he get poisoned too?

It looked like his eyes were watering already. Her mom was sniffing and blinking. But Hairy and Tuxedo seemed immune to the sludgy air. The moans turned to cat screams and the fur flew for a few seconds before they backed off to see if the other was properly intimidated.

But the only way out was sudden death on Seventh Street.

Bill ordered Charlie to pull over and stop. "Told those critters to stay outta here." He aimed the needle at the cats. Libby giggled under her tape when he glanced down at it as if surprised to find it wasn't a gun. That's when Libby's mom hit him upside the head with both fists clenched together and so hard she jumped in the seat to hit her own head on the roof. Way to go, Mom.

The kiddie latch was on the driver's side and Charlie had the door open and the hypodermic out of Bill's hand before he recovered. She rolled away with it and hit the road on her belly. On a workday, even this early, she'd have been dead by car tire before she had the presence of mind and enough balance to slam the door in his face. Today she was alive, on her feet, and running around to free Libby before she realized she'd done something dangerous and had no clue as to how to continue the heroics.

The fog was thinning and growing patchy, but the car's exhaust huffed ghastly breath in Charlie's face as she passed the wagon's back door, which looked like a mouth with a black tongue sticking out.

And that's as far as she got before the vehicle shot off up Seventh, Tuxedo and Libby staring back at her and both, in a very short and smoky moment, managing to convey utter astonishment at Charlie's stupidity. Hairy, from across the alley, sprang at his adversary, who was too busy being astonished to pay attention, just as the wagon turned onto Cherry and headed north.

And Charlie. Charlie stood in a lapsed T-shirt. White sweatpants meant for the garbage truck. One of her Keds hadn't bothered to escape with her. She stood there unwashed. Unshampooed. Uncombed. *Sans* makeup. A hypodermic needle poised in a hand that connected to her hip via an elbow. Watching a madman drive off into the fog with her daughter.

It was, of course, at this moment that a police car pulled up beside her. Still in a stunned trance, Charlie watched the officers' calmness as they took in the needle and her grooming . . . as if they saw people who looked this way every three minutes. The white guy got on the phone, the black one out of the car—but warily, she noticed with some relief. If they couldn't see the possibility of a surprise here, they wouldn't be a lot of help.

"You want to give that to me?" the black officer said gently, one hand out, the other discreetly raising the flap on his holster.

"Yes." Charlie handed over her weapon and threw herself at the poor guy. "Thank God you were so close."

"We got a hostage situation. Young blonde. Female. And a couple of cats. Black and hairy," Officer Warren warned softly and oh-so smoothly—into a small cellular.

Charlie was relieved they and several other police cars hadn't come screaming in with sirens like they do on live TV cop shows like *Good Guys, Bad Guys*. It was her kid out there among the white and black marble tombstones with a madman.

She hadn't been able to tell them the license plate of Bill the Abductor's car but the description of the "black tongue," a beat-up, greenish station wagon with a man in front and a blonde in back, had soon brought a response from other cars converging on the area.

"Let us not become heroic here. SWAT's on the way but I need careful assessment and reasoned reporting. Who is seeing what without standing up? And don't nobody shout, okay?" He might be a uniform, but Charlie was getting the impression this was not your ordinary patrol cop. She huddled with him behind a plaster monument. Plaster?

They'd found Libby's abductor and his car in a controversial cemetery on Signal Hill, just off Willow. The old pioneer cemetery that had been neglected long enough to raise the ire of local historians and fuel the local press for a minute. It looked spiffed up to Charlie, who hadn't paid much attention to the shortlived media brouhaha, but plaster seemed too temporary a fix—even for Long Beach.

The fog here was definitely of the wispy variety—snaking around angels and obelisks, burning off in patches above, still thick over the city below.

"Suspect has uncovered a strip of sod to reveal a sheet of plywood. Which he removed to reveal a hole the size of a grave," Officer Warren repeated in a whisper what another officer was reporting to him. "He has backed the vehicle up to it and is pulling the alleged coffin out."

"Where's Libby?" Charlie had all she could do to not race over there and push the jerk into the grave and the coffin in on top of him. The more she thought about it the angrier she was getting. "The alleged blonde?"

Officer Warren repeated the question to his contact, but before he could get an answer, good old Tuxedo came sniffing around the plaster tombstone.

"What a gorgeous kitty. Is it . . . ?"

"Yeah, alleged Tuxedo. Want him?"

But Tuxedo bit the guy's thumb and drew blood.

"He had his shots?" The policeman sucked on the wound.

Charlie assured him the animal was legally without preventable disease as the cat licked a shoulder wound of his own and somebody was talking to her cop again. She exchanged meaningful glances with the cat, who broke off the stare to segue to the inside base of his tail.

"He's short-haired. I thought you said he was hairy."

"That's the other cat. He's a long hair, named Hairy. What did he say? What about Libby?"

"She's on the ground outside the vehicle."

"Can't somebody pick him off with a rifle?"

"Whoa, aren't we getting bloodthirsty."

"The guy's a lunatic and that's my kid." Charlie made it to her knees, tensing to push herself up and run when he pulled her back onto her butt with enough force to jar her incisors.

"Your kid's pulling her torso and legs through the circle her taped wrists made of her arms," he repeated the message relayed to his ear, "and now she's pulling the tape off her mouth and ankles. Between the two of you heroines, you are going to get her killed before SWAT even gets here." He went back to sucking his thumb, but grabbed Charlie again when she started to move. "Greg, what non-lethals you guys got going there?"

"Non-lethals? What is this, a TV show?"

"Well, it was supposed to be. Before you, your kid, and your cat came along."

"You're not a patrol-type cop."

"I was when this big show went down, Mrs. Greene. And finally I'm going to get my fifteen glory minutes and tape an *Ultimate Cops.* But on my way I meet you wearing prison underwear and carrying a deadly needle. And your cat, who's carrying God knows what. Teach me to stop for pedestrians on the way to a shoot."

"On the way to a shoot," Charlie repeated helplessly. Seemed like everybody in California talked like that now. "I don't want Libby caught in any crossfire."

"And you are worrying about non-lethals?"

Besides a smooth talker, this guy was damned good-looking. Charlie noted now some of that had to do with special grooming. While she and her backsliding sweat pants were on their knees, he squatted so as not to mess his uniform. "They're going to tape a show with plaster tombstones?"

"Re-create a crime scene was the intent, I believe." Really big eyes, large head, intense expression, total control. He was talking to her and listening to somebody named Samuel. Every time Samuel came on the line, Officer Warren blinked once. "Silly Putty."

"Excuse me?"

"Samuel is armed with a can that shoots Silly Putty. Sticky Silly Putty. In webs, like a spider weaves. Or adhesive pasta strands. Totally incapacitates the victim."

Charlie tried to get up and running again. She came close to making it, too. Tuxedo took off like a cannon.

"Wait. Officer Stone has a Whizzer."

"That's supposed to give me confidence?" Charlie's struggles were so desperate Officer Warren came to his knees in the damp grass. "You're talking to a mother here."

"A Whizzer is a sonic device that incapacitates the perp sonically, like a bat might take on a mosquito or a moth. Now tell me more about this Bill. You say he's a screenwriter?"

"You know anybody around here who isn't?" And Charlie happened to know more about bats and mosquitoes than that. Her mother was a batty biologist who went on about such things interminably. "Yeah, apparently he submitted a treatment . . . actually I think he said a whole screenplay and he hadn't heard from me, so he got desperate and—"

"Went looking for it in your home."

"We've got pretty good security at the office. But according to him it had been only about two years, and if it is there, it hasn't surfaced yet. So he decided to take matters in his own hands and—"

"*Only* two years?" Officer Warren lost his control, and Charlie made it around the fake tombstone and out of reach.

Bill tipped the coffin into the hole. It shuddered when its occupant hit the top end.

"It's not empty," the Hollywood agent's daughter said behind him. "I thought—"

"You thought I was going to bury you in it? And your mother?" Bill Palmer was reminded by some kind of birds singing in the huge old oak trees of a similar morning when he had announced to his parents that he was moving back to the family home in order to eat while he established himself as a successful screenwriter. He assured Dick and Jane Palmer that when he made it, they too would live in luxury beyond their wildest dreams. Dick and Jane looked at each other, bit their lips, and broke up with laughter anyway. That same kind of bird sang the same kind of song in the backyard in Huntington Beach and you could smell the sea salt on the breeze. "Actually I'm going to bury you on top of him—wishing it were your mother."

Jane's first words had been to her husband, "He'll grow out of this too. He's just slow. Be patient."

"Slow? The kid's thirty," was Dick's reply. Well, the kindest part of his reply. Bad enough to have parents named Dick and Jane, but to have a dad who was a stand-up comic made life a one-liner misery. They'd given him six months and then insisted he find a day job. So he ended up with Jerk Angalini.

"But maybe this will hurt her more."

"Why would you want to hurt Mom? She's nobody."

Jerk Angalini had told Bill to get an agent. Jerk was the producer of the now-defunct *I Love a Good Murder* series. Bill, a lowly construction grip, had managed to get the great man's attention in a weak moment, for just a moment. And then only because Jerk had been in Vietnam. And because the producer had fallen through a fake plaster rock on the set and been forced to listen to a three-minute pitch from the construction grip trying not too hard to free him.

Bill didn't realize how much of his thoughts he'd spoken aloud until the beautiful brat with the braces on her teeth leaned around him and said, "You actually got the chance to leave home and you went back so you could write screenplays? What are you, crazy? Do you have a clue how many people out there are writing screenplays? Like, you could have had a life. You can't believe how much I want to leave home."

He refocused from the shocking depth of the grave and the coffin that sat tipped to bow still—its stern hung up somehow—to the brat and registered that she was loose and talking and walking. "Well, kid, I'm going to make your dreams come true."

But she grinned and pushed him off balance. Bill Palmer reached for her a nanomoment too late. He'd have pulled the slut in on top of him but was thrown further off balance and out of reach when he tripped backwards over a screaming cat. Bill could see it clawing its way back up the crumbling embankment as he hit the coffin prop he'd made himself, finally adjusting its angle to perfection.

The cat barely made good on its scramble to freedom and Bill Palmer could barely breathe after the shock of his landing. The writer in him noted the rectangle of sky above, the two cats and the brat making shadowy bumps in its symmetry.

Six eyes blinked above him, all seeming eerily iridescent in the shadows, which couldn't be—because the girl's were dark-colored. The short-haired black cat with white chest and toes moaned displeasure or warning or whatever. The long-hair studied Bill as a curiosity. But the brat settled on her stomach between them at the edge of the grave she would soon occupy instead of him, all long platinum hair, huge eyes, and scorn. "Right, so who's in that box under you?"

"Jerk Angalini. And it's all because of your mother."

"You know Jerk Angalini?" The kid looked impressed. "My mother knows Jerk Angalini?" she asked the cats for backup. They did not look impressed. "The producer-director of *Ultimate Cops*?"

Bill Palmer was halfway up the slippery earthen wall to the daughter of the woman who had ruined his chances to become a billionaire and show Dick and Jane some real reality when a new face appeared above him. Charlie Greene herself. Jerk had pointed her out as a new agent in the field who wouldn't be loaded down with clients yet. "Just in from New York," Jerk had said. "Send your stuff to her at Congdon and Morse fast. She's not going to be hungry long in this town."

Bill did and waited patiently, politely. For two years he waited. And heard nothing. Yesterday morning Dick and Jane threw him out of the house. Yesterday afternoon he found a way to corner Jerk Angalini, now producing *Ultimate Cops* and for whom Bill still worked. Angalini didn't remember Bill existed and had never heard of Charlie Greene, Hollywood literary agent.

No more Mr. Nice Guy, son of Dick and Jane. Still, he'd tried to give Charlie Greene one more chance. She might have his manuscript on her bedside table.

Bill was holding onto the edge of the grave and about to pull himself to freedom when the same Charlie Greene pushed him back in and her daughter said in disgust, "Mom, we were talking about Jerk Angalini. Will you stop with the hero stuff? You always ruin everything."

When both cats screamed and disappeared from the edge of the grave, Bill was in the process of falling back into it and landing upon the coffin on his aching back again.

When amorphous strands of spaghetti swirled down on him and almost hid the cop heads ringing Angalini's grave. Trust a damn cop to be early for a shoot.

The All-American

Peter Crowther and Stewart von Allmen

God only knew where he was . . . and God wasn't telling.

D. P. "Deepy" Daniels had chased the animal out of the pet room, along the White House's labyrinthine first-floor corridors and up an endless grand-paneled staircase before scampering—yes, *scampering*—the full length of a second corridor, a curved affair of polished marble flooring upon which his shoes clack-clacked like a drummer's rim-shots and the slippery surface of which threatened to send him his full length.

He rounded the corner and stopped as carefully as he could, a singularly simple procedure under any other circumstances but which here, because of the icelike conditions underfoot, necessitated a ridiculous pinwheeling arm movement which made Daniels feel for all the world like an ancient aviator negotiating the air currents. The corridor ahead stretched to a two-over-two-panel sash window, which sent strange angles of shadow across the marble and up the wooden wainscoting of the wall opposite. More importantly, it was empty. Socks was nowhere to be seen.

"And now I lay me down to die," Daniels muttered.

The trainlike wheeze of George Bearson and the guttural grunting of Izzy Mennix rounded the corner behind him and grew steadily louder. Without taking his eyes from the corridor, Daniels, now somewhat more confident at having retained his balance, waved an arm to silence them. They drew up alongside him and waited, listening, Izzy leaning against the wall as though he were being frisked and

George Bearson suffering from the cumulative effects of several years' intake of a daily pack and a half of Herbert Tareyton.

"Where'd he go?" The question's delivery, puffed and panted out by the 240-pound Assistant Deputy Security Manager, confirmed the aptness of his name: he was indeed every inch a bear's son. He was also several other members of its family all rolled into one.

Daniels shook his head and took a single step forward, his head cocked to one side as he strained to hear the faintest sound . . . like a convenient meow or an indistinct mewling. But there was nothing.

Bearson shrugged his jacket and hiked up his pants, pushed more closely toward the floor by his ample belly than mere gravity could ever achieve. "What the hell were you doing?" he snapped across at Mennix, now regaining his wind.

Israel Mennix turned around and slumped back onto the corridor's wall. "I . . . I just don't know what the hell happened," he said, shrugging to amplify the accuracy of the statement. "One minute he's there, and I'm putting down the bowl with the . . . the gunge in it . . . and the next thing I know is he takes a powder. Whoosh . . . gone!" Mennix slapped his hands together like cymbals.

Daniels turned and glowered at his colleague.

"Oh, sorry," he whispered, grimacing.

"He has to be here somewhere," Daniels said softly, taking another step and cutting in alongside the right-hand wall.

"It's a dead end down here," Mennix pointed out.

"Hey, good thing we brought you along, Cochise," Bearson muttered.

They stood again in silence and hoped Socks would reveal himself. After a moment Mennix muttered, "Are you sure he came this way?"

"If I was sure," Daniels whispered sourly over his shoulder, "I wouldn't be standing here like a motion detector waiting for the pittypat of cat feet."

Then Daniels sniffed his fingers. "Least he could've done is bolted *before* I got this stuff all over my hands. I'd run too if I had eat this crap twice a day!"

Impatient now, Bearson said, "Okay, then, let's start checking the rooms." Then he added brightly, "They say the cat's pretty smart, you know—a good American cat. Maybe he can open doors."

At that precise second one door did indeed open, along on the left, but instead of a cat, a woman in a tight-fitting blue suit strode out into the hallway. She pulled the door closed behind her and, seeing the three men, all of them staring fixedly down at her legs, stopped, frowned, and cleared her throat.

"Ma'am," Bearson said, mopping his brow with a gaudily colored handkerchief that would have made a neat cloth for an average-sized picnic table.

The woman nodded once, curtly, and shifted her eyes across them in turn.

Daniels studied her.

She was a little too old for a cheerleader and a little too young for a debutante, but she had equal measures of tease and confidence vying for control of her face. A thick batch of papers nestled under her right arm and pushed her jacket and emphasized her bosom. If he'd have had his 'druthers right then and there, D. P. Daniels would have reincarnated as that sheaf of paperwork. No question. In her left hand, she carried a faded brown leather valise that looked serious enough to contain the Armageddon remote button.

"Can I help you gentlemen?" She made the question sound like *Take a hike, guys,* but it would probably have turned out as *Why don't you chaps run off and play in the traffic?* The accent was unmistakably English, and her expression told Daniels she was used to getting results.

"We're . . . er . . . we're—"

Daniels pulled his jacket aside and said, "Daniels, ma'am, Security." She didn't seem impressed. He let the jacket fall back over the pass clipped to his shirt pocket.

Mennix stepped away from the wall and smiled winningly. "We're looking for Socks."

The woman nodded, eyes checking them out again. Around a thin smile, she said, "You've checked your underwear drawer, I presume?"

Bearson hung his head and sniggered around a meaty hand.

"He's a cat, ma'am," Daniels said, knowing the information was superfluous. "The President's cat? You know?"

The woman's face beamed now in contrived understanding, and then a frown started on those magnificently controlled eyebrows.

"You've lost the President's cat? My, whatever will the President say when he finds out?"

"It's not lost exactly, ma'am," Mennix started.

"Oh, you know where he is, then?"

Mennix cleared his throat and checked his shoes.

"You mind if I ask you what you're doing here, ma'am?" Daniels said.

For a second, the woman looked genuinely hurt. *Me,* the expression said, *li'l ol' me?* But the voice told a different story. "*I* am taking some papers for urgent completion," she said in a measured tone, "and while I cannot elaborate on that statement, I would be happy for you and your colleagues to accompany me." She smiled, and for a moment, Daniels expected a warming of the ice maiden. But he was disappointed.

"Then you will be able to address your inquiries to my superiors." She smiled and nodded as she moved to pass the three men and then stopped. "After all, who knows what other creatures have been allowed to roam freely."

Izzy Mennix bit into the inside of his cheek to stop the smile he felt forming.

Bearson looked at Daniels and then at the woman. Then back at Daniels.

Daniels shrugged his shoulders and smiled, waving a hand. "Hey, I'm sorry if we got off on the wrong foot here, Miss . . . ?"

The woman simply watched him and waited, giving no indication of providing her name unless she were specifically requested to do so. Even then, Mennix thought, it would be a close-run thing.

"No, you go on about your business," Daniels continued after a reasonable pause. "We'll . . . we'll just . . ." The sad truth was that he had no idea of *what* they would do now. Instead of finishing the sentence, Daniels waved his arm towards the far end of the corridor and nodded.

The woman smiled again, sharp and thin, turned her back, and strode purposefully along the corridor the way the men had come.

Daniels watched her sashay and, as she turned out of sight, looked at Mennix and Bearson. Izzy Mennix waved his right hand in front of his mouth and blew on it as though it had been severely burned. "Wow, quite a cool customer."

"Just rude," Daniels said.

Bearson smacked his lips. "Know what she needs?" he asked nobody in particular.

"Yeah," Daniels snarled as he walked to the door of the room the woman had been in. "Etiquette lessons."

"I thought the British were supposed to be polite," Mennix said.

Daniels tried the door. It was locked. He should have guessed. "Good and bad, Izzy, like everywhere else."

Bearson frowned.

Turning from the door, Daniels saw him. "What's up?"

The big man shook his head. "Aw, nothing probably."

"Go ahead, George, you got something to say then spit it out."

"Well," Bearson said slowly, "she made out like she didn't know about the cat, yeah?"

Izzy nodded. "So?"

Daniels shrugged. "She was just playing with us, George; we knew it and she *knew* we knew it. Nothing in that."

Bearson nodded and mopped his brow again, still recovering from the exertions of the past few minutes. "Yeah, that's fine, I know that." He put the gingham cloth back into his pants pocket and smiled. "But then why do I suddenly have a tuft of short white hair on my sleeve," he said, "right where she brushed past me?"

Now it was Mennix's turn to frown. He grabbed Bearson's arm and, like an impatient tailor, spun him around. Sure enough, it was cat hair. Mennix squinted his eyes, cocked his head, and looked up at Bearson. Clearly having some trouble in believing it, he said, "How do you know this isn't from sometime before?"

Daniels was having no such trouble, and he fumbled in his pocket.

Bearson smiled, "You know me, Izzy. I always keep my uniform real clean."

And it was true. George had a huge appetite and was a messy eater, but his uniform always seemed to remain spotless. If on the off chance a stain *did* result, a half-hour later Bearson would appear in the course of his rounds in freshly pressed and clean clothing.

Daniels had once asked to see inside Bearson's locker to count how many ready uniforms waited George's need, but the big man had adamantly refused. "It's private in there," he had explained, and though his face had betrayed a hint of amusement, there had been no mistaking the resolve in his voice. *No way* was the message coming through.

But Bearson had no such qualms of privacy as he solidly planted himself in front of the door the woman had closed moments before.

Daniels quickly looked along the corridor as he wrestled his intercom from his pocket. Pursuit at this stage was pointless: the woman would have reached the elevators by now. He pressed the red button and stepped away from the door. "Break it down, George," he said.

"You calling it in? You think you should?"

Daniels turned to Izzy Mennix and frowned. It was a good point. What did they have to go on? He glanced at Bearson's sleeve as the big man prepared himself to charge the door: a few white hairs . . . that was all, just a few white hairs. If he was wrong . . . what had the woman said? *You will be able to address your inquiries to my superiors.*

Unless those superiors included either Saddam Hussein or Boris Yeltsin, he would be on car-park duty for the next thirty years.

A hazy voice sounded from the two-way. Daniels lifted it to his mouth and told the security officer to forget it. He dropped the intercom back into his jacket pocket. First they would check the room. Maybe the cat was in there.

He nodded to the waiting Bearson and cringed as the man ran at the door. Izzy Mennix marveled at the sight. The door flew open and crashed against something behind it, knocking out one of the inset panels, while the entire lock section of the jamb pulled away from the wall and snapped cleanly in the center. Bearson stumbled on for a few feet and pulled up short at a large filing cabinet.

Daniels stepped over the door panel and wood shards into the room.

It was dark until Mennix flash-rubbed a hand along the wall and popped the light switch. Then the three men could plainly make out the nondescript contents. It was a small office that seemed to be in current use as a halfway house for a number of different items like lamps, rolling file cabinets, a teepee of rolled projection screens, a couple of abused bookshelves, and an easel among some other less obvious items.

Mennix slipped by Daniels and into the room where he examined one of the filing cabinets on wheels. "This must be where the woman must have gotten her files." He leaned against the frame of the cabinet and prepared to riffle.

"What are you doing?" Daniels hissed. "You can't go grubbing your way through that! There might be top-secret material in there."

Mennix sheepishly backed away from the cabinet, pushing the drawer closed.

"We did break in here, after all." Daniels had suddenly become aware of what they had done, where they were and what they were about to do. Did the U.S. Government have a posting equivalent of Siberia? Alaska sounded likely . . .

"But we're looking for Socks," Bearson reminded Daniels.

"In a goddamn *filing* cabinet?"

Mennix, too, cringed at the thought of violating top secret information simply because they were chasing a cat. Okay, maybe it *was* the President's cat, but even that would still sound pretty silly on the front page of the *Washington Post.* He pictured the headline:

"NO COMMENT," SAY FELINEGATE INTRUDERS

and the tagline beneath the inevitable line-up photograph . . .

Come on, boys . . . Cat got your tongues?

"Yes," a smiling D. P. Daniels announced, breaking Mennix's train of thought. "We started out looking for Socks . . . but maybe now there's *more* to the *outfit."*

"Ouch!" said Izzy Mennix.

"Yeah, now we're *unraveling* a mystery," George Bearson added.

"And again," said Izzy.

Daniels chuckled. "Once we *tie* all the—"

"Shaddup!"

She had walked the first forty paces as normally as she could. The second forty, when she could be sure she was out of sight of the Three Stooges, she had taken a little faster, with considerably less restraint.

Reaching the elevators, she had pressed the call button and

switched the valise to her right hand. It was suddenly heavy. *Damned* heavy.

Adrenaline flow, she thought.

She glanced back the way she had come and listened. There were no sounds of pursuit. She was out of trouble and now she was feeling the pressure. Like those stories of people lifting cars to free their children. She felt as though she had lifted a Greyhound bus.

She allowed herself the luxury of a couple of deep gasps, low-down emptying gasps . . . rejuventating gasps. It had been close.

She could hear his voice . . .

You mind if I ask you what you're doing here, ma'am?

The tall one. Not bad-looking either, she thought. For a jock. She smiled. Kevin Costner in *The Bodyguard,* but without the flair. Where did they *find* these people?

Finally, her slender body shuddered in a way that would have made any of the three security guards forget Socks (and perhaps all cats in general). If not that, then surely the long, cool sigh that trickled from her throat as her fingers unknotted and the valise slipped to the ground and she slumped against the wall. That would have done the job.

In a display of energy that surprised her, particularly considering her drained condition, the woman readied a high-heel-fitted foot to kick the brown leather bag. But then she thought better of it, or perhaps weariness overcame her again, and she melted toward the wall and relaxed.

"Bastard," she whispered. She glanced back down the hall the way she'd come as though the word were aimed at one of the guards she'd just spoken with, but then she leveled her gaze at the valise. That was the problem right there; that was the cause of her dilemma.

This fact would have become abundantly clear to even the most disinterested passerby as she squatted, most unladylike, beside her cargo, absently set the sheaf of papers in her hands to one side, twisted the triple-numbered lock recessed under the hard brown handle of the bag, and popped it open.

A new sound, mewling and feline and not so unlike the lady's gasps after all, trembled from inside the bag. When a furry paw slipped out and stroked at the woman's hand, a look of concern washed quickly across her eyes, though a hint of irritation and fatigue was still settled around her mouth. She opened her valise wider and deftly flicked hands inside to grasp Socks under his armpits and his butt—the only way to lift a full-grown cat safely. She rocked the cat until he rolled onto his back, looking just like a baby in her cradled arms.

Brushing at a few loose cat hairs on her blouse, the woman realized she had actually risked implicating herself by holding this glorious All-American animal. Usually she didn't worry about the hairs, but that was during playtime. Playtime with Socks was well-coordinated and meticulously planned. She did not like being interrupted.

Fortunately, she had actually brought in a "recipient" cat—something she did not usually do, relying instead on administering a mild mixture of concentrated testosterone and sedative and then manually extracting the semen for later use—and so she had her cat-bag with her.

It's a dirty job, she had once told a friend of hers, *but someone's got to do it.*

She smiled to herself as she thought of Socks making his own way to the room before she had even had the chance to go and get him. Thank God she had heard him scratching at the door when she did; otherwise he might have given the game away completely.

More thankfully still, those oafs had been noisy, grouching among themselves long enough outside the room for her to restrain Socks and administer a little shot of downer in his leg so he wouldn't give them away or ruin their rendezvous. Socks was perhaps less aware of the implications of this, but the woman was not. That little-used office was her breeding ground and, like any good mother, she intended to protect it.

Good mother. She smiled at the phrase. The last thing she had ever wanted was children. Who could think of bringing children into a world like this? She shook her head to the empty corridor. "Not me," she whispered, tickling Socks under his chin. He purred affectionately: this was, after all, his den mother. This was the woman who scored for him.

Sure, he purred. Who wouldn't?

Right now, however, he was licking his leg where she had jabbed him.

There had also been time to administer a larger dose of sedative to the other cat. A weakling-breed cat like that female would be out for hours, perhaps even until morning, as a result of such a dose.

She set Socks down and let him accept his own weight. After a slight push to get him moving, the cat balanced himself and trotted, albeit a little shakily, down the hallway in the direction in which the woman was recently heading—and, thankfully, away from the rendezvous room.

With a contented smile, the woman watched Socks as he visibly regained both his strength and his confidence. With a quick backward look that might have been his way of saying *Thanks, catch you later,* the cat bounded away from her. Maybe she didn't charge enough for those genes.

On the other hand, she hated to soil a cat like Socks with contact with the likes of the Persian Blue knocked out (but not yet *up,* unfortunately) in the bottom of the valise, but that cat would now mother a cleansed litter . . . with not a single moggy in sight.

She lifted the folder and checked the sleeping cat. It was out for the count.

There was enough imperfection in the world without adding to it. The work she was doing would make it just a *little* better. She closed her eyes and rolled her head back, savoring the way she had handled a potentially difficult situation. Maybe it was just one small step, she thought as she got to her feet and smoothed out her skirt. But then, every great journey started this way.

As the elevator doors opened she heard a loud crash from up along the corridor. She lifted the valise, stepped inside, and hit the down button quickly.

Minutes later she walked by the front desk and out into the watery winter sunshine.

It was Friday. The third Monday in February was now four days away.

Between now and then, Donald Penrose Daniels—his mother was one of the Concord Penroses—had a weekend to contend with, a weekend comprised of two luncheons, an informal brunch for one of Hillary Clinton's charity concerns, and a full-blown dinner for visiting dignitaries from some distant corner of the globe, the name of which ended in *-istan*: *Godonlyknowsistan,* maybe, or even *Whothehell-caresistan.* Daniels could not remember and could care even less. He had never been able to figure why America needed to get involved in these far-flung regimes, but then he didn't need to know. All he needed to know right now was what was happening with the room on the second floor.

Socks had been found a little after they had discovered the panel. That was yesterday afternoon.

The news had been announced by Izzy Mennix, who had intercepted the call to Daniels on his own intercom. "The aliens have returned the cat," is what he had said. At that point, Daniels had been jammed into a neatly cut hole behind an exotic-looking firescreen rummaging about amidst trays of bottles and what looked like specimen jars, each neatly labeled.

Carefully backing out of the hole, Daniels had dragged one of the trays with him, balancing it on one hand while he pushed himself backwards with the other, swaying side to side as he went. "You ever thought of becoming an exotic dancer?" Mennix had asked.

Daniels had grunted. "It could be an option . . . particularly Hawaiian," he had muttered, his voice sounding strangely distant and hollow. " 'Cos if anything happens to screw up the weekend's arrangements, my ass is grass."

Then he had emerged with his treasure.

That was yesterday.

Now the three men were sitting in Daniels's office with an array of bottles and jars covering the conference desk.

Israel Mennix was leafing through a printout containing the names of all personnel on the premises the previous day, each one accompanied by a computer-generated photograph. Qualitywise, the pictures were not exactly Ansel Adams, but they did at least contain sufficient detail to enable Mennix to satisfy himself that the woman they had encountered was not among them. It was the fourth time he had gone through the sheets.

Meanwhile, Daniels and George Bearson had produced a list of names—he assumed that was what the labels were—from the four trays of bottles and jars. They had got just about as far as they could get, and still none of it made any sense. Bearson lit a cigarette and scanned the list again.

"Okay, George, give me it so far." Daniels leaned back in his chair, kicked off his shoes, and plopped his feet on the window ledge.

Bearson sucked on the cigarette and blew out a thin plume of smoke that looked set to carry on for hours. "Okay, the story so far. We have thirty-seven bottles, phials, flasks, and specimen jars, some with contents, some without. The jars are numbered and labeled, the labels containing what appear to be names—probably animal names."

"Cats?"

Bearson shrugged. "Cats, dogs, pythons . . . who the hell knows? I mean—" He flicked down the list. "Bubbles? Nobody I know ever called their kid Bubbles, but—" He scanned the list some more. "Abigail, Gena . . . there are names here that could relate to humans."

"All female, though," Daniels observed.

Bearson nodded. "All female names, yes."

"And the contents?"

Mennix walked over to the water cooler, pulled a conical cardboard cup from the dispenser, and filled it. "Jism," he said. "Lots of it. Well, twenty-two containers, anyway. Good grade-A quality sperm."

"But not human?" Daniels said.

"We're waiting on the lab report," Mannix said, "but, no, we don't expect it to be human. If it is, then most of the male employees in this wing must be spending too much time in the john with girlie books."

"Or boy-ey books," Bearson muttered.

Daniels ignored the remark. "How long does it keep fresh? And how old is it anyway? Will they be able to tell us that?"

"They'll be able to tell us everything barring what the . . . what the donor was thinking about at the time."

"Probably sardines," said Bearson.

Daniels sighed. "George, why do I feel you're not taking this as seriously as I'd like? You working up to a one-week slot in Las Vegas or something? Or is it just your long-winded way of handing in your resignation?"

Izzy Mennix sniggered as Bearson's smile faded. "Sorry," they both said in unison.

Daniels picked up the telephone as soon as it rang and snapped into the mouthpiece. "Daniels. Sure. Go ahead." He sat up in his chair, reached for a pen and started scribbling. "Yes . . . okay . . . yes . . . only one? Geez! Yeah, yeah, I got it. Yes, thanks. Say hi to Carol for me. Sure. Talk to you later." He replaced the receiver on the cradle and looked at the other two men.

"What I want you to do, George, is run down that list of names again and see if any of them could be surnames."

"Surnames?"

Daniels frowned. "Like Bearson?"

Bearson nodded, cringing, and wrote himself a note.

"Some folks often give their pets their own surname," Daniels explained to a puzzled-looking Izzy Mennix. "Then check the directory and see how many of that name you can find. Then—"

"Make some calls? See if they have a cat?"

Daniels nodded. He turned to Mennix. "Izzy, can you find out if there's some kind of institution . . . like a cat protection league, something like that? There must be *something*, for crissakes. Then find out if they have any members whose animals' names tie up with our labels. Okay?"

"I'm on it." Mennix crushed his cup and tossed it into the waste.

"What did Ed say?" Bearson asked, nodding at the telephone.

"He said it *is* cat sperm . . . and get this, it all comes from just one animal."

George Bearson whistled. "That must be one tired papa cat."

"Picture it," Izzy said as he opened the door. "A regular feline sperm bank and only one donor."

"Yeah, but five'll get you ten he ain't complaining."

Some hours later, the three men reconvened in Daniels's office. All three looked tired and ready for the week to be over.

Unfortunately, with all the functions at the White House, as well as preparation for Presidents' Day on Monday, there was still a lot to be done. At least with this mystery they were up against something new. Far better, they all thought, than to have to battle another pigeon that had slipped inside and was making (at least in the minds of some of the staffers) a beeline for the Oval Office.

Daniels asked, "So what do we have?" His feet were propped up on the desk and his hands cradled his head.

George Bearson cleared his throat, obviously proud of something and wishing to draw attention to it. "I may have something."

"Shoot," Daniels said around a big smile. Bearson rarely *had* something, though Daniels would be the first to admit that, despite the man's size, his larger-than-life colleague was the one who always seemed to grab the pigeon.

"Well, none of the labels seem to relate to surnames." He paused for effect and frowned thoughtfully. "I did some thinking, though, and figured that the names might be coded with something other than the person's real name. That's when I remembered one of the night security men talking about his kid brother shacking up with a woman called Bubbles."

"Bubbles?"

Bearson shrugged. "I know, I know . . . maybe she has that kind of a personality. Who knows?"

"Could be a coincidence," Mennix suggested.

"Could be," Daniels agreed, "but maybe George is on to something. Either that or we think seriously about making this whole thing into an *X-File*."

"I am," Bearson said. "On to something, I mean. Because there's more."

"Oh, by all means," Mennix chuckled sarcastically. "Do tell."

Bearson glared at Mennix and then puffed himself up again. "I called John Hendrickson—the night guard—and he was in bed. But it was his brother that answered the phone. So—"

"So you asked the brother how we can reach Bubbles."

Bearson nodded. "It also happens that Bubbles owns a cat."

"I bet everyone named Bubbles has a cat," Mennix said, the sarcasm still plain.

This time Daniels too shot a withering glance at Mennix. "Maybe there's something in this, George. What else?"

"Nothing much. Turns out that Hendrickson's brother has already moved on from the Bubbles woman because—his words—she's a little flaky."

"Flaky?"

"Yeah. Seems she's a real weirdo when it comes to her cat. He wouldn't say anymore. That's it."

"We don't know *how* weird?"

"Uh-uh. Hendrickson wouldn't say."

"Okay. We know where we can reach this woman? Bubbles?"

"Sure." Bearson flicked the pages of his notebook. "She works over in the big photocopying store—Quickprint—it's on Third Street."

"I know that!" Mennix said. "It's across from the Jewish Museum."

Bearson nodded. "Her name is Bevins, Sandra Bevins."

Daniels frowned as he took in all that he had heard and then turned his attention to Israel Mennix. "Izzy?"

Mennix smiled coolly. "As Holmes said when Watson discovered him painting his porch yellow, 'Lemon entry, my dear Watson.' "

Bearson and Daniels laughed as Izzy Mennix continued.

"Turns out there are several cat groups. Everything from the Humane Society to some group in Harrowgate called—"

Daniels frowned. "Harrowgate? Where the hell's Harrowgate?"

"England. The group is called Ninth Life . . . they say they can tell you who your cat was in a former life if you spend three to five nights in their hotel while they do some tests on your animal. I didn't check any of the names with any of the groups, though there are a couple here in DC that could stand a little more investigation, I suppose."

"You didn't ask them if Bubbles was a member?" Bearson feigned shock.

"Like I said, wiseguy, they probably all have a Bubbles. Both cats and people."

Daniels nodded. "We could at least check these groups in DC for a Sandra Bevins, though, huh?"

"Yeah, yeah, sure," Mennix said. He glanced at his watch. "I better get right on it. Just give me ten minutes." He climbed to his feet and left for the phone in the next-door office.

When Mennix returned, he found Bearson asleep with his chin on his huge chest and Daniels flipping cards into an old top hat on the floor that he kept just for this purpose. It certainly wasn't a hat to be worn.

"You won't believe this."

"Try me," said Daniels as he flipped the queen of spades into the hat. When the card bounced back out, he looked up.

"Bevins is a member of a group called—" He paused to glance at a small slip of paper "—Cleaner Cats. At least I guess she is, since she's running for secretary this year. There was no one at the office—or no one answering, anyway—but the voice gave me a whole load of information . . . sound bites, not much more . . . and then numbers to press for more details." He shook his head. "You stay on the line long enough, I figure you could get the weather in Des Moines and Dr. Ruth's recipe for gefilte fish.

"Anyway, I punched some number, then the machine rolled me over some message listing everyone running for office." He shrugged, hands outstretched and palms up. "And *voilà* . . . Sandra 'Bubbles' Bevins, young hopeful of the year."

"Cleaner Cats?" Daniels asked.

Mennix shrugged some more. "Beats me. Maybe they all have get-togethers, wash their cats at the same time."

Bearson was waking up just then. "You figure maybe that's why they call her Bubbles?"

Daniels and Mennix both looked at him and shook their heads slowly. "Right," said Mennix.

Daniels stood up, stretched, and yawned, his suit more crease than cloth. "So let's pay her a visit."

"I already checked about that," said Mennix. "She left today. Around noon."

"Seems a bit suspicious, I guess," Daniels conceded.

Izzy Mennix waved his hand. "No, she's just gone for the weekend. She went north somewhere to ski. No one in the store knew exactly where."

Daniels shrugged his shoulders. "I guess we wait until Monday, then."

Bearson wondered out loud. "Isn't that a holiday, though? Presidents' Day? Maybe she's gone for three days."

"Not according to the guy I spoke with. The store is open as normal on Monday morning—seems they have a lot of copying work on—and Bevins will be in then."

"Gefilte fish . . . hmm," George Bearson said around another yawn. "Sounds good to me."

❁   ❁   ❁

Sandra Bevins was indeed back at Quickprint on Monday morning, though she acted as though she thought she should have had that day off, too.

The snow had been really good, she told them, adjusting the bridge of her spectacles every other word and occasionally chuckling . . . though at what, the three men had no idea. Aside from the lengthy weather report, Daniels, Mennix, and Bearson learned little from her other than the name and address of the current president of the organization and the fact that she, Bubbles, was running for secretary because "this group is really worthwhile, because without them my baby's kittens would be as sick as their mother is when they turn three."

None of them really knew what she meant, and she seemed just a little too far out there to expect much more from anyway. She insisted that if they wanted to know more they go and talk to the President. "Well, not *the* President" she corrected herself, chuckling, her left index finger spearing the bridge of her glasses with such vigor that George Bearson feared she was about to give herself an impromptu lobotomy. "I mean *our* President . . . Samantha Morris."

Izzy Mennix nodded on behalf of them all and smiled.

"Delightful lady," Bubbles Bevins added. "But then the British have such class about them. Do you know what I mean?"

Daniels gave a broad grin that widened in line with the woman's puzzled expression. "Indeed we do," he said, glancing down at the address on his notepad. "Indeed we do."

Pennsylvania Avenue is a bad place to be hungry and broke.

They drove slowly, checking the numbers, while George Bearson stared out of the window at the passing eateries . . . all of them exclusive, all of them expensive.

They were on the west side of Washington Circle, home to Marshall's West End, The Bristol Grill—where Bearson had once fallen so in love with a plate of mesquite-grilled chicken he'd ordered seconds while he was still a couple of forkfuls away from the end (the guy he was with swore up and down that George had actually had tears in his eyes)—Brasil Tropical, Donatello, and One Step Down, Daniels's favorite, but more because of the music, very accessible jazz ("Not this 'just blow and see what happens' shit," he delighted in telling people), than the food.

Samantha Morris's house was a sand-cleaned six-step walk-up complete with brass plaque—

CLEANER CATS
For Our Feline Future

—it read, and mahogany balustrades leading up to the door.

They parked the car and strolled up the steps. Pulling the old-fashioned bellpull, Izzy Mennix said, "If a tall guy with a pasty face and neck bolts answers, I'm outta here."

As the door opened, Daniels beamed a wide smile. "Ma'am, you have no idea how pleased I am to see you again," he said, flashing his I.D.

Samantha Morris's face drained white on the spot and she tried to slam the door. But George Bearson's right foot was in the way and the door bounced back into her arm. "I wonder . . . might we come inside, ma'am?" George asked softly. "We can talk better off the street."

As stories went, Samantha's was neither of the sob variety nor the inspirational kind. It was just a way to make money off gullible people who spent more time trying to cure the country's ills by responding to wacky newspaper advertisements than in actually getting up off their backsides and rolling up their sleeves.

The elitist mentality of Cleaner Cats was just one step away from Old Man Schicklgruber's kid's plan for a New Order for the Third Reich some sixty years earlier. No matter how the dainty and admittedly classily spoken Mizz Morris dressed up the facts, it all came down to the same thing in the end.

In addition to making a lot of money out of a lot of misguided people, Cleaner Cats aimed to restore purity of breed to the feline species. The advertisement in the organization's newsletter—the ad had also appeared in several local journals and papers up and down the country—said it all. In a hysterical display of hollow promises, veiled threats, prophesies of doom, split infinitives, and misplaced exclamation marks—the ailing syntax of the fanatical and the deranged—the copy offered "true blue" salvation (the true identity of the lone donor was not disclosed) for the feline members of the American race.

"It's kind of like the ads in the old comic books," George Bearson observed as he handed the copy back to a pleasingly red-faced Sandra Bevins. "Things like growing your own monkeys . . . and glasses that enabled you to see through clothing."

Mennix nodded. "No, those things never worked," he said sadly.

The singlehanded—though Bearson suggested another part of the anatomy might be more appropriate—effort of Socks, frequent visitor to the knee of our much venerated President and the First Lady, was considered by Cleaner Cats to be an inspired means of raising the standards of the cat population . . . though all of the men wondered how long Bevins had expected it to take.

But inspired it had been.

Samantha Morris went on to show the intrepid—if incredulous—trio documentary evidence and letters by the fileful, some articulate, some angry, some avowed . . . but all bigoted. They found the letter from Sandra Bevins, who wrote—passionately and at some considerable length—about saving the cat world from the inferior classes. John Hendickson's brother had clearly understated the case when he had accused the woman of being flaky.

One or two of the other correspondents appeared to have learned to write just the morning of the day on which they posted the letter. And for all of these, further lessons were clearly needed. Vitriol and stupidity, the ingredients of the most lethal cocktail of all, oozed from every page in almost equal measure.

The system went his way: a phial of Socks's sperm—treated with a special preservative to ensure sufficient longevity for it to be "utilized"—was sent to anyone writing in and enclosing two things: a check for $99.95 and a return address. Daniels had to admire—albeit reluctantly—the fact that Cleaner Cats could have sent just any old cat sperm but instead chose to do the honorable thing and supply only the real McCoy. Further proof, if any were needed, that there was nothing more dangerous than the fanatic.

They took the files with them—along with Samantha Morris—and Daniels called in for White House security staff to give the Cleaner Cats headquarters a complete going-over. He also asked for the Chief Security Officer—the guy in charge of organizing visitors' passes—to be at his office at 8:00 A.M. the next morning. Daniels expected one of the team would also have some connection to Cleaner Cats. He would know for sure when they had had the chance to go through the organization's files.

After dropping the woman off at police headquarters, the three men sat silently in Daniels's car as they returned to the White House.

"You know, just when it looks like we're moving forwards . . . something rotten always turns up," Izzy Mennix announced to nobody in particular as he leafed through one of the files. "It scares me that there are still people out there who can think like this."

George Bearson grunted his agreement.

"You know what scares me more?" Daniels asked.

Mennix shook his head.

Daniels nodded to the file. "All of those people get to vote."

The three returned just in time to help with final preparations for the President's Presidents' Day address.

Before long, Clinton was in full swing, his voice trying to make the words sound improvised but not quite making it. The speech was obviously—and hopelessly—read.

After some nonsense about how he shared many characteristics with Washington (who was president before political parties even existed) and Lincoln (who was a Republican), Clinton was on to the heart of the matter: Bosnia.

"You all know about it," the President concluded, "the rapes of the women, the murders of the children, all these things you have read about. We've got to try to contain it. I can tell you folks: we're not going to make peace over there in a way that's fair to the minorities that are being abused unless we get involved. If the United States now takes a leadership role, there's a real chance we can stop some of the killing, stop the ethnic cleansing."

Daniels and Mennix and Bearson all added to the applause.

As the President hurried out the back of the press room, the three men regrouped and shuffled back to Daniels's office.

"Can we call it a day?" Bearson wondered.

Mennix looked hopefully at Daniels.

"Probably," he said. "Just hang around long enough for me to finish the report on this last case. You'll both need to sign it, and I want to get it out of the way."

Bearson and Mennix nodded and wandered away when Daniels turned to enter his office.

It didn't take long.

Deepy Daniels slipped his summary report into a folder for the case he'd codenamed *Little Serbia*.

He was about to call it a day when he received the call.

One minute later he had buzzed his colleagues. "Come on, guys," he shouted into the intercom on his desk. "Another pigeon is terrorizing the White House. It's time for all good men and true to come to the aid of the party."

"Tell Socks," quipped Mennix. "Shouldn't this be *his* job?"

The Old Man Who Saw Newgrange

J. N. Williamson

On the afternoon before St. Patrick's Day it was only natural for Mara McShaney—sole proprietor of the bar called Derry's—to count her blessings. St. Pat's had been a very special holiday for her, Derry's, and Mara's husband Mike as recently as last March 17 when droll and sweet-tempered Mike had still been tending bar.

Now redhaired and thirty-six-year-old Mara sighed as she counted her blessings and got as high as two: her bar and the one other meaningfully connecting link she had to the days that were good and golden, her striped cat Aloysius. Sad-faced Aloysius, her fellow helpless spectator at the fatal shooting of Mike when Derry's was held up—watchful Alley, as Mara occasionally called the animal (who hated it), her beloved companion who sometimes scanned the faces of patrons as if searching for Michael Kelly McShaney. Poor Mikey, doomed to be thirty-eight years old forever.

Maybe the blessings list stood at three if Mara wished to add Timmy Corbett, the big-shouldered, soft-spoken bartender she'd hired and found a reliable employee and loyal chum in the year since Mikey had . . . departed. On occasion Mara even imagined Corbett, whose hair was a curlier and more carroty version of her own, had a yen to be more than an employee and chum. But he was a romantic fellow in the old-fashioned, idealistic way, a constant book reader who believed everything he read, and she was *years* older—at least two.

Best to keep things on the business plane, Mara told herself, dropping Aloysius behind the little gate through which she and Timmy

Corbett entered and exited the bar area. Of course, there were regulations against having a pet on the premises, and of course, Alley could clear the gate whenever he felt like it. But Mike McShaney had been a widely liked cop before buying Derry's, no one had ever registered an objection, and Aloysius had never felt like jumping the gate. Instead, he preferred to keep close to Mara—and Timmy Corbett, whom he tolerated—and to make sure there would never be a mouse or crawling insect with wanderlust that showed itself to a customer.

And to pop his beautiful little head above the bar gate from time to time in his apparent quest for another glimpse of Mike.

Mara had arrived early and she managed to complete most of the set-up work before Corbett or the waitresses, Tia and Shawna, came in for the evening shift. It was the eve of St. Patrick's Day and, while it was not a large tavern, some of the regulars liked getting a bit of a head start on the holiday. Business was brisk on March 16 and tomorrow, as always, would justify Derry's opening earlier, at eleven a.m. After greeting Timmy Corbett, Mara found herself staring at his broad back, reminded of poor Mike and what he had believed about St. Pat's: "Things may get boisterous, but basically everybody's in fine spirits so things don't get out of hand."

But they had, when a man at the cash register produced a gun, and suddenly Mike McShaney was basically dead. Dead and unavenged, for the authorities had never even turned up a suspect. Mara shuddered and went back behind the bar with Alley and Timmy Corbett, who was resplendent in green shirt, green tie, and green pants.

"I should have worn more green than a blouse and shamrock," she said.

"Nonsense," Corbett said with a snort, glancing up fleetingly from an order he was filling. "You wear those emerald eyes of yours three hundred and sixty-five days a year, Mara. Now how does a person get more Irish than that?"

Mara laughed. One hand pushed back a straying lock of red hair, but she was aware only that her bartender was as charming as ever and that a difficult night and busier next day were off to a relaxed beginning.

In fact, the evening stayed like that—customers steady but amiable—until eight-thirty or so. She'd taken time to show her pet some attention and was seated on a chair scratching Aloysius's ears when his body tensed and his head came up, his fascinating eyes clearly on alert. A familiar but seldom-heard rumbling sound rolled around inside, but of most concern to Mara, he made no effort to reach his vantage point for an inspection of what was alarming him.

Mara stood and turned, peered out from a location a couple of yards down the long bar from where Timmy Corbett was filling pitchers with green beer. She was trying to take in the tavern's newer arrivals.

Almost no time was needed to discover the source of Aloysius's agitation.

First was the man, settling himself down onto a bar stool midway between Corbett and her. Although Alley had not seen him, anyone doing so would find herself or himself looking back at him, because he was a study in contradictions. Towering several unguessable inches above six feet, he also appeared to be nearly four feet wide and none of it resembled fat. He was the fortunate man who could carry upwards of three hundred pounds and be that much more masculine of demeanor for it. His legs were smokestacks, his torso, thanks to a black leather pea coat, a great belch of dark and suffocating smoke. The rest of the contradiction was that his enormous head was encased in a bristling white mane and beard; in short, the customer was very old, perhaps in his eighties.

The primary cause of Aloysius's anxiety, however, was certainly the big cat clambering onto the lap of the master he resembled. Mara gaped almost open-mouthed at the feline. Nearly the size of a bobcat, it had a dark brown, muscular body with legs that rippled with power—and its huge head and stilettolike whiskers were the color of newly fallen snow. Mara, who adored all cats, wasn't ready to make an exception, but she would have hesitated to stroke this beast's pate.

Behind her, a scrambling noise startled Mara into a swift glance. All she saw of Aloysius was the tip of his striped tail, which he hadn't yet managed to tuck in with him beneath her desk. What he was doing astonished her; she felt twinges of dismay and angry shame as well. Alley was her co-spectator at a murder, he was her dearest friend and a source of confidence during the life without Mike, even—however unreasonable (and human) it was—a provider of courage to go on. She would have demanded that he come out from under the table except that Derry's newest customer was calling to her.

"Irish whiskey, Madame, if you please." The bearded old man eyed her appraisingly from beneath white brows bushier than all the hair on the heads of most men his age. "If it's genuine, you may leave the bottle."

"Sir," Mara said immediately, "local ordinances forbid us to serve patrons with pets." She had to take a breath, surprising herself by a rise of apprehension. "If you'll put your cat in your automobile for your visit at Derry's, we'll be happy to welcome you."

Only one eye was in view as a brow descended, creating a ferocious squint. "I might be in error," he said, rumbling deeper than Aloysius had been able to produce, "but I daresay you were patting your *own* cat as Brownie and I approached, before the poor creature"—he pronounced the word *crayture*—"bolted in fright." He massaged Brownie's Alp-like dome with an immense palm. "Madame, I assure you that neither of us means you, your pet, or your establishment the slightest harm." The two tiny eyes widened, twinkled. "Surely two citizens of the Emerald Isles shall not be turned away on the eve of St. Patrick's because each of us is . . . large?"

Mara rumpled her long red hair with a hand, indignant on behalf of Aloysius but also wondering how the ancient giant had seen her stroking the cat's ears. Then she realized the answer lay in the very word *giant.* That he had merely been tall enough to notice them on the other side of the bar. "Timmy Corbett," she called, falling into an Irish idiom that was quite natural to her, "will ye be kindly servin' this gentleman our best Irish whiskey?" But she also gave him a wink, their signal to track a customer's behavior closely while he was at Derry's.

When the old fellow had his bottle and a glass, he seemed content enough, and Mara decided the only problem was her cat's. Aloysius had simply never seen one of his own kind three times his own size. *Except,* she thought while refilling several table bowls with a variety of free snacks, *he never* saw *that cat, Brownie. Did he actually* sense *its size—or was it the old man who frightened him when he peeked at us?*

All seemed well, then, except that the bearded old man hummed incessantly as if listening to some irresistible music no one else could hear. Eventually Mara realized that his enormous cat Brownie raised his snowy head and cocked it at certain points in the humming serenade, listening attentively and purring a feline reply. The appearance of elderly man and trusted pet sharing a strange conversation made Mara smile.

But she wondered about the charm of the peculiar duet when, not long before closing, Timmy Corbett and the old giant raised their voices in what certainly wasn't song.

"What do you mean, sir," the latter demanded, "I can have nothing more to drink?" His bass voice ascended in volume. "Have I not paid the establishment with the proper coin of the realm and in the correct amount? Is a man to go thirsty?"

Corbett's carroty hair color seemed to wash into his face. Mara knew he had yet to encounter a visitor to Derry's whom he couldn't hush or hustle out, if necessary; but this customer was old enough to be Timmy Corbett's grand-da. Worse, she thought with a pang, the big old man might be too much even for her bartender to handle. "What I mean is that you've exceeded your limit, Pop. If you're thirsty, we can give you all the water or coffee you want, maybe even a glass of milk!"

An expression of scorn and insult at the reference to water became one of benign hope at the end of Corbett's sentence. "Why, milk would be fine," he said with raised brows, pronouncing the word *foine*—"*if* you have it." He read Corbett's own expression and added, beaming at the younger man, "Especially if you won't put a limit on the blessed stuff!"

Mara spoke up with a grin. "What kind of woman would I be, as Aloysius's step-ma if I didn't keep milk on the premises?" A tilt of her head sent Timmy Corbett back to the walk-in refrigerator.

"I could not answer that, Madame," the customer murmured, rising slightly from his bar stool to acknowledge his gratitude. "But you *do* have the blessed stuff, and that makes you a considerate as well as lovely hostess in my book!"

The minutes slipped away, and at closing time, their interesting customer also departed. Mara and Corbett found generous tips for them on the bar. "He and his cat are eccentric," she said, pleased too by what the place had taken in the night before St. Patrick's Day, "but he seems to be a good-hearted enough soul."

"I wouldn't be too sure," Timmy Corbett said as he tugged on his full-length coat. It was still March and no sign of spring had presented itself. "To tell the truth, Mara, I'm suspicious about that one."

"Why, for goodness' sakes?"

He clapped a cap on his head, set his jaw firmly. "I could never trust a man whose belly lets him switch from Irish whiskey to milk," he retorted, shuddering. He took three paces towards the front door, hesitated. "And there's more. I'm going to check something out in a book I read. When I come in for work tomorrow, it bein' St. Pat's and all, I mean to be prepared—just in case that old boy and his cat come back!" And he was out the door, a whisper of winter slipping inside before he had closed it.

All the while Mara was busy locking up the day's receipts, collecting Aloysius, going upstairs to the flat over the bar and changing into a nightgown for bed, she felt somewhat uneasy about what her well-meaning bartender had told her. Except, of course, he hadn't pinpointed anything whatever that was sinister about a man eighty years of age or older. Her late husband Mikey had also been known to have his hunches, but he was a policeman. Timmy Corbett, just as eager to defend her and Derry's, was merely superstitious. This time he'd gone too far about an old gent with the good sense to switch from booze to milk instead of making a quarrel.

Mara sat in the kitchen with humiliated Alley, deriving comfort from her little friend as usual, smiling as she coaxed the cat onto her lap. She tried to imagine John Walsh or Robert Stack on TV, grim-faced as they showed photos of a white-bearded ancient, law enforcement's quarry from coast to coast. "I think we've seen the last of him and his monster tabby, baby," she told Aloysius to cheer him up. "There are plenty of bars where he can go on downing 'em till he's too polluted to attend mass!"

Tired from so much time on her feet, she slept like a child except for a few baffling dreams she didn't remember when she awakened. She roused herself on St. Pat's and made it downstairs to the bar by eleven.

Depositing a similarly sleepy Aloysius over the entry gate, she read

for the umpteenth time the plaque Mike had mounted above the bar
the day before they opened Derry's under their ownership:

> St. Francis and St. Benedict,
> Bless this house from wicked wight,
> From the nightmare and the Goblin
> That is hight Good Fellow Robin.
> Keep it from all evil spiretes,
> Fairies, Wezles, Bats and Ferrytes,
> From Curfew Time to the next Prime.
> —William Cartwright

Mara didn't know who Cartwright was—neither had she or Mike
known what most of the creatures whose presence was not desired
happened to be—but the prayer had worked just fine for them—

Every Prime to Curfew except for the one when she had been
widowed, a year ago. Surely it was a suitable plaque to have posted
on a day that honored a man who drove the serpents from Ireland
and killed Pishta-More, the Monster of the Lake.

Then, after a wonderful lunch hour and early afternoon, Mara was
filling orders for the barmaids Bernadette and Erin when, sensing
something, she glanced up from behind the bar and saw the enormous old man from last night making a path toward her. *And Timmy
Corbett isn't due in for almost an hour,* she thought automatically.
He found a stool a yard or so away from her with a table of two loud-
talking younger men at his back.

Mara turned her head to catch a glimpse of Aloysius. Although it
was obvious the cat's demeanor was changed—he no longer looked
drowsy but on full alert—he held his ground and didn't try to run and
hide.

That was when the redhaired human recognized what Aloysius had
realized without his having craned his neck to see the bar room: The
old fellow's immense cat wasn't with him today.

"Where's Brownie?" she inquired after taking his order for Irish
whiskey. "I hope I didn't really chase him away—and I had no business suggesting you leave the poor guy in your car."

"I understood perfectly," the white-bearded man fairly purred. His
broad face reflected his concern. "But as for Brownie, I have no idea

where he's gone. When I arose this morning he had simply . . . left." He brightened. "Knowing Brownie, I'm confident he shall return." His brows rose as he looked past Mara. "Hello, what have we here?"

Aloysius's sleek, striped head was visible above the gate as he stood on tiptoe to peer at the powerfully built old man, then at Mara and, deeply curious, back to the customer.

"He almost never shows any real interest in anyone but our bartender and me," Mara marveled. Further surprising her, Aloysius lightly vaulted the entry gate into her lap. He nuzzled his head against her but kept his gaze on the old man.

Chuckling, the latter made coaxing noises in his throat and with his lips. To Mara's astonishment, Alley listened for a moment, then jumped over to the aged customer's lap! "I'm sorry, sir," Mara said. "Get back here, Aloysius!" She put out her arms to retrieve her pet.

But a massive arm circled Aloysius, almost tenderly. "If you wouldn't object, Madame," he said, "it would ease my anxiety about Brownie to hold your darlin' friend awhile." He tilted his huge head, began to hum as he had to his cat. "Don't fret, I shall not let him venture into the rest of your establishment."

Mara shook back her lovely red hair in a motion of smiling acquiescence and went back to preparing drinks for the growing number of other customers. *So much for Timmy Corbett's old country superstitions,* she thought. *This old man is a pussycat!*

Then Corbett himself arrived for his shift twenty minutes later and his gaze was on Mara all the way from the front door through the room to the bar. She noticed it but ignored him until he was standing beside her, glancing disapprovingly at the sight of Aloysius in the company of the big, snowy-haired man with his Irish whiskey.

"I copied something out of that book I mentioned," he told Mara under his breath. "For you." He slipped a note to her along the bar, wouldn't release it until her hand was covering it. "What I thought about ol' Santa Claus's father there—well, don't get too close to him. Maybe he'll just leave after a bit."

"I'm too busy to read this right now, Timmy Corbett," Mara said, "and so are you! Besides, I think he's a nice gentleman who loves cats and milk, so—"

But the carrot-topped bartender had promptly headed for his end of the bar after hearing her admonition. She carried the page with the quote he had copied out by the microwave oven and, trying to put both her friend and the aged customer from her mind, resumed her own duties.

Two youngish men at the table to the white beard's back sounded as if they were at the stage in their drinking when they were trying to show off their knowledge of obscure facts. Mara attempted to tune them out, but they were both speaking too loudly for that. One said, "A skunkworks is not a think tank. It's a place to develop things to blueprint, build, and put to work—fast."

"I know *that,* Ned," said the other. "A fellow named Kelly Johnson created 'em, and made the first American fighter plane to top five hundred miles per hour in forty days."

"Well," said the first man, "did you know the University of Chicago took the same chemical compounds that light up fireflies and some fish and made a terrific explosion?"

"Everyone knows that, Ned." A sloshing sound as if draft beer filling glasses drifted to Mara. "It's little-known facts we're supposed to be discussin'."

"Such as, Will?" Ned demanded, taking a noisy slurp. It sounded challenging.

"Cold viruses stay alive in introverts' noses longer than extroverts'. Like that one?" Will chortled. "How about the safest hours to sleep? Midnight to six a.m., that's when! And most folks die when it's time to get up. *Now* who buys the next round, Neddie?"

Mara was startled when Aloysius was suddenly deposited in her arms with a hurried but gracious *"Thank* you, Madame." She whirled around in time to see her immense customer hauling up a chair at the young loudmouths' table. "Let me in on the bet, boys, and I'll tell you a really *impressin'* Irish tale in keeping with the day!"

Ned and Will clearly couldn't think of a way to leave him out, and despite herself, Mara leaned her elbows on the bar, shamelessly eavesdropping.

"Ye ever hear tell of a marvel thirty miles from Dublin called Newgrange?" asked the oldster. It was obvious they hadn't. "It's a tomb built a thousand years before Stonehenge was completed, maybe that long before the Egyptian pyramids." He crouched forward conspiratorially but without lowering his voice. "Yet—Newgrange is more then a tomb, lads." He caught a suspenseful breath. "It's also a cathedral to the life force of the sun!"

"Mara, you read the stuff I gave you yet?" Corbett asked. She shushed him with a wave.

"Imagine a mound of earth two hundred and sixty feet in diameter, more than thirty feet above the ground." The old man's eyes grew big beneath his bushy white brows. "Imagine a wall of shining white quartz, an entrance marked by stones weighing upwards of twelve tons. You walk inside the passageway toward a cruciform chamber. And at the end, you find a vertical openin'. Then, *through* it, you see . . ."

The increasingly curious younger men saw their uninvited guest pause to slug down more Irish whiskey. "Yes, yes?" Ned cued him, bent forward from the waist.

"You see—sunlight," said the aged one. "But *only* for a week or so, before the winter solstice and about a week after! In fact, a chap named Tom Ray from the Dublin Institute for Advanced Studies proved the sunlight would have been *perfectly* aligned with a midwinter sunrise . . . *five thousand one hundred and fifty years ago!*" He sat straight, beaming. "Now, boys, was that great tomb built to celebrate Christmas before Christ was born, in the hope of reawakenin' the dead, or to provide them with light to see where they were goin' as the Irish of old went on their way to the afterlife? Or why *did* a people more than five thousand years ago work so long and so hard to arrange for the *only* light in Newgrange tomb to fall upon the dead—once each year, perhaps for eternity?"

"You win the round," Will assured him, "but what's the answer? And how can you be so sure that light gets through the way you say it does?"

The bearded ancient smiled. "I know it does, for I have been there, lads," he murmured. "My home *is* Ireland. As for the answer to your question, the only ones who know it may be our eldest ancestors." He pushed back his chair. "Save your money—just pay for my round by keepin' it a mite less noisy. This bar is run by a lady." He began ambling back to the bar, bottle and glass in hand.

"Your story was great," young Ned called to him, "but we were swapping facts, not guesses. Where's the reality to that Newgrange place?"

The white-bedecked giant paused as he sat on his stool, but just briefly. "I gave you boys the reality of an ancient mystery, a chance to solve a puzzle no one else has solved. The longer I live, the more I prefer mystery to facts any day of the year—especially St. Patrick's Day!"

Mara, hearing the entire conversation, was utterly fascinated with the old fellow's story and his gallant way of persuading the other customers to hold it down—for *her!* She thought for an instant of going to read Timmy Corbett's presumably sinister quotation in the note he'd given her, just to enjoy a laugh! But she realized she shouldn't tease him just now when his feelings were doubtlessly hurt by the way she'd told him to hush.

The evening dwindled slowly but steadily, people came and left— or stayed put, a testimony to her late husband's plan for Derry's and to her employees, she felt—and what had happened to Mike a year ago slipped into the recesses of her mind.

But surprises were still coming. A man bundled up enough for the far colder nights of six weeks ago entered the front door and, in his wake, the enormous cat belonging to her oldest customer was trotting in the direction of the bar. Brownie had returned to his kind-hearted master and Mara was delighted to see the cat leap straight into the old fellow's lap. The latter hugged him and immediately there was an exchange of humming and strange feline sounds, almost as if Brownie was being asked to explain his whereabouts! *In an odd way, though,* Mara reflected, *it nearly sounds like music.*

While Timmy Corbett was greeting the newest customer, she turned to soothe Aloysius, thinking he'd be just as upset—and per-haps hiding—as he had been yesterday. Instead, Alley had propped himself up on the entry gate and appeared to be engrossed in the activities of Timmy Corbett and his bundled-up patron as well as Brownie and the old man. The four of them, standing or seated, were grouped within a few feet of one another, and Aloysius's attentive striped head was shifting minutely from left to right and left again.

"You can go to hell," Corbett said loudly, and Mara saw the veins in his muscular neck standing out. Why did his words sound so famil-iar? "It's not going to happen!"

Startled by the bartender's resistance, the stranger put his hand into a pocket of his heavy coat. In the process, his coat collar flipped down and Mara gasped. This man, as tall and well-built as Timmy Corbett, was no stranger.

"What are you doin' with my cat?" the old man asked incongruously, pawing in a motion that seemed drunken at the younger customer's arm. "Did you kidnap him?"

Mara saw a handgun the angry man reached for halfway out of his pocket, as if showing Timmy Corbett he was armed, and in her mind she heard Mikey say once more, *"Go to hell! You're not stealin' our hard-won profits!"* This was the *same* hold-up man, the one in all her nightmares; but now he was telling the bearded giant, "Leave me alone, you old lush! That's *my* cat!"

Shaking, wanting nothing to happen either to her friend Timmy or to the aged customer, Mara walked toward them. A year before, she had simply frozen. Now she saw the uncharacteristically angry expression on the old man's face as he crooned to Brownie, saw Timmy Corbett pull from under the bar the shillelagh he kept for just such emergencies, and saw her husband's murderer free his weapon from the coat pocket and begin to aim it at Corbett.

Aloysius cleared the gate, flashing past Mara at a speed he'd never achieved before. He was scurrying toward the killer of his master, Mike, at precisely the instant the heavier cat, Brownie, hurled himself—claws raised—at the gunman's wrist. His yowl of pain might have awakened the dead when Aloysius clawed at his face.

The handgun was jarred loose and skimmed along the surface of the bar directly into Mara's hand. Snatching it up, she heard the sickening sound of something very solid against human flesh and bone.

Unharmed but in the pose of a baseball slugger completing his swing, Timmy Corbett seemed for a moment to have connected with nothing whatever, for nothing and no one was standing before him.

Then Mara saw the hold-up man and murderer sprawled on the other side of the bar, clearly unconscious.

She scooped up her valorous friend Aloysius, handed Timmy Corbett the gun, and said she would go call the police.

But when she was sitting at her small desk in the privacy of the area well behind the bar, she said a brief prayer of thanks first and then promised Aloysius enough treats to make him as big as Brownie. "Does that old man really *talk* with ol' Brownie, and did Brownie tell you what the two of you were going to do? And how did your new friend just happen to return at the same time as that terrible man? Or did he and the old man sense last night who he was and get him in here so we could catch him for Mike?"

Aloysius, peering at her with his head charmingly cocked, said something that sounded considerably like a purr of contentment—and pride.

Mara placed the call to the police from her desk, being assured of prompt assistance when she mentioned the name Mike McShaney. Hanging up, she started to go back to the bar to help Timmy with their prisoner, then she saw the sheet of paper he had given her at the start of the St. Patrick's Day shift.

Unfolding it, Mara read the quotation from a book of Irish mythology:

> The nobility of both the Irish and Scottish fairies, the *Sidhe* is the largest, the oldest, and the most powerful of all fairies. They prefer their pets—sometimes Brownies in animal form—and making music to dwelling in palatial mansions. All they consume is milk and Irish whiskey.

Mara paused with her mouth open and new respect for her friend Timmy's imagination filling her heart.

> The *Sidhe* feels obliged to avenge any insult, and a single touch of one—if he wishes—can drive a mortal man mad or cause severe illnesses or wounds. On the other hand, his touch can create courage and unity.

Mara jumped up from the desk, hurried back to the bar.

Everything was the way she had left it—the hold-up man who had once more tried to kill in order to steal their money remained unconscious—except that many customers had already departed, obviously not eager for a chat with the authorities.

The frost-bearded giant of an Irishman—whose name they had not even known—had also left, along with his huge and helpful cat.

"No, I didn't even see 'em go," Timmy offered, reading Mara's expression. "But he left us each another tip."

Mara found hers—it was twice as much as the day before and a shamrock lay atop it—and also found tears in her eyes. "I should have listened to you, Timmy Corbett," she said, and went to give him a hug.

"Funny," he answered, keeping the gun trained on the unconscious killer, "I was about to say the same thing to you. Remember? 'I think he's a nice gentleman who loves cats and milk'—that's what you said. Maybe his mystery is like *that*," Timmy admitted, pointing.

Two glasses were set on the bar before the oldster's bar stool, Mara saw, one with a few drops of amber liquid in the bottom, the other glass stained as white inside as their aged customer's hair and beard.

"You're a deep one, Timmy Corbett," Mara said, her arms around his waist. "I think it will take quite a while to figure out your mystery, too"—she laughed merrily—"but maybe it's time I started tryin' to do just that!"

The Easter Cat

Bill Crider

Let me give you a little piece of advice: Never stop to help the Easter Bunny change a flat tire. I would never have done it myself except that it was obvious that he was totally incompetent and no one else was even giving him a second glance. Besides, I thought I recognized him.

So I drove on by and coasted to a stop by the curb about half a block in front of the Bunny's pre-war Chevy. It was the same model as mine, in fact, a 1940 model, but mine was in better shape. The Bunny obviously wasn't a very good driver.

I got out of my car, stretched, and took a deep breath. It was a beautiful California day, all blue skies and sunshine, low humidity, and the smell of oranges drifting in from one of the groves that still remained nearby. If I'd had any sense at all, I would have kept right on driving. But then no one ever accused me of having any sense at all.

I walked back to the Bunny's Chevy. The passing cars ignored both of us. We were out near the studios, and you don't have to live in Hollywood for very long to get used to some pretty strange sights out there. Or anywhere else, for that matter.

The Bunny was trying to loosen a lug nut. He was down on his knees, straining so hard that his long pink ears were quivering. As I watched him strain, his hands slipped off the lug wrench. He keeled over on his side and hit the pavement.

"Goddammit," he said, which I thought was pretty strong language for the Easter Bunny, and I told him so.

"Yeah? And who the hell asked you?" He didn't bother to get up.

He just lay there on his side with his puffy white tail sticking out toward the traffic.

"Nobody asked me. Nobody asked me to stop and help a bunny in distress, either."

He sat up then, and turned to look at me through eyes narrowed against the sunlight. He was who I'd thought he was, all right, Ernie Wiggins, dressed out in a bunny suit. Rabbits' noses were supposed to be pink, I think, but his was a bright shiny red.

"Ferrel?" he said. He put a hand up to shade his eyes. His eyes were a little red, too. "Bill Ferrel, private dick?"

"It's me, all right," I said. "And better a dick than a bunny rabbit. You got a part in something?"

It was a natural question. Ernie Wiggins was a has-been comic who'd started out with a couple of bits in Leon Errol shorts and then done one with the Three Stooges. Someone at Gober Studios spotted him in that one and gave him a try as the comic sidekick in a Rick Torrance jungle epic, *Johnson of Java,* I think, but it might have been *Benson of Borneo.* I can never remember which one came first.

Torrance and Wiggins hit it off, and Ernie had been funny enough to get a couple of good mentions in the trades. Not only that, but the box-office take was a little better than Torrance's last picture. So naturally they put Ernie in another movie with Torrance, *Johnson* or *Benson,* whichever, and it looked like Ernie was on his way.

He was on his way, all right—on his way out. As it happened he was a lush. Now that's no big thing in Hollywood, of course. If they fired all the lushes tomorrow, every studio in town would close down. But Ernie was the wrong kind of lush. He started showing up drunk on the set, forgetting his lines, and missing his marks. Even that might not have been so bad on some pictures, but Rick Torrance's directors weren't exactly top of the line. They preferred the methods of William "One Shot" Beaudine. So after one more picture, *Andrews of the Amazon,* Ernie was out on the streets.

And not only that. Now he was dressed like the Easter Bunny.

Ernie stood up, none too steadily, and brushed haphazardly at the knees of his bunny suit. He didn't say anything about having a part. What he said was, "Can y' gimme a hand wi' th' tire?"

Even the exhaust fumes from the passing cars couldn't disguise the fact that he'd been sipping on the Old Overholt, or whatever he favored. Did I say sipping? He'd probably slugged down a fifth of the stuff by now, and it was only a little after noon. He'd never get the tire changed by himself.

So fool that I was, I said, "Sure."

I took off my hat and jacket and laid them on the hood of Wiggins's Chevy. Then I picked up the lug wrench and got to work. Ernie stared vacantly off into space and leaned his back against the car as if he needed a brace to help him stand up. While I worked at getting the wheel off, he slid slowly down the side of the car, an inch at a time.

I got the wheel off, put on the spare that Ernie had left lying in the street behind his car, and tossed the flat into the trunk. By that time Ernie had slid all the way down the side of the car. He was sitting in the street, his back to the Chevy, snoring heavily.

I jacked down the car, tightened the lug nuts, and threw the wrench and jack into the trunk with the flat tire. I slammed down the trunk lid as hard as I could, hoping the noise would wake Ernie up. It didn't.

I wiped my hands off on my handkerchief, then put on my hat and jacket and looked down at Ernie, who was still snoring. He'd drawn a bunch of little black lines straight out from the sides of his nose. Whiskers, I guess.

I kicked one of his feet. Gently. I'm not some tough peeper like Bogart in *The Maltese Falcon.* "Wake up, Ernie," I said.

He opened one eye. "Ri'. Wakey, shakey. Gotta job."

If he had a job, it wasn't at Gober Studios. I'm on retainer to Gober, the big cheese himself, and I know the casts of every picture on the lot, which is how I got to know Ernie in the first place. Wayward starlets, oversexed leading men, pregnant ingenues—I'm the one who tries to keep them out of trouble and, when that fails, to keep their names out of the papers.

In fact, I was on my way to do a little job for the studio at the moment, or I was supposed to be. I didn't think Mr. Gober would appreciate my helping out the Easter Bunny.

"Where are you working?" I asked Ernie.

"Rick's place. Kid's party. All I can ge' 'ese days."

He shut his eye and began snoring again. I hunkered down beside him and slapped him on both cheeks, gently. That didn't work, so I shook him. Gently, of course.

"Stop," he said. "Stopstopstopstop."

"Not until you wake up."

"Can't wa' up."

He slumped forward into my arms, and I shoved him back against the car. He opened one eye again. "Gotta ge' to Rick's. Gotta be bunny a' party."

I couldn't just leave him there, so I dragged him around to the passenger side of the car and held his head up by the ears to keep it off the street while I opened the door. Then I tried to get him inside. It was like working with a very heavy dummy filled with flour dough, but I finally managed it. Of course his feet were in the seat and his upper body was on the floor, but at least he was in the car. His head was practically up under the dash.

I shut the door and looked down the street at my own car. It would be all right where it was for a while. I could drive Ernie to Rick's house. Maybe he would sober up on the way.

Sure he would.

And maybe MGM would call me to replace Robert Taylor in some big-budget foreign intrigue film because I was so much better-looking than he was. My nose has been broken twice, I'm going bald on top, I'm a little overweight, and my eyes are too close together. You figure the odds.

I sighed, walked around to the driver's side of the Chevy, and slid in. As it happened, the little job I was supposed to do was at Rick Torrance's house. It seemed that there was some kind of dispute going on, and Mr. Gober wanted me to settle it. He hadn't said what it was, which is why I wasn't in much of a hurry. It apparently wasn't an emergency, and I didn't like settling arguments. That wasn't my idea of what my job was all about.

But I was going to do it. That's what I got paid for.

Rick Torrance lived not far off Sunset in Beverly Hills. I'd been to his place once before, when some starlet had nearly drowned in his pool, where she'd fallen after being goosed by a chimpanzee that had wandered in from Rick's private jungle.

The house was a big, three-story stucco job, painted pink and set back from the street behind a pink stucco wall on a couple of acres of ground, only a little of which was given over to a well-manicured lawn and a drive lined with bougainvillea bushes. The rest was covered with the jungle: three or four kinds of palm trees, banana trees, creeping vines, climbing vines, and a few varieties of exotic flowers.

God knows what the water bill was, but it didn't matter to Rick. The studio paid it. The jungle was good publicity, giving the place the semblance of the kind of terrain Rick Torrance was supposed to prefer.

Anyone familiar with Rick knew that he actually preferred the terrain of a nice shady bar to a jungle anytime, but most of the ticket-buying public didn't know Rick at all. Instead they read about his private jungle in the fan magazines and had fantasies about his running around among the palm trees with his shirt off. Most of his pictures didn't require big wardrobe. He never wore a shirt if he didn't have to, and I didn't blame him. If I had pecs like his, I'd go shirtless, too.

I stopped Ernie's Chevy at the gate in the pink wall. The gate-keeper, an old geezer with bifocals and white hair growing out of his ears, recognized me from the last time I'd been there. He was willing to let me inside, but he wanted to know who was on the floor.

"The Easter Bunny," I said.

The geezer wasn't surprised. "Oh, yeah, him. He's late. Mr. Torrance and Mr. Gober are having a fit."

"He's a little under the weather," I said. "You say that Mr. Gober's here?" I hadn't realized that Gober was calling from Rick's place.

"In the flesh," the gatekeeper said. "He's the kid's godfather or something. He's fit to be tied because the bunny hasn't showed up. If I was you, I'd do something about your buddy there and get him ready. Mr. Torrance and Mr. Gober, they don't want the kid to be disappointed."

I didn't want the kid to be disappointed either, and I didn't want Ernie to get into any trouble. But I didn't know what to do about it.

The gatekeeper had a suggestion, however, which is how I wound up in the bunny suit, walking up the drive with a basket of colored eggs in each hand. The eggs and baskets had been in the Chevy's back seat, and now and then I stopped along the drive to hide an egg or two in a bougainvillea bush.

I was careful not to wander off into the jungle. There was no telling what was in there. I thought I could hear spider monkeys calling to one another, and then there was that chimp. So I stuck to the drive.

The gatekeeper and I'd had a hell of a time getting Ernie out of the bunny suit, and I was having a hell of a time wearing it. It was hot, it was too tight, and it smelled a lot like Ernie. I wasn't a happy bunny when I hammered the brass knocker against the front door of Torrance's house. Ernie, lying asleep in the gatehouse in his underwear, was considerably happier than I was.

No one answered my knock on the door, so I tried the knob. It was open, and it swung back into the house.

I looked inside just in time to see a familiar-looking man hurtling down the hallway toward me. He had a cat in his arms, a huge tabby that was dark and light gray on top, with a lot of orangy gold mixed in, and a solid white stomach. It was colored almost like an egg—sort of an Easter cat.

I thought maybe it had something to do with the party, and I was trying to get a better look when there was a thunderous explosion and the door frame shattered above my head.

Maybe the little dispute Mr. Gober had called me about was more serious than I'd thought.

I looked around for a place to run, but before I could move, the man from the hallway crashed into me. I'm pretty sturdy, but I don't think I slowed him down much. It was hard to tell. I couldn't see very well because I was lying flat on the tiles in front of the door. There were colorful hardboiled eggs all around me.

There was another explosion and I raised my head cautiously. I could see Rick Torrance back in the hallway. He had an elephant gun to his shoulder. At least it looked like an elephant gun. Maybe it was only a .30–.30. Pistols I know a little bit about; rifles are something I don't generally have to deal with.

I squirmed out of the way before he could run over me too. He ran past me and headed down the drive. Then Mr. Gober, who must have been behind him, came outside. He stopped and looked at me.

"You're not Wiggins," he said. Studio heads have to be perceptive.

"No, sir. I'm not."

He recognized me then. "Goddammit, Ferrel, what are you doing in that outfit?"

He always says that. *Goddammit, Ferrel,* I mean. I'm thinking of having my first name changed, since he can't seem to call me anything else.

"I'm taking Ernie's place," I said, standing up.

I started gathering up the eggs. Most of them were cracked, but I put them in the baskets anyway.

"Goddammit, Ferrel!" Gober said. "You're not supposed to be playing with Easter eggs. You've got to stop Rick. He's going to kill somebody if you don't."

"What about the party?" I asked. I didn't want to disappoint the kids, not after I'd gone to the trouble of getting dressed like a bunny.

Gober, however, didn't care about the kids. He was more interested in his star. "Forget the party. The kids have waited this long; they can wait a little longer."

"Where are they?"

"They're in the back yard. Peggy's with them. They're fine. Now get going!"

"I need to know what's going on here first," I said.

Mr. Gober took a deep breath and tried to control himself. Patience wasn't his strong suit. "The guy that ran you over is Lawrence Berry. Rick's going to kill him."

I didn't think so. It was widely known that Rick was a terrible shot. But I was curious. "Why?"

"He got Felicia pregnant, that's why. Now—"

I interrupted him. "Felicia? I thought Rick's wife was Penny Turnage."

Gober's face was turning a truly amazing shade of red. It was almost the same color as Ernie's nose. I wondered if Gober had been drinking. He took another deep breath.

"Felicia's the cat," he said. "Rick's cat."

"And Larry Berry got her pregnant? Illicit pregnancy is one thing, but bestiality? And cross-species breeding? Wow! Wait till the fan mags get hold of this one! Not to mention *Scientific American!*"

Berry was a well-known womanizer who generally played the villain's role in films. He'd been in a couple of Rick's pictures, playing an evil white hunter in *Kent of Kilimanjaro* and a murderous guide in *Clive of the Congo*. Or maybe he was a guide in *Kent* and a hunter in *Clive*. As I said, it's easy to get confused. The pictures are a lot alike. Plenty of shots of Rick with his muscles showing, and lots of stock footage of crocodiles sliding off sandbanks into rivers—things like that.

"Not Berry, you idiot!" Gober yelled. "He didn't get Felicia pregnant! His *cat* got her pregnant! Berry lives next door, and the cat comes sneaking over the wall to assault Felicia."

"Was that his cat Larry was holding?" I asked.

A rifle boomed.

"Yes! Now are you going to do something to earn your retainer, or do I have to turn things over to the Continental Agency?"

I handed him the Easter baskets. "Hold these," I said.

As an Easter Bunny, I was more of an urban type of animal. I didn't really belong in the jungle.

For one thing, my ears kept getting caught on the vines that dangled from the palm trees. It wasn't so bad once I realized what was happening in time to extricate myself, but once or twice I'd nearly jerked my own head off.

For another thing, the ground was squishy and wet underfoot. Rick had some kind of irrigation system for all the plants, even an overhead mister, and it was doing a very efficient job. Water dripped down out of the palms and soaked into my fur.

And for still another thing, I didn't like the noises, especially since I didn't really know what kind of wildlife Rick Torrance had stocked the place with. There were rumors in the fan magazines that monkeys weren't the only things in there. Pythons had been mentioned more than once. And boa constrictors.

Of course snakes don't make noises. That's one of the things I don't like about them. They're very sneaky, snakes are. But lions make noise, and one article had hinted that Rick had a lion on the property. I wondered if lions liked to eat rabbits.

Even though I wasn't exactly an old jungle hand, it was easy to follow along behind Rick and Larry. They were crashing along like a couple of rhinos in rut, and now and then Rick would let off another volley with his cannon.

When he did, a screeching like nothing I'd ever heard in real life would arise, and the trees above me would come alive with terrified monkeys. They weren't any more terrified than I was. I was afraid that if Rick saw me, he'd shoot me. He probably didn't have any rabbit heads mounted on his trophy wall.

Larry was probably even more frightened than I was. Rick was actually trying to kill him, which he'd done often enough in the movies but never before in real life. It was pretty stupid considering the circumstances, but then Rick probably hadn't taken the time to think about that. Maybe it wouldn't have made any difference even if he had.

There was a sudden frenzied fluttering off to my right, and I jumped about five feet straight up. I was a credit to the bunny clan. It wasn't a lion, however; it was only a bunch of colorful birds that were no doubt as scared as I was. They were cockatoos, which reminded me of my last case for Gober. That one had involved a cat, too. I was beginning to think that everyone at Gober's studio was nuts, though even that wouldn't be big news in Hollywood.

I looked down at my shoes, which I'd managed to force onto my feet over the bunny costume. They were ruined, naturally. I'd put them on the expense account, but I was still upset.

What with the noise and my shoes, I momentarily lost track of Rick and Larry, but then I heard something that sounded the way Tarzan might yell if he'd pulled a hernia. When I looked up, Larry was swinging toward me on a thick vine that he had gripped in his right hand. He had his multi-colored cat cradled in his left arm.

This time I was able to get out of his way, but I didn't really have to. From somewhere in the jungle a rifle roared, the vine parted, and Larry splatted on the wet ground, flat on his back.

He didn't fall far, but he was stunned. He lay there in the dappled shade with his eyes rolled back into his head. His cat, demonstrating the loyalty for which cats are renowned, took off for the tall timber.

Rick Torrance came crashing through the undergrowth, his rifle at the ready.

"All right, you son of a bitch," he said when he spotted Larry, "say your prayers."

"That's more like a Monogram Western than a jungle epic," I said.

Maybe Torrance had seen me on his stoop or maybe not. At any rate, he seemed pretty surprised to see a six-foot bunny in his jungle.

"Jesus Christ," he said, and I didn't bother to reprimand him for it. It seemed appropriate enough, considering the season.

What didn't seem appropriate was the barrel of the rifle that he had leveled at me. It might not have been an elephant gun, but the bore looked big enough to stuff a python into.

"Who the hell are you?" Rick asked.

"Bill Ferrel, private bunny."

He didn't laugh. "What're you doing in that outfit? I thought Ernie was supposed to be here."

"It's a long story. Why don't you give me that rifle and we'll talk about it."

"Forget it." He aimed the rifle at Larry's head. "I'm going to plug this varmint."

"Monogram again," I said. "Or maybe Republic. Have you ever starred in a Western?"

"No, but I like to watch 'em. Now why don't you just get out of here and let me do what I have to do."

Larry's eyes were no longer rolled up in his head. They were wide and bulging as he stared into the rifle barrel. I think he was holding his breath. He'd looked into plenty of rifle barrels in his movies, being a villain most of the time, but he wasn't used to them when he wasn't acting.

"Killing Larry would be bad publicity for the studio," I said. There was no need to bring morality into it; stars don't understand morality. So I was appealing to his practical side. "And bad publicity for you, too. What about that picture you're working on now?"

"*Manfred of Madagascar*? What about it?" He moved the rifle, pointing it at the wet ground, and Larry let out a slow hiss of air.

"Think how it would look to the fans if you murdered your co-star," I said. "Larry's in the picture, isn't he?"

"Yeah, he's in it, but I wouldn't call him a co-star. He's just the bad guy. I don't have co-stars."

"Right. But it still wouldn't be a good idea to kill him, not over something as silly as a pregnant cat."

The rifle barrel came up. Now it was pointing at me again. Right at my pink bunny stomach.

"There's nothing silly about a pregnant cat," Rick said. "Especially not about Felicia. She's a pedigreed Siamese, really expensive. Very classy. I've got all the papers on her. And now she's been polluted by alley trash."

"You should've kept her locked up. That's what people usually do."

"She was in the backyard. She likes to get out a little in the daytime. Get some exercise. There's a fence, so she should have been safe. Besides, Berry's the one who should have taken precautions."

Torrance turned the rifle barrel back toward Larry. I have to admit to feeling a guilty twinge of relief. But I can never resist asking questions when I shouldn't.

So I said, "What precautions?"

"He could have had his alley cat fixed."

"I thought about that," Larry said.

His voice, always firm in his movie roles, quavered just a little. Not that I blamed him.

"But I just couldn't do it," he continued. "If I had a wife, she could probably have had it done, but I just couldn't."

It was clear that Larry had certain psychological problems that we weren't going to be able to resolve for him. Or it was clear to me. Rick seemed to think he could resolve them easily enough.

He pointed the rifle in the general direction of Larry's reproductive organs and said, "I could fix *you* right here and take care of the cat later."

While Rick was focused on Larry, I made my move. I'm not generally a very quick guy, but maybe the bunny suit inspired me. I jumped to Rick's side and grabbed the rifle, trying to twist it out of his grasp.

He didn't want to give it up, and he twisted back, which caused both of us to fall to the squishy ground. Luckily, I landed on top.

We thrashed around for a while, but neither of us could get the advantage. Rick's muscular chest wasn't just a movie illusion, though. He managed a powerful roll that turned the two of us over and put him on top. Then he began slowly wresting the rifle from my grip.

I thought that if I could hold out long enough, Larry would get up and help me out, but I was wrong about that. You can never trust a villain. I heard the frantic rustling of palm fronds, and I knew that Larry was leaving the area. Possibly he was extremely worried about his cat and wanted to find him as soon as possible. More than likely, however, he didn't really care what happened to me, just as long as it didn't happen to him.

I could tell it was going to be up to me to rescue myself, so I resorted to low bunny cunning.

"Rick," I gasped.

He didn't stop trying to get the rifle, but he said, "What?"

"Are there any tarantulas in this jungle?"

"No." He sounded a little nervous, which was good. "Why?"

"Well, there's a couple of big hairy black spiders on your back. I thought maybe—"

"Spiders? Spiders?"

Rick let go of the rifle and jumped to his feet, brushing wildly at his back with both arms.

"Did I get them? Where are they? Step on them! Step on them!"

I stood up, holding the rifle. My formerly fluffy white tail was soaking wet, and it dragged down the seat of my suit. I was willing to bet it wasn't white anymore, either.

"The spiders are gone," I said. "They probably weren't tarantulas, anyway."

He seemed happy to hear that, but he kept looking around anxiously until he noticed who was holding the rifle.

"You son of a bitch," he said. "You're going to let Larry get away."

"He probably won't leave without his cat," I said. "Let's see if we can find them."

It didn't take long. We found Larry at the base of a tall palm tree, trying to coax the cat down with a toy mouse. I didn't bother to ask where the mouse had come from. Larry probably carried it around in his pocket.

Rick and I stood quietly behind a banana tree until Larry had the cat safely in hand. Then I took over.

We marched back to the house with Rick in front, Larry and his cat behind him, and me bringing up the rear. A guy wearing a bedraggled bunny costume and carrying a rifle. I felt like an escapee from an Abbott and Costello set.

To add to the fun, Rick and Larry yapped at each other all the way to the house.

"You'll regret this, Berry," Rick said. "I'm going to get you and that cat if it's the last thing I do."

"Fat chance. As soon as I leave here, I'm calling my lawyer. I'm going to sue you for every cent you've got. You'll be living in a jungle, all right—a hobo jungle!"

Stuff like that. I didn't try to keep them quiet. I knew someone who could do that for me when we got to the house.

And he did. Four or five words from Gober, and they were sitting in a pair of leather-covered chairs, as quiet as a couple of rocks. Larry's cat was spread out all over his owner's lap, sleeping calmly.

"That's better," Gober said. Then he looked at me. "Goddammit, Ferrel, you've got to settle this. I can't have two of my stars running around trying to kill each other."

"I didn't try to kill anyone," Larry said. "It was Rick. He—"

"Shut up!" Gober roared.

Larry shut up.

"Larry's no star!" Rick said. "*I'm* the star. I—"

"You too!" Gober thundered, and Rick was quiet.

Gober turned to me. "What about it, Ferrel? You're a fixer. Fix it."

One of my ears kept flopping over my eye. Probably got broken by one of those stupid vines. I pushed it out of my face and said, "Well, Mr. Gober, I think we can take care of things. The way I see it, there's been no crime committed here. Rick got a little excited, but that can happen. He didn't hurt anyone, after all. And I'm pretty sure Larry's cat isn't guilty of anything."

Rick jumped to his feet. "The hell he's not! He . . . he *raped* Felicia! He—"

"Shut up and siddown!" Gober shouted.

Rick shut up and sat.

"I can't swear that Larry's cat— By the way, what's his name?"

"Slim," Larry said with a straight face.

I didn't smile, either. "I can't swear that Slim didn't have his way with Felicia. But I'd be willing to bet my month's retainer from Gober Studios that he didn't get her pregnant."

Rick jumped up again. "That's a lie! He—"

This time Mr. Gober didn't say a word. He just looked at Rick, who sat back down. I wished I could look at people like that.

I went on as if I hadn't been interrupted. "I'd be willing to bet that Slim didn't get anyone pregnant because I don't think he's capable of it."

Larry was incredulous. "Not capable? Are you kidding? Look at the size of his ba—"

Gober glared. Larry shut up.

"It's not the size that matters," I said. "The truth is that cats with as many colors as Slim are usually females. And when they're male, they usually can't reproduce. They're sterile."

"Is that really true?" Larry asked. I guess he had a suspicious nature.

"Of course it's true," Gober said. "Ferrel knows his cats. Isn't that right, Ferrel?"

I didn't really know all that much about cats, but I nodded. I'd heard something like that once, and it might even have been true.

Rick looked as if he believed me. Or if not, he believed Gober.

"So who knocked up Felicia, then?" he asked.

"I don't have any idea. But if you think a fence is going to keep male cats away when a female's in heat, you're crazy. You may have caught Slim with her, but you missed the others. And I'd bet there were plenty of them."

"I did hear some howling out in the back yard earlier," Rick admitted.

"So there you are," I said. "If you want pedigreed kittens, you'll have to make the proper arrangements. And if you want no kittens at all, you'll have to keep Felicia locked up or get her spayed."

It took a little more persuasion, but Rick eventually admitted that everything was mostly his fault, not that he ever came right out and said so. He even apologized to Larry, sort of, for trying to kill him. And then he asked him if his cat could stay for the party. With Felicia safely put away in the house, of course.

The party was a success. I looked pretty crummy, even for a fake Easter Bunny, but the kids didn't care. I'd hidden the eggs, and that was all they really wanted. They ran down the drive looking for eggs in the bougainvillea bushes, yelling happily every time they found one.

But the real hit of the party was Slim, who was billed by Rick as the Easter Cat, the Easter Bunny's special guest and helper. Slim had the coloring for it, all right, and he wasn't the nervous type. Even after all the excitement he'd had, he let the kids rub him and scratch behind his ears and under his chin. I could hear him purring from ten feet away.

When the party was over, I went back to the gatehouse. I took a couple of hardboiled eggs with me, a blue one and a pink one. I figured on having them for dinner. I might as well get something out of my day's work.

Ernie was awake but still in his underwear. He was drinking coffee with the gatekeeper and looking right at home.

"Damn," Ernie said when he saw me. "What did you do to the bunny suit? It's rented, you know. You're going to have to pay for having it cleaned."

I gave him a look. It wasn't as good as one of Gober's, but it was a pretty good one.

"Ernie," I said, "I've never killed a man before. But I've never worn a bunny suit before, either. There's a first time for everything."

Ernie smiled weakly. "Oh. Yeah. Right. I see what you mean. I'll take care of the suit. Did you get my check?"

I reached inside the suit, pulled it out, and handed it to him.

He gave it the once-over, started to stick it in his boxer shorts, then thought better of it and just held it in his hand.

"Great," he said. "Thanks, Ferrel. I mean it."

"Sure," I said, and I started peeling myself out of the bunny suit. "You're welcome."

"You know," he said, giving the gatekeeper the elbow, "you look pretty cute in that outfit, Ferrel. You ever think of getting into the movies yourself?"

They had a good laugh at that one, and while they were guffawing, I reached down and got the pink egg from the basket. It would have made a nice dinner with a little salt and pepper, but I had a better use for it now.

Holding the egg behind my back, I walked over to Ernie and said, "Open up and say *Ah*."

For some reason, he did it, and I shoved the egg into his mouth, slapping away his hands when he reached for it.

"M-m-m-m-m-m," he mumbled.

"Happy Easter, Ernie," I said.

About the Authors

GARY A. BRAUNBECK has sold more than sixty short stories to various mystery, suspense, science fiction, fantasy, and horror markets, including *Careless Whispers* and *White House Horrors*. His first collection, *Things Left Behind,* is scheduled for hardcover release this year. He has been a full-time writer since 1992 and lives in Columbus, Ohio.

JON L. BREEN has written six mystery novels, most recently *Hot Air* (1991), and more than seventy short stories. He contributes review columns to *Ellery Queen's Mystery Magazine* and *The Armchair Detective*; was shortlisted for the Dagger Awards for his novel *Touch of the Past* (1988); and has won two Edgars, two Anthonys, a Macavity, and an American Mystery Award for his critical writings.

RICHARD T. CHIZMAR is the author of more than forty published short stories and is the World Fantasy Award–winning editor of *Cemetery Dance* magazine and numerous anthologies, including *Cold Blood, Thrillers, The Earth Strikes Back,* and *Screamplays*. His first single-author collection, *Midnight Promises,* was published in hardcover earlier this year.

BARBARA COLLINS'S last appearance in the *Cat Crimes* series was "Cat Got Your Tongue" in *Cat Crimes III*. She has made appearances in numerous anthologies, including *The Year's 25 Finest Crime and Mystery Stories* and *Celebrity Vampires*. She lives in Muscatine, Iowa, with her husband, author Max Allan Collins, and their son, Nathan.

BILL CRIDER won the Anthony Award for his first novel in the Sheriff Dan Rhodes series. His first novel in the Truman Smith series was nominated for a Shamus Award, and a third series features college English professor Carl Burns. His short stories have appeared in numerous anthologies, including *Cat Crimes II* and *III, Celebrity Vampires,* and *Werewolves.*

Since the World and British Fantasy Award–nominated *Narrow Houses* (1992), **PETER CROWTHER** has edited or co-edited eight anthologies, continued to produce reviews and interviews for a variety of publications on both sides of the Atlantic, sold fifty of his own short stories, and has published *Escardy Gap,* a collaborative novel with James Lovegrove. A solo novel, a short story collection, more anthologies, and *Escardy Gap II* are all currently under way.

CAROLE NELSON DOUGLAS is the author of more than thirty novels, in such diverse genres as mainstream, historical, mystery, and science fiction. Her rise in the field began with her quartet of historical mysteries featuring Irene Adler, the female counterpoint to Sherlock Holmes and the only character to outwit him. Recently her novel series involving the detective Midnight Louie has monopolized her time, and the feline sleuth makes an appearance here.

JAN GRAPE is no stranger to the *Cat Crimes* series, having appeared in *Cat Crimes III, Feline and Famous,* and *Cat Crimes Takes a Vacation.* She also writes excellent short fiction that doesn't involve cats, as can be found in *Santa Clues* and several other anthologies. She lives in Austin, Texas.

NICK HASSAM divides his writing between the dark fantasy and crime genres. He lives in Yorkshire, England, with a cat who indirectly provided the idea for this story.

JEREMIAH HEALY'S mystery fiction has been translated into five languages and nominated for the Shamus Award eleven times, winning in 1986 with *The Staked Goat.* He has served as a judge for both the Shamus and Edgar award committees and was elected vice president and president of the Private Eye Writers of America. He accomplished all of this while working as a professor at the New England School of Law.

MORRIS HERSHMAN lives in New York City and has published a wide variety of fiction in several genres. Other work by him appears in *Murder Most Irish, Santa Clues,* and *Crimes of Passion.*

TRACY KNIGHT is a psychologist who writes with grace and style about some of the darker aspects of the human psyche. When combined with an "American" small-town setting, as in this piece, the result is unsettlingly effective. More of his short fiction can be found in *Murder Most Delicious* and *Cat Crimes Takes a Vacation.*

JOHN LUTZ writes two fine mystery series, one about a powerless deadbeat named Nudger, the other about a cop-turned-private-detective named Carver. Before that, he wrote short fiction for the first ten years of his career, winning an Edgar Award for the story "Ride the Lightning." Other short fiction by him can be found in *Careless Whispers, Murder Is My Business,* and *Mistletoe Mysteries.*

GRAHAM MASTERTON is the author of more than fifty bestselling horror novels and thrillers as well as dozens of short stories. His first book, *The Manitou,* was made into a movie starring Tony Curtis, Burgess Meredith, and Stella Stevens, and a later novel, *Walkers,* is currently in production in Los Angeles. He has won a special Edgar from the Mystery Writers of America and two Silver Medals from the *West Coast Review of Books.* He lives with his wife, Wiescka, near the famous Derby racecourse at Epsom in Surrey, England.

CHRISTINE MATTHEWS is the pseudonym author Marthayn Pelegrimas uses when writing mysteries. Her work has appeared in *Deadly Allies II, Ellery Queen Mystery Magazine, Lethal Ladies* and *For Crime Out Loud I and II.* She is currently co-editing *Lethal Ladies II* and writing *Murder Is the Deal of the Day* with her collaborator, Robert J. Randisi.

MARLYS MILLHISER is quickly becoming a name in the humorous mystery genre. Other fiction by her appears in *Funny Bones* and *Murder, She Wrote,* and she has written nonfiction articles about the mystery field for numerous publications. Her series character is Charlie Greene, a Hollywood literary agent.

BARBARA PAUL uses her experience as a former drama and English teacher to good advantage as a novelist. Her two series are as different as night and day, one featuring the singer Enrico Caruso as an amateur sleuth, the other a New York City policewoman named Marian Larch. Other notable novels include *He Huffed and He Puffed,* a wicked mix of larcenous characters whose only desire is to protect themselves at any cost. Her short fiction can be found in the anthologies *Future Net, Murder Most Delicious,* and *Santa Clues,* among many others.

NANCY PICKARD is a Macavity, Agatha, Shamus, and Anthony award–winning author who just seems to get better with every story she writes. Her long-running novel series features Jenny Cain, director of a philanthropic organization in a small New England town caught up in a recession. She is a past president of Sisters in Crime, and her short fiction also appears in *Careless Whispers*; *Murder, She Wrote*; and past *Year's 25 Finest Crime and Mystery Stories.*

ROBERT J. RANDISI has had more than 275 books published since 1982, having written in the mystery, western, men's adventure, fantasy, historical, and spy genres. He is the author of the Nick Delvecchio series and the Miles Jacoby series, and he is the creator and writer of *The Gunsmith* series, which he writes as J. R. Roberts and which presently numbers 185 books. His newest novel, *Alone with the Dead* (1995), received a starred review from *Publisher's Weekly* and is currently in its second printing. He is the founder and executive director of the Private Eye Writers of America.

STEWART VON ALLMEN is the author of a 70,000-word novel, *Conspicuous Consumption* (1995), which he wrote in three weeks, and a second project published for a Bosnian relief charity in 1996, *Saint Vitus Dances Eternity: A Sarajevo Ghost Story,* which is a 15,000-word novelette that consumed a year of his time. He is now working on a science fiction project he hopes will combine the length of the former and the quality of the latter.

J. N. WILLIAMSON has had over 150 short stories published in a variety of genres and anthologies. Recent work by him appears in *White House Horrors, Murder Most Delicious* and *Holmes for the Holidays.* His most recent novels are *Bloodline* (1994) and *The Hunt* (1997).